THE RAVEN AND THE JACKDAW

A Novel

ANTHONY MCDONALD

Anchor Mill Publishing

Anthony McDonald

The Raven and the Jackdaw

All rights reserved. Copyright © Anthony McDonald 2015

www.anthonymcdonald.co.uk

Anchor Mill Publishing

4/04 Anchor Mill

Paisley PA1 1JR

SCOTLAND

anchormillpublishing@gmail.com

Artwork on cover: Copyright Rawpixel.com. © Shutterstock. 'Gay Couple love Home Concept'. The individuals depicted in this artwork are models. No inference in regard to their sexual orientation may be drawn from the content of the book.

Anthony McDonald

Dedicated to the memory of Antony Linford

And to Nigel Fothergill

The Raven and the Jackdaw

ONE

I first fell in love with my brother when I was six. I fell in love with him because he was beautiful and full of charm, and sensitive as well as bold and brave. I fell in love with him because it was in my nature to do so. I fell for him because he loved me too.

He was two years older than I was.

We shared a room in which we had one small bed each. There came a night when a violent storm raged outside. Lightning turned the room a brilliant eerie blue again and again. The thunder cracked and the whole house shook with it. The storm must have been, at least for a few minutes, directly overhead. Our mother came in to see if we were awake (we were) and if we were frightened. We said that we were not. After she had gone, reassured at having reassured us, the room continued to flash and boom as if we had gone to bed by mistake in a fireworks box. My brother, whose name was Jason, suddenly said, 'Do you want to come in with me?' I did want to. I got out of my bed and took the few paces across the room that were all that were necessary. He rolled back the covers to make it easy for me, I climbed in alongside him, he covered us both up snugly, and that was the beginning of it.

It wasn't as though we had never touched each other before. We'd played together half naked and had bedtime mock fights. From time to time we'd grabbed each other's willies, half by accident and half for the fun of it. But this, tonight, was different. As soon as Jason had covered us up I wrapped my arms around him, pretending I was more frightened than was actually the case. He wrapped his arms round me then protectively and we cuddled, rocking back and forth. Soon we were competing to see who would lie on top of whom. There was no real contest. Jason was two years older, bigger and sturdier. Of course he ended up on top.

I was conscious of our two pyjama tops between us, the warm fabric, and two sets of buttons making hard indentations in both our chests. I wanted then to feel Jason's soft warm skin against my own, and discovered immediately that the same desire had been born in him. Together we worked to undo the buttons of our pyjama tops, then pulled them apart. Jason sank his naked chest and tummy onto mine, tenderly as a bird pushing itself down onto its eggs. He ground his soft warm skin against me. He exhaled, a little overcome by the intensity of the experience. 'Ahh…,' his breath murmured, and I felt his milk-sweet breath against my face.

It wasn't enough to have undone the buttons of our pyjama shirts, we soon discovered. We wanted the lower bit also, and soon undid the single button – one for each of us – that stood in the way of that. Pyjama bottoms were soon disposed of, kicked down into the capacious vacant area that was the Bottom of the Bed. Our thighs pressed against each other's and we lay quietly together,

The Raven and the Jackdaw

savouring this. Bellies too, and we lay quietly also savouring those. But there was something else, something that neither of us knew how to speak of, if indeed we ever were to speak of it. We were enjoying above all the sensation of pressing together our two small cocks.

After a few minutes of lying together in this thoughtful stillness we became aware that the thunder and lightning had stopped. Perhaps inspired by our example the elements had also found stillness and peace. I didn't want to say it but I had to. My voice was coloured with reluctance. 'I better get back to my own bed.' Jason didn't comment. He eased himself off me to make my departure easier, and I left his bed and returned to mine. I found it was no longer quite as warm as his. But I snuggled down in it anyway, and that was that. At least, as far as that night went.

The next day was a school day. Perhaps that was just as well. We had our quick breakfast with our parents, then our father drove off to work, dropping Jason and me at the bus stop. We were very quiet in the car but dad, or Daddy as we called him then, didn't seem to notice this. He presumably had work-related preoccupations of his own: a fact of adult life of which we were still blissfully ignorant.

In the bus we sat a couple of rows apart with friends from our different classrooms, and the same went for the school day as a whole. It wasn't until bedtime and we were tucked up snugly in our two beds that we were really alone together. And this time it was I who started it.

'Do you think it'll thunder again tonight?' I asked, pretend casually. There was no chance of thunder this night, and we both knew it. Last night's tempest had cleared the June air magically, and the low bedtime sun was still beating at the closed curtains.

'It might do,' said Jason, also feigning insouciance.

'Perhaps I better get into bed with you just in case it does,' I said.

'Perhaps you'd better,' said Jason very correctly. He'd presumably been taught recently that the expression had a *'d* in it.

I made my way easily across the half lit room. I found that Jason had burrowed deep down into his bed and was curled up in a ball at the bottom of it. I plunged in to join him. Head-first.

By the time we encountered each other Jason had somehow already contrived to unbutton his pyjama top and let down the trousers. He pushed himself upwards as I continued to dive downwards, somehow managing to undo my own top buttons as I went. As my warm chest encountered Jason's chest and then his tummy I felt Jason dealing with my own pyjama trousers.

The next thing for me to do seemed suddenly very obvious. I found my brother's penis with my lips. It felt quite springy, like softish India-rubber. It filled my mouth almost to the point of discomfort, but I was excited by the taste of it. Sweet yet salty, it had something of the sea about it.

Jason said, 'Mmmm,' which on paper looks non-committal. But his tone of voice suggested pleasant surprise that bordered on ecstasy. A moment later I felt Jason's warm wet mouth engulf my own small thing and then I knew exactly what the 'Mmmm' meant.

Not till many years had passed did either of us realise that we'd discovered something that most people come to rather later in life, and that adults had a name for – a name that was also a number.

We stayed where we were for a considerable time, meditatively sucking on each other, but eventually the

The Raven and the Jackdaw

position grew uncomfortable and the lack of oxygen beneath the bedclothes became stifling. By unspoken common accord we released each other; I turned round like a fish in a jam jar and together we swam up for air. But, having surfaced, we found ourselves loth to part from each other. We continued to hold and touch and caress until the little midsummer night had well and truly fallen, and even then we only parted company – me hopping back to my own sheets and blankets – for reasons of prudence. For although neither of us had at that stage any sense that there was anything wrong or transgressive about what we'd been doing, some deep-rooted instinct told us – heaven knows how – that we'd be in very serious trouble if we were caught at it.

It was on the bus going to school the next morning that I felt compelled to turn round and look at Jason, two seats behind, talking animatedly with his eight-year-old classmates. It was at that moment that – like a newly hatched duck imprinting on the first thing it sees and giving its whole unwise heart to it – I knew I loved him.

TWO

When I was in my early twenties, I tried to make sense of it all by writing a fictionalised account of it. But I was frightened of the subject by then. Very, very frightened. My account (it took the form of a novella) was very sanitised, very idealised and, of course, self-censored. In a way I wanted everyone to know about Jason and me, and would have loved lots of people to read my story. Yet, inconsistently, I was also terrified of people finding out about us. (This was only partly due to the fact that by then I was a little bit famous.) The novella was never published and only a small handful of people ever read it. When two of those people did read it that had major consequences for all of us, but I shall come to that part of the story later. Here is the ever so safe, warm and cosy opening of the first chapter. It burrows back in time to an era of innocence some three years earlier than that cataclysmic night of the thunderstorm. It hardly needs saying that 'Raven' was Jason and that I was David. I was 'the Jackdaw'. (My real name's Barnaby, by the way. Barnaby Whitcomb.)

****

It was Sunday. Which meant Church. Raven was looking at his hymn-book with the discerning eye of one who has just learned to read, Mary was tracing the grain of the dark oak pew with her thumb and David was peering upwards in all directions because when you are between two and three feet high upwards is the only direction in which you can profitably look. All those people, standing, sitting, kneeling, with books in their hands. All looking terribly serious – a little worrying, this, because they were mostly very nice and jolly when they spoke to you in the ordinary way. This was the

The Raven and the Jackdaw

disconcerting side of grownups. It made you wonder whether they were really very nice or whether they just put it on for your benefit. But anxieties about the true nature of adults were put in perspective by the sheer scale of the church. Adults weren't so tall here. In the farmhouse the grownups stretched all the way up to the ceiling and the tallest ones would crack their heads on the beams... That was their own fault for being too tall. But here there was still an awful lot of church above even the tallest of them. Rough whitewashed walls rose high above their heads and tall wide windows let the bright autumn sunshine in through grimy panes. Stone pillars strode down the nave where, in the centre of the church, the walls rose even higher in the giddy darkness that no daylight reached. It was lit instead by the mysterious reverberant sound of the organ, which seemed to David to flicker round among the rafters and to glow like flaming spirits. The height of the ridge-pole, where age-black beams met in the noisy darkness, was too awful to contemplate.

Far better to focus the attention on the efforts of a red butterfly to transport itself by sheer will power through the leaded windowpane. There were two sorts of butterfly: white ones, which were nasty and ate cabbage (a thing David only ever did under protest) and red ones, which were good. You weren't to kill red butterflies or attempt to catch them by their wings, but should you let them batter themselves to death against church windows?

Most of the people appeared not to have noticed the butterfly, though it was making quite a clatter with its brittle wings on the glass. Auntie Jean had noticed it, though, David was sure. He had seen her eyes surreptitiously following its non-progress. But even she made no move to rescue it – no tripping along between the pews, trampling on people's toes, cupped hands outstretched... Even she, the most perfect person among David's acquaintances and relations, seemed sadly altered by being in Church.

Then Church was over and the butterfly forgotten. Everyone filed out into the sudden glare of the sunlight, the three children taking exaggerated care not to step on the strangely shaped door-sill at the porch gate. Mary said it was the lid of a medieval coffin. Medieval sounded worse even than ordinary evil; the word crawled with unthinkable horror, like the stone itself. The children stepped high over the sun-warmed slab with involuntary shudders. The brick path shone pinky-red in the bright light, pinky-red like the butterfly... The butterfly! 'Mummy, Auntie, what'll happen to the butterfly? Can't we go back? Can we go back?'

Patiently Auntie Jean explained to David that winter was approaching and the butterfly had gone inside to find somewhere warm to sleep till spring. When the sun stopped shining it would go back to sleep again. You had to leave it alone, Auntie Jean said, and let nature take care of it. David imagined a huge gentle hand like his mother's soothing the butterfly to sleep on the window-sill and watching over it while it slumbered until spring.

Raven had already raced across the churchyard to his special tree. Long ago, when the old forests of oak had been used up in the iron-smelting furnaces they had been replanted with Spanish chestnut. A circle of these had been planted round the church to ensure a blessing on the new timber crop. Now this ring of trees was itself ancient and the huge gnarled trunks were full of holes where owls, bees, squirrels and jackdaws nested. One tree was so rotten and hollow that Raven could climb in at ground level, scramble grubbily up on the inside and poke his head out of a hole nearly ten feet up. He did this now. A jackdaw that had been sitting on a branch

The Raven and the Jackdaw

nearby flapped away in surprise, calling Jack? Jack? Jack? as it went.

'Oh Raven! His new Sunday trousers!' Isabel directed all her reserves of outraged motherhood at her elder son but Auntie Jean turned to David and said,

'Did you see that? A raven and a jackdaw in the same tree. Wasn't that funny? A jackdaw is rather like a raven isn't it? A raven is big and black and sleek, and a jackdaw is smaller, with bright blue eyes and lots of curiosity, rather like you. Perhaps we ought to call you jackdaw. I shall, anyway.'

By lunchtime the name had gained general currency. It was, 'Jackdaw, please pass the mustard,' and, 'Jackdaw, we do not put our fingers up our noses at table.' ('Jackdaws have beaks, not noses.' 'Thank you Mary; that will do.') It was a good lunch. After the roast joint there was autumn pudding, David's favourite, a mass of blackberries steaming under a hot suet crust that was crimson with juice and, though it was not Christmas, there was a bottle of red wine in honour of Auntie Jean's visit. The children were allowed to taste it.

'I prefer white wine,' said Mary grandly. 'Red's not nice.'

'Red butterflies are nice,' said David abstractedly, still thinking blissful thoughts about Mother Nature.

'They don't make wine out of butterflies, silly.'

'Mary, stop it.'

David tasted the wine and winced. The glass was passed to Raven. He took a hearty slurp, rolled it around his mouth noisily, then cast his eyes heavenwards and swallowed. 'It was so lovely,' he said.

'He's only pretending,' said Mary.

****

Well, some of that was true and some of it wasn't. Like most pieces of fiction it was cobbled together from a basket of memories, stitched with the elastic thread of imagination and overlaid with the varnish and polish of fantasy and wish fulfilment.

Yes, we did have an Auntie Jean. (Her real name was Sonia.) She was our mother's much younger sister. She made no further appearances in the story as I wrote it. The real life Auntie Sonia died of breast cancer while still in her forties. And I used the memories of that sadness when later I came to describe, in my "novella", the fictional death of our mother.

There was no sister called Mary. No sister at all. Just my brother and me. Though we did at that time have two parents. But we didn't live in a large farmhouse. We had a rather small cottage on the edge of the village, which backed onto a neighbouring farm's fields.

That first chapter ended with a sequence that was set nearly two years later in time: with a panegyric to the month of June, a lyrical description of haymaking as it was carried out in the mid-nineteen-sixties, and the first intimation of something a bit special between the two brothers – on the Jackdaw's side at any rate...

****

In June he changes tune. But still he sings all day. June. It's the most magical, marvellous month of the year, especially when it's your last one, your last proper one that is, because you know perfectly well that before this time next year something will have happened that stops anything from ever again being as it was. The best years of your life will be gone. The cuckoo will never again sound so carefree, the world will never again be so gentle and well-disposed towards you, nor the grass so green or the sunlight brighter. You will never more

The Raven and the Jackdaw

have the luxury of not knowing what time of day it is, what day of the week or month it is, what year it is or how old you are growing. You will never again be unaware that it is all passing so quickly. For, suddenly, you are aware of that now. School is coming for you. Coming to get you with its cutters, spinners and balers. Coming for you. School. You know already, instinctively, that school is the end of everything. From then on nothing will ever stand still for you again. Time will spin you away and on through life, faster and ever faster, and you won't be able to stop, go back, get out, or even look around you...

But this is June still. You've already had four Junes without knowing what they were. But this one you're going to appreciate and in the years to come will long to escape back into. In your fond memory the grass will grow longer and greener, the sun warmer, the sky bluer, and the Raven's grin wider as he peers down from the hay cart at you from a distance measured in galloping years. And the image will grow ever more vivid as time leaches the accidents of mundane reality out of it and leaves you with... With what? With the essence of a smiling face, sunlight on his black hair, and a sky of the deepest, hottest blue.

Once they get you to school they're going to make you a grownup, and then the rest of your life is just a post-script. It's those first years that matter and you're only beginning to realise this now, now that they're slipping away. Your last June, Jackdaw. Make the most of it.

'The machines'll be here in a day or two.' Isabel pointed towards the endless sea of waving grass. 'Remember the machines last year, Jackdaw?'

'She means tractors,' said Raven, scornful of his mother's euphemisms. And of course Jackdaw remembered tractors. How could you forget something as marvellous as tractors? Jackdaw knew everything *there was to know about tractors. Raven had told him the whole of it. The blue ones with red wheels were Fordsons, the grey ones were Fergusons and the red ones Massey-Harris. Their exhaust pipes stuck up in the air and they smelt of hot oil and straw: liberal quantities of both those commodities were wrapped around their axles together with a good deal of mud. Nobody spent their Sundays washing tractors and they were driven by people with big boots. The tractors were coming. Haymaking was about to start.*

Beyond the fence at the bottom of the garden the green-blue grass heads waved higher every morning in the hot breeze. Then one day the tractor was there even before breakfast, with one swathe cut already, right round the field.

The long blade shivered through the grass, invisible save for the wooden guide at its outer end, ploughing through the green wave like a shark's fin and aligning the slain stems in a neat unending ridge. Slowly the tractor circled the field, hugging the curves and angles of its perimeter, at each circuit a few more feet from the edge, gradually altering the field's appearance beyond recognition. At lunchtime Jackdaw sat in the shade of a tree talking to the driver as he ate his sandwiches and drank from his Thermos near the resting tractor. The driver's name was Joe, he told Jackdaw between mouthfuls, and he came from a country called Poland, which was farther away across the sea even than France. By the time Raven returned from school only a small central square of field remained uncut. Polish Joe was going to finish it later in the evening. 'And tomorrow if it is sunshining we have the acrobat here,' he said.

'Who's the acrobat?' asked Jackdaw.

'You make sure it don't rain in the night and you see tomorrow.'

The Raven and the Jackdaw

The field wasn't finished until Raven and Jackdaw were in their beds. Jackdaw could hear the tractor's engine still going as he drifted towards sleep. Grownups could stay up and out of doors so late.

The Acrobat turned out to be a set of bright red and yellow revolving wheel-rakes attached to the back of the tractor. Tossing the new-mown grass skywards it gave it a chance to land in a different position and dry its other side. By Saturday, a day on which Raven didn't have to go to school, the grass was no longer green but lemon-gold and sweet smelling. Then the baler came, large, red and cumbersome, nearly getting stuck in the entrance to the field. More men came with it, and other tractors and trailers. Raven and Jackdaw followed the baler around the field as it snorted, shuddered, snatched, rammed, and tied the bales with orange string as if by magic.

At teatime the children lay in the shade alongside the men, accepting offers of biscuits out of paper bags and watching oily tea being poured into cracked cups and swallowed noisily. Watching the men the boys thought that was how they wanted to be when they grew up: stubble-chinned, with hair matted with sweat, their trousers torn, boots caked with mud, and lying on the flattened grass beneath the willow saplings while bees buzzed among the thistle flowers and beetles crawled mating up the grass stems. And teatime would last for ever.

*

The baling was finished. The remaining bales would have to be picked up later in the evening for the trailer was loaded as high as it could be without overbalancing. Raven was allowed to scramble up on top of the load and ride back across the field. He climbed like a monkey up the bars that leaned outward from the back of the trailer to keep the load in place and soon he was securely in position on top. Mary had said emphatically that she would prefer to walk. Jackdaw stood on the ground looking from his sister to his brother and back again. There was his brother miles above him, grinning like a gargoyle, framed in hay and sunshine and a vast blue sky. There was the picture that he would keep for ever. There the grin, the snub nose and the laughing brown eyes. There was his brother suddenly calling out, 'Come on, Jackdaw.'

'I can't,' said David wretchedly, and he looked back at his sister who was preparing to set off across the stubble on foot. The tractor driver started the engine. Suddenly one of the other men leaped down and lifted him up, they hauled him up from above, and there he was atop the load. There he lay with Raven and the men, his heart thumping and his clenched fists holding on with the grip of panic, but happy beyond belief. They started off and the load swayed alarmingly as it struggled slowly towards the gate. David could see his home just beyond the fence. How small the house looked from up here. He could see his parents, tiny figures, watching from the garden. He could see Mary tramping along beside them, far, far below. He clung tightly to the bales he lay on and felt an exhilaration he had never known before. High on this perilously rocking, sweet smelling mountain of hay, under the cloudless blue dome of the sky, close to his brother in the afternoon sun, this was where he had to be. Here he had found what he most desired and now he wanted the ride never to end. Raven and he could ride on top of the wain till the end of time. For at the end of the ride lay the end of everything. This time next year he would be at School.

****

I set that scene two years earlier than the night of the thunderstorm. Partly because I wanted to make a point

The Raven and the Jackdaw

about the brutal interruption of an idyllic early childhood by the get-real necessity of school.

One of the things that strikes me on reading that final passage now is of course the health and safety issue. A five-year-old and a seven-year-old riding ten feet up in the air on a load of hay with no side-railings, bouncing over a rough field in the care of total strangers. The cliché springs to mind: it couldn't happen now. Rather a shame, that. Because back then it did – and it was rather wonderful.

The other thing about the passage is that it suggests that Jackdaw's first rush of feeling for his older brother came when he was barely five – that is nearly two years younger than I was at the time of the thunderstorm and the moment two days later on the bus. So had it really started for Jason and me in mistily remembered, rosily remembered, earliest childhood? The answer is almost certainly yes. It had just needed that thunderstorm to firm it up.

THREE

On the third night we didn't bother even to pretend there might be a thunderstorm. As soon as our mother had said goodnight to us and returned downstairs my brother got out of his bed and took the three steps towards mine. I could see in the subdued, curtain-filtered daylight that he'd taken the very practical if risky measure of removing his pyjamas in advance. He walked towards me naked, and with a miniature erection. He got into my bed alongside me and methodically peeled my own pyjamas off me. Then we did again what we had learned, untaught, the night before.

****

'Pity he can't go to school by tractor instead of the bus,' Hector observed drily. Jackdaw didn't like school much and looked on it as a waste of time that might have been more profitably occupied among his own pursuits, which were outdoor and nature-oriented. Mary had taken to school readily and the Raven had gone with an attitude of stolid indifference that was to serve him till the day he left. He, James, the Raven, was not particularly good at Reading, Doing Sums and Paying Attention but excellent at playing football and making friends – the two usually went together. And he had one further talent: he was very good at drawing. Always had been, graduating from aeroplanes and trains to people playing football – which was far less easy. He was mildly surprised to find that time was set aside for this pleasant activity and further surprised to find that he was easily the best draughtsman in the class. School had little effect on James: he neither liked nor disliked it. Jackdaw, though his teachers thought him rather bright, loathed it.

The Raven and the Jackdaw

One day as David boarded the bus that took them to school in the next village, the driver's ticket machine ran out of tickets just as it was David's turn to pay. 'Well now,' said the old driver, 'it looks as though they forgot to load this old thing this morning, don't it? Would you like to take this?' David was handed the ticket machine. 'And when we stop outside the garage in a minute, run in and ask Mr Prentis to put a new roll in. Can you do that?'

David had never been entrusted with such an important errand before. He was conscious as he got off the bus that all eyes were upon him and also that the bus could not go on its way before he got back, so he ran all the way, clutching the silvery box to his chest, down the slope that led to the ramshackle sheds that were the headquarters of Prentis Bros., Bus and Coach Co. Ltd.

The sliding doors were almost shut but David squirmed through. There, in near darkness, he discovered a new world. Buses stood tall and mysterious in the gloom and beyond them a light beckoned. It came from a welding torch that was being held by a man wearing dungarees and goggles. David had seen nothing like it but he advanced on the man and asked, 'Is Mr Prentis in?'

'Mr P.' the man called over his shoulder. 'A very young gentleman to see you.'

Mr P. shambled over. He was bespectacled and bent, with a very red face, a small quantity of frizzy grey hair, and hands and voice that shook. 'What can we do for you?' he asked.

'It's this.' David held out the ticket box. 'Mr Larkin says it needs a new roll.'

'Then we'd better see what we can do.' Mr P. picked up a roll of tickets from the workbench beside him, opened up the box and tried to thread the paper into it.

His hands shook, the paper crumpled; the bus was waiting.

'Let me try,' said David, and threaded the machine first go. That evening he told his astonished parents that he intended to make a career as a bus driver.

Every Saturday now would find him at the bus garage. He learned how to check oil levels with the dipstick, he swept the interiors of the buses meticulously with dustpan and broom and was even allowed, under supervision, to start the engines. And he learned not to try to talk to Mr Prentis after Saturday lunch, when he could usually be found snoring on the back seat of one of his buses. Buses had quite suddenly replaced tractors in Jackdaw's pantheon. He never became much of a mechanic ... but he was at last reconciled to going to school.

****

Some of that was drawn from life. Jackdaw's sudden interest in buses and his Saturdays at the depot were my own. I did not loathe school however. I was mildly interested by it. And the assertion that Jackdaw's brother was very un-academic would have been a calumny if applied to my own brother. Jason actually did very well at school. He was particularly good at mathematics – which I wasn't. As for being good at drawing ... in the real story of our lives that went for both of us. But I didn't invent the bit about my brother being good at football. The real-life Jason was much better at it than I was, and enjoyed it much more than I did. Playing football with his friends was what he did with his Saturdays. That's why I was left alone to go and play with the buses.

My brother Jason got renamed James in my story. This was fairly transparent. The name was only two letters

The Raven and the Jackdaw

different from his real one, and I loved him too much to be able to relinquish the other letters. To our parents I gave the names Isabel and Hector because I thought the name Isabel rather lovely, and Hector appealingly outlandish. Their real names aren't needed for the present. But if I clung fast to Jason's real name in calling him James, I took the opposite approach when naming the younger brother. The name David is far removed from my own moniker of Barnaby. No doubt – I look back now with twenty-twenty hindsight – this was part of a subconscious attempt to distance myself from the character I was writing about.

****

It did not occur to Hector, who was deputy head of the local Comprehensive, that there was anything illogical in his decision to send Raven to private boarding school. Raven was getting big and bumptious and was accordingly told to anticipate his removal thither as soon as he reached the age of ten. The news washed over him like almost everything else. Jackdaw, though, thought his brother must be remarkably brave and even Mary began to look at him, against her usual inclination, as a bit of a hero.

'They'll have a drawing master to teach you properly at last,' Hector told his older son, 'and there'll be decent football coaching. First eleven and second eleven, and in the Easter terms you'll learn to play Rugby. A real gentleman's game that, and a sight tougher than your old soccer.'

James began to feel rather pleased at the new recognition he was getting from his family: pleased that he was being singled out to become a man. Much preparation was required. There was an outfit list of horrifying length, and Cash's name-tapes to be sewn on absolutely everything – though by Isabel, not by Raven. A suitcase was required and so was a trunk. The latter would come home to roost only once a year; the suitcase would accompany the boy back and forth each term. But as the preparations gathered momentum, and as Jackdaw watched his elder brother getting ready for his launch into the unknown, the realisation gradually and unpleasantly dawned on the younger boy that one day he would be expected to follow him.

****

Hmm. That was only half of the truth. The reality – for yes, Dad did send us both to boarding school, thanks to a timely legacy from a childless aunt – was that much as I dreaded being sent away from home in a year or two's time, I knew I was going to miss my brother terribly. Especially at night.

I notice that in that extract I've used the old-fashioned word thither. The only time in my life that I've ever used it. I thought about changing the sentence in the quoted extract in order to modernise it a bit… Thought about it, and then decided that I wouldn't.

****

It was the last Saturday before Raven's departure. He had been playing football with friends while Jackdaw had been by the pond in the field trying to catch dragonflies. It was his ambition to mate a blue one with a red one and produce a brown one. Returning via the hole in the garden fence Jackdaw found Raven curled up behind the garden shed in a state of extreme misery. Raven didn't often cry but when he did he seemed to give way to the tears completely in a way that made it seem to Jackdaw to be that much worse. 'What's the matter?' Jackdaw asked.

The Raven and the Jackdaw

'It's Richard,' his brother managed to say, *'and Michael, and Raymond ... and Barry ... and Keith ... and Bill ... and the rest.'*

'What've they done?'

'They won't let me be captain any more. They won't even let me be in the gang at all.' They had called themselves a team for the past year or so, but Raven in his distressed state inadvertently returned to the old title – the gang. *'Because I'm going to boarding school. And they all went against me. They said, wasn't their school good enough for me any more? And I said it was. They said I didn't have time for them any more and I said I did. Then they just...'* Raven stopped talking and started crying again. He couldn't bring himself to relate the most humiliating thing of all. That when he could no longer face the rest of the gang, couldn't argue with them any longer, knew that he was beginning to cry and therefore had to turn his back and walk away, someone had kicked the ball at him and had hit him hard on the back of the neck. He hadn't even turned round to see which of his friends it was.

They both sat in silence for a while. Jackdaw wondered whether this was an indication of what life in the outside world was really like. This was not the kind of loyalty his family upbringing had taught him to believe in. Would boarding school be like that? he wondered. Would friendship? Was that the way perhaps that grownups behaved among themselves when they weren't being nice to you because you were a child? He would not put too much trust in the outside world, in other people, he decided now. You were too likely to get hurt, like Raven by his football team. But at least Raven should have his loyalty. He turned towards him but could think of nothing to say so, rather diffidently – for he expected a rebuff – he put his arm round his brother's shoulder instead. Raven didn't say anything or attempt *to shrug it off. He acknowledged the gesture with the faintest flicker of a smile. It was the first time Jackdaw had put his arm around his brother in that protective sort of way and it would be a lifetime before he did it again.*

****

I cheated rather. Wrote about an event that Jackdaw didn't witness – the football being kicked at James as he walked away – in the middle of a long passage that is all narrated from David's point of view. Ah well, I was a young and very inexperienced writer when I wrote it.

The bit about David catching dragonflies rings true, though. I always dreamed of mating incongruous animals and producing something fabulous, like the beasts of heraldry. And I knew a little bit about the birds and the bees by now. There is an intimation of this back in the first chapter of my "novella". David – Jackdaw – is four during this scene. The fictional sister Mary is about eight.

****

'And that one's a chaffinch. You can tell by the white bars on its wings.'

'What are the bars made of?'

'You are silly sometimes,' said his sister. 'They're just a colour. They're feathers, aren't they?'

'They seem too real.'

It was spring. Mary told him it was the fifth spring he'd lived through but somehow he didn't have a very clear memory of the others. He could remember snow, could remember having had that twice, and he could remember picking blackberries twice, which meant autumn apparently. But he couldn't remember all this

The Raven and the Jackdaw

before – buds swelling on the birch twigs, downy catkins opening on the sallow (pussy willow) and "lambs' tails", dangling masses of yellow dust, on the hazels. He didn't remember the water squelching under your wellingtons as you walked under the cold clear sky, nor how the primroses appeared in the sheltered places where the clay was mossy and moist. And he didn't remember the lapwings doing aerobatics high above them as they crossed the fields, diving to within inches of the ground before soaring up again, making strange bubbling noises the while, all in order (Mary said) to show off to their mates. 'What's mates?'

'Boyfriends and girlfriends, sort of.'

'I see,' said Jackdaw, who did see – sort of. They sat down on the ground and Jackdaw began to pick blades of grass in an abstracted way. He had something on his mind. They sat silently for a while, doing nothing much except getting a little damp and Jackdaw going on picking grass stems. Eventually he asked, 'Why do we wear clothes when the animals don't?' He had asked his mother the same question some time before and no longer needed to know the answer but he thought it might serve as a useful introduction to a subject on which he did want information. So he waited politely, patiently, while Mary explained that some animals needed fur or feathers to keep them warm, while others had cold blood, so didn't feel the cold at all, but that none of them needed coats or scarves even in the coldest weather. When she had finished David asked his supplementary question in one long sentence without pausing for breath once. 'I take my clothes off when I have a bath and you've seen me having a bath lots and lots of times but I've never seen you having a bath never seen you with no clothes on it's not fair.'

'I've seen Raven in the bath too,' said Mary with a superior air.

'Everyone's seen Raven in the bath: that's nothing,' Jackdaw replied in what he intended to be a crushing tone. Then he added quickly, *'Will you take your clothes off now, here?'*

Mary did not seem put out by the request but put her head on one side as though weighing up the pros and cons. 'I don't think I will,' she said after some consideration. 'It'd be much too cold out here. Perhaps in the summer I would've. There's not much to see anyway.' And with that, as Mary stood up to go, Jackdaw had to be content.

*

In the hawthorn hedge the blackbird's nest at last contained an egg. The nest had already captured David's imagination; it created a whole new world of ideas. It had come there so suddenly, so secretly. You never saw it being built because the birds took grass and leaves into the dark recess only when you weren't looking. One day he was lifted up and shown the inside, glistening with wet mud, smooth as something on a potter's wheel. The next day it was all upholstered with finely shredded grass. Less than a house, more than a bed, created in only a few days yet looking as though it had always been there, so snugly did it lie in the hedge with the many-branched twigs woven into it.

And now the egg. It was an egg all right, like the kind you ate for breakfast only it was so small, green freckled with brown, shiny and beautiful. But there was something else about it, something you couldn't understand but that made you want to be alone and sit and think. Next day there were two eggs, then three, then four. They were going to hatch. Whatever that meant. David repeated the word to himself over and over in the hope that that might clarify his cloudy understanding. The hen blackbird sat on the nest all day now. One day David caught sight of her eye. It was large, round, dark

The Raven and the Jackdaw

and liquid and it seemed to see in all directions at once, seemed to see everything. It was fearful and fearsome at the same time. It was wild, and he ran away.

One day they lifted him up again. A black shapeless mass writhed in the nest, clawed with skeletal arms and stretched blind heads towards him. David cried at intervals for the rest of that day, inconsolable in the discovery that not everything was beautiful that lived under Nature's great tender hand.

****

My fictional alter ego was learning bit by bit about the birds and the bees just as I had done. Though Jackdaw would have been astonished to know that his real-life counterpart would one day be presenting the mating rituals of the African mammals on television, to a worldwide audience.

Yet what interests me most as I re-read those last extracts is the scene behind the shed in which eight-year-old Jackdaw tries to comfort his older brother after he's been kicked out of the football team. It comes over as a rather strongly written scene, I think. And yet for the life of me I can't remember if that episode ever actually took place, or if I made it up. Either way it seems to express quite neatly the closeness of the bond between us. But as for the way the scene ended... *It was the first time Jackdaw had put his arm around his brother in that protective sort of way and it would be a lifetime before he did it again...*

Honestly! In those last days before Jason went off to boarding school we grappled with each other in bed each night with an urgency that bordered on the violent, so desperate were we to make the most of each other before our enforced separation. In writing so coyly about that diffident hug behind the shed, was I trying to deceive an imagined horde of future readers – should the thing ever by some remote chance be published – or was I trying simply to deceive myself?

The Raven and the Jackdaw

FOUR

I knew in advance that I would miss my brother when he went away to board at prep school but the experience of that missing was even worse than my expectation of it. I felt as if my world had been punctured like a bicycle tyre and all the air let out. My parents showed me Jason's first letter to them. It began, *Dear Mummy and Daddy, I am very happy here although I miss you very much.* It didn't mention missing me. Perhaps that was just as well. I might have broken down and cried in front of my parents if it had. The letter ended, *With lots of love, Jason.* Then: *PS Give my love to Barnaby. Lots.*

Lots of love for me. Did he really mean that? So much in letters was formulaic. I already knew that. Letters to total strangers began with the word Dear, even letters of protest or complaint. I chose to interpret Jason's message in the most optimistic way I could. It was the first time he'd put the word love and the idea of me in the same sentence, either in writing or in speech. I chose to think it meant that Jason felt the same way about me as I felt about him. Even if the silent vocabulary that framed my thoughts about him didn't yet include the word love.

In bed at night, in the short but long-seeming time before I went to sleep I would fiddle with my penis, delve into my groin with fingers, and caress my tummy and the insides of my thighs, trying to pretend that it was Jason doing this. I fantasised about the pair of us, trying to think forward to a future that contained just the two of us and nobody else. I saw a nature programme on television which showed the activity inside an underground bumble-bees' nest. It looked wonderfully cosy. The bees had made a soft bed of moss and wool on which to build their fragile honey pots and then sleep at night. I imagined that Jason and I might nest in such a place, approached through an inconspicuous mouse-hole in a cornfield. Safe and hidden in our underground fastness we would cuddle and fumble our way through life, always naked. We'd live on the honey in the honey pots. I gave us a pair of wings apiece, to help us get about, though they would considerately disappear when the fumbling was about to start. Nobody else was involved in this fantasy. Our whole world comprised just the two of us. Needless to say I never told Jason about this.

Jason returned for half term at mid-day on a Saturday. We all drove to the station to meet him and his suitcase. He seemed bigger and there was a new look in his brown eyes. His look was stronger, harder, a little more distant. But we played together during the afternoon, re-established physical contact in the course of our horseplay, and the new look in Jason's eyes somehow seemed to thaw out. By bedtime he was his usual familiar lovely self. Bedtime was exceptionally late. Jason hadn't seen much TV in the last six weeks, and our parents let him – and me – stay up and watch the Benny Hill Show as a special treat. When at last we got into our two beds and put the light out the room was November dark. There was silence for a minute or so. Neither of us moved a muscle. The silence began to ache. Then Jason said, with a diffidence in his voice that had been absent all day, 'Do you want to come in with me?'

'Yes,' I said. My voice surprised me by coming out all charged up and husky. I pulled my pyjamas off in rapid motion and leapt eagerly in with him. He too was naked. We pressed tummy against tummy and wrapped arms and legs around each other and it seemed the best moment of my life.

****

The Raven and the Jackdaw

David assumed that, as he was two years younger than his brother, it would be two years before he was expected to follow James to boarding school. He had reckoned without his own academic reputation. Being bright, he found to his dismay, meant that this upheaval would follow in less than a year's time. David would be nine and a bit.

The September day on which David set off for his new existence was blazing hot. He felt awkward and uncomfortable in his new unfriendly uniform and rather envied James his with its worn, comfortable look and, presumably, feel. They had lunch early, James, David and their mother, and then set out for the station, which was a good few miles away.

Why did it have to be such a beautiful day, David wondered, when it was going to be the worst one of his life? The fact that Isabel had taken the trouble to cook a special lunch at which his favourite dishes appeared (liver and bacon with thick gravy, bread and butter pudding) made the whole business even worse. He wondered as he glanced from time to time at James whether his brother had felt the same, the previous year, as he, David, did now. Certainly he hadn't shown it but then, David wasn't showing what he felt now either.

They stopped for ice-cream at a village shop. It was too hot not to. David realised with painful clarity that this would be the last ice-cream for who knew how long. It wasn't that going without ice-cream was a hardship. There was something else he knew he would be doing without: it was his own identity, though he couldn't have defined it so precisely at the time.

Goodbyes were said on the platform; final and half-expected bags of sweets changed hands; the waving arms receded into the distance. David kept his eyes glued to the window for the whole long journey. What he was intent on seeing was the physical link between home and school: the geographical fact of one field coming next to another one; each station following another one and existing with its predecessor in the same world. Had he taken his eye off the slowly unrolling tapestry of the landscape he would, he felt, have snapped the thread, have found himself in another place instead of being simply in a distant part of the same one. He didn't think he could cope with the first idea – the second he might just about manage. So whenever James spoke to him he had to reply out of the corner of his mouth, leaving his gaze fixed upon the golden filament of countryside outside the window, which must not be broken at all costs.

James had been given a pound note to get them both a taxi to the school. He was a little nervous about the prospect as he had never taken a taxi on his own before and hoped he would have the necessary nerve to get one, especially because he had his image in the eyes of his little brother to consider. But in the event it proved easier than he had anticipated. Taxis hovered around the station as though they were actually anxious to be hired. They did not play hard to get as he had feared they might and once he had got himself and David inside one he found himself wondering where he had imagined the difficulty would lie. It occurred to him that other things in life might prove to be like that too. Things that appeared as insurmountable obstacles at a distance often melted away as you got up to them and when you looked back you wondered why you had been anxious or frightened. For you had coped with the situation somehow and it had never been all that difficult. Each day James was growing to be more of a man – he now took taxis when he wanted to – and it was not proving such a difficult thing to be.

The taxi turned left, right, left; plunged through residential estates... The thread broke at last for David.

The Raven and the Jackdaw

For all his efforts he had lost track of which direction they were going in. Thoughts of escape would be no comfort now; he wouldn't even know the way to the station. He was in a different place.

The taxi turned in at big gates and swept round a courtyard to the front door. James paid the driver with a manly flourish. 'We don't use the front door except at the beginning and end of term,' he explained to David. 'It's out of bounds most of the time. In fact most places are out of bounds.' A long hall stretched into the distance, chillsome, tiled and slithery. Halfway along it three boys were unpacking trunks.

'What are their names?' David asked. Despite his assumption that life ahead was going to be hell he had decided to take as positive an attitude as possible. Getting to know people's names seemed a good start.

'Ridgeway and Belt. I don't know the thin one. He's a new boy.'

'Like me.'

'Like you? There'll be hundreds like you once the school train from London gets in.'

'Hundreds?'

'Well, thirty or forty. Come upstairs. We'll look at the dormitory list and then you can unpack.'

The matron, whom they bumped into at the top of the stairs, saved them the trouble of looking at the list. 'You're in Dorm Four this term, Rhodie ma.,' she said. 'Your little brother's in Dorm One. Show him where to go. And mind you look after him now.'

David had seen the dormitories before, when he, James, and their parents had been shown round the school over a year ago. Then the strange little rooms with a dozen or so beds in had been curiosities: things to look at and wonder at – but from a distance, as though in a glass case in a museum. Now David was actually going to live in one. It seemed somehow impossible. 'We *call it the babies' dorm,'* said James. *'Of course you're not a baby, being nine. But a lot of the new boys are only six or seven. You'll be with them I'm afraid. At least to start with. Next term they may put you in Dorm Two. Lights-out in Dorm Two isn't till eight o'clock. I was put into Dorm Two straight away. But then, I was ten.'*

David wanted to say, 'It all looks so uncomfortable,' but was well aware that it would have been inappropriate as well as serving no purpose. So he said nothing. There was a lot to take in. There was the bath rota, lockers, a shelf in the linen cupboard, pigeon-holes, timetables, rules, games lists, dinner-table lists, tea-table lists, house lists...

'Brothers are always put into different houses,' said James. *'I'm already a White, so you'll be a Black. Whites have won everything worth winning for years, I'm afraid.'*

'I don't think I'll ever get the hang of all this,' David said.

'You'll get into it.'

'How long did it take you?'

'A few days. A week or two.'

'Do you actually like it, though?'

'Oh, school's school. Nobody likes it. But it's all right. You want to get into one of the junior house teams. Then you'll be OK.'

'But you know I'm not that good at football.'

'You'll just have to get better, I suppose. I don't know any other way.'

The school train crowd arrived. The place swarmed with people and noise, and much attention was focused on David's brother. David realised suddenly that James was a popular figure here: he was a good talker, at ease and able to hold his own in a boisterous crowd. David was none of those things; he was small for his age and at this moment feeling very self-conscious and a little

The Raven and the Jackdaw

uncomfortable. James occasionally made a move to introduce his friends to David but after a curt hallo they would always turn back towards the brighter star. David was not given to jealousy. Otherwise that is what he might well have felt now towards his brother.

'Well,' said James when they were alone again. 'I mustn't go on calling you David any more. You're Rhodie mi. now and I'm Rhodie ma.'

David felt panic and puzzlement. 'Can't I even call you James when we're alone?'

'It wouldn't feel right somehow. Not here. Anyway, we won't be together much. Being in different classes, in different dorms, on different tables, you know. Anyway I must go off and do my own unpacking. It's nearly teatime anyway now.'

'But what do I do?' David was horror-struck at this impending desertion. This really was turning out to be the worst day of his life. 'What do I do?'

James looked a little uncomfortable. He was not insensitive and he had some idea that he was behaving meanly but he did not really see how things could be otherwise. People didn't mollycoddle their brothers here and James was no nonconformist. 'You'd better meet up with some other boys, I suppose. You'll be getting to know them sooner or later anyway.'

'Right, well, that's what I'll do then,' David said uncertainly and then added, 'See you in tea,' hopefully, before walking away. He went outside to where boys were roller-skating on the concrete and others were playing on the grass beyond. Spotting the thin boy he had seen earlier he walked up to him and said, 'Hallo. You're new too, aren't you? I'm Rhodie mi.' He was surprised at the cheery confidence with which he managed to invest the words. A few moments later he had met several other new boys and discovered that they were all in the same dorm and all equally unsure of

themselves. They ran races across the playing field and David actually managed to win one of them. The sun was still shining and the grass had just been mown and it still smelled sweet when it was trampled. By the time the bell rang for tea David was cautiously thinking that he might be enjoying himself.

'Bless us, O Lord,' said the headmaster crisply when the rustling had died away, 'and these thy gifts which we are about to receive from the fruit of thy bounty through Christ our Lord, Amen. Sit down. Tea is eaten in silence.'

The Lord's gifts consisted of a spoonful of red jam on the side of each plate, dishes of bread and margarine which swept up and down the table on a tide of moving hands, and tea with the milk and sugar already in it. This was dispensed from huge green enamel jugs by Florrie who, David was reliably informed, had a glass eye, if not two glass eyes and consequently did not always judge the distance between jug and cup too accurately, so that cups and saucers tended to be filled to the brim and beyond. David always drank milk at home. He detested tea. But here was this rule of silence and no opportunity to discuss the matter – and now his cup was filled to overflowing by tall businesslike Florrie with her glass eye, so there was not much to be done except drink it. It was not pleasant, though such a consideration, David realised, was out of place here. At one point during the meal David caught his brother's eye across the room. The Raven winked at him. Delighted and surprised the Jackdaw winked back.

'All new boys stay behind. Tomorrow morning you will go to Form One and Miss Thinn will give you some tests to see whether you'll stay in Form One or go into Form Two.' There was something abrasive in the way the headmaster pronounced the word tomorrow. It made it quite clear that tomorrow would be much worse than

The Raven and the Jackdaw

today. David found himself looking forward to bedtime and the hours of sleep that would fill the gap between the grim present and the grimmer future. Sleep at least was the same everywhere. You didn't have to struggle with life when you were asleep. The rest of the time, when you were at school, it seemed to require so much willpower even to exist.

It was still light outside. There were more new faces. More roller-skating. Then the bell rang again, for junior supper. They filed along the corridor in twos. The boy next to David smelt. One luckless individual burst into tears en route. The others heard him in appalled silence, each one thinking, it might have been me, and each one glad that it was not. Supper was a slice of bread and margarine and a plastic cup of milk. Nothing else. It was eaten standing behind one's chair at one's table place. In silence.

Alone in bed at last David was annoyed to find that when the lights went out a dim red night-light was switched on in their stead, its curled-up element glowing pink and un-winking in its fluted shade. When he buried his head under the covers it seemed to burn through the blankets and when he shut his eyes it burned into his brain.

Two people could be heard sobbing in a muffled sort of way. Perhaps they were the six- and seven-year-olds. David would not have forgiven himself if it had been he and not they who had given way like this, but he knew he would have to choose carefully the thoughts he might dwell on over the next few days if he were to avoid following their example. He thought now about his brother, rather crossly. He saw him for the first time as just another grownup in a grownup world: one who had let him down at the precise moment when he was needed most. There was a kind of cowardice in James that David hadn't seen in him before. Yet James was popular and successful. David was proud of him. And he had winked at him during tea. For that he could perhaps be forgiven anything. David felt less cross. He fell asleep.

*

David became, over the next four years, a rather quiet, serious schoolboy who lacked his brother's gift for easy laughter and conversation and the popularity that went with them. There was an aloofness about him which, with the passage of time, grew into an intimidating quality that seemed to demand respect from others. Nobody knew he had once been called Jackdaw.

To his surprise he was made house captain in his final year at prep school. In this last year James was no longer with him; he had scraped into public school at last. David had to admit that life had become easier now, in spite of his rather so-so performance on the sports field. He could not be bullied or intimidated by older boys: there were none. Staff confided in him, junior boys looked up to him, and kitchen staff found him choice titbits to eat. Life could become more comfortable if you were prepared to do a bit of waiting, he thought. In fact, by the time he was due to leave, at age thirteen, and join James at senior school, David was almost beginning to enjoy himself.

****

David's disillusionment at his brother's behaviour towards him on his first evening at boarding school seems perhaps disproportionate. It was real enough – as was the whole description of that traumatic day – but its cause was somewhat different. Jason came with me to find the bed I'd been allocated (beneath that infernal nightlight!) in the new boys' dormitory, then, when we'd deposited my suitcase on top of my bed we went along the corridor together to find his new place in dormitory

The Raven and the Jackdaw

four. Inside his dormitory we found ourselves alone. I remember the two of us standing on either side of his bed, on which his suitcase now sat just as mine did just three rooms away. I looked Jason very squarely in the face for a moment, wondering if he was going to say something about a certain subject. He looked back at me but remained silent. He looked uncomfortable. He knew very well what that certain subject was. Faced with his silence I brought the matter up myself.

'We're only going to be three rooms away,' I said. 'When it's really late and everyone's asleep I could come along the corridor and...'

'No,' Jason interrupted me firmly, a horrified expression appearing on his face. 'It's far too risky. There's never a moment you could be sure that everyone's asleep. Somebody would notice, and sneak to someone. We'd be expelled. There'd be a scandal.' He paused. 'You do understand that, don't you?'

I said, 'I know what a scandal is.' My voice stayed level, in command of itself. But inside me everything was suddenly shaken up as if by an earthquake. I'd dimly realised that we must never get caught in bed together by our parents, and I'd kept my feelings towards my brother very much to myself. Yet the things we did together seemed so natural to me, so integral a part of me, so much a part of *us*, that I'd never had any sense of guilt about them, no sense that we were unusual or (though this was not a word I knew) deviant. But I did know the meaning of scandal; I knew about politicians, even churchmen, having to resign their posts because of scandals. I was deeply shocked and unsettled now to hear the word used by Jason in connection with *us*.

I went on quickly, 'I suppose you're right. We could never be sure everyone was asleep in both dormitories.' Then I was suddenly anxious. 'But you'd still want to, if it was possible, I mean?'

Jason reached across the bed and put one hand on my shoulder for an instant. An uneasy smile flickered across his face. It was a smile whose brief intensity, like an electric shock, hurt both of us. 'Yes,' he said. The smile vanished and he withdrew his hand. 'But it's quite impossible. We mustn't. Never try it. Never come along the corridor to find me in the night. Never, never. We have to be patient. There are half-terms and then there are holidays. Like last year.'

I turned away then and left him to his unpacking. Went outside and found the other new boys. Ran, and won, a race.

The Raven and the Jackdaw

FIVE

My written story leaves a gap of seven years between that mainly true account of starting prep school and the next events that it reports. It was hardly the case that nothing happened in those seven years, though. My brother and I both hit puberty for a start.

One half-term when I was ten and he was twelve Jason returned to my bed at home, from which he had been unavoidably absent for six weeks. He had learned a new skill. He tried it out on me and I found I liked it enormously. 'It's called wanking,' my brother explained. 'All boys do it in their teens.' Until this time we had fondled and fiddled with each other's erect cocks as well as sucking them. Jason's new technique was something extra. 'When you get a bit older, stuff comes out,' he told me.

'What?' I queried. 'You mean like pee? Wouldn't that wet the bed?'

'I think it's thicker,' he said, pausing for a moment in his stroking of me. 'I've never seen it, only heard about it. I think it's more like toothpaste. And the quantity's not as much as pee.'

'How old are you when that happens?' I asked.

'Thirteen,' said Jason authoritatively. 'That'll be next year for me, then you two years after that.'

I thought it was pretty sensational already, even without toothpaste. The tingling and the throbbing that I got... I knew it was the same for Jason, because after a while the exquisite torture of my attentions to his dick would make him beg me to leave off. By the time he got to that stage I would already have reached the same point – about a minute earlier – and would have begged him too to leave off. We were always good to each other abut this: when asked to, we always did leave off.

Jason's dick had always been bigger than mine; he was older and bigger than me; I accepted that detail as a matter of course. But from this time on, the expansion of his penis accelerated far more quickly than the growth of the rest of him. Nor was it long before a little seepage would occur, just after I stopped massaging it. Jason assured me that this was just a preliminary watery emission, not to be confused with the toothpaste-like substance which could be expected when he reached thirteen. He'd learned from older boys that that had a name. Or rather three names. I found it interesting that all three names began with S.

Jason's learned friends weren't exactly right about the timetable, it turned out. Jason had to wait till he was fourteen before he could come properly, while this stage occurred for me – to my surprise, as I was still smaller, and hairless down there – when I was only twelve. To Jason's chagrin. It meant that he saw and felt my first outflow of semen before his own. Though happily for both of us he caught up with me within a fortnight. Both our rites of passage occurred during the same school holiday and we were glad about that. There was now though the problem of what to do with the ejaculate we produced together in bed. Jason found the answer on my very first night. He licked me clean like a cat. And when, two weeks later, we had to deal with Jason's own first spillage, I copied his example. I found the taste unpleasant at first, and the texture disconcerting, but I got used to it as time passed.

The wonders of my brother's developing nether regions, and of my own, were not the only aspects of biology that fascinated me. Over the years my interest in wildlife continued to grow and develop. When we started to do biology as a school subject, when I was thirteen, I found my attention gripped, and my curiosity

The Raven and the Jackdaw

excited, to an extent that had happened with no other school activity. Our biology teacher was a real enthusiast for his subject and his laboratory was stocked, at different times, with Martian-eyed locusts in a glass-fronted cage, and live gerbils and mating frogs in tanks. We dissected cockles and mussels (alive, alive-o, I guess) and we watched in awe as our teacher split open the eye of a dead sheep. So exciting was this that I decided to try it at home.

Jason was slightly startled when the two ox eyes turned up. I had asked my parents to ask the butcher to deliver them along with the meat. 'You never told me about biology,' I said to Jason a bit accusingly. 'You never told me what fun it was.'

'It's just another subject,' he said. 'Like physics or chemistry. You just have to do it.' But his dismissive attitude was a pretence. I knew that he was one of the best in his class at all three subjects. (I, on the other hand, though good at biology, was a duffer at the other two subjects. It was as much as I could do to keep a Bunsen burner from going out.) And when I set about cutting up the ox eyes he was right beside me, even helping me to get the razor blade through the sclerotic coat, which was extremely tough. Together we identified the aqueous humour (it simply ran out) the lens and the iris. The jelly-like vitreous humour that filled the main cavity; the optic nerve and the blind spot. We thought about tasting the vitreous humour but in the end did not. We swallowed each other's semen nightly, but drew the line at that.

On another occasion I dissected a dead wood-mouse and again, Jason wanted to be with me when I did that. Although it was my idea, my mouse, it was Jason who proved better at identifying and naming the tiny parts. It was a male, with miniature cock and balls to prove the fact.

My career as an anatomist came to an ignominious end though. The cause of this was a dead adder that I'd found under a hedge in a nearby field while out on one of my solitary nature walks. I had it in mind to extract the skeleton, then assemble and mount it. To do this I would have to boil the meat off the carcase first. I borrowed the old saucepan in which our mother used to boil our dirty handkerchiefs...

Reader, you can have no idea of the abominable foulness of the stench of boiled adder unless you've boiled one yourself.

It hung about for days. The whole house stank. Our clothes smelt. Fortunately it was summer and the windows could be kept open day and night. Yet that barely helped. Even my schoolmaster father, who had eagerly encouraged me in my researches, lost faith in me at that point. I could go on dissecting animals, he told me, provided they were dead and that I hadn't killed them expressly in order to do it, but none of my cadavers must ever, ever again be cooked.

As for Jason, he was thoroughly disgusted with me. 'How can I bring friends round while the place smells like a charnel house?' he said. 'You ought to have known it would never work.' He pointed to the putrid mess of skin and hundreds of ribs and bits of flesh. It looked like a half-digested fish that a seagull had puked up. 'You can't assemble that.' I didn't even try. My tail between my legs, I took the snake's mortal coils out into the garden, got a spade from the shed, and buried my failed experiment. Jason did have the decency to thank me for doing that, at least, but he continued to complain. 'You've made the house unliveable,' he said. 'To think we've got to eat here, and go to sleep in this stench.'

I thought that Jason might be so annoyed with me that he would refuse to come to my bed that night, or refuse to allow me entry to his. But I was wrong. He did let me

The Raven and the Jackdaw

into his bed. And when we had both come, and we'd licked each other ticklingly like two kittens, he held me in an embrace that seemed – I don't think it was my imagination – more tender and more protracted than any cuddle he'd given me in the past.

****

It was late September and the sun had risen, blazing. So far there had been no frost. The garden still had a look of summer about it; forget-me-nots still flowered extravagantly, the rose trees were still thick with blooms and a few flies still disported themselves, in defiance of the laws of gravity, on the white-painted weatherboarding in their zeal to take maximum advantage of the warmth of the sun. Only the heavy dew, which had not had time to disappear before the sun surprised it and which still lay, thickly sparkling, over everything in sight – only the boughs of the ancient Bramley apple tree, weighted almost to the ground with their burdens of brown-green fruit – only the length of the shadows at half past eight in the morning – only these gave the lie to the illusion of high summer sustained for ever, as though paradise had materialised on earth and kindly stopped all the clocks.

It was a Saturday. The boys, sixth-formers now, had been back at school for a fortnight and Mary already lived away from home. Hector sat at the garden table, which had not yet been banished to the garage for the winter. It was laid with the gaily striped kitchen cloth and all the familiar breakfast things. From the open doorway came the smell of toast and the quiet noise of Isabel stirring round in the kitchen. In a minute she would emerge into the sunlight, bearing the final tray. She would be looking as radiant and as lovely as she had done on the day they met. She would sit beside him and before she had time to pour the coffee he would put his hand over hers. She would turn towards him and smile and neither would need to speak.

Hector peered into the deep shadows under the hazel bushes at the bottom of the garden. A lot of it could do with cutting back. You forgot about things like that for years and then you realised suddenly how overgrown everything looked. That was something he could tackle this weekend perhaps. The garden did look good at this time of year, though. Especially this year with its Indian summer that showed no sign of breaking up. The grass was as neat and trim as those uneven lawns allowed it to be. The borders were ablaze with colour. There were bees in the air, still going about their tasks with ponderous dignity. This was not a weekend for hurrying; it was a time to savour. The smell of coffee wafted suddenly from the kitchen door.

Hector had not been born in the country but in a small garden-less house in Edinburgh. But his grandfather had been a farmer; he had kept a small windswept cliff-top farm in Berwickshire. The buildings were ugly, functional, rain-blackened stone and slate but Hector as a child had lost his heart to that farm. To spend holidays there was magical. In later years the farm had lost money and had had to be sold, but Hector had kept alive the vivid, hard-edged memory of it. As a student, as a teacher, as a soldier, he had cherished the improbable hope that he would one day live in the country and rear children there.

The war had ended. Years later Isabel had materialised. The deputy headship in the south of England had come a few years after that. And then, Hundredhouse Farm. The house had been parted some time before from the land that had once belonged to it; it lay up a long winding lane. They had both fallen in love with it at first glance one bleak March day. It was of

The Raven and the Jackdaw

warm pink brick with leaded windows. The garden was ramshackle, full of old fruit trees, un-pruned roses, and tumbledown sheds that deceived you into thinking they held endless possibilities but which could only in fact be useless to the point of luxury.

So they bought it. With the help of an opportune legacy on Isabel's side. 'You're mad,' people said. 'You'll never be able to afford the upkeep.' But somehow they did.

Three fine beamed rooms ran along the front of the house, two of them retaining their original open hearths. At the rear was a long kitchen with an ancient range in it. They replaced it with an Aga. Bit by bit the house was made habitable, while the garden astonished them with its fecundity. What would they do, they wondered, with the dairy and the game larder? By the end of their first summer the question had become instead, where would they put it all? There were redcurrants – for jelly; angelica growing like hogweed by the back door, waiting to be crystallised; elderberries lazing in inky drupes among the derelict pig-sties, to be turned into wine; runner beans to be salted down for winter; nasturtium seeds to pickle...

One summer had followed another. The three children came along. Big teenagers now. And Hector had risen from deputy head to head of his Comprehensive school. He had had a number of articles published in History Today over the years, and his prize-winning shallots and cucumbers were the envy of the whole population of regulars at the Red Lion.

Now a wagtail bobbed across the lawn as though on a string, while Isabel came out of the doorway with the toast and coffee. She put down the tray, then sat down herself, soberly. Hector reached out his hand and clasped hers. She turned to him at once with a suddenness that surprised him. 'Darling,' she said, 'I've bad news. I have to go into hospital – on Monday.'

*

It was good to be able to laze away the day over endless cups of coffee and cigarettes and intense, world-righting conversations about everything from the Labour party to the headmaster's latest regulations about haircuts, and then to read Nineteen-Eighty-Four and King Lear before collapsing into bed in the small hours only to discover at breakfast that you had no recollection of either. Somebody had had his eyes put out. But who? And in which book? Life was not altogether unkind to sixth-formers.

James found the lifestyle suited him. People had always considered him lazy even when his timetable had given him no opportunity to be. Now at last he had the chance to justify his reputation. He played in the First Fifteen sometimes – though not all the time; that would have been too much like hard work. He grew to enjoy the feel of a pint mug in his fist, and he discovered the charms of womankind. More precisely, womankind discovered the charms of James.

He had lost his virginity at sixteen. Lost it was the right phrase. He hadn't struggled to rid himself of it the way most men do. One day it simply wasn't there any more and he hardly noticed its disappearance. He still had the black hair that had given rise to his childhood nickname. He had an olive complexion that set him apart from the rest of his family and a fine pair of brown eyes that were humorous, cheeky and sexy at the same time. And he had his smile. It would begin lazily, slowly, sensuously, and it would expand into an impressive display of brilliant white teeth. To say the performance was effective would have been an understatement. Opinion was divided over the smile. Some thought James knew to a nicety the effect it had on people, others

The Raven and the Jackdaw

believed that he was so unaware of things in general as to be completely innocent about the smile and the effect it had: namely that girls of previously unimpeachable reputation went weak at the knees when they beheld it. The truth lay somewhere in the middle. He never practised the smile in front of a mirror (as some people suggested) and might not have always been conscious of whether it was in operation at any given time. But he knew about the smile all right.

Self-assurance and confidence enhanced his good looks. At eighteen he was nearly six feet tall and had the kind of slim muscularity that is admired universally. Grown women flirted with him outrageously.

Most adolescent boys concentrate on seeking sex with a singlemindedness that would be regarded as commendable if aimed in any other direction. Not so James. He had no problem finding sex; it always found him first. He took it as it came, smiled his irresistible smile, enjoyed it, and that was that. It never became a preoccupation.

Neither did his school work. Even his drawing and painting, much as he enjoyed them, occupied little of his energy. His mental and emotional apparatus coasted through these teenage years as some people coast through the whole of life, in neutral gear or as if in sleep. In later years it would seem to him that he remembered very little about his schooldays.

David was about as unlike James as one brother could be to another. He was rather less than average height at sixteen and not physically very well developed. His eyes were blue, his hair mouse-coloured and his general appearance nondescript. He still lacked his brother's aptitude for games and he excelled in none of his school subjects, though he was reasonably competent in just about all of them. 'You're the man with the ten talents,' one of his teachers flattered him. 'No,' he replied, 'I'm *the man with one. I just got given it in small change, that's all.'* He was becoming prone to epigrammatic statements. A few people found this endearing, most, simply irritating.

It did seem, though, as his schooldays neared their end, that David was beginning to acquire a little personality and even the rudiments of charm. Though shy and, particularly with girls, diffident, he could at times be witty and even entertaining to talk with. He seemed to be at his best when the shyness and wit were equally balanced. He was enjoying the experience of sharing in his brother's easy popularity, of being included, being listened to. How he would develop from here it was hard to say.

*

That Isabel was ill was something dreadful. Beyond belief. But there was worse for Hector than that. She hadn't told him. She had suffered those first suspicions alone, stifled her nagging fears, and when she could have reached out so easily for his reassurance and comfort had chosen to hide her thoughts from him. He couldn't have done anything in practical medical terms but he could have been with her, sharing the anxiety and pain. Yet she had chosen to be alone. It was as if she had said, 'We have shared everything we could but now here is a place where you cannot come. Deep down here where the pain is I have to be alone.' It was a bitter discovery. Life had designed Hector for sharing and he had believed that years of marriage might be a training for just such a time as this: when two hearts that had become one could tackle the unspeakable together and – who knew? – perhaps even win. This might have been the moment he was created for but Isabel had denied him it. He had wanted to share in another's suffering and was not allowed to. It made a nonsense of his life and he found no purpose in it afterwards.

The Raven and the Jackdaw

Isabel went into hospital. She was operated on. She was given ray treatment. She faded. Hector drank more than he had used to.

Isabel remained in hospital until the early spring. Then one day, as the buds were bursting on the horse chestnuts outside her hospital window, she was dead. Her two sons stared blankly, that Easter holiday, as her coffin was inched into the ground and wondered what they ought to feel, wondered what they did feel, wondered numbly if they felt anything at all.

SIX

In fact neither of our parents died at this stage of our lives, though as I mentioned earlier, very sadly our Aunt Sonia (Auntie Jean) did. I've written the word *lives* meaning my life and my brother's. But that plural applies equally well to the way those lives were divided, to an almost schizophrenic degree, between school and holidays. At home our situation was rural to the point of loneliness. Not many of our pre-boarding-school friendships had survived the years during which we'd been away from home in term-time. And most of those friendships belonged to Jason: he was the more sociable and extrovert of the two of us. He would take a bus into town sometimes and hang out with a friend or two there, or go off with a couple of mates on bicycles. I was often content to wander the fields by myself, observing the wildlife (and no doubt being in my turn observed by it). I found coveys of partridges and would track pheasants to their hidden nests in the hedge bottoms, collect frogspawn in early spring, and watch the courtship rituals of ducks and dabchicks.

I built a catch-it-alive trap and – though not always easily – caught bank voles and wood-mice, which I brought home and kept in large, excitingly designed, cages that incorporated nest boxes and tree branches. I used to study their behaviour and, by handling them often, tame them. They had names, some of which I remember: Minimoss, Triumph Nimrod and, simply, Mouse. Occasionally I would still find the corpse of some animal or other and take it home and dissect it. Though out of respect for my parents' and Jason's wishes – as well as my own olfactory memory – I would never, ever, boil it.

Our cottage had three bedrooms. My parents had one, Jason and I the second one, while the third was a spare

The Raven and the Jackdaw

room, available for the occasional visitor. When I was thirteen and my brother fifteen our mother said that we could have separate bedrooms if we wanted. I could move into the spare room and make it my own, with the proviso that when anyone came to stay I'd give my room up for the duration and move back in with Jason. When this proposal was put to us one evening Jason and I looked at each other for a split second with something like panic in our faces. We had no chance to confer or formulate a strategy or even discover if we were in agreement. I hoped we were, though, and took it upon myself to answer very quickly, 'I think we're quite happy with the way things are.'

To my huge relief I heard Jason chime in with, 'I don't mind going on sharing with Jackdaw. It's nice sometimes, you know, to have someone to talk to in bed. To say things that don't get said in the daytime.' I thought that was brave of him.

Our mother looked rather narrowly at both of us and I saw the idea flicker quickly through her mind – though it was snuffed out equally quickly – that we might have a hidden agenda here; that we were covering up for nocturnal activities that were less innocent than adolescent conversation. After all, she would have worked out, or our father would have told her, that we both were old enough to masturbate and that we probably did so, despite the lack of evidence. For we still disposed of the evidence by the foolproof method of swallowing it.

And so, despite often spending our daytimes separately, we went on as before after lights-out. One night when I was fourteen and Jason sixteen he asked me as we lay together, in a rather throaty whisper, 'Would you turn round, I mean your bum towards me, and let me fuck you?' I wasn't sure about that and said no that first time. But when he repeated the question a week later I relented. It wasn't a success, though. I was as tense as a coiled spring; it hadn't occurred to me that I would need to relax myself. While it didn't occur to Jason that he would need to use spittle or some other lubricant. He did the next best thing on that occasion, pushing his dick between my thighs, which he asked me to clench for him. As he rodded that artificial crevice I put my hands in front of me to catch his ejaculate. With this technique, we realised, there was a much bigger danger of making a mess of the sheets but somehow, through the years that followed, we managed it.

Once Jason had shown the way I was ready to follow. We spent about two years doing this during the school holidays, almost nightly. Not always precisely turn and turn about, but almost. We found we could do it either front to back, or looking into each other's faces. We did eventually learn to fuck each other properly, just before Jason went off to university, thanks to both of us having lessons from other people. Though our sexual experiments with others diverged in nature. Mine were exclusively with those of my own sex, while Jason's sex partners were female.

Who said anything about love? Who knew anything about love? Our parents seemed to have the idea – they didn't preach this at us, but it was apparent in their reactions to the newly unbuttoned world of the sixties and seventies that was all around them – that teen love was not the full ticket. Real love came later, and came to its full strength with the development of a long-term relationship like marriage. I know now that I felt romantic love for my brother; that I had done since I was six, and that it had deepened. I didn't know at the time, though, that romantic love was the name for what I experienced. My parents might talk about the shallowness of teen relationships, but nobody mentioned romantic love between brothers. I had no role-model situations to go on, no precedent to copy. Through all my childhood and teen years I never said to my brother, 'I love you,' and waited for him to return the compliment. It was beyond my power, just as it is beyond a dog's power, to articulate the concept.

I think I only knew I'd been in love with Jason when I fell out of love with him. I fell out of love with him when I was sixteen. When he got himself a serious girlfriend. I fell out of love with him quite simply because I was jealous.

It happened during school term-time. She – her name was Clare – was at a girls' boarding school on the other side of town. They met by coincidence on a visit to the cinema, with other friends of them both. This happened twice by chance. The third time the two of them, just the two of them, went together. They would meet up then in the evenings, sneaking out of their respective schools, leaving friends to cover for them. How and where they found places to be together, to have sex together, I don't know. In all the years afterwards Jason never told me.

I was in the lower sixth form by then, and Jason in the upper. We each shared a study bedroom with a boy of our own age. My roommate was a boy called Edward. We'd known each other all our schooldays and, though we'd never been close friends, got on well enough. I didn't mind sharing the room with him.

One evening Edward and I were sitting in our room doing prep together. Jason had sneaked out to be with Clare. Edward stood up from his desk and crossed the room towards mine. He stood at my side and laid his hand on my shoulder. He had never done this before, and it surprised me. But what he said then was even more surprising. 'I guess you miss your brother, now he's out most evenings.'

I then gave myself an even bigger surprise. 'Yes,' I said. I wondered if Edward had guessed about my relationship with Jason, even though for years we'd never shown to anyone at school any physical sign of it. I put that thought out of my mind at once, though. I put my hand on top of the hand that Edward was resting on my shoulder.

From then on it was one surprise after another. Edward let his hand, with mine still riding piggy-back on top of it, slide down the front of my shoulder. It paused for a moment at my shirt-covered nipple and very gently tweaked it. Then it went on down... There was a limit to how far Edward's hand could travel while he still stood and I was sitting. Edward slid slowly down onto his haunches. This was all wonderfully easy, I thought. No need for us two to sneak out of school for clandestine meetings in chilly weather. We shared a room. It was gorgeously cosy. That first evening we took the precaution of wedging a chair under the door-handle but then simply crashed onto Edward's bed, opened each other's flies and gave each other a hand-job. Because of the novelty of this and our excitement it took only about a minute. Later that night, when we'd undressed for bed, we climbed in together naked.

When that Easter term ended and Jason and I returned home I guessed that we wouldn't be doing anything in bed together. Jason was now a paid-up member of the heterosexual community and my experiments with Edward about four nights each week had made me feel differently towards Jason, both emotionally and physically. And for three days nothing happened between Jason and me in our shared bedroom. Nothing had happened there at all actually: I hadn't masturbated during those three days and I was pretty sure that Jason hadn't either. Then, on the fourth night, I heard Jason calling softly from his bed, his voice plaintive in the

The Raven and the Jackdaw

darkness. 'Do you want to come in with me? We always used to. Remember?'

I don't remember crossing the room. I seemed to arrive at his bedside in an instant. Then I was in bed with him. But if I'd thought that everything would now be the same as it had used to be, well, it wasn't. Our encounter was fulfilling sexually, physically. But it was somehow different. On my side (I only knew my side of things) the romance, the passion, had gone out of it.

We made the best of it of course. Got into bed every night of that Easter holiday, and either sucked or jerked each other, or came between each other's thighs, as we had always used to. We no longer needed to lick each other clean, though. Jason had found a private towel, which he hid somewhere, and we wiped our nightly emissions away with it. Anyway, we were no longer quite so kittenish. Jason was now six feet in height and I was three inches behind him.

Then the holidays ended and we returned to school for Jason's last term there. So our last summer term together at boarding school began. We slept separately again, as had been always been the case since my first night at prep school seven years earlier. In the days that followed Jason took up again with Clare. But I beat him to it. Within four hours of our return to the sixth-form accommodation block I was back in bed with Edward.

****

Sunday lunchtime was the best bit of the week. There was a tradition associated with it called Going to the Bell. The Bell was of course a pub. It was actually called the Railway Bell, for reasons that became obvious when conversation was regularly drowned by the din of goods engines shunting and hooting at some ten yards' distance. The Bell was less handy than the posher Angel on the corner but there was always the possibility of an embarrassing encounter with members of staff at the Angel. Staff knew that sixth-formers frequented the Bell and so kept to the Angel by unspoken agreement. To force an issue over this particular breach of school discipline would have been considered ungentlemanly by both sides. So at twelve o'clock each Sunday a party of schoolboys that varied in size and composition from week to week would appear on the Bell's doorstep. Also on the dot of twelve would arrive an elderly, dapper gentleman in a three-piece suit, with a gold watch-chain across his ample middle, and in a trilby hat. Each week he would nod a courteous greeting to the youngsters, order a pint of Tankard and sink into a chair by the window, where he would sit sipping his beer and surveying the goods yard with an expression of unsurpassable tranquillity and contentment on his smooth pink features. Though he never spoke, everyone seemed to know he was called Henry. David thought he might have been Sunday lunchtime personified.

For a whole hour it was possible to forget school and schoolboy status and, for the price of two pints of bitter apiece, join the ranks of adult manhood. Life then seemed more mellow and spacious, the future more promising and the past more rosy, while the ideas and thoughts exchanged over the dimple mugs became charged with a significance out of all proportion to their actual content. Then the journey back to school would become a romp with James, usually the instigator of these outings, leaping over the pillar-boxes en route and David, not to be outdone, turning cartwheels on the pavement.

It was after lunch on one of these Sundays that a boy called Bob Belt looked up at the roof of the sixth-form block. The roof at the front of the building was masked by a parapet against whose inner side they were all

The Raven and the Jackdaw

accustomed to rest their feet as they sprawled at a forty-five degree angle on the slates, catching the sun as they revised for exams in the summer. David had once persuaded himself to walk along this parapet, which was only about two feet high on the inside but dropped the full height of the three-storey building on the other. This was unusual for David: bravado did not play a large part in his make-up. But having done it once he took to doing it every day, just to show off. He knew the performance made him look brave, though he reckoned that it merely looked dangerous. There was no reason why you should fall – assuming you didn't faint, or trip over your own feet.

At the back of the building there was no parapet. The roof rose steeply pitched above the rear wall, over the jutting bathroom block and, lower down, the remains of a conservatory that was now almost roofless thanks to the depredations of generations of schoolboys. Below lay the jungle of a garden where boys now sat drinking post-prandial Nescafé out of chipped mugs. The garden was the principal venue for such events as mock duels with fencing foils, serious hostilities that involved fire-extinguishers, and the celebration of birthdays with the time-honoured custom of tossing the unfortunates aloft in a blanket. There were also bonfires when there was anything to burn. Usually A-level notes when exams were finished.

It was from this ragamuffin garden that Bob Belt looked up at the roof-line that day and a-propos of nothing idly wondered aloud if it would be possible for someone to climb the back wall of the house by means of the drainpipes, scramble up the slope of the roof without falling, and tumble safely down the other side to land against the familiar parapet.

Everybody looked up. A lad called Richardson, somebody said, had accomplished this very feat two years previously. Richardson, who had now left, held a place in school lore as a representative of a vanished breed of senior boys that had seemed infinitely daring and had terrorised the authorities in those far-off days when the present crop of sixth-formers were still leading frightened little lives at the darker, lower end of the pecking order. Bob pointed out that legends had a way of growing with time and he rather doubted if Richardson had actually done it.

'There would be one way to find out,' said James laconically. 'If it was possible then, someone could do it now.'

'Like people crossing the Atlantic in pseudo-Viking ships?' said Bob. 'That would settle the matter one way or the other. Anyone fancy it? It won't be me. I can tell you that now.'

'Nor me,' said David. *That was taken up and echoed, as a general murmur, all around.*

'So we shall never know,' Bob said.

'Yes, we shall,' said James matter-of-factly.

Everybody looked at him in surprise. 'You're not offering to try it, are you?' *someone said.*

'Don't sound so astonished,' said James. 'Why shouldn't I?'

'You just won't,' said Bob. 'I know you and I know you won't do it. You're not a fool. You're not reckless like Richardson.' *It was true that James had no reputation for physical bravery. Athletics was one thing, and so was bold talk but heroic exploits had never been much in James's line and they all knew it.*

'You mean you think I haven't got the guts.'

'No, I don't think you haven't got the guts,' said Bob. 'Well, yes, all right, I do think you haven't got the guts. It's nothing to be ashamed of. I haven't. Everybody else says they haven't. I don't believe that Richardson…'

The Raven and the Jackdaw

James said, in a very quiet voice, 'I have got the guts, you know.'

'No you haven't. Don't pretend. Or if you have, go and do it. Put your guts where your mouth is.'

'Why should I?' James's tone was still casual, laconic. 'I could do it. I know that. Why should I need to prove it?'

'Of course you need to prove it,' said Bob. 'We want to see you do it. I dare you. Go on. Do it now.'

James didn't reply though he looked as pale, suddenly, as his olive complexion would allow. He took off his jacket and laid it on the grass. Then he walked towards the wall. Bob and David exchanged glances, then Bob went after James and caught him by the arm. 'Don't be stupid. You know I didn't mean it.' He paused but there was no response so he went on, 'All right, you probably do have more guts than the rest of us. And you don't have to prove it. You've made your point. Don't do it.'

James turned to Bob and smiled. 'I know I don't have to prove it. But I'm going to do it anyway. Just for kicks.' He began to survey the network of drainpipes on the wall of the building.

'James, don't.' It was his brother who had come up behind him. 'You heard what Bob said. You're not expected to do it.' David paused, then said very emphatically, 'I don't want you to.'

But James simply turned to him and said, 'Don't worry, I won't be long.' Then he began, rather inexpertly, to clamber up the outlet pipe that led down from the first-floor lavatories. After some time and a bit of a scramble he got onto the rickety roof of the old conservatory. He crossed it gingerly on all fours and reached another part of the wall where a more slender drainpipe led on upwards. In the minute or so since James had announced his intention of tackling the climb the crowd in the garden had grown considerably and windows had been thrown open all the way up the wall. Heads appeared in each one and every head offered conflicting advice as to the next hand- or foothold.

James was now edging his way along a sloping pipe, his hands on a windowsill near his waist. Then he reached up, caught at the sash and stood on the sill. Now he made another lunge, sideways, at a rainwater pipe that nestled in a corner. His hands found the pipe and held it tightly. The rest of him swung to and fro. There was an audible gasp from the spectators below. He kicked off his shoes and they fell with two cracks onto the concrete. Now the crowd below was silent as he went hand over hand, three storeys up, gripping the pipe with his socks. He stopped just below the eaves and the gutter, clinging like a monkey.

'Somebody go up and get onto the roof the other side,' said a voice. 'He may need a hand over the ridge.'

'If he wants to go on,' said another voice and Bob added, 'James, are you sure you don't want to come back down this side?'

James spoke for the first time. 'I can't go back.' He didn't try to disguise the fear in his voice. But now there was already a head looking over the roof ridge from the far side, looking towards him anxiously, holding out a hand. Then James sprang suddenly to life, clutched and clawed at the bottommost slates and, more it seemed by willpower than by effective effort, scrambled onto them, spread-eagled himself against the slope and inched painfully upwards.

'Come on, James.' The face across the roof-ridge spoke encouragement and the proffered hand was stretched even further in his direction. Seconds later the hand was grasped, gripped hard, and the Raven was helped up the final two feet between himself and safety.

David, who had watched as if frozen in a trance until now, came back to life the instant James disappeared

The Raven and the Jackdaw

over the rooftop, and raced indoors madly. He leaped up the stairs crazily, first two at a time, then three at a time and burst into the attic room whose skylight formed the access to the familiar, parapet side of the roof. His brother was just coming down through it. He shook uncontrollably. David stood back and tried to look as if he had just strolled casually upstairs. 'Well, well,' he said in a jokey sort of way, 'you're quite a brave boy really, aren't you?' It was a poor camouflage for a whole nest-full of feelings. Both of them knew it.

James looked at his brother and the unmistakeable look of admiration of David's flushed face made him feel good. Then he felt strangely uncomfortable and a shiver ran down his spine. Unknown to him, David experienced the same sensation and simultaneously each looked away from the other with an involuntary frown. Then the room was filled with people and their voices and the episode was finished.

'Why the hell did you do it?' David asked James later.

'I don't know,' said James. 'It just seemed – suddenly – as though it didn't matter any more what happened. I didn't care really whether I lived or died.' He peered intensely into David's eyes. 'Do you never feel you may as well gamble everything on something really futile just for the hell of it? I do. Perhaps it's boredom. Perhaps it's just me. Perhaps I shall end up throwing my life away on something completely worthless.' He smiled a smile that David found hard to fathom, though he thought the smile beautiful. 'Maybe everybody does,' James finished thoughtfully. 'One way or another.'

****

No explanation is given as to why James should have felt at that point in his life that he didn't care whether he lived or died. But the episode is based on a real one and I described it pretty accurately from memory when I wrote my story some five years later. My brother Jason really did climb over the school roof at colossal risk to himself. He had just been dumped, earlier that week, by Clare, the girl he was seeing in the town in the evenings. While the moment at which our eyes met just after he came down from the skylight, trembling all over… That was the moment I fell back in love with him.

The Raven and the Jackdaw

SEVEN

That evening a crowd of us left the school after supper and went to a nearby pub. Exams had finished, term was nearly over and the authorities were prepared to look with a lenient eye on what the senior boys got up to; many of them would be leaving in a fortnight. On the walk back to school after two pints of beer I found myself walking alongside my brother. Found myself there? All right, I engineered it. I said, quietly but boldly, 'Will you sleep with me tonight?'

'Are you mad?' he said. 'Where do you suppose we'd do that? All hell would break loose.'

I said, very coolly, 'I'd ask Edward to sleep in your room, in your bed, for the night. No-one else would need to know.'

'My roommate Michael?' suggested Jason with a touch of sarcasm in his voice.

'Michael and Edward were both in the garden. They saw what happened this afternoon. They'd think it the most natural thing in the world that we'd want a private talk tonight.'

'They wouldn't think it the most natural thing in the world that we needed to go to bed together to have it.'

I argued a little more but in the end I was defeated, and I saw Jason's point. Two pints had made me bold to the point of losing all caution but my brother, two years older, was more practised at handling his drink.

We didn't sleep together that night. But something else happened, which I did not expect. Jason and I parted for the night outside the door of the room I shared with Edward. Unusually there was no-one else on the landing or the stairs at that moment. I saw Jason rapidly check that this was so. He said, 'Sorry, Jackdaw,' very tenderly and with a shrug of apology. Then he quickly put one hand behind my head, the other behind my shoulder, pulled my head towards him and kissed me on the lips. I was too astonished, and the moment too fleeting, to kiss him back. He let me go as quickly as he'd caught hold of me and nipped up the stairs towards the room where he slept.

In all the years since we first shared a bed together we'd never kissed. I stood on the landing rooted to the spot. It took me a full minute to compose myself sufficiently to enter my room and banter with Edward, while we both got ready for bed, without showing the traces of this seismic event on my face. Eventually I managed it but later, when Edward showed signs of wanting to get into bed with me to have a mutual wank, I said I wasn't in the mood for it that night. Edward said he understood. He might not have seen the kiss but he'd seen my brother climb the roof and presumably could guess that it had been a big deal for the two of us. I sometimes wondered in later years if he'd made a shrewd guess about our sexual relationship. I spent that night alone in bed at any rate, and it seemed to take years to get to sleep.

During those days, towards the end of that term, there was a spirit of "anything goes" about the place. So I was hardly surprised that on one of those nights Edward asked me if I'd ever been fucked. I answered, just about truthfully, that I had not. Nor had I ever fucked anyone else, I added, with self-revealing candour. Edward, admitting his own lack of experience, said the same went for him. 'Shall we try it?' he asked brightly, in a way that sounded amused as well as businesslike.

We did. We might have lacked experience but it was clear that we'd both been thinking about it. Edward had thought about it sufficiently hard, it next appeared, as to have invested in a jar of Vaseline. That night we managed successfully to roger each other, although

The Raven and the Jackdaw

during what was left of that term we never repeated the experiment. But before term ended I bought my own jar of Vaseline, and when the time came to pack for the return home for the holidays I put it in my suitcase.

I wasn't the only one. When I got home and at last found myself in Jason's bed and in his arms I discovered that he had made a similar optimistic purchase.

We tried not to be noisy that first night of the holidays. It wasn't easy. We were no longer a pair of elf-sized six- and eight-year-olds, but two nearly full-grown men attempting anal intercourse in a single bed. Jason had first go, of course. He rather assumed that as a right that didn't need to be negotiated. Because he was older; because he was experienced with women, which I was not...

I let him. I wasn't going to argue the toss, especially as we were trying to be quiet about it. We did it lying on our sides, spoon-wise, with Jason at my back. If Jason was surprised at how easy I was to deal with he didn't say so. His cock was noticeably bigger than Edward's, but not by so much as to cause me pain or distress, and when he climaxed inside me I felt not so much physically stimulated as proud of him for doing it; the burning feeling inside myself seemed an apt symbol of the heat of our relationship.

He would have brought me to my own climax by hand and left it at that, but I wouldn't let him; I was determined to do to him what he had done to me. This surprised Jason somewhat; I could feel his surprise in the twists and turns of his body and in the quiet grunts he made more than in anything that he said. Unlike me he'd never been penetrated in this way and seemed doubtful and apprehensive at first. However, he went along with it. It helped that my cock was still a good deal smaller than his was: he must have felt reassuringly unthreatened by it. Again his body showed his surprise at the discovery that I knew what I was doing, though he didn't question it. As for me, I was vastly more excited than I'd been when I experimented in this way with Edward. To say that I was radiant with delight would not have overstated it. For this reason I climaxed very quickly; even more quickly than Jason had, and he'd been quick enough.

A little later we had to take it in turn to creep along the landing to the lavatory and after that we returned to our separate beds. On my way to my own I nevertheless leaned over Jason, snug in his bed, and gave him a quick kiss. He didn't return it, but he didn't object.

It was while we were getting dressed the next morning that Jason spoke. 'You seemed very competent last night. Had you been practising with Edward?'

His hitting the nail so squarely on the head surprised me into a laugh. 'Yes,' I said. Then Jason laughed too, smiled into my eyes a moment, and didn't say anything else. I was amazed at how easily and economically the subject had been broached and then packed away again, astonished at how well we'd dealt with it.

We went down to breakfast with light steps and light hearts, even if slightly sore between the legs. The last thing we were expecting was a bombshell over breakfast but a bombshell there was.

'I'm moving you into the other room,' our mother said to me. 'It's all ready for you. I let the two of you share last night as you'd just got back. But you're grown men now. Jason's no longer a schoolboy. It's time he had his own space.'

I stared at my mother, appalled as well as astonished. I could see no trace of logic in the string of sentences she'd just uttered. The only thing I could think was that she or Dad had heard us getting it on during the night, made a guess at what was happening and had

The Raven and the Jackdaw

determined, though she wanted to avoid confronting us directly, to put a stop to it. I was so sure that this was the case that I found myself unable to argue or even find a word to say. I said, 'Oh,' quite simply and tried not to let the collapse of my inner world be seen on my face. My brother's face was also a mask. He too found himself nearly speechless. He said, 'Oh. Right.' And that was it. Our mother had staged her coup. We'd caved in and collapsed.

We made the best of it. But the best wasn't very good. We could only be intimate with each other throughout those summer holidays on the few occasions when both of us were in the house and both our parents were out. A family holiday in the Lake District did give us a final chance, though. We shared a room in a Bed and Breakfast, like any pair of brothers, for reasons of cost. It was lovely to be back together again. I at any rate thought it was. But there was a sense of ending about it; a feeling of melancholy pervaded my happiness just as it had done when I'd gone haymaking at the age of five in the weeks before starting school.

Shortly after the end of that stay in the Lake District I went back to school to find myself promoted to head boy. I shared a room with another prefect. He was a perfectly decent fellow but I didn't find him remotely attractive and it was clear that he had no sexual interest in me. Edward was sharing a room with someone else in another house. I didn't have my brother with me. I looked forward to a grim year without love, support or sex. I heaved a large sigh metaphorically, put my head down, also metaphorically, and just got on with the tasks in hand: being head of school and preparing for A-levels.

My brother's A-level results had been impressive. In maths, chemistry and biology. Had his interest in biology had something to do with me? I sometimes wondered that. Those days of dissecting dead mice and the eyes of oxen... At any rate he had set his sights on a career in medicine and, having been accepted by Cambridge, set off there that autumn to read organic chemistry at St. John's College. I didn't see him again till Christmas.

By that time I was gagging for sex. Sex of any sort. I was climbing trees and humping the branches in order to bring myself off in my pants. Being back at home with Jason was wonderful in a way, but now that we had separate rooms that tantalising proximity also made things worse. I cornered him on the landing outside the bathroom on my second night back 'We've got to do something,' I said. My voice was a half whisper, for reasons that were mainly practical. 'It's been too long. We need to find a moment to get into bed.'

I'll never forget the look that appeared on Jason's face. I could see that he'd known I was going to say that but wished to heaven that I'd left it unsaid. More than that, he hated knowing that my need for him had been so desperate as to force me to say it.

'We can't any more,' he whispered sharply. Now there was a look of something like terror on his face. 'We're not kids. We can't pretend any longer that we don't know what we're doing. It's not just about the risk of getting caught. It's against all moral codes – deeper than law, deeper than religion...'

'It's your girlfriend been telling you this,' I said. He'd talked of nothing but his new girlfriend Cheri in the last day and a half. I didn't want to know about Cheri. I was insanely jealous.

'Cheri telling me?!' If he hadn't been whispering – from necessity – it would have come out as a roar. 'As if we'd be discussing something like that... As if I'd have told her that!'

The Raven and the Jackdaw

Through all the smoke of our heated exchange I managed to register that our thing was still a secret between us; I reached out and held fast to that, and took some pathetic comfort from it. But I turned away abruptly at that moment. I was afraid of breaking down in front of him and I didn't know how I could have handled that. I tried again three or four more times during that Christmas holiday but met with no more success. I slept alone and had little contact with Jason during the daytimes. At night I masturbated often and desperately and, occasionally, wept.

I took my A-levels the following summer. I was only seventeen, and so was not expected to go to university that autumn. Instead, it was agreed that I should spend one final term at school, preparing for the Oxbridge entrance exam, and then have a gap half-year before going to whichever university – Oxford or Cambridge or other – would have me.

I was advised not to make applications to both Oxford and Cambridge. Whichever of those two institutions I put second on my list of preferences would consider itself snubbed and would not even give me an interview. I thought long and hard about this choice. Cambridge had already snubbed me, in the person of my brother. I'd had no sex with him for over a year now, and had not spent much time with him doing anything else. I'd had no sex with anyone else either, and for all that I remained head boy at school – a position that I should have been proud of and an achievement that should have made me confident and happy – I was becoming emotionally withdrawn and increasingly lonely. It would be sensible to make Oxford my number one choice, I thought. Oxford would give me a new start in life, I realised: an opportunity to put the past behind me. But in the end I changed my mind. I allowed my sore heart to triumph over my head, allowed hope to triumph over experience. I decided that for better or worse I would try and follow my brother to Cambridge.

To his credit Jason was supportive. When I went to be interviewed there that next winter he met me at the station, helped me find the room I'd been allocated for the night – it was in a beautiful old wing of St. John's College – he showed me around the town and took me to a pub, with some of his friends and his current girlfriend, in the evening. And he was caring enough to not allow me to drink too much or stay out too late, wanting me to be in good shape for my interview the next morning.

I can't have shone too brightly at that interview, I guess. At any rate I wasn't accepted by Cambridge. Instead I was offered a place by my university of second choice, which was Bristol. I would be going there – eighty miles away from home and some hundred and seventy from Cambridge – the next autumn, to read zoology.

These days the idea of a gap year brings to mind thoughts of back-packing round the Far East, doing voluntary service in Africa, or basking in a cultural exchange with some rich kid from Argentina. None of those options was available to me that winter in the early nineteen-eighties. I went to work two miles away from where my parents lived, on a farm that housed a frozen foods packing station among its outbuildings. I was picked up from outside our cottage by the farm's minibus at seven-thirty every morning.

Cold, cold, cold, is my memory of that period. The cold of going to work early in the morning in the winter. The cold of the deep-freezers when I entered them with my pallet-loader to pull out the next pallet-full of frozen vegetables for the women to work on. At first it was Brussels sprouts. We blanched and bagged them. Then, as the season advanced, we moved on to cabbage. I

The Raven and the Jackdaw

didn't only drag pallets about. I joined the teams of women at the metal tables and with a big kitchen knife I helped to shred cabbage after cabbage after cabbage.

Fluted carrot rings followed, then last year's frozen raspberries. At tea breaks we sat on upturned crates and discussed the news as reported by The Sun newspaper. A bit of an eye-opener, this. We'd had The Times at school, and my parents took the Daily Telegraph. I had little sense of the passing of time. Spring was late that year, and it still seemed like winter when suddenly, one day, Jason was back from Cambridge for the Easter vacation.

My expectations were low, concerning Jason. But he had a surprise for me. We'd only been exchanging news for ten minutes or so, sitting in the living-room before family supper, when he said, looking at me rather curiously, 'If you want to get out of cutting cabbages in the freezing cold, there might be a job for you for a few months in Cambridge.'

My heart leapt crazily. Not at the thought of a new job – I didn't know yet what kind of a job Jason was proposing: it might not necessarily be any more congenial than freezing cabbages – but at the idea that Jason would welcome, or at least would not take exception to, my presence at Cambridge. I tried not to show my feelings. I wanted to leap on top of Jason as he sat beside me on the sofa and smother him with kisses, slobbering over him like a puppy. Instead I said in a guarded tone, 'What kind of job exactly?'

'I know someone who knows people who work at the theatre. They're shortly going to be looking for a day-man.'

'What's a day-man?' I asked.

'Search me,' said Jason. 'But I'd guess it's a jumped-up title for a dogsbody.' Be a dogsbody in a professional theatre? I'd leap at the chance. Wouldn't any seventeen-year-old? Be invited to share the life of the beautiful little town that was inhabited by Jason? My heart wanted to burst. Wouldn't that of any boy who felt for his brother as I felt for Jason? 'How can I get in touch with them?' I asked urgently. I was almost bouncing up from the sofa. If I'd had wings I'd have spread them there and then and flown immediately to Cambridge.

'I've got a phone number,' said Jason, like some magic being in a modern fairy story. 'You can call them later this evening. They know to expect to hear from you.'

How had Jason known I'd want the job? How had he known I'd want it so much that he could reasonably have asked them to hold it open till they heard from me? Could it be ... I tried not to think this ... that somewhere deep inside him, perhaps in a place he didn't know existed, he wanted me to be with him? I said simply, 'What time shall I phone them?'

They interviewed me pretty thoroughly over the phone, but they did suggest I came to Cambridge if it was at all possible, so that we could see the whites of each other's eyes before committing ourselves. They suggested Saturday. My end of the conversation was fairly public. Jason astonishingly volunteered to drive me up if Dad would lend him the car for the day and my father nodded his agreement to that. I might have been able to drive myself, only I'd failed my driving test a month earlier and hadn't got round to re-taking it. Jason by now had his full driving licence.

Actually Dad was so pleased at the thought of my getting a job in Cambridge – a useful foretaste of university life, he said, and he harped on the cultural life of the place – that he gave Jason the money for the petrol. As for my mother, if any worries about our relationship had lingered on after she'd so firmly

The Raven and the Jackdaw

separated us a year and a quarter earlier, well, she suppressed them and wished me luck.

It was noticeable during the couple of days between my brother's return home and our drive together to Cambridge that Jason made no reference to Cheri. Gone were his previous refrains of Cheri thinks, and Cheri says. I assumed that they'd split up but didn't ask. Not until we were in the car on the way to Cambridge did he volunteer the information that that was the case. 'I'm very sorry to hear that,' I said, and left it at that. Actually I wasn't at all sorry. His announcement had let a little ray of hope enter my place of darkness, though by rights I should not have entertained that hope. I made sure to keep my delight out of my voice as I made that little show of commiseration, and hearing myself do it successfully thought what a good actor I was.

'Where would I stay?' I asked just as Jason was negotiating the town's outskirts. 'The pay's obviously not going to be much. It'd need to be somewhere cheap.'

Without taking his eyes off the road, and very casually, yet without a split second's hesitation, Jason said, 'You could stay at our place. It might mean a sofa in the living-room, but it wouldn't cost.'

'That'd be great,' I answered, trying to keep my tone as level as Jason had kept his. But then I added, 'Brilliant in fact,' just in case I hadn't sounded keen enough.

The interview was a formality. I knew, and the woman who interviewed me – her job title was production manager – also knew, that I'd already got the job. I was asked to start in three weeks.

Hope? I didn't dare to. I forced myself not to think of anything like that. I knew what I felt for my brother. I knew what it was called, though I never named it. I never said the word to him. I didn't even use it silently to myself. All the same, the word lay buried like a splinter in my heart.

Did the same word lie buried deep inside Jason? I couldn't fathom that. For if I couldn't allow myself to acknowledge even my own feelings about the two of us, how much less could I expect to know my brother's thoughts?

I worked my notice at the frozen foods packing plant. The weather played a wicked trick during that time by turning unseasonably warm at the end of March. We workers now took our tea breaks, and spent our lunchtimes, lazing in the sunshine by the pond. The males among us took our shirts off and we threw the crusts from our sandwiches into the water to make the carp rise slurpingly to share our lunch. Those midday moments made me regret, each day for a few aching minutes, that I was going to move away to a city to do an indoor job. True, I'd be with Jason. But I still wasn't allowing myself any over-reaching expectations of what that meant.

Nothing happens until it has happened. So nothing happened to change my modest expectations of Jason as a housemate until the first night I joined his household in Cambridge. We had supper with the others – someone cooked us all omelettes – we watched a bit of television and then went off to our separate rooms. Well, Jason and the others did. I realised as I made up my bed on the living-room sofa that there was a downside to my economical sleeping arrangements. I would always have to be the last to go to bed, whether I wanted to be or not. However tired I felt.

I suppose I'd fallen asleep. I was suddenly aware that I wasn't alone in my living-room bedroom, despite the Stygian dark. Someone was disturbing my sheets and blankets. A head was close to mine. Then to my astonishment – though it was such a wonderful astonishment that I nearly cried at it – I heard Jason's whisper and smelt the toothpastiness of his breath. 'Come on,' he said. 'Budge up.'

EIGHT

My first job was to sweep the stage. My second was to sweep the area outside the dressing rooms where flats were stored against the wall. An area known as "the cut". I've heard apocryphal stories since, about stage-struck youngsters who have been required to carry out these tasks with a toothbrush. Luckily for me I was given a broom with a width of about a metre and a half: luckily, because I wasn't as stage-struck as all that. But even so I loved it. I took turns answering the stage-door phone and writing messages for actors. If a delivery arrived in the foyer in the morning – of Coca-cola, say, or toilet paper – I had the job of transferring it to the appropriate store-room. If the stage managers had work to do up on the fly-floor among the hemp-lines, I climbed the ladders with them and helped them do it. I worked on get-ins and fit-ups before a new show opened, and on the strikes and get-outs after they finished. Occasionally I had to work late into the night, but more usually I was free in the evenings. When Jason was.

He'd never before been like this. Openly showing the world that he enjoyed my company. Just a few months ago he'd pushed me away. 'We can't any more. It's against all moral codes,' he'd said. What a difference a girl makes. But what a difference not having one makes. Now, if he went to a pub with friends he made sure to ask me along with him. At supper time we ate together. All who shared that house of ours took it in turns to cook for whoever was eating in each night. I learned to cook. Cheap things, usually. Herrings. Mackerel. Liver and onions. Stuffed vegetable marrows. Spaghetti Bolognese with more tomatoes in the sauce than meat. At night when the house was quiet Jason would creep down the stairs and join me under the bedclothes on my sofa in the

The Raven and the Jackdaw

living-room. We would pleasure each other for an hour or so and then he would return to bed.

I was in paradise. I loved my job, I loved my brother, I loved Cambridge. I look back on those wonderful months there – through spectacles that have grown rosier-tinted with the passing years no doubt – as one of the happiest times of my life. The epithet, city of dreaming spires, was originally coined for Oxford but it suited Cambridge equally well. There were the lofty pinnacles of King's College chapel, whalebone white; the wrought-iron peaks of Clare College gates; the towers of Trinity and St. John's gatehouses in glowing brick, the turret-crowned church of St. Mary the Great. Cambridge was a city of aspiring dreams too, and when it rained it became – for a whole day sometimes – a city of dire streamings. It was beautiful even then, though, its towers and buttresses gleaming through their wash of wet. And when the rain was finished and the sun came back out the grass in the city's meadows shone all the more brightly for it. In May the hawthorn blossomed whitely everywhere, and cow parsley flowers ran riot along the river's banks. White and green were everywhere you looked, replacing the apple blossom's April pink.

There came a weekend in May when, quite by chance, all of our housemates went away – to their parental homes I suppose – and Jason and I were left alone in the house. We ate supper together, just the two of us. Jason cooked. It was a sort of all-day breakfast. Bacon, tomatoes, sausages, fried eggs, mushrooms, black pudding, and fried bread. The fact that he was going to try and become a doctor and so presumably knew all about healthy eating was never allowed to impinge on his activity in the kitchen. Thank God. After we'd eaten we sat about, drinking beer till it was time for bed. There was always homemade beer in the house, just as there was always homemade bread. On the inside of the door of the kitchen cupboard were two hand-written recipes, one for beer and one for bread. Whoever had time to kill was expected to set to and make one or other of the two staples whenever we were running low on stocks. It was a comradely arrangement and helped to bond the six of us.

I was too timid to say it. Jason did it instead. 'We could spend the night together, if you liked,' he said pretend casually, some time after ten o'clock. 'In my bed.'

'Yep,' I said, pretending this was not the most wonderful thing that had been said to me in my life. 'That'd be nice.'

So we slept together. Though we did other things first (and did them noisily for the first time ever, our first time together in an empty house) the sleeping together was the best part of it. Drifting off together, lightly cuddling and in contact. Half waking in the darkness to feel my brother's soft warmth and breath. I'd never spent a whole night in bed with anyone before that night. Jason and I had always been careful to go back to our own beds when we shared a room at home, fearful of going to sleep together by accident and being discovered by our parents. For the same reason I'd never actually gone to sleep in Edward's arms at school. The thought of being found together in the morning by the duty prefect…

I've written that the sleeping together was the best part of that night. Maybe it wasn't. Maybe waking in the morning was. That gradual dawning of the knowledge that I was not alone in bed. The sweet smell of him, the warm touch; the early day forming silver lines of highlight along his nose, his chin, his cheeks. The thick black lashes like curtains to his silky eyelids, guarding his lovely private dreams and shutting out the night. At

The Raven and the Jackdaw

this moment, gazing at his sleeping face I knew I'd never felt more happy, never felt more safe. I felt a lump come into my throat.

His eyes opened slowly. They gazed into mine oddly for a second as his brain sorted out where he was and who with. Then he smiled at me and I smiled back. I knew what the lump in my throat was. It was three words trying to get out. I didn't say them. I couldn't. I was afraid I'd ruin everything if I said them. I longed to hear Jason say them, though. If he had done I would have said them back to him. But he did not. Or could not. I didn't know which.

That weekend absence of our housemates allowed us a second night together. And two long mornings in bed. And then our housemates came back; the wonderful time was over, and it disappeared into the past. Things returned to the way they'd been before. With Jason slipping into bed with me on my living-room sofa when the coast was clear four or five nights a week. It was still good, but that weekend experience of spending whole nights together, of going to sleep together and waking up together, had spoiled me. I knew what I'd been missing up to then, and wanted more of it.

I didn't get more of it. After a few more weeks even what I had began to dry up. Jason met a girl again. Her name was Anna. I found I liked her. Couldn't help liking her, despite the fact that I wanted to dislike her because she was my rival and would take Jason away from me. I knew that she would, and in time she did. I don't know where Jason first had sex with her but I knew when he did. He simply didn't come downstairs to me on two consecutive nights. As with a pregnant woman who has missed a period, it was the second one that clinched it. And then the third night and the fourth...

Jason continued to be a lovely friend in his role as brother. I got included in many of the social things that he and Anna and their other friends did. The fact that I could get us all free tickets for the theatre from time to time helped here of course. But then the end of term came and Jason went off to stay with Anna, while I stayed on in Cambridge for another couple of weeks – until the theatre closed for its own summer break.

Jason and I caught up again at our parents' home later in that vacation. I did a few weeks' work back on the frozen foods packing plant (it was less of a penance during the summer's heat) while Jason earned some cash manning a till in the local town's small supermarket. At no point did we have sex together, while I at any rate had none with anybody else.

The semi-fictional story I wrote about the Raven and the Jackdaw covers none of the above. I didn't attempt to make sense of anything that happened between the time of Jason's (or the fictional James's) climb across the school roof and the Raven and the Jackdaw starting university an unspecified number of years later. I fiddled with the timeline to make things tidier, sending them off to their respective seats of tertiary education in the same autumn. My story also parted company with real-life events when it came to where those places of study were to be found on the map. And whereas Jason and I had both in reality chosen scientific disciplines, I allowed our fictional counterparts a much more artistic bent...

****

James achieved a place at St. Martin's art college in London and entered upon his new life with much enthusiasm. He maintained his now well-tested policy of doing just enough work to get by and devoted most of his time and energy to enjoying himself, London and the people he met there. He made love to all the women who

The Raven and the Jackdaw

came his way – which they did – but all feminine plans to make a permanent capture of him failed dismally. Why be tied down when you were young and handsome and life was full of tomorrows?

David went further afield, to university at St. Andrews. He had never been to Scotland before and was not sure that he would enjoy it. In the event he found that the little grey-roofed town appealed to him greatly. His contemporaries regarded him as something of a loner: someone who enjoyed solitary rambles on the rocky, limpeted shoreline among the oystercatchers and turnstones, who spent long hours gazing out to sea but who kept the results of his contemplations to himself.

Happy enough with the town, David was less enthusiastic to begin with about university life. After the initial challenges of settling in were over, life moved into a routine that was rather less stimulating than he had expected. People were less exciting than he had imagined they would be and the pace of life less exciting than it had been at school. Something was missing. Something he could not pinpoint for the moment.

Then a small thing happened. David saw a notice announcing that the drama society would shortly be holding auditions for its first production of the year: Ibsen's Ghosts, David had quite enjoyed taking part in plays at school and he went along, although not very hopefully, to try his luck. And lucky he was. The postgraduate student who was going to direct the play thought he would be ideal for the role of Osvald and offered him the part.

He had only just recovered from his surprise a few days later when a total stranger made himself known to him, said he had heard what a fine actor David was, and would he accept a part in his forthcoming production of Robert Bolt's A Man for All Seasons? Despite the fact that the two plays were to be presented within ten days of each other, the confidence that flattery induces overcame all caution and David said yes. Academic work suffered, hardly anyone else saw him, rehearsals preoccupied him entirely. But the results seemed to justify his incautious venture. He was hailed as a rising star by the university newspaper, strangers stopped him in the street to tell him how much they had enjoyed his performances, and he never had to go to another audition all the time he remained at St. Andrews. To his own astonishment the solitary rambler of the shoreline was a big shot now, in his very first term at university. And all without really trying. The world of student drama was a very little one, it was true, but at the time that seemed to bother nobody...

****

Why did I send Jackdaw all the way to St. Andrews, a place I'd never visited, when I actually went to Bristol, half a thousand miles away from the Scottish university? Partly, I suppose, in order to distance myself from the character of David. Partly, I have to admit, because I'd seen teams from St. Andrews competing in University Challenge on TV, and was very taken with the scarlet academic gowns they wore when they took part. But as for David's interest in student drama, that was a real enough part of myself. A few months of working as a humble day-man at the Cambridge theatre had given me the bug. I really did play Osvald in my first term at university, though A Man for All Seasons (I played Thomas Cromwell!) didn't come along till the second term. A lot else happened in that second term, but I'll come to that later. It didn't happen in the first. If people thought me cold and withdrawn during that first term they were right. I was trying to recover from the loss of my brother to Anna, trying to understand the pain I felt,

The Raven and the Jackdaw

and trying to understand myself. The last thing I wanted was to get involved with a new person, of either sex: the only thing I could imagine happening were I to do so was that I would end up being hurt.

My account tries to deal with the nature of my feelings for my brother at that time. In the next extract the subject is approached obliquely. (In the extract that follows it, in the next chapter, I tackled it head-on. But first things first.) The Raven and the Jackdaw have returned home after their first terms at art college and university respectively…

****

James hadn't missed the countryside or even looked forward to returning there but he found himself, this December, seeing it as though for the first time. He actually proposed a walk one cold but sunny afternoon – this rather astonished everyone for he was not usually attracted by the idea of rural scrambles. Neither Hector nor Mary offered to join him but David went along willingly enough.

The previous night's frost still coated the grass and the shady side of the tree trunks. The fields looked a trifle gloomy in the chilly light of a winter's afternoon but beautiful for all that. Here and there stood groups of cattle, steaming like hot dinners. Pheasants called abruptly from the dark copses. The two young men walked in silence, feeling suddenly a little anxious or oppressed. Perhaps it was the cold. At the bottom of the sloping meadow they came to the chalk stream and began to follow its reedy course. It almost encircled a tree at one point, so close to the trunk that the roots were exposed, plunging straight down into the water. Rounding a bend they came upon a standing copse of long-dead trees. Their bark-less trunks rose like the pillars of a roofless hall and the frosty light lent them the colour of old ivory. In the spring woodpeckers would drum here but today the dead forest was mute. Until a jackdaw flew into the derelict place and, with its cry of Jack, Jack, broke the silence.

From time to time now, as they left the stream behind them, the rooftops of a farm could be seen rising out of a little hollow in the hillside above. They followed the upward-winding course of a hedgerow, bright with scarlet rose-hips and occasionally sibilant with the tiny noises of field-mice that climbed in search of the shining fruits. Then they became conscious of a commotion. They stopped. The noise stopped. They moved on and now heard it again but close at hand: a noise halfway between a mutter and a growl. Then what they saw stopped them in their tracks.

There was a gap in the hedge where the branches were bruised and bark-less. In the centre of the wreckage a badger as big as a spaniel strained against the fox wire into which it had blundered and which now held it tight around the chest and kept its forepaws lifted a foot off the ground. Its fur was matted with blood. There were large raw patches where there should have been fur and skin. The animal bared needle-like teeth and snarled dementedly as they approached.

Trying to get close to the badger only made it claw the air frenziedly, until exhaustion drove it down again onto its girdle of wire with a hiss of pain. David and James looked at each other helplessly. Then, after a few minutes of indecision and the exchange of some futile ideas they realised they must go to the farm and get help.

A trek of a quarter of a mile brought them into the farmyard, an old-fashioned one where mongrel ducks swam placidly on a pond among glass-thin floes of ice and where sparrows assiduously devoured the corn that had been scattered for the indifferent chickens. Outside

The Raven and the Jackdaw

a barn two men were peering into the gearbox of a tractor with an air that was less suggestive of mechanical know-how than of hopeful experiment. They did not look up until the boys were almost upon them.

'Excuse me,' said James rather formally. 'I wonder if you could help us.'

'That rather depends,' said the older of the two men, 'on what it is you want.'

'There's a badger caught in a wire in your field ... in someone's field ... just down the hill there. It's badly hurt. Struggling.'

'Badger?' said the younger man.

'Go on, Reg,' said the older one. 'Badger. Two hammers you want. Bang 'em together on the wire, it'll snap, and your badger'll be off like a shot.'

'Sounds a bit chancy to me,' said the other. 'All right. I'll go. Just let me get two hammers and a gun.' And to show that there was more than one person around who could hand out advice he nodded meaningfully towards the gearbox and said, 'You want to get some of that muck out of there.'

It took a minute or two for him to equip himself with hammers, wire-cutters, a double-barrelled shotgun, cartridges, pipe, tobacco pouch, matches and cap. Then they set off. 'Don't much like the sound of that hammer business,' confided the farm man, filling his pipe as he walked. 'I'm not getting clawed by no bloody badger.'

'There it is,' said James as they reached the spot. The badger snarled through curled-back lips.

'Christ almighty!' said the man from the farm. 'You'd never get near that. That one's had it anyway. He'd never get far even if he did get free.' He raised the gun to his shoulder and looked along the barrels. The badger became quite still. It even lowered its snout as though it knew what was happening and was preparing itself resignedly for death. The report was deafening, the aim

exact. A round black spot appeared in the middle of the white stripe of the animal's forehead. The body jerked momentarily on the wire and then was still. The black spot grew a little bigger and turned red. Then it crept down towards the nose.

All the way home David didn't speak. It was not that he didn't want to talk about the badger. There was something he suddenly realised he wanted to say but couldn't. Perhaps this shared experience of death in the hedgerow had brought things into focus, for surely this thing that now struck David so forcefully had been there all the time. David glanced sideways at his brother as they strode back over the fields towards home. He saw his brother's thick hair and his new, close-cropped black beard, remarked his turned-up nose, his thoughtful frown and his dark eyes that stared straight ahead. He looked back down at the ground they walked on and only half saw his own boots pounding the rimy grass.

The Raven and the Jackdaw

NINE

Christmas Day was coming to an end with a whimper. The Red Lion had been packed at midday and James and David had been bought drinks by nearly all who knew them there. The sun had shone and the boys had romped home across the fields in high spirits. Mary had created an excellent dinner and Hector had produced some fine claret and Sauternes. Now it was over and Hector and Mary had both retired to bed. The log fire still blazed in the great hearth and sitting, or rather sprawling, on the floor in front of it were James and David. The room was lit only by the flickering firelight and on the table stood a bottle of Cognac that at dinner time had been very nearly full but was now very nearly empty.

The conversation taking place on the floor had lurched from one topic to another, uncertain where it had come from and whither it was bound. Now it blundered, accidentally it seemed, into the subject of James's love life. This was not a topic habitually discussed by the brothers but now, eloquent with brandy, James launched into it in all seriousness and frankness. He talked about his conquests and his occasional failures. He talked about his uncertainty as to where it was leading, his uncertainty about what he really wanted in life. He sounded untypically pessimistic, untypically thoughtful. He didn't believe, he said, that anyone in the real world actually fell in love. He believed that what passed for love was a self-induced state engineered to produce a romantic backcloth to decisions of practical necessity or convenience. Maybe, he conceded, he was wrong. Perhaps other people really did fall in love. They were lucky if so. He, he was fairly certain, couldn't.

'Well, that's a lot about me you haven't heard before,' he said eventually. 'Enough for now, I should think. But what about you? You never tell me anything about what

happens at wild St. Andrews.' His tone was one of affectionate banter mixed with a rather tipsy prurience.

David was quite drunk now though he wasn't showing it much. He had been listening intently. He was conscious of a multitude of things besides James's words. He was sharply aware of the hot fire at his elbow and the quiet sizzle of the embers. He was aware of his brother's face and the bold relief into which the firelight threw his fine features. He saw, as if he had never seen them before, his lustrous brown eyes. And then he could feel his heart beating wildly at the bars of his chest like some creature that agonised for release. When he opened his mouth to reply he had no idea what would come out, nor what it was that he really wanted to hear himself saying. 'Oh, you know me. I'm not exactly the Don Juan of the university…'

James cut him off. His tone had changed. 'No, I don't know you. I don't know you one little bit. Not in that way.' Then he was his smiling, nonchalant self again. 'Tell me. What do you get up to? I'd love to know you just a little bit better.'

David was silent again. James began to be irritated. He had been suddenly, strangely, aroused, sensing that he was about to learn something new, perhaps something sensational, about his brother. 'Talk to me, for God's sake.'

But David looked at him with a face of such misery that he drew back. He wished his question unasked, wished that he could be somewhere else, anywhere else; wished he hadn't drunk so much. From the look on David's face he knew that whatever his brother had to say would be somehow catastrophic; that after it was said – if it was said – nothing could ever be the same again.

David looked at the floor and began pulling little pieces of fluff from the hearthrug. He began to talk,

The Raven and the Jackdaw

tremulously, as if under strain. James had no alternative but to listen. It was too late to say stop.

'I've not been too successful at getting girls into bed,' David began. 'The one time I scored I felt lousy afterwards... Maybe I should go for blokes instead. Never have. Too timid to try, I suppose. But I don't really think I'm like that... My God, as if that mattered!'

The last sentence was delivered with great vehemence. The two looked at each other for a moment. James made a final effort to defuse the time-bomb. 'Look, don't go on ... if you don't want to. Tell me another time, or don't tell me at all if you'd rather. Look, let's just forget this conversation.'

David ignored that. 'I've actually tried sometimes to make myself fall in love with people. Imagine! But it never works. Why? Not for your reason: not because there's no such thing as falling in love. It doesn't work for me precisely because you're wrong. There is such a thing as falling in love. I'm in love with somebody already. I've been devoting more effort and energy to denying that one fact than I have to anything else. But it won't let go of me. I can't pretend to myself any more.'

It seemed frighteningly cold to James as he sat alone with his younger brother in the firelight. His stomach seemed to be full of lead and he wished he could stop his ears and rum madly away; wished he could hear nothing and run for ever. But he could do nothing of the sort. David had stopped talking. James had to ask the question. It could not be escaped. The words came out as a croak. 'Who are you...?'

'With someone too close, too near ... here ... now...'

'God help me, God help me.' James didn't speak the words. They cannoned in his head and David read them in his brother's eyes as they looked at each other in agony in the firelight.

'You.'

James made a little involuntary whimpering noise. Something in him made a superhuman effort to continue a rational conversation. 'Me... And in that way too?'

'In that way too. In every way. Fuck it.'

Conversation disintegrated. David began to mumble, 'Shouldn't have said that, should have kept it to myself...'

James kept repeating, 'Must go to bed. Sorry. Can't stay here. Must go. Sorry. Sorry.' He rose uncertainly to his feet, staggered to the door and distractedly, drunkenly, fumbled for the way out. He made his way upstairs and collapsed on his bed, his mind beyond coherent thought.

David lay on the hearthrug where James had left him, reaching out, writhing, opening his hands for what wasn't there, the most beautiful thing in his world, the thing he could never have. He heard himself start to sob.

****

The episode involving the trapped badger was a real event, in which Jason and I participated along with a local farm lad, although it took place in the spring, not around Christmas. It's not something I could have easily made up. However I did make up the painful conversation of Christmas night. Made it up in the sense that I never actually said all that. I used my story – as real writers also do, I know – to express the unsayable on paper: the real feelings for Jason that were inside me but could never be translated into speech.

In reality I experienced an additional torture that Christmas after my first term at Bristol. Jason spent a week of that holiday away at Anna's but then, after we'd all had our family Christmases, Anna came to spend a few days with us. Although Jason was now twenty our parents would not let him share a room with Anna under

The Raven and the Jackdaw

their own roof because – my mother's words – they had, 'shown no sign of getting engaged yet.' This meant that Anna had to have the spare room, which was also my room when I was at home; and I returned, for the first time in eighteen months, to the second bed in the room that had once been ours but which now belonged solely to Jason. As I've said, those few nights were a double torture to me. I can't help wondering if the same thing went for Jason. He never said. But neither did I, of course.

At Bristol I shared a house with other students, just as Jason did at Cambridge. My experience of sharing that Cambridge establishment turned out to be a useful rehearsal for the Bristol experience. I actually introduced the idea of bread and beer making; I wrote up the recipes on the inside of the kitchen cupboard door, and we had a whip-round for the few necessary items of equipment – they included a plastic barrel with a tap at the bottom – that were not already present in the house.

A big difference between Bristol and Cambridge, whose impact became very noticeable to anyone who spent more than a few hours in both cities, was that Bristol was extremely hilly while Cambridge was dead flat. Cambridge students and dons coasted around the streets on bicycles, while the alumni of Bristol did not. Our house, in the district of Redland, was perched on the top of a steep hill. I quickly made three observations concerning this. First, that walking up and down between Redland and the centre of the city would keep me pretty fit. I wouldn't need to take up jogging, go to the gym or get involved in a team sport. Second, to judge from the constant grinding and crunching noises made by cars negotiating corners on the hillsides, you'd need to shell out quite often for new gearboxes if you drove a car here. Which I did not.

The third thing I noticed – although perhaps it was really the first – was that young male residents of the hillside terraces had pleasingly well developed muscles in their thighs and buttocks. At that time I boasted no such adornments; at eighteen I was still a rather skinny kid. I wondered if that would change during the time I lived at Bristol. I would be here for three years, and wondered if that would be long enough for such a transformation to come about. But I stopped wasting my thoughts on such unprofitable speculation a little way into my second term. On February the eleventh to be precise.

Bristol was home to a drama school as well as a university. The drama school shared its name with the city's beautiful old quayside theatre. Both were called The Old Vic. The postgrad student who was directing us in A Man for All Seasons had a friend at the school of drama. He was in his final year. His name was Byron. Our director asked this friend of his if he'd be kind enough to sit in on one of our rehearsals and perhaps offer us, and him, some handy tips.

I couldn't take my eyes off Byron. His own eyes were bright blue and his face finely chiselled. As far as I could tell he had a fine, quite animal, physique. We ran the trial scene for him. It contained my – I mean, Thomas Cromwell's – great speech, as imagined by Robert Bolt. *...Gentlemen of the jury, there are many kinds of silence. Consider first the silence of a man who is dead...* It was as much as I could do to remember the words, let alone act the theatrical moment. My eyes kept wandering back to Byron's attentive face, however hard I tried to keep them fixed on anyone else. And his face was attentive. He had trouble focusing his eyes on anyone but me. I could see him dutifully wrest them away towards another character from time to time, but they kept coming back.

The Raven and the Jackdaw

When the scene ended we sat around on the floor – cast, director and Byron – and Byron gave us his notes. He'd found out what my name was and kept using it as he spoke. 'Barnaby, just a little idea here…' or, 'I liked the way Barnaby used his space…' and things like that. When he gave a note or word of praise to anyone else it was just *you*. Nobody else got their name called out. It was very noticeable to everyone else. I would have been horribly embarrassed by being singled out like this if I hadn't been thrilled to bits.

Afterwards a few of us went for a drink. One by one the group said their goodnights and left. It was as though an onion was being peeled or a stick whittled away. At last, as everybody knew would happen, the group was reduced to Byron and myself. Byron looked around the nearly empty bar. 'It's getting a bit quiet here,' Byron remarked. 'But it's even quieter back at my place.'

'Then let's go there,' I said.

At that time I couldn't have imagined myself taking a guy I'd got off with back to the house I shared in Redland and coolly taking him up to the bedroom while my housemates watched TV or sat about chatting downstairs. But that was exactly what Byron did with me that evening. I guessed that drama school students were more open-minded than most university students of the time. Or perhaps I underestimated my own housemates. Anyway I went upstairs at Byron's place that first evening. We took our clothes off in a businesslike way, then admired each other's physical shapes for a minute before getting onto his bed. Of course I liked the look of Byron. He'd spent two years more in Bristol than I had, and had the typical Bristolian's well-developed buttocks, thighs and calves to prove it. But I was more surprised, and very moved, almost shaken, to see that Byron was also admiring me.

He loved the touch of me, and when we explored each other on the horizontal plane of his mattress I found we were having sex – oral on that first occasion – in a way that almost brought to mind the expression *making love*.

Almost, though not quite. For the very obvious reason that I still loved the brother who had spurned me in favour of a woman. And I found it difficult to explore the contours of Byron's body and enjoy the lightly musky smell of him and the taste of his cock without comparing those things with their counterparts in Jason. Nevertheless I enjoyed the experience. It had been six months since I'd last had sex with another person or touched anyone in this intimate way and I was determined to make the most of it – in case another six months were to pass before it could be repeated.

After we had come – in my case, for obvious reasons, all too quickly – we got dressed and went out to get a Chinese takeaway. We ate it quite unselfconsciously – I followed Byron's lead in assuming an air of casualness – on the downstairs sofa, chatting with the one remaining member of Byron's household who hadn't gone to bed yet. Then Byron and I returned upstairs to Byron's bedroom and slept in his single bed together.

I didn't know what would happen in the morning. Neither, I think, did Byron. We ate bowls of Cornflakes in the early kitchen. I had to borrow Byron's toothbrush to clean my teeth with before going off to lectures. For me this whole ever so common scenario was overwhelmingly new and giddying. When I came downstairs from the bathroom Byron met me in the hallway. He looked at me then very shyly and mumbled, 'I don't suppose you'd like to meet for a drink this evening?'

I didn't try to affect nonchalance, pretend that I could take him or leave him. I said, 'I'd love that.' I knew then

The Raven and the Jackdaw

that, for better or worse, I'd taken a first step into a relationship.

That evening I went back to my own place to get overnight things: a change of clothes and my sponge-bag. 'Ah,' said one of my housemates. 'Do we take it you've got yourself a girlfriend?'

'Not exactly,' I said, and darted out of the door before he could probe further.

The days passed and turned into weeks. Byron was clever and witty, in my eyes at any rate. Everything he said seemed either funny or brilliant. I saw him in a drama school production of The Merchant of Venice, playing Shylock. He was dazzlingly good. His performance knocked my own modest talent as a student actor into a cocked hat. If I had any private lurking thoughts that I might, instead of qualifying as a zoologist, have tried to become a professional actor I wisely abandoned them at that moment.

I became something of a little mascot among Byron's circle of friends: the boy who was two years younger than they were. They found me cute (one of them told me much later) and charming. In return I loved their adult-seeming attention. I was eighteen and they, including Byron, twenty.

My refusal to come clean with my own friends and housemates about Byron could not be maintained for ever. I was hardly anonymous or invisible among a community of students. The cast of A Man for All Seasons had all seen what had happened between us on the occasion of our first meeting; they'd left us alone in a pub together. And now we were more and more often seen in public together, with or without Byron's other drama-school mates. What happened next was interesting from an anthropological, social studies, standpoint. It was also (looking back on it) quite amusing.

The apostle Peter famously denied Christ three times. In a reversal of this paradigm I was forced three times to acknowledge my relationship with Byron. A girl on my zoology course, whom I often sat next to at lectures, asked me point-blank one morning, 'I saw you with a very handsome man last night walking by the quayside. Is he your boyfriend?'

'Yes,' I said without pausing for thought. 'He's a drama student. His name's Byron.'

'How lovely,' said my fellow zoologist, smiling.

I have to admit that it made it easier, his having a heavenly name like Byron. Nobody else on my course ever needed to ask me the same question. The news was evidently conveyed by osmosis and the relationship became official.

Exactly the same happened among the cast of A Man for All Seasons. The chap playing Thomas More said to me very casually at the end of a rehearsal, 'That drama student, Byron, who came to watch us, do you still see him?'

'Yes,' I said and, emboldened by the reception my news had got in the zoology department, I added, 'He's become a sort of boyfriend.'

'Good for you,' said Sir Thomas.

And then the housemate with whom I'd been less than candid that evening when I'd gone back to Redland to get my overnight things said pointedly, 'I keep seeing you around the place with a gang of students I don't know. Drama school aren't they?'

'Yes,' I said. Then, getting braver by the day now, 'the best-looking one's my boyfriend.'

'I thought so,' said my housemate. 'You don't need to hide him away, you know. Have him round here when you want to and introduce us. Nobody cares what you do in your own bedroom.'

The Raven and the Jackdaw

Again, it was noticeable that no other member of the cast of A Man for All Seasons or of my household found it necessary to ask me the big question. The news was out, and so was I – at least as far as the University of Bristol went – and to my surprise my news and I, and my boyfriend, were readily accepted.

We were still an item (though that was an expression I hadn't heard back in 1980) when term ended and we had to part for a few weeks. Back at home I mentioned Byron's name occasionally – I couldn't help it: my tongue always itched to pronounce it – but always casually, as I mentioned the names of other friends. I didn't tell my brother or our parents that we were enjoying a homosexual relationship. Enjoying would have been the right word, though. I had no expectation that the thing would last for ever. From the little I knew about such relationships, and I knew very little indeed about them, those things normally didn't.

Similarly, I hadn't talked of my feelings about Jason when Byron and I had opened up, as new lovers do, about ourselves, our families and (most of) our inmost thoughts. Byron knew that I had a brother, and would have gathered from the way I spoke about him that I was close to him, but that was as far as it went.

The proximity of Jason during that Easter vacation was something I'd half longed for and half dreaded. Again there were a few days when I had to share Jason's bedroom with him, during a visit from Anna. I wished the two of them would get engaged soon, so that I wouldn't have to go on doing this. But I discovered something I hadn't expected. My feelings for Jason hadn't gone away but they were suddenly more manageable. Loving him these days didn't hurt quite so much as it had done. I'd been inoculated against the Jason bug by my relationship with Byron. Despite whatever was going to happen to the Byron and me thing in the future I would always remain grateful to Byron for that at least.

Summer terms at school or university ripen relationships just as the summer ripens fruit. They brighten and take colour, they grow and swell... Quite often, like overripe fruit, they simply burst. Byron and I became a well-known couple around Bristol as that summer warmed up and life was lived more and more in the open: in the city's streets, around the quaysides and in the parks. We deliberately made ourselves conspicuous as we swanned about, wearing each other's clothes quite ostentatiously, wanting to make other people talk.

In the middle of the term Byron told me excitedly that he'd been offered an audition in Glasgow, at one of the UK's most prestigious theatres, which was situated in the notorious Gorbals Street. He was very excited by this. The end of his drama school career was looming and the summer looked like leaving him no longer in full-time education – and so without a job. He asked me if I'd travel up to Scotland with him. The audition was over a weekend. It was doable, if expensive. The theatre was going to pay Byron's travel expenses and find him a place to stay overnight. He offered to pay half my own train fare, and to ask the theatre if, when they found him somewhere to stay overnight, they could find a place that would take the two of us, pointing out that we would only need a single bed.

That weekend in Glasgow was an eye-opener. I won't go into it here, as an extended story about life at the theatre in the Gorbals (partly fictionalised) became the centrepiece of my Raven and Jackdaw novella and is quoted in full a little later in this book. It gives an account of an affair that is based loosely on my relationship with Byron and describes, albeit with

The Raven and the Jackdaw

different details and circumstances, the ending of our time together.

What happened to Byron and me was so commonplace, so usual, that the story hardly needs telling. The end of term parted us. Byron got his job at Glasgow, four hundred miles from where I was. I travelled up twice during the autumn to see him. We shared a bed on both occasions and though our cocks were up for it our hearts were not. We'd moved on. He moved in a new exciting circle, had new friends, would have new loves. I, for my part, had met someone else. He was twenty years older than I was. He was gay, I found out gradually, but though we became close friends he was never my lover. But thanks to him I was offered (and I accepted), while still a student, the most wonderful and exciting job I could have imagined in all my life.

TEN

In my second year at Bristol my peer group and I were taught by, among other people, Will Lumsden. His name may not be widely remembered now but at the time he was a well-known figure in the wider world thanks to BBC television and radio. He presented many programmes about natural history through both those media and was hugely popular with the public. His style was quite flamboyant; he wore huge straw sombreros in summer and had a beard that came and went. He made complex information about plants and animals accessible and easy to grasp and somehow communicated his own delight in the subject as well as its awesomeness. He was fun to listen to, often funny also, and fun to watch. We second-year students were excited at the thought of having him as a lecturer and tutor and in the event he did not disappoint.

At my second tutorial with him (there were four in our little tutorial group) it was my turn to present the paper that was discussed. I had been disappointed, I have to say, with the topic I'd been given. The others got the fascinating subjects of the migration of eels between the River Severn and the Sargasso Sea, the distribution of big wild cats on the African continent, and humming-birds in Ecuador. I was asked to research and write about snails' teeth. But I made the best of it, shrugged my shoulders, accepted and carried out the task with good grace.

In fact my paper was quite a success. It stimulated the interest of the others, the discussion that followed my reading of it was lively, and Doctor Lumsden (as we were expected to call him) made some very nice comments about my work. When the tutorial was finished and we students rose to leave the room Doctor Lumsden called me back. 'Shut the door,' he said. Then,

The Raven and the Jackdaw

'Don't look so nervous.' He grinned at me and I grinned nervously back. 'Sit down. I want to pay you a compliment.'

'Oh,' I said.

'I saw you in A Man for All Seasons last year. Thomas Cromwell. An intelligent as well as an arresting performance. And I also saw you in A Midsummer Night's Dream.'

I had done that back in the summer. I'd played Puck. Byron had given me some invaluable tips on how to play the part.

Lumsden smiled and said, with what looked like a naughty twinkle in his eyes, 'You were a very good Puck.'

Was that some kind of double-entendre at which I was expected to laugh? I didn't dare do that in case it wasn't. I said, 'Thank you,' instead.

'The two parts could hardly have been more different,' Lumsden went on, rearranging his face so that it looked more serious. 'And now this term I was surprised, though pleasantly so, to find you at my lectures and in my tutorial group.'

'Why surprised?' I asked.

'Most student actors come from the arts departments, do they not?'

I saw his point. 'Yes,' I said. 'There are a few scientists among us, but you're right. The sample as a whole is weighted pretty heavily in favour of the English department.'

He was kind enough to laugh at that.

'Now I'll come to the point,' he said. 'I'm looking for a young chap with a good understanding of natural science to front a little item on garden wildlife for one programme in my next series. It's just a one-off. Ideally the person should be about your age, should be able to present himself nicely, like an actor does and – not to beat about the bush – have an appealing face.' He gave me the alert, no-nonsense look of a terrier who thinks it's time to go for a walk. 'Would you like to do it?'

The BBC Natural History Unit was based in Bristol. There was no need for me to travel to London for the job; I simply walked to Whiteladies Road. They checked out what I'd look like on camera and listened to what I'd sound like over a mike. On the day itself – warm, clear-skied and windless – we went to a sweetly overgrown garden a few miles outside the city; it belonged to a friend of Lumsden's, and contained a large pond. I wore – as agreed in advance – a pair of white gym shorts, white plimsolls without socks and a pale blue top. I had recently turned nineteen; I looked considerably younger than that.

We worked with what was available. With what was in the garden, and with what flew in and out. There were dragonflies of several sorts – I named the species easily and off the cuff. Luckily for me no difficult ones turned up. We found a toad quite by chance, and some late caterpillars of the small tortoiseshell butterfly, feeding on nettles. It was probably too late in the year for them to stand a chance of successfully pupating but I didn't tell the viewers that.

I took my plimsolls off and waded into the pond with a net. It was autumn and the possibilities were limited, yet by some sort of miracle I caught a frog. There were moorhens, always good for a half-minute's footage, bobbing their heads as they swam, while their reflections did the same thing underneath. We carried on till daylight failed us and I began to feel chilly in my shorts. Then we packed up and drove back.

I tried not to think too much about my forthcoming one-off TV appearance, though I phoned my brother and my parents to tell them to make a note of the date. I also

The Raven and the Jackdaw

left a phone message for Byron at the stage door in Glasgow. He actually replied with a one-word telegram. *Congrats!* My housemates, course-mates and fellow members of the drama society also knew, of course.

The programme went out at half-past six on a Tuesday. I sat and watched it with a couple of my housemates. We had glasses of our home-made beer and I held a cushion on my lap, ready to put it over my face if the embarrassment of the experience became too much. First there was Lumsden, doing a major story about seals in the Wash. It must have been recorded during the summer vacation, I guessed. Then, for the last ten minutes of the thirty, there I was.

I looked rather good, I thought, and sounded natural. My shorts-clad legs looked fine; my year of walking up hills in Bristol had seen to that. And for once I'd managed to move gracefully, I noticed. I didn't flounder in the water or stumble about the place. I didn't need to put the cushion over my face. My housemates were lovely about it, and one of them joined me in a second glass of beer.

But it was the next day that I felt the full impact. On my walk down the hill to my morning lecture I was stopped by no less than three mothers with children who all told me how much they had enjoyed my last night's TV appearance and asked if I'd give their kid my autograph. The programme had gone out nationwide. I wondered if the same thing would have happened if I'd decided to go to London that morning and walk down Oxford Street. I didn't put this to the test.

A round of spontaneous applause broke out when I walked into the lecture hall. To my astonishment. I signed two further autographs for children that day. It seemed that I'd become famous (for five minutes) overnight.

A week later a little batch of letters arrived, forwarded from the BBC studios. There were five from teenage girls. This was very flattering. And there was one from a fifteen-year-old boy. That one had a different effect. It caused a pang, brought an ache to my heart.

The Raven and the Jackdaw

ELEVEN

When I came to write my novella, to which I eventually gave the rather obvious title The Raven and the Jackdaw, I wrote about my extraordinary stroke of luck, though I disguised it somewhat by placing it in the world of the theatre. I made use of my visits to Byron in Glasgow to create the background, and gave my imagination free rein with the idea of becoming a professional actor – something which I, prudently, hadn't done in real life. I let the character of David, the Jackdaw, become an actor in my stead.

****

It was raining at Euston. It was raining at Bletchley, it was raining at Rugby, and it fell in sheets upon Crewe. David, alone in a train of strangers, wondered what in the world he was doing. He must be mad, he thought. He was twenty-three.

James lived in London. He'd married a barmaid when he was still at art school. 'For God's sake,' Hector had said, 'if you young people can't manage to behave these days, at least ... at least you have every opportunity to take some precautions. At least you could have avoided ... this. Some girl who's just anybody. She may well manage to make you unhappy for a whole lifetime. You may do the same for her. Fine set-up for a child to be born into. What kind of a world will you have prepared for it? Have you thought of that? Have you no sense of responsibility at all?'

'Yes Dad,' James had said tiredly. 'I have. That's why I'm getting married.'

A small squalling bundle had arrived soon after the wedding guests had gone, looking as if he meant to stay. They'd called him Richard. He was four now and had a younger brother of his own. James worked for an advertising agency. He had a room with no windows, a desk with his own sketch-pad, and a telephone that could not be used for outgoing calls.

Mary had disappeared to Canada the previous year with a young man named Lawrence. It was a move that had taken her brothers by surprise and upset Hector considerably. He now lived alone at Hundredhouse, a sense of disappointment in his children leaving him as liable to be irritated by their occasional presence as depressed by their habitual absence.

David had contributed at least as much as the others to his father's state of dissatisfaction. Returning home at the end of his first year at St. Andrews he had announced baldly that he would not be going back. 'What a bloody waste,' his father had said, and David still recalled vividly the atmosphere of that conversation. The fact that David had gained a place at drama school for the autumn and a scholarship to go with it cut no ice with Hector. Weren't there enough good actors out of work already without David swelling their ranks? And what guarantee was there that David would rise above the ranks of the mediocre anyway? Whereas with a university degree... And then there was the question of the taxpayers' money that had been invested in him by the state...

Happily James and Mary had been less dampening. James had been positively enthusiastic. He did not share his father's reverence for university qualifications and the thought that David was standing up to his father's displeasure and striking out after something he wanted to do gave him some satisfaction. He was also quite excited by the idea that someone in his family might perhaps become a familiar or at least an occasional feature of the TV screen. He'd kept saying, 'Jackdaw's going to be an actaw,' till the grotesque rhyme drove the

The Raven and the Jackdaw

others to distraction. But there had been a touch of admiration in the way he said it.

Mary had tried – or so David imagined – to adopt what might have been their mother's position in the matter. She'd said things like, 'I'm sure that if he's thought about it so hard, and gone to all that trouble ... auditions, scholarships...' and, 'So long as it makes him happy...' Privately they must both have wondered how much the sudden U-turn of his career had been influenced by what David now thought of as "that Christmas". David wondered that himself.

That Christmas. That Boxing Day. David, in his train in the rain, smiled weakly at the memory. (Carlisle was outside now. It waited in the rain and dusk of the November afternoon for a minute or two. Lights were coming on in the streets. Then the town disappeared into the past.) That Boxing Day he'd come downstairs and found Mary tidying up in the kitchen. She'd looked at him and said, 'You look dreadful. Are you all right?' He'd gone straight out into the garden and thrown up.

From the garden he'd heard Mary say to James a few minutes later, 'What have you done to him?' The question's multiple ironies were echoed in James's repetition of it with changed inflections. 'What have I done to him?!'

Nobody spoke much that day, except for Hector who raged tirelessly about his empty bottle of brandy and managed, incredibly, to make the atmosphere even worse. Over the next few days Mary had tried to elicit what had happened from both brothers by turn. Without success.

But the days had passed. The injuries that James and David had both sustained eventually healed to a degree that was liveable with. Normal relations were resumed. If anything between them could ever be normal now. The conversation of that Christmas night had never been referred to in the years that followed it...

It wasn't actually raining under the glass roof of Glasgow Central; it only felt like it. David struggled up the long platform with his luggage. The taxi rank was empty; that was what rain did. At last one taxi arrived and took David to the address he'd been allocated. The taxi departed and David rang the bell. There was a dramatic pause and then the door opened, and David's future with it.

'David?' asked the bright and bouncy young woman who opened it. Behind her the house was light and warm in contrast to the rain-driven darkness behind him. 'Did you have a good journey up? Isn't this unspeakable?' She gestured towards the rain that lashed the beginning of the night. 'Isn't it dire? Now look, there's been a change of plan. It looks as though you'll be sharing a flat with Alec – and Wendy, who's up here for the panto. They're both as new as you so you can all three feel lost together. What's happened is that our flat has been more or less commandeered by Robert who's playing Dame. He's just split up with his boyfriend and has nowhere to live. He's got his old flat of course, but his previous ex-boyfriend was murdered there last year in the living-room. You probably read about it. He's not too keen to go back there, obviously, so everything's a bit topsy-turvy at the moment. Everyone's over at Jessica's tonight watching Streetcar on the telly. I'll drive you over there and you can go back with Wendy and Alec.'

By now they were already in the car. David peered between the windscreen wipers and the raindrops at grimy side-streets. They drove down Sauciehall Street. 'Christmas lights are up already. Aren't they just so too ghastly for words it's wonderful?' said his driver. 'I'm Deborah, by the way. Publicity and Marketing. I should have said.'

The Raven and the Jackdaw

David was nervous, cold and hungry. Nevertheless he was in the theatre at last and on the threshold of his first job. The thought did not do much to cheer him up. He was an actor now but it didn't feel much like it. All those letters, those auditions... finally the terse postcard asking him to turn up at a church hall in London and dance. Dance! It had been the least of his talents as a drama student. But now his first job depended on it. He had gone to the audition with a determined desperation that masked his lack of expertise and to his surprise... Well, now here he was, ready to sing and smile for his life in the chorus of a pantomime in Glasgow.

'This is David.' The room was full of people, in chairs, on the sofa, on the floor, their faces lit only by cold television light. 'Meet Jeremy, Caroline, Alec, Tom, Monica, Kate, Tony, Jessica, Will, Chris and Wendy.' Nobody looked up. One or two grunted and someone, indicating the flickering screen, added, 'And Mr Brando.'

Any desire to make an impression melted at once in the heat of an even stronger urge to fade away unnoticed. 'Have you eaten?' This was Jessica, crawling towards him across the floor.

'I had a pork pie on the train,' David said brightly, trying not to sound pathetic.

'Oh darling, you must be starved to death. I'll do you an omelette. Won't be a minute. You'll find the pepper and salt in those two china pigs. You shake it out of their snouts.'

David ate his omelette kneeling. The two pigs looked up at him from the carpet. When the film was over and David was just realising that he had a pounding headache an elflike person of about his own age came over and said, in a broad Yorkshire accent, 'I'm Alec. Would you like to go home now?'

'Yes, I would,' said David, perhaps replying to a deeper question than the one that Alec had meant.

'We can stop at the chippie on the way back. That omelette didn't look too big.'

'Are you in the panto?' David asked as they walked along the street. Alec insisted on carrying David's luggage for him although he was smaller than David.

'Me? In the panto? No. I wish I was. I'm the front of house manager. I'm new though. In the job three days.'

'What does a house manager do exactly?' David asked.

'Deal with the public and the usherettes, spend a lot of time counting money and entering figures. Are you having haggis or fish? Repairing the loos of course. Theatres are always falling apart.'

They ate their haggis and chips in a shop doorway, looking down at the River Kelvin and the rain that fell like javelins into it. 'You're not gay, are you?' Alec asked, suddenly serious.

'No,' said David. It was the only answer he could think of.

'Thank God for that,' said Alec, sounding relieved. 'I was beginning to think I was the only bloke here who isn't. Not that I've anything against them. I wouldn't be in this business if I had. But here nearly the whole company is. The panto company at any rate. You'll find you're the only straight guy in that lot. I mean, you heard them this evening, going on about how many telly stars they've had it off with. Gets a bit much. Give them half a chance and... Anyway, it'll be nice to have someone in the flat who bats for the same team. The guy who's just moved out...'

'Tell me about the girl. Wendy?'

'Came up yesterday. Been going around all day in a sort of sailor suit tucked into red wellies. Got the biggest

The Raven and the Jackdaw

bum this side of the Humber. Can't wait to see her in tights.'

'Hmm,' said David.

'Actually, I'm looking forward to the panto,' Alex went on, using chips for commas and full stops. 'Loved panto since I was a kid. Used to sit in the gallery at the Alhambra – I'm from Bradford by the way – and we used to belt out the song-sheet and throw toffees onto the stage.'

'Bet you were really favourite with the actors,' said David.

*

Three weeks were gone in an instant and the pantomime opened. There were two performances daily and three on Saturdays. Sundays were for sleeping. A feeling of unreality set in. David would make his way to the stage without any clear idea of which scene it was until he got there; he would hear the audience moving about and be unsure whether it was the interval of the second performance or the beginning of the third; he would wonder whether, had there been a window, it would have shown daylight or darkness outside. He learned to change his costume like lightning at the end of the evening and so manage to catch a drink in the stage-door pub before the deafening ten o'clock closing-time bell drove customers out of the door before it could drive them mad. He would fall into bed numbed with exhaustion and then lie awake with the pantomime songs spinning in his head in a never-ending loop.

After Christmas fatigue lowered resistance and the company was swept by flu. Policeman number one had to go on as Dame when the leading actor went sick and David had to replace the policeman. He was so nervous that he could hardly sing his quickly learned number and had to be rescued by Policeman number two. But by the following day he was well in control and was disappointed when Policeman number one's recovery a day after that sent him back to the chorus. Another day he was 'off' himself and had to spend a miserable day alone, in bed in the flat. Alec brought him some supper while Wendy, whom both David and Alec disliked, complained about people bringing germs to the place. At the height of the flu outbreak there were only two people left in the chorus, the others were either filling the shoes of those too ill to work or off sick in their own right. The show went on for a gruelling five weeks. It played to packed houses and took enough money to keep Alec at his desk cashing up till after midnight. It was reckoned a major success and David wondered if it would ever, ever end.

Towards the end of the run an entirely new company of actors appeared, to start rehearsals for the repertory season that would follow. Their contracts would run for six months. 'Lucky sods,' said the panto actors, as they looked forward to the dole queue in a few days' time.

Just ten days before the pantomime ended the theatre director put his head round the dressing-room door and asked David to look into his office before going home. 'What have you been up to?' his dressing-room mates asked.

Knocking at the director's door brought back memories of the headmaster's office. David felt nervous and tired. He opened the door when the director's 'Come in' rang out, and found himself facing not only him but the theatre's administrator and the author of the play that was beginning to be rehearsed.

'Sit down,' said the director. 'I liked your policeman the other day.'

'Thank you.'

'I fired an actor today. He came back from lunch drunk. Silly boy. It leaves us with no-one to play the juvenile lead in Take Two Letters.'

The Raven and the Jackdaw

There was a hiatus during which David could manage to do nothing except look startled.

'We'd like you to read a couple of scenes for us,' said the author of the play, and thrust a script towards his face.

David read well, to his own astonishment. When he'd finished he looked up at the three faces opposite him, hardly daring to think.

'We'd like to offer you the role,' said the director, unsmilingly and in a businesslike tone of voice. 'But only if you're sure you can learn it very quickly, and rehearse every minute you're not on stage while the pantomime's still going. We need you to say yes or no right now, I'm afraid. Time's getting short.'

David said the first thing that came into his head. 'Yes.'

The administrator handed him a contract and asked him to sign it. She smiled as she added, 'Better read it first.'

*

'Can't hear a word you're saying, sweetheart,' called the director from the stalls. 'You're not in a drama school hall now. Have you any idea how many seats there are out here?'

David did know. Alec had told him. 'Eight hundred and forty-three,' he yelled back. There was general laughter.

Looking back on his stroke of fortune David reflected that luck had turned up rather backhandedly and less than gloriously. He wondered for the first time if good luck usually arrived like that.

Six months passed before David had a chance to pause for thought. It seemed to him that he had barely paused for breath. He had been in every production between February and August. For the time being he had no need any longer to prove himself. He had kept his head down and been almost unaware of anything outside the scope of his work. It had been a good-natured joke among the company that he was so engrossed in his work that you could try and seduce him and he would never notice. One or two of the girls and rather more than one or two of the boys had in fact tried. And it was true that he hadn't noticed.

There was something else he hadn't noticed. The flat he shared with Alec was now also occupied by a woman called Caroline – she'd replaced the pantomime actress Wendy. Not until the season was as good as ended did David realise that Alec had been bedding Caroline for months. He was a little shaken by this discovery. 'I didn't think you liked her particularly,' he said to Alec.

'I don't like her particularly,' Alex retorted, 'but for heaven's sake, here we are in the same flat... It seemed obvious really. Inevitable, if you like. It's convenient...' He came to a stop, reading something close to disapproval in David's face. 'Well, fuck it,' he said defensively. 'I was lonely. People do get lonely. Ordinary normal people, that is. People like you, perhaps not. Now that your great career has taken off. Ever since you got your first decent part you've no ears or eyes for anyone ... or anything ... except your bloody work. Nice for you if you can fill every nook and cranny of your existence with a job you're besotted with. But don't be so shocked by the rest of us – by those of us who can't. Your acting must be very satisfying for you. But what about me? What do you expect me to do? Rot away totalling cheques and ticking off delivery notes against ice-cream consignments and never go to bed with anyone I'm not in love with?'

The Raven's grin grows wider as he peers down from the hay cart, from a distance measured in galloping years. The essence of a smiling face, sunlight on black hair and a sky of the deepest, hottest blue.

The Raven and the Jackdaw

****

I was very unkind to the Raven in that extract. Having him knock up a girl from a pub and having to get married at twenty-one. Putting him in a windowless office in his place of work... Of course none of that happened in my real-life brother's case. That was me taking my revenge on him for what I considered his betrayal of me and his rejection of my love. For he did get engaged eventually – and eventually got married. To his by then long-standing girlfriend Anna. Whom I couldn't help but like.

TWELVE

'What do you do about fan letters?' I asked.

Will laughed. (I called him Doctor Lumsden in tutorials and in front of other students, but he was Will now, when we were talking about TV work.) 'Have you been getting thousands?'

'I've had six,' I said, seeing the thing in proportion now and feeling a bit small as I said this. 'Teenage girls.' I wasn't going to complicate things by saying that one was from a very young bloke.

'Answer them if you can manage it,' Will said. 'You can probably handle six.'

'How many do you get?' I asked him.

'Fewer than thousands,' he said. 'But more than six. OK, I have a secretary who helps me deal with my post. But you need to be careful. For a start, don't give away your home address. I'll get you some letterhead from the Unit that's designed for the purpose. The BBC Bristol address is on it but not the phone number. You just say you appreciate their kind comments and tell them when you're next appearing on TV or what your next project is.'

'I don't have a next TV appearance,' I said, 'or a next project.'

'You do have actually,' said Will matter-of-factly, 'but I'll come to it in a minute. If they ask to meet you just ignore that. Pretend their letter didn't mention it. Whatever happens, don't think you could have sex with them if you wanted it and then forget about it. You might forget but they won't. I've known people, prominent people on TV or in entertainment, who've had a miserable time of things, pursued down the years by people they thought they could have a bit of fun with when they were little more than kids. You have to keep

The Raven and the Jackdaw

your nose absolutely clean if you work at the BBC. If not, you're all over the tabloids and your career's finished.'

I felt very sobered listening to that. But I said, 'A career at the BBC? You said something about…'

'Well, I can't offer you a career yet,' said Will, looking a bit alarmed, realising he might have raised my hopes by accident. 'But we can talk about a second TV appearance. The powers that be at the Unit were very impressed by your performance. They want you to do a second Nature in the Garden slot. To tack onto my programme next week.'

'Next week?' I was astonished. The last one had taken weeks to process.

'They'll rush it through,' Will said. Even so, I thought, it was now November. There would be nothing of interest in most gardens, unless I was expected to disinter hibernating hedgehogs. I certainly wouldn't be able to wear shorts. I told Will some of this.

'You'll be doing it in a greenhouse,' said Will. 'At Slimbridge. Peter Scott's Wildfowl Trust.'

I'd heard of that, of course. It was less than an hour's drive from Bristol. But a greenhouse? I said, 'I thought it was all ducks and geese.'

'There's a tropical house, glassed in and temperature-controlled. Full of humming-birds and butterflies. A few other stray insects and some tree-frogs. You might have to brush up on the relevant species in a few books.'

'Wow,' I said. I wondered if they'd like me to wear my shorts.

I replied to the five fan letters I'd had from young girls exactly as Will had told me I should, as soon as he gave me the BBC letterhead. The letters had arrived from as far afield as London and Cheshire though two, including the boy's, were from the Bristol area. When it came to answering the boy's letter, though, I hesitated. Were I to brush him off with the standard formula I would hurt him; I somehow knew that. I knew too that I would also hurt myself. I didn't reply to him before going to Slimbridge, and I still hadn't answered his letter when the programme went out.

The day at Slimbridge was fun. I'd asked about the shorts a bit sheepishly, thinking they might laugh at me, but with perfectly straight faces the director and cameraman said yes. And it was rather like a taste of paradise to find myself being filmed among jewel-like hovering humming-birds, pointing out the different species (which, yes, I did have to look up in advance) and big bright butterflies that obligingly settled on my arms and shoulders as I talked. It was warm and cosy in the tropical house. It felt even more so when a small thunderstorm broke overhead and rain lashed the glass roof. Some years later a structure that was similar in concept to Slimbridge's tropical house, though twenty times its size and twenty times as ambitious, would be built in Cornwall. It struck me as absolutely right that it should be called the Eden Project.

I finished my piece to camera with an observation that was completely off my own bat. They could cut it if they liked. Not everybody could have a garden like the tropical one I stood in, I said. But you only needed a square yard of outdoor space, a bit of lawn or a weedy patch, and a magnifying-glass, and you could go on safari every day, just outside your back door, at no cost. There were wonders to be seen everywhere, even if sometimes very small wonders. All you had to do was look.

They kept that bit in, I saw, when I watched the finished programme on TV later that week. I was pleased about that. I felt even more pleased when, a few minutes later, the phone rang and it was my brother,

The Raven and the Jackdaw

calling from Cambridge. 'You were super,' he said. 'For the second time. And you looked nice. Anna and I watched it. Both really proud of you, mate.' That really made my evening. It was only the fact that the compliments came from Jason and Anna jointly that made them bittersweet.

A few days passed and then two letters came from the Natural History Unit. One was from a senior producer. The Unit had taken note of my "square yard" suggestion, and thought it would make a good basis for a series. Though the idea was still at the discussion stage. If it did happen they would start filming in the spring of next year. If it went ahead, they would ask me to front it. Would I be interested in doing that?

A ripple of something ran all through me. Down my arms and legs. Dopamine I suppose. As if I'd inhaled deeply on a spliff. The sensation was almost orgasmic. Although I could see at once that a part of the appeal of such a series was that it would cost almost nothing to make, that did nothing to diminish my feeling of excitement. I was still tingling down to my toes and fingers when, without looking very hard at it, I slit open the second, forwarded, envelope.

It was from the boy. The boy whose letter I hadn't answered. His name was Alastair. I hadn't forgotten that.

Dear Barnaby

I wrote to you a couple of weeks ago but you may not have got it. I saw you again on television last night. I thought you were great. I like your square yard idea and think I'll try it. Next year when the weather warms up.

Then the letter lurched into a different gear. Alastair left restraint behind him and pitched forward as though suddenly unable to stop himself.

I think you must be someone who is like me. Someone who likes the same things and thinks the same thoughts. I'd love to meet you. You seem kind and gentle. It would be so good to meet and talk. I really hope you will write back.
Yours
Alastair (McNeil)
P.S. I think you look very nice.

My heart was thumping. On top of the amazing letter from the BBC producer – this! The boy was clearly bright: his hand-written letter hadn't contained – or so it had seemed during my first rapid perusal of it – a single spelling or grammar mistake. I had a very vivid impression now of him rapidly folding the page and sealing it in an envelope, not daring to read it over in case he lost his nerve and couldn't send it. I felt the sudden sting of tears behind my eyelids.

I replied to Alastair's letter at once. My hands and my legs were shaking as I wrote. I put the address and phone number of the house I shared at the letter's head. I told him I'd been very touched by his kind words. If he would like to meet, well, I was going to be free all the following weekend. Would he like to suggest a time and place? He could do that by phone if he liked. I didn't stop until I came to the valediction. What should I put? After a half-minute's thought I followed his own example and wrote *Yours, Barnaby*. Then I folded the letter very quickly and sealed it in an envelope before I could get cold feet.

Some of our lecturers and tutors would invite students to their houses occasionally, for a meal or a drink. It was generally known that Will Lumsden never did that. Probably because he was a TV celebrity, we thought, and entertained – if or when he did entertain – at a

The Raven and the Jackdaw

higher level than that. So I was surprised when he called me back after our tutorial that week and invited me to lunch for the following day, giving me his address. He prefaced the invitation by asking if I'd dealt with my fan letters yet. I told him I had. 'How does your girlfriend feel about you getting letters from girls all over the place?' he asked.

'I don't have a girlfriend,' I answered.

'Ah,' he said. It was then that he invited me to lunch.

His house was big and pleasantly chaotic. He didn't have a girlfriend, either, or a wife. He lived with a man called Jeffrey, who was about the same age as Will was. They were convivial and entertaining hosts, generous with the food and wine. It was the first time in my life that I'd seen a mature gay couple at home, although I'd seen plenty of younger gay relationships in progress on my short visits to Glasgow to see Byron. Jeffrey and Will had been together for twelve years, they told me, and I found comfort and encouragement in that. They didn't ask me about my own love life. They seemed to know about me without having to ask. Perhaps it had something to do with those white shorts. Nor did they ask me not to broadcast around the university the information that Will Lumsden lived with a man. They were good judges of character and knew that I would not. And I did not.

Meeting the couple at home had given me plenty to think about, but my thoughts were all very positive. I walked back to Redland in a very cheerful, as well as slightly tipsy, state. When I walked into the living-room of my shared house the only other occupant of the room, a chap called Martin, said, 'You just missed a phone call. Someone called Alastair. He left his number and asked if you could ring him back.' A slight frown of puzzlement overcame his brow. 'He sounded very young.'

'Ah,' I said. 'I think he may be a young fan of mine.' My housemate looked even more puzzled. 'From my TV appearances,' I said.

Martin didn't seem reassured . 'How the hell did he get this number? Are we going to have thousands of people ringing up? You must have been seen by a million people at least!'

'God knows,' I said, feigning innocence. 'How long ago did he phone?'

'About five minutes.'

'Give me the number,' I said. 'I'll call him another time perhaps.' Martin handed me the piece of paper on which the number was written, then I walked out of the house. My actions as well as my lies must have been totally transparent but I was too far gone to care about that. I walked round two street corners and found a phone-box. From there I called Alastair up.

His voice sounded lovely. Very genuine. Very sweet. 'Do you still want to meet at the weekend?' I asked.

'Yes,' he said. His voice had gone husky.

'When and where?' I asked.

'Saturday morning?' he asked back.

'How about eleven o'clock? Somewhere in the city centre?'

'Yes,' he said. He'd got tongue-tied.

I picked a place at random. 'Outside the front of the Old Vic theatre then,' I said. There was a pub right next to the theatre. I'd gone there with Byron often enough. I could hardly take Alastair into a pub, but there were plenty of places around there where we could go for a coffee. It was an area that was heavily frequented by students as well as by locals and tourists, but that couldn't be helped. I'd say he was my little brother if anyone asked. He accepted my choice. 'See you Saturday, then,' I said.

The Raven and the Jackdaw

After I put the phone down I discovered that my heart was thumping in my chest. I also realised that I had no idea what Alastair looked like. I had such a vivid image of him in my mind – slender, beautiful and blond – that I hadn't thought to question it. It now occurred to me for the first time that he might not be attractive to look at. He might be very spotty, very skinny, or very fat. He would recognise me though. I wouldn't be able to check his appearance out from a distance and turn on my heel if I didn't like what I saw... I at once reproached myself for even thinking that. I'd agreed to meet him. I owed it to him to keep to that. He was a boy who wanted to talk about wildlife. I wasn't going on a date.

I saw him at once. He saw me at once. There was no mistaking him. There was no mistaking what, at that moment, we both felt. It was as much as either of us could do not to rush into each other's arms.

Alastair was slender, beautiful and blond. Four years younger than me and about two inches shorter. His physical development was a bit more advanced than mine had been at that age. Climbing those Bristol hills might be responsible for that. I fell for him when I first looked into his eyes and read there that the same thing had happened for him. This had happened to me only once before: with Byron nearly a year earlier. (I can't include Jason in the comparison: between brothers who'd lived together since they were babe and toddler there could hardly be love at first sight.) And as for Alastair, I guessed this might be a first.

We stood and looked at each other, too surprised by each other to speak. We didn't shake hands. Then Alastair stretched out a hand slowly and touched my bare forearm with a fingertip.

'I'm real,' I said. 'Don't worry. You're Alastair, I guess.' I smiled at him and he smiled back.

We went to the nearest coffee shop and sat and talked. We didn't talk about square yards or TV programmes. We turned ourselves inside out and laid our lives out for inspection as if on the table between us among the plates and coffee cups.

I longed to touch him but of course could not. I wondered how long I could expect to have the pleasure of his company. What time were his parents expecting him back? I didn't have to ask him: he volunteered that information himself.

We finished our coffees and looked at each other across the table. He said very quickly, very nervously, 'I told my parents I was meeting friends. That we'd get a sandwich and go to a matinee at the cinema. I said that just in case…'

'I'm free for the rest of the day,' I interrupted, needing to put him out of his agony as quickly as I could. 'We could have a sandwich together. Then in the afternoon, do what we like.'

We walked along the old harbour quays that were now given over to restaurants and shops. We looked at and talked about the boats that were tied up. In the end I did take him into a pub – I was behaving like a madman, I knew that – and we had a ploughman's lunch each, for which I paid, of course, and I got him a Coke with ice and lemon in it, while I had a pint. One or two strangers looked at me, not because I was with a younger boy but because they'd seen me on TV. By now I knew that look. Then we climbed the grassy slope of Brandon Hill and looked down at the city from its height. It was still warm and sunny but it wouldn't remain so for much longer. I said, 'Would you like to come and see my place?'

Of course he wanted that.

There was no harm being done to anyone, I told myself. We were just two teenagers spending an

The Raven and the Jackdaw

afternoon chatting together. Though of course I also knew that I was longing for sex. I'd only had sex twice since the summer: the two times I'd been to Glasgow to see Byron. The second of those occasions had been a month ago. I was missing Byron and missing sex.

I was still technically a minor. Sex with Byron, who was twenty-one now, was technically an illegal act. The law didn't seem to cater for the situation that had existed between Jason and myself since I was six. Alastair and I were just two more underage teenagers, I told myself – or would tell myself if it actually came to it.

It was quite a long walk from Brandon Hill, past the university, back to Redland, but Alastair didn't seem to mind that. Yes, we did walk among the buildings of the university. Amazingly we didn't come face to face with anyone I knew. I must have thought I was leading a charmed life. We came to the house I shared. 'Just a student house-share,' I said apologetically. 'I'm just a student still. Not a TV star yet.' I turned my key in the lock.

'I know that,' said Alastair sweetly. 'You don't need to apologise.' We went into the house. I was bracing myself for the inevitable encounter with one or more housemates in the living-room and thinking what I would say to them but there was no-one. It seemed that Alastair and I were alone in the house. There was, though, a letter conspicuously placed on the coffee table. Addressed to me, forwarded from the BBC, it bore the postmark of Peterhead. That was in the north of Scotland, I vaguely thought. I slit it open with a forefinger, grinning apologetically at Alastair. 'A fan letter, I think,' I said.

'Do you get many of those?' Alastair asked.

'This is the seventh.' I read it quickly. It was from a girl. I let Alastair read it.

'Do you reply to them all?' he asked.

'Yes,' I said. 'Briefly, and on BBC letterhead. I never suggest that we meet up.'

'Were the others from girls?' Alastair asked.

'Yes,' I said.

'You made an exception for me, then.'

'Yes,' I said. 'Can you think why that was?'

'Because I live locally?' he asked.

I looked at him intently. 'You know that's not the reason,' I said.

We kissed.

Did I initiate that? I don't think I did. Did he? I don't think he did. It just happened to both of us at the same instant, just as with our first exchange of looks at eleven o'clock.

I didn't do anything with my tongue; I didn't want to startle him. Though if he had gone down that route…But he didn't, and I let it go at that. Already this was more than good enough. He did, however, put his hands very diffidently, loosely, lightly, round my waist. I put my arms, equally lightly, around his back. Very, very slowly I increased the pressure, gently, ever so gently, tightening my grip. I felt him relax into the embrace. His arms round me grew gradually more confident. He too tightened his grip. Then he was pressing his crotch against mine. It was definitely he who started that. Though I quickly pressed back. I could feel the ridge of his hard little dick through our two pairs of jeans. I could feel my own, too, of course.

'Do you want to come upstairs?' I asked him. I hadn't intended the question to be a whisper, but that was how it came out.

'Yes,' he whispered back. I ruffled his blond hair as we came un-clinched in preparation for the journey ahead of us.

The Raven and the Jackdaw

An hour had passed by the time we came downstairs again. It was time for Alastair to be heading back home if questions were not to be asked. 'I'll walk with you down to the bus stop,' I said. Again there was no-one in the living-room and I breathed the more easily for that. But as we were heading for the front door through the hallway I heard the sound of the key in the lock just three feet ahead of us. Alastair gave way to panic for a second. I felt him start, and he clutched at my sleeve. He took his hand away quite smartly a moment later, but not before my housemate Martin had opened the door and clocked it.

'Oh, hi,' I said, grinning stupidly to cover my embarrassment. 'This is Alastair. One of my fans. Alastair – Martin, one of the guys I share the house with.'

'Hi, Alastair,' said Martin, sounding startled. Alastair could only manage a grunt. Neither of them attempted a handshake.

'Taking Alastair to the bus stop,' I said to Martin, who stood aside to let us pass. We went out through the still open door and shut it behind us.

'Wow,' said Alastair when we were out in the road.

'He didn't see us come downstairs,' I said. 'He can't know what we did.'

'He'll guess,' said Alastair glumly. Then, in a babes-and-sucklings moment of insight, added, 'Don't people always do that?'

THIRTEEN

I had to face Martin when I got back. He greeted me with a look that hurt. 'Are all your fans as young as that?' he asked.

'Not sure,' I said. 'He's the only one I've actually met.'

'I think you need to be a bit careful,' he said.

'Really?' I blustered. 'He's just a youngster who's interested in wildlife. All we've done is talk. It's not as if we were going to have sex.'

Martin looked at me very piercingly. 'If you're going to be a telly star – and good luck to you, because I hope all that side of things works out brilliantly for you – we all do…' He'd rather lost track of his sentence by then and had to make a new start. 'The thing is, for anyone who's anywhere near the media, it's not what you do, it's what people think.' He shrugged and smiled wryly. 'Sorry. Of course you know that. No offence intended.'

'No offence taken.' I said. 'You're absolutely right. Sometimes we all need to have the obvious pointed out.'

And that was that. I breathed a quiet sigh of relief. But clearly I couldn't bring Alastair home again. And in the city centre we would be all too conspicuous. Hundreds of people at the university knew me, at least by sight, if only because of the plays they'd seen me in. To say nothing of the numbers who'd seen me on TV twice. I would have to think long and hard about where the two of us could safely meet next.

We had had sex, of course. Though no penetration had taken place. We hadn't even put each other's cocks in our mouths. We'd taken our clothes off, kissed and cuddled, and masturbated each other to orgasm – Alastair had actually come twice. Perhaps by tomorrow Alastair would have changed his mind but at the moment

The Raven and the Jackdaw

of our parting, when his bus pulled in to the bus stop, he was as eager for a second meeting as I was.

I was lonely. That's why it had happened, I told myself. Alastair too was lonely. He had no brothers and sisters, he'd told me, and felt somehow different from the other boys at his school. Yes, it was because we were both lonely. I imagine that every person who does what I'd just done comes up with that excuse.

I brought the theme of loneliness into my attempt at a novella, though my writing of it still lay a few years off. By then I had plenty of experience of loneliness to draw on. Here is the Jackdaw, still at Glasgow, about three years older than I was when Alastair and I first met.

****

David got used to it. This was to be the pattern of his life. To work, to act, to devote himself so wholeheartedly to his job that no extraneous thoughts and desires could force their way in. Though they did. What did you expect people to do? Rot away totalling cheques? There were times when David cried, deep down, where the most painful, unseen tears are shed. Tears dry and bitter from love of an elder brother, for the frustration of a childhood and adolescent passion that was unresolved, undiminished by the years, painfully non-transferable...

Spring, summer and autumn came with renewed contracts.

'You're good news, David. We want you to stay till the New Year at least.' David could smile now at the memory of his apprehensive self watching Streetcar on a wet night in a strange town a year ago. He was almost a fixture now. Senior and confident. Acting grew easier for him.

A November morning, bright and sharp. The Clyde shone like abraded lead. David had nothing to do, for once, until the afternoon. The grind of work sounded faint today. The underground train ran scowling, welds and rivets yawning on the curves, through its mouth-wrenching stations: Cowcaddens, St. Enochs, Govan Cross. The newsagent was as precise as ever. 'There is no Guardian today. The Times? What Times would that be? The Beath Times? Oh, the London Times. No, not today. Carmunnock and Springboig Times? No sir? A good morning to you then.' And before he knew it David had arrived at the theatre.

There it sat, tall and shapeless among the slum clearances, exposing an exterior view its architect had never intended should be seen. Out-juts and lean-tos bled off it in all directions. Once those had tunnelled between surrounding buildings, now demolished, that had dictated their shapes and lent them a decency they could no longer pretend to. Now the building stood in a wasteland where tramps warmed themselves in front of bonfires fuelled with garbage, and threw nooses of barbed wire at you by way of a welcome. It made a good metaphor, David thought, for the theatre's place in the world and for its purpose.

The inside of the building presented a very different picture. David sat himself in the quiet of the stalls in the half-dark. It was like being inside a chandelier, he thought, or a wedding cake that had been pulled inside-out like a glove. A silhouette came through the pass door from backstage. It was Alec. 'What are you doing?' he asked.

'Admiring the view,' said David. 'I've got a morning off. Glasgow's beautiful today. I've just found the time to realise I like it.'

Alec perched on the back of a seat near David. A little gingerly. The seats were liable to pull away from their moorings without warning. He said, 'I've got a new job.

The Raven and the Jackdaw

I've just heard. I'm going to be general manager of a fringe theatre in London. It seats fifty.'

'That's what you want?' asked David.

'It's what I want next. After that...?' He shrugged his shoulders. 'I'd just decided I like it here too. I find that's the time to move on generally. The day you come in to work, hang your coat up and say, "I'm home now:" that's the day to put your coat back on and go straight out again. Anyway, that's what I think.'

'Sounds a bit restless.'

'Pots and kettles. You're just the same. I do know you a little bit by now. You won't be here much longer. You won't be content to be a grand old man here, unknown to anyone more than a hundred yards from the Clyde. And you won't stop in any one place for long. You won't stop running.'

'Am I running?' David was genuinely surprised to hear this.

'I wouldn't presume to know what you're running away from, but you are running.'

'You do talk some rubbish,' said David untruthfully.

*

'What now?' Alec asked, emptying his glass of champagne. A month had passed. Alec would be starting work in London on Monday. This was his leaving drink, in the theatre bar after the show on Saturday. 'What's to become of you now?'

David, to whom the question was addressed, laughed. His hair was still wet from the shower, he looked lean and healthy and his eyes shone with a confidence that owed nothing to champagne. He said nothing. Alex pursued him. 'You had an audition on Tuesday. You kept it very quiet but I could tell you had. Tonight you heard something. Good news if I'm not mistaken.'

'OK,' said David. 'You can be the first to hear it. I'm going to Manchester after Christmas. They're doing Romeo and Juliet. They want me...'

'To play...?'

'Romeo.'

Alec groaned theatrically. 'You should have said so at once. You must be over the moon about it.'

'For once in my life, yes. I am over the moon about it.'

'Then tell everyone, you dumbo! What's the matter with you? Crack open another bottle. Enjoy the bloody moment. It might never come again.'

'You're probably right,' said David thoughtfully but Alec wasn't listening. He was standing on a chair and broadcasting the news to the company.

****

It wasn't only my loneliness that I handed over to the fictional David like a used coat. His little string of successes was mine also. I was still humble enough – though perhaps only just humble enough – to count myself lucky in that.

A few days after my encounter with Alastair I got a phone-call from the Natural History Unit. The square yard series was going ahead. They wanted to check if I was still interested in presenting it. I said I was, of course. The programme would be called The Square Metre, though, the producer went on to say. Yard had other meanings and connotations apart from being a unit of measurement. Prison yard, Scotland Yard, back yard, et cetera, and the word square attached to any of those might have a ring of old-fashioned or out-of-date about it. Square Metre was modern, streamlined and clear. I totally agreed with that, and was impressed that people should give so much time and thought to the title of a TV series. (I was only nineteen.) 'Good,' the producer

The Raven and the Jackdaw

said. 'There'll be a letter, making a formal offer, in the post. We'll start filming in March when the bugs start to come out, and go on until late summer, all being well.' The programmes would go out in the early evening, twenty-five minutes' worth a week, about two weeks after each episode was shot. (It would be like Coronation Street with a population of slugs and insects, I thought. I did not say this.) I put the phone down. I could feel my excitement in all my nerve endings, crawling in my skin and making my heart pound.

One day later a cheque arrived. I'd almost forgotten I was expecting this. It was payment for the two garden slots I'd fronted for Will. It wasn't enough to retire on, but for two days' work, it knocked the money I'd been paid for being a theatre day-man, and for chopping cabbages, into a cocked hat. It would have been enough to buy an old banger with. I had passed my driving test at the second attempt over a year before, and regularly drove my parents' car in the vacations. But I wasn't going to buy a car. I had no need of one in Bristol, where everything was in walking distance, and walking kept me fit. For the time being I left the money in the bank.

That Saturday I again met Alastair outside the Old Vic. At two o'clock in the afternoon this time. We'd agreed this before we parted at the bus stop the previous week. To have repeated the eleven o'clock assignation might draw unwanted attention from his parents. We saw each other from a little distance, hurried towards each other and this time had to restrain ourselves from greeting each other with a kiss. We made do with a blink-or-you-miss-it hug. Alastair's excitement at seeing me was actually visible in his trousers. Ah, to be fifteen! Even though I was only four years older my reaction time was no longer quite as quick as that.

I told Alastair at once about my conversation with Martin and explained that we couldn't go back to the house. 'What did you tell your parents you were doing this afternoon?' I asked.

'I said I was going to the cinema with a friend,' he said.

'Then you're going to do exactly that,' I said. I grinned at him. 'No lies for once. Have you seen Chariots of Fire yet?'

He hadn't and I hadn't, so that was where we went.

We sat in the back row – just the two of us – and, running the very big risk of being picked out by a torch beam, unzipped each other and did the obvious. Afterwards I took him to a tea-shop and bought him tea and crumpets. Christmas holidays were looming. We had to discuss that. 'Is it all right if I send you a Christmas card to your parents' address?' he asked. I said that would be fine. 'But I'd rather you didn't do that to me,' he went on. 'You're expected to have fans. I'm not.'

'I'll make sure I give it to you in advance. But we need to find a way of keeping in touch without falling foul of your parents or my housemates.'

Alastair looked round the café quickly. 'And of the nation's TV-watchers,' he said.

'I don't think you need worry too much about that,' I said. 'They have short memories and I haven't been on the box for over a fortnight. It's days since I was last stopped in the street.'

Alastair knitted his brows thoughtfully. 'How do you feel about that?'

'Mixed feelings,' I said. 'It's a relief in a way. The fact that nobody in here is taking a blind bit of notice of us is rather welcome, but I'm vain enough to have a bit of a feeling of regret.'

'Never mind,' he said. 'You've all next year to look forward to.' My contract to present The Square Metre

The Raven and the Jackdaw

was one of the first bits of news I'd told him about when we'd met. 'Then you'll be a mega-star and mega-rich.'

I laughed. 'I don't know about that,' I said. Then I took a deep breath. 'I may be heading up to Glasgow for a day or two over the Christmas break. See Byron.' Alastair knew all about Byron. When we'd poured out our hearts to each other the previous week Byron was one of the big things I'd told him about.

I'll never forget the look Alastair gave me as he asked, 'Will you be having sex with him?'

'Probably,' I said. 'Would that upset you?'

'Probably,' said Alastair.

I felt a quick sigh escape me. 'I'll have to think about that.'

We still hadn't thought up a safe and foolproof method of communication when the time came for me to walk him to the bus stop. (Oh for the miracles of mobile phones and text messaging! But we'd be in our forties by the time those came about.) Our route this time took us past Alastair's school and then the obvious struck both of us. The tried and tested method that, for all I knew, went back to the Ancient Greeks: the message wedged in the school gates. Though actually, in this case, slightly more discreetly, in a crevice between two out of the way bricks.

At the bus stop we agreed to meet the following Saturday. It would be the last one of term, of my term as well as his. 'Give me your hanky,' I said as the bus came into sight.

'Why?' he asked.

'You know why,' I said. 'I'll get it washed and ironed along with my stuff and give it back to you, clean next week.'

He giggled as he handed it wetly over. 'Thank you very much,' he said.

I only went near the school after it was dark and the school was shut. If no-one was about I could extract any note from Alastair there might be and put mine in its place almost without breaking stride. There wasn't a note from Alastair every day, obviously, but I walked past there every day just in case.

A wild idea entered my head about this time. The Square Metre was intended to appeal to a youthful audience. I thought one day how wonderful it would be if I could have Alastair as my co-presenter. A kid of fifteen whom young viewers could identify with... Happily I didn't share this idea with anyone at the BBC – or anyone else. My motives would have been horribly transparent. Nobody, but nobody, when they are offered a job out of the blue, asks if they can do it as a job-share with a fifteen-year-old friend before they've even started work. And the third thing was that they didn't need a kid for young viewers to identify with. I was that kid. In my shorts. I was that bait. I never told Alastair about my thought. He might have been thrilled at the possibility, then disappointed in me for not proposing it.

I had other news for Alastair when we met the next Saturday, though first I returned to him his white handkerchief, cleaned, ironed and neatly folded. 'What are you doing on Thursday?' I asked him. Thursday would be the third day of his school holidays, and by coincidence the second day of my Christmas vac.

'Nothing at the moment,' he said.

'All my housemates are going away on Wednesday,' I said. 'I've checked. I plan to stay up a couple more days. Head home on the Friday. I won't be able to put it off much longer than that or my parents will be asking questions too. But it means that I have the house to myself on Thursday. We could spend as much time there together as you think you can risk.'

The Raven and the Jackdaw

'Wow,' he said. 'I'll see what excuse I can dream up. See how much of the day I can be away for, without them smelling a rat. I'll keep you posted the usual way.' He meant, via the bricks near the school gates.

I put my hand in my jacket pocket and fished something out. I handed it to him. 'Your Christmas card,' I said. 'I'm delivering it today in case Thursday doesn't come off.'

'Thank you,' he said. Then he looked probingly up at me – a shock of blue. 'Will you be going up to see Byron in Glasgow?' he asked.

'No,' I said.

'I love you,' he said, almost under his breath.

'I love you too,' I said.

We went to see Raiders of the Lost Ark. This time I cleaned him up myself, sharing my own handkerchief.

The most obvious thought hit me as I was walking home after seeing Alastair onto his bus. I'd told myself I didn't need an old banger for driving around Bristol. True, I didn't. But Alastair and I did.

I stopped off on the way and bought a local paper. Back at home I looked through the used car ads. Martin, who was no more experienced than I was when it came to buying cars, helped me with the task and gave advice which might or might not have been valuable, about prices, condition and so forth. I took the plunge and dialled one of the numbers. Yes, the car was still there. Could I come and look at it in the morning? Yes, I could. It was actually in Redland and just a few blocks away from where I was. In the morning Martin very kindly came with me and we looked it over together with eyes of ignorance. It was a Mini, about four years old, dark blue and on sale at three hundred pounds. Its owner was the wife of a retired policeman. I thought that sounded safe enough. The banks were closed, as it was Sunday. I asked if she would keep the car for me till eleven o'clock the next morning, by which time I would have got the cash. She said yes and we shook hands on it. The next morning I parted with my money and drove away, with hands that shook against the steering-wheel, in the first – and thus the most memorable – car of my life.

Thanks to the school-gates communications system I was able to let Alastair know that he wouldn't need to catch the bus into town on Thursday. If he would draw me a map I'd pick him up two blocks away from the house in Clifton where his parents lived.

When Thursday came it showed me what heaven, if it existed, would be like. I picked Alastair up at the corner we'd agreed to meet on at ten thirty in the morning. As we drove Alastair laid his hand confidently on my thigh and, crossing my arm over his, I returned the compliment. At the empty house – it had taken just two minutes to get there – we kissed in the hall and then immediately went upstairs, took each other's clothes off and got into bed. We didn't do anything we hadn't done previously. Nothing adventurous. No sucking. No penetration. What made that next hour special was the simple fact of lying together and sharing our young bodies. It was something I knew very well already. It was better than the orgasmic aspect of sex; it went deeper than that.

For Alastair this second time in my bed was his second experience of the situation full stop. Before meeting me he'd never shared a bed with anyone in the whole of his life. I was his first bed-mate, his first sex partner, his first lover, his first love. Unlike me he'd never been to boarding school. Had never had a brother.

Eventually we got up. I cooked us a bacon omelette for lunch, and we ate it with new bread and butter. I gave Alastair a prudently small glass of beer with it. I only had a slightly larger one myself. We ate and drank in

The Raven and the Jackdaw

dressing-gowns, looking at and occasionally touching each other. Then we went back upstairs and got into bed again. I set the alarm-clock for four o'clock, to be on the safe side. But the alarm-clock was unnecessary; we didn't go to sleep.

The drive back to my parents' was alarming. I'd never driven on a motorway before. I'd never driven eighty miles all on my own before. In a Mini you were looking out, eye level with the hub-caps of lorries that passed you doing seventy, or at the hub-caps of lorries doing fifty which you passed. But it was a universal rite of passage, like falling in love. You got through it. I arrived safely, and wondered what I'd been worried about.

Jason had finished at Cambridge back in the summer. He was now studying medicine proper at Guy's Hospital near London Bridge. He shared a two-bedroom flat – he and Anna had one bedroom, another young couple, both fellow medics, had the other – at Stockwell, just a few stops away on the Northern Line. During that Christmas vacation I went up there and stayed a couple of nights. And Anna came down to our place. Mum no longer fretted about her and my brother sharing a room now that Anna had a ring on her finger, so I didn't have to share with Jason but kept to my old room. I was quite happy about that.

I missed Alastair. We were of necessity out of touch. He knew my parents' address, though, and I'd given him the phone number – just in case.

The phone rang towards the end of Christmas dinner, just as we were getting into the port and the nuts. 'I'll get that,' I said. I knew, I knew absolutely, who it was.

'I really miss you,' he said.

'Where are you?' I asked.

'Sitting on the stairs. The parents and grandparents are watching telly. I thought I'd give you a buzz.'

Give me a buzz? Where had he got that bit of slang from? But he was right. He was certainly giving me a buzz. 'I can't talk for long,' I said. 'It's just lovely to hear your voice. And I need to know that you're all right.'

'I am all right.'

'Then hang on and I'll be back with you. Just two more weeks. Think you can manage that?'

'I think I can. I'm better now I've talked to you.'

'You'd better hang up now, sweetheart,' I said.

He said, 'I love you,' quietly and quickly, and then hung up before I could say anything else. So he could hang on a couple more weeks, he'd said. Just then I wasn't sure whether I could. I gave myself a few seconds to compose myself before re-entering the dining-room.

'That was obviously for you,' said my mother, smiling. 'Who was it? Or shouldn't I ask?'

'Just a fan of mine,' I said airily.

'A fan?!!' My father sounded as affronted as if I'd used another word that began with F.

'Yes, I have fans these days,' I said sweetly. 'They come with the job.'

FOURTEEN

As I drove into the outskirts of Bristol a few days after the New Year I found myself slowing down every half minute. Every time I saw a group of kids I peered into their midst to see if Alastair was among their number. Each time I saw a youth sitting alone (and, I imagined sentimentally, disconsolate) on a wall I would look at him in the hope that it might be Alastair. I couldn't bring myself to drive straight back to Redland but meandered, moping, around the city's outskirts, all around Redland and up to Clifton. I drove across the high suspension bridge, turned at the roundabout a little way beyond it and, re-crossing the bridge, drove back into Clifton. There on a low wall sat one young lonely male person. I slowed. I stopped. Because it was Alastair.

I will never forget the light that came into his face. 'You'd better get in,' I said.

We nearly dislocated every joint in our two bodies as we renewed our contact – hugging and squirming in the front seats. I drove us to a high grassy headland overlooking the Bristol Channel that would have been tourist-swamped in summer but on a January early evening was unfrequented. We made love in the car, across the gear lever, not wasting time removing ourselves into the back seat and, for the first time, sucking each other's cocks. I had no hesitation in drinking down everything that Alastair had to offer. To my surprise – and it came as a great boost to my ego – Alastair, who had never done this before, reciprocated in every particular.

The car, my dark blue Mini, liberated us. We met every two or three days over the following weeks, laughed at the cold outside and were often grateful for the fog on the inside of the car's windows.

I would be doing our relationship a grave disservice if I allowed the reader to think that it was all about sex. We continued to talk about ourselves, to turn ourselves inside-out and to devour, each of us, what the other offered. I don't mean only in the physical sense. I learnt all about the changing cloudscape of Alastair's school friendships, and he learnt all about my friendships, my doubts about myself, my insecurities and my aspirations. Where I could I offered Alastair advice and words of help and comfort. I, who was only four years his senior. As for me, without expecting words of advice or wisdom from him, I told him everything about my essence and existence, except for the fact that my life was a total mess because I was infatuated with my brother. That was something I neither would nor could tell anyone. Until, of course, I came to write it in a book.

We filmed the first of the Square Metre programmes on February 14th. St. Valentine's Day. Traditionally the first day of spring, the day when the birds start mating and looking for places in which to nest. Everyone at the BBC seemed to think the date appropriate. Even the new breed of super-administrators who were known disrespectfully among us as the bean counters. I didn't discover till much later that there had been high-level discussions over whether there should be three similar-looking square metres in three separate gardens, in order to avoid the risk that went with putting all our eggs in the one basket. If inspection of one of the sites failed to discover anything interesting on a particular day, ran the pragmatic argument, we could simply move on to one of the others. It had been Will Lumsden who had strenuously argued against that. In the first place, he'd said, it was simply cheating the viewers. It would be better ... he liked to take things to extremes in order to make a point ... to show the viewers twenty minutes of

The Raven and the Jackdaw

grass being ruffled by the breeze, with nothing else happening, than to lie to them. In the second place (and I was deeply touched when I eventually heard this) he said that they had found in me a brilliant presenter. I would find something interesting to talk about even if I had to pick open a dog turd (apparently he actually said this!) and I could be relied upon to make an interesting programme however unpromising the situation might appear at first sight. Perhaps the impact of my presentation to his tutorial group on the dental apparatus of the snail family had reached further than I'd thought it would.

I didn't wear shorts in early February. I wore faded denim jeans which I'd ironed carefully the night before, though without putting creases in them, and a rather butch pair of lace-up boots that were loaned to me by the BBC's wardrobe department. I'd turned up in plimsolls and white socks, but they were deemed inappropriate for the season.

The square metre had been set up in the garden belonging to Will Lumsden's friend: the garden from which I'd made my first broadcast in the autumn. It was marked out by four galvanised metal rods that stuck out of the ground about eighteen inches, and by two wires that connected them, to give an indication of the four straight sides of the area. One wire ran round near the top, the other near the bottom. They would not impede the free movement in and out of the square metre of any creature much smaller than a sheep-dog.

Cannily the square had been set up at the edge of the pond, and one of its corner posts actually stood in the water. This would give an opportunity for aquatic plants and animals also to invade the area and to be exhibited to the viewers.

All of us, producer, technical crew and I, were nervous: we had low expectations about what we might expect to find so early in the season. A first quick inspection in the morning of that Valentine's Day seemed to confirm our worst fears: there was nothing to see, nothing to film, nothing for me to talk about. Our cameraman set his camera optimistically rolling, though, in a fairly long shot, like a fisherman lazily casting his line into empty water, and then, within seconds the most wonderful thing happened. A thrush dropped down into the centre of the square metre, picked from between the grass roots a snail we hadn't spotted and promptly started to smash its shell to bits on a stone by the edge of the water.

I started spouting extempore, excitedly, on the habit of thrushes of breaking snails in this way in order to gain access to the meat in their centres, and went on a little bit about how snails themselves usually spent the winter. I left the details of their dentition out of this for the time being: I might need that information to fill a gap with at some future date.

It was as if the thrush had turned a magic key and unlocked the square metre for us. Things happened at a rate from then on. The first yellow butterfly of the year, a brimstone, alighted at the edge of the pond, unfurled its long proboscis and took a sip of water. An earthworm crawled into the square along the surface, found a soft bare inch of soil and slowly burrowed down into it. A bank vole took staccato steps between the grass stems, its short tail shaking and long whiskers twitching, and had a good drink of water. Above, an ash key that should have fallen in the autumn lost its connection with its parent tree and came down spinning like a helicopter crashing...

Most of the work was done, and most of the skill was demonstrated, by our wonderful cameraman and by the director. All I had to do was to think on my feet, talk informatively about what I was seeing, and look

The Raven and the Jackdaw

attractive while I was doing it. We wound up some time before dusk fell. The cameraman had got more than a can-full. The director seemed crazily happy with the result of that first day's filming. He told me I'd been brilliant, and he bought me two drinks when we all went to a pub afterwards. The next day I had a tutorial with Lumsden. Before it even started, and in front of my fellow students, he turned to me and said, 'I got a phone-call from Malc last night,' (Malcolm was the Square Metre's producer) 'and he said you were bloody fantastic.'

The programme went out less than a fortnight later. By that time we'd shot the second in the series. On that occasion even more wonderful things had happened for us. A dabchick had put its tufted head between the wires to peck at something, and there had been a three second's visit – miraculously captured by the cameraman – from a kingfisher. After that first programme, though, the phone in the house I shared rang several times. My housemates didn't complain about this. They were all delighted for me. Byron phoned. So did my brother. And, on behalf of my father and herself, my mother. And of course, so did Alastair. I took his call rather publicly. Martin almost certainly guessed who it was but very kindly said nothing.

A week later Byron came down on a visit. He didn't stay with me, however, but with old friends from drama school. When it came to sex these days I was only interested in Alastair, and I think Byron sensed that there was someone new in my life. We spent time together, though, very amicably; had drinks and dinners together. Late on his last evening, when my tongue had been considerably wine-loosened, I opened up to him. 'I'm having a thing with one of my fans,' I told him indiscreetly.

'Male or female?' asked Byron.

'Male, obviously.'

'And why haven't you introduced us?'

'That's the difficult bit,' I said. 'It has to be kept a bit secret. His parents…'

Byron frowned. 'How old is he?'

'Fifteen,' I said.

'Bloody hell,' said Byron.

'That's only four years less than I am,' I protested. 'Only two years more age difference than between you and me.'

'That might not be how others would see it,' Byron cautioned.

'We're in love with each other,' I said, drawing myself up on my bar stool. 'There's no more to be said.'

'Not by you, perhaps,' said Byron. He reached out a hand and ran it affectionately down my upper arm. 'For God's sake, darling, be careful.'

That was the first time that anyone except for my mother had ever called me darling.

The following morning I spent some time with Byron. We walked by the quays and talked happily of other subjects than Alastair. A few people recognised me, I could tell, but they didn't try to talk to us. 'Hmm,' said Byron. 'Recognised in the street now, are you? That only happens to me in Glasgow.'

'Get away,' I told him, and gave him a mock punch, laughing. Later I walked with him to the station.

I went home around midday because I had some course work to do. I found the house was empty – except for a letter that lay on the hall carpet. It was postmarked Bristol and the envelope type-written like the letter inside it.

Dear Mr Whitcomb

Your disgraceful behaviour has been brought to my notice. It would appear that you are a sexual predator of

The Raven and the Jackdaw

the most despicable kind and that my son Alastair is the object of your interest.

My first reaction, on hearing about your sordid, wicked seduction of my son was to go at once to the police. However Alastair has begged me, in tears and more, not to do this. I have decided that, for the moment, I shall not do so. Principally because an inevitable result would be the intrusive questioning of my son, and I do not wish him to suffer more distress than he already has – at your hands.

But secondly, I am a teacher (as Alastair has told me your own father also is) and so am more conscious than most of the fragility of the psyche of the late adolescent. You are young and – perhaps, but only perhaps – deserve a second chance. You have, Alastair has told me, a promising career at the BBC ahead of you. Were I to involve the police at this stage, or at any future date, believe me, that opportunity would be lost in an instant.

I shall therefore do no more on this occasion than demand that you make no further attempt to contact my son. Bear in mind that he will remain under age until 1987, six years from now. Should you choose to ignore this demand of mine, whether that should involve even one single letter, phone-call, Christmas card or message at the school gates, I will contact the police at once and ask them to instigate criminal proceedings against you. I will also inform your employers at the BBC that you are a danger to impressionable children and request that they remove you from your post before I inform the press of your conduct.

Before reaching my decision I found myself wondering if you were also grooming other young boys in the same way that you did Alastair. Alastair assured me vehemently that this was not the case. I'm not sure that he would know. People of your kind are wily, expert at lying, and manipulative. But for the present I am prepared to give you the benefit of the doubt on this issue.

However, believe me when I say I shall be watching you closely. Any suspicions I may have reason to entertain at any point in the future concerning you will be reported at once to the police, with consequences to you which I have already spelled out.

I shall end by expressing the hope that you will change your ways before disaster overtakes you, and that at some future date you may be a credit both to your employers and to your own parents. That is something which you are not at the moment.

Keep away from my son.
Ian McNeil

I went hot and cold as I read even the first sentence of that. By the end I was in tears of distress and terror. I couldn't stop the noise that was coming out of my mouth. Thank God I was alone in the house. I ran upstairs and threw myself face-down on the bed, ramming my head into the pillow to muffle my noise, in case one of my housemates should come home or the neighbours hear and wonder what was happening. In fairness to myself I was crying and in terror not only for myself but also for Alastair. I thought of the desperate loneliness of his situation, tried to imagine what he was going through, and found that it was literally unimaginable. My imagination hit a brick wall every time I tried to do it.

Two hours passed before I was sufficiently in control of myself to move around the house, wash my face, and look at myself in the mirror without crying hysterically. My mind was a maelstrom. I had no idea what I was going to do. There was no-one in Bristol I could talk to. Not Martin or any other of my housemates. Certainly not Will Lumsden, who had warned me sternly not to get

The Raven and the Jackdaw

involved sexually with fans, and whose advice I had ignored wilfully. I thought perhaps I should rush to the station, follow Byron up to Glasgow, throw myself into his arms and beg his understanding. But something told me I couldn't even do that. He too had warned me just hours earlier about the fire that I'd been playing with.

It was mid-afternoon by now. Suddenly, after what seemed an age of not knowing what to do or where to go, something clicked in my brain and I knew exactly what I would do, and knew I would do it immediately. I packed overnight things, left the house, got into my car and drove out of Bristol. The demands of driving safely forced me to concentrate so hard that I actually became calmer. I drove the hundred miles along the M4 to Hammersmith and then burrowed my way into central London. I could only guess which would be the best way to go. I followed the main route to Victoria and then to Vauxhall. At last signs began to appear that arrowed Stockwell. Once I got to the tube station there I knew where I was going. I'd been there at Christmas, travelling by train and underground, and so now recognised the surrounding streets. By driving around a bit I managed to find an area of unmetered parking, with a space amongst the other cars that was big enough to take a Mini. I jammed my Mini into it.

'Good God,' said Jason, when he opened the door and saw me standing there. 'What brings you here? Not that it isn't good to see you, of course.' Then he peered into my face. 'You're not all right, mate. Are you in trouble?'

'Yes,' I said. The simplicity of his question combined with the truthfulness of my answer combined to bring me to tears again.

'Look, come in,' Jason said. The other couple, Garth and Susie, were cooking in the kitchen. I could hear their voices wafting out. After a moment's indecision Jason said, 'Let's go up to the bedroom. Private for a moment.'

The bedroom Jason shared with Anna, which I'd only glanced into through a half-open door on my previous visit, had a feminine smell about it. In any bedroom shared by a man and a woman the smell of the woman's cosmetics always predominate. This bedroom smelt like our parents' bedroom, though a generation more up to date. We sat down side by side on the bed. 'Where's Anna?' I asked, as though she should by rights have been there behind us in the bed.

'She's away tonight. At her parents'. Now tell me what this is all about.' Jason clapped his hand on my thigh, but in a manly, no-nonsense way, removing it smartly after about a second.

'Remember that phone-call from a fan I had at Christmas?' I said.

'Yes,' said Jason.

Without saying more I took the letter from the inside pocket of my denim jacket and passed it to him. He took it out of the envelope, unfolded it and read it. It seemed to take him ages. Willing myself not to read it again over his shoulder I tried to imagine, second by second, how far he'd got. At last he finished it, refolded it and handed it back. 'Phew,' he said. Then, 'I think what you and I both need is a drink.' He stood up and patted my shoulder. 'Come on, let's go out.'

He could have said, 'You bloody fool,' or, 'You total fucking idiot,' but he had not. He could have said, 'Get away from me, you pervert,' but he did not. I loved him for that.

We sat together at an out of the way table in the Brewery Tap. 'Do you think I should reply to it?' I asked.

'No,' he said, with calm decisiveness. 'No, you should not. The chap's set it all out very clearly. He's told you

The Raven and the Jackdaw

what not to do, and said what he won't do if you abide by that. From reading him I'd guess he'll keep his word. Was it Henry Truman who said, "Never explain, never regret, never apologise."? Whoever said it, it's a very good principle for this case. Just make sure you never go near the kid again and you'll be all right.'

'He needs me,' I said. 'He's hurting dreadfully. He needs me to comfort him…'

Jason actually touched my hand with his across the table. 'You can't do him any good. You could only stir things up and make it worse for him. I understand that he's hurting. Of course he is…'

'I love him,' I said wretchedly.

'Of course you do,' said Jason. He said it with what I can only describe as tenderness. 'But unless you plan to go the whole hog and elope with him to Mexico you can't do anything about that. Do you plan to elope to Mexico?'

'Nope,' I said.

Jason half-smiled at me. I half-smiled back.

'It's typical of you – and very good in you – to think about the boy hurting,' Jason said. 'But someone else around here is hurting. Someone who I care about. That's whose hurt I need to deal with. Come on, let's move from here. I think we should get you something to eat.'

We went Indian, as one did in Stockwell. We talked and talked. Not all the time about deep and serious things, yet I felt as though I was emptying a store-room that for years had been needing a clear-out. We were both a little tipsy by the time we got back to the flat. Garth and Susie were sitting on the sofa watching TV. They were also cuddling, but sprang apart when we walked in on them.

'Here's Barnaby,' said Jason. 'Sorry we scooted off a bit rudely when he first arrived. But there was family stuff we needed to talk about.'

'Does he – sorry, Barnaby, do you – need a bed for the night?' Susie said this, looking around the living-room. When I'd come here at Christmas she'd turned the sofa into a put-u-up.

'He can bunk up with me,' I heard Jason say. I could hardly believe he'd said it. I was flabbergasted – no other word will do. I was almost in shock. 'I don't think Anna's going to mind, for one night,' Jason said smoothly. Then he looked at me. 'Or two, if you need it.'

'I think one'll probably do it,' I said. 'I'll need to get back.' I gave him a pretend supercilious look. 'Filming the day after tomorrow.'

'Typical bloody movie stars,' Jason said.

I was in Jason's bed again. It was nearly two years since those two nights when we'd slept together at Cambridge. And only a few weeks had passed after that before he'd met Anna and we'd stopped having sex altogether.

In the darkness beneath the duvet Jason grasped and explored my erect cock. 'It's grown, kid,' he said.

'With a little help from others,' I said. 'But mostly I've had to work on it myself.'

'Sorry about that,' said Jason and sniggered.

I said, 'What do think of my legs?'

He gave them a careful feel, like the doctor he would soon be, carrying out a lower limb examination. 'They're coming on nicely,' he said. 'I noticed them when you were on TV in the autumn.'

'So did half the population of Great Britain,' I said. I couldn't help boasting about that. 'It's walking up the hills of Bristol that's done it,' I said.

The Raven and the Jackdaw

'Perhaps I'd better come there myself,' my brother said, and chuckled.

Jason's physique had always been far better than mine and it still was. 'Nothing wrong with your legs,' I said. 'But come to Bristol anyway if you want.' I giggled. I held his cock and reacquainted myself with its contours. It too had grown somewhat since I'd last held it. I said, 'And there's nothing whatever wrong with this.'

That night I got fucked by it. Fucked for the first time in two years by Jason. For the first time by anybody at all in five months (Byron had been the last). And in the small hours I returned my brother's compliment.

As I drove back down the motorway I tried to make sense of the way life worked. My heart and cock had got me into trouble. The result of that – in the form of Alastair's father's letter – had caused everything to fall apart inside me. Yet it was the workings of my heart and cock, combined with the workings of Jason's that had, up to a point, repaired me. I felt strong enough to deal with life because I'd slept with, and had sex with, my brother last night. I didn't know if any of the ancient philosophers had identified such a paradigm in their writings. I didn't know if anyone else in the world had had a comparable experience.

It was all very well, though, my feeling better as I drove back towards Bristol. My brother's healing of me, temporary though it might prove, could have no impact at all on Alastair and his state of feeling. There was nothing I could do for Alastair. Jason had reiterated that strongly this morning over breakfast. He had made me promise *him* not to try and contact Alastair again and I had solemnly made him that promise. I knew he was right. That if I tried to get in touch with Alastair it would cause the boy more pain in the long run. The thought of not being able to make that contact was almost unbearable. But bear it I would have to. There was no alternative, and the same went for Alastair. I wished then that I could take Alastair's suffering upon my own shoulders and so spare him. But that was impossible. That only happened in religion and in myth.

My night with my brother had been wonderful. Like the lighting of a warm fire in a cold dark room. But I couldn't take the fire with me back to Bristol. I couldn't take my brother away from Anna. Eventually the room would grow cold again and I would again be alone in it. I had no alternative but to get back to my interrupted work on the university essay I was supposed to be writing and to prepare for tomorrow's filming. Life went on: I had to go on with it.

FIFTEEN

When I came to write my 'novella' a couple of years later I found that in the first several chapters I had made David, the Jackdaw, a somewhat sexless character. He came over as quite sensitive but also austere, obsessed by his love for his brother, but sublimating his desire through his work. He had told his brother (on the night of "that" Christmas) that he had once had sex with a woman (something that I had not myself experienced) but that it hadn't done it for him. He'd said on the same occasion that he wondered sometimes if he ought to try having sex with men, but didn't think that would work either when it came to getting his feelings for his brother out of his head. Again, that was a bit different from my case. I'd had a certain amount of sexual experience with men or boys other than Jason, even if my experience in bed with my brother outweighed and outclassed the rest of it. But I had this in common with my fictional alter ego: the other experiences had generally failed to drive the ones I'd shared with my brother out of my head and heart.

At any rate, I thought it was time I gave David a chance. Against the background scenery of a theatre in Manchester, where David had gone to play the part of Romeo, I wrote the only sex scene in the short book. I drew upon my experiences with Byron and Alastair, as well as on my feelings for my brother. The passage is quite a long one, so I have devoted the rest of this chapter to it. It boiled down to a simple equation in the end, though. *Love = Loss.*

****

David was a newcomer once again, adrift in a strange town and nervous this time not because he was a chorus boy but because he wasn't. This would become a routine: Sunday evening: find the digs, find something to eat, try the local pub. Monday morning: meet the new faces, wonder if he'd be up to the job – console himself with the hope that perhaps some of his youthful fellow actors were secretly wondering the same thing.

'I haven't fenced since drama school,' he confessed.
'Neither have I,' said Tybalt with a rueful smile.
'Nor me,' said Mercutio.
'I'm glad we've all got that off our chests at least,' said the fight arranger, handing out rapiers as though they were pencils in a drawing class. 'Very slowly to begin with. One, two three and lunge...'

'You're going to be a bit good,' said a voice at coffee break. David turned round. It was Mercutio. The actor's name was Howard, a handsome black-haired young man, older than David by a year or so, and taller by an inch.

'Thank you.' David was pleased, and surprised. Although he tried to tell himself the compliment was no more than his due, the fact that it should have been offered at such an early stage was flattering. He felt relaxed enough to say to Howard, 'You're pretty good yourself,' and was rewarded by a bright-eyed smile in return: a smile that showed off a pretty array of pearly teeth.

David did not usually think the word pretty in connection with men. Perhaps it would have been truer to say that he tried not to. Yet Mercutio's – Howard's – teeth were quite something, David had to admit. And those eyes of his too.

The break ended. The rehearsal continued, with David counting, 'One, two, three, lunge,' under his breath, and showing his teeth a bit competitively when called upon to smile at Juliet.

The Raven and the Jackdaw

'What a lovely actor you are to work with,' said Sian, who was Juliet, at lunchtime. 'Your smile is something other. We're going to have a great time. You're so giving.'

She was very attractive herself, David thought, registering simultaneously the twin novelties of being complimented so boldly, and his own new sensitivity to the attractiveness of others. Did it have something to do with the role he was playing? He had found Mercutio's smile attractive as well as enviable, if he were honest. And Sian, well, she had the loveliest deep-set hazel eyes above her high cheek-bones. As for himself, he had never thought that he was especially good-looking. Average height, average build, average facial features. And, as far as his limited knowledge went, an average-sized cock as well. He'd never made a point of looking at other men's, though he saw them from time to time – in showers or at urinals; in theatre dressing rooms. He'd rarely seen another man's full erection.

But when he was on stage everything became different. If his character was handsome, then so was he, and he could make the whole audience, and himself, believe it. The same held true if he were playing someone ugly of course, but this month, while he was Romeo, that thought could be laid aside. Things were starting well, he thought. He'd managed to charm – and had decided to like – two new people in one morning. As he donned the mantle of Romeo it was as though life was changing up a gear. A sepia-tinted phase of it was giving way to a Technicolor one.

*

Other people were nervous on first nights. Not David. He could be terrified on the first day of rehearsal, shy with new fellow actors, but soon his performance would take on a momentum of its own. The presence of an audience might change it a little, would usually improve it, but it would not disturb him or make him anxious. Audiences didn't suddenly materialise on first nights anyway. The first dress-run would find the wardrobe mistress sitting in, the second would furnish design staff and carpenters too. The technical rehearsal would leave David in a private world, able to polish what he had not had time to do before: a little gesture tweaked, a new way to give meaning to a phrase... Nobody would be paying attention to him. Everyone would be busy with lighting, cueing, snagging, focused intently on props and buttons, leaving him to pursue his own inner goal: the perfect performance of his given role. Eventually...

'Half an hour please.'

'Oh God, I'm right out of powder. Anybody got some?'

'Got any carmine?'

'What play are you in, darling?'

'Quarter of an hour please.'

'I'm shit-scared. Look at David there. Cool as a whatsit.'

'Anybody else get a card from Viv?'

'Beginners please...' David and Uncle Tom Cobley and all to the stage please.

It went like a dream. All that had been good in the three weeks of rehearsals came together in that evening's two hours' traffic. David came off after his final curtain call feeling ten feet tall. The supporters' club had drinks laid on afterwards. David and Sian were feted, toasted, separately and together. A magical new stage partnership had been born, people said.

'Party back at Simon's,' word went round. 'Get away when you can.'

'I don't have a bottle,' David said.

'Come anyway.' David went. An hour or two later Sian was sitting on his knee and making him recount his life story. There was much to be said for playing Romeo, he thought, aware of his own excitement.

The Raven and the Jackdaw

'I'll get you some more wine,' Sian said disappointingly, and got up. There was a knock at the door, welcoming voices. *'Tom, we didn't know you were back. How did it go?'*

Sian introduced Tom to David. He could hear in her voice the pleasant uncertainty of one spoilt for choice. Then she took Tom away to the kitchen to get him a drink. David remained in his armchair.

'Some you win, some you lose,' said someone who came and perched on one of the arms. It was Howard, Mercutio.

'Your Queen Mab speech was magic,' David said. He really meant it, but the words came out without enthusiasm.

'Aren't you the kind one? Do you know what you were?'

'What?'

'Fucking ruddy brilliant from beginning to end.'

'You're pissed,' said David a bit more kindly.

'So are you.'

'I am?'

'I think so,' said Howard. *'I can tell by that smile of yours. I didn't notice it when I first met you, but it's grown day by day. Now it's bigger than you are. Must be the wine smiling, I thought. Seems to have worked a treat with Sian anyway.'*

'I don't know about that.'

'Why not?'

'I'm not sure,' David began, uncertain what he was going to say, uncertain whether it would make any sense, but vaguely sensing that it wouldn't much matter, *'what this smile is doing for me. Or what I'm supposed to be doing with it.'*

'With Sian, you mean?'

'Anyone. Anything.'

'Probably the wrong thing,' Howard suggested, *nodding his head at his own shrewdness. 'Most people do.'*

'Probably,' said David, without knowing what he was agreeing with.

'Perhaps you should be looking in a different direction.'

This woke David up somewhat. 'If you mean what I think you do, the answer is no.'

'What do you think I mean?' asked Howard teasingly.

David only laughed in reply so Howard tried, 'Your glass. You haven't got one.'

'Sian took it out to the kitchen. I think.'

'To fill it up and give it to that Tom fellow. How diabolical. Perfidious. I'll get you a new one.'

'I've had more than enough already,' said David, but Howard had already set off towards the kitchen. David watched him go. He certainly was a good-looking man, as well as a good actor. David had admired his panache and his smile and had made a point, as Romeo, of copying them. Now Howard had paid David the compliment of admiring the reflection.

'David, you should be circulating,' someone said.

'I daren't,' he answered. 'I'm afraid the room might, too.'

Howard returned with two glasses of something. It no longer mattered what. There was a new warmth in his eyes that David found appealing. He wanted to say, 'You remind me of someone,' but he couldn't remember who, so he left it. Big Norma passed by. Big Norma who had played earth-motherly roles up and down the country for years (she was the Nurse in this production) said, 'I didn't know about you two.' For Howard had somehow half slipped off the arm of David's chair and looked to be nearly in David's lap.

The Raven and the Jackdaw

'Just good friends,' said Howard lightly and rested his spinning head on David's shoulder.

'Exactly so,' said David, and completed the tableau by leaning his own head against Howard's.

'Well, well, well,' said Norma, and gave them an old-fashioned look as she walked away.

'She'll have forgotten by the morning,' said Howard from somewhere near David's right ear.

*

'I'm rat-arsed,' Howard volunteered as they spilled out into the street.

'I'll walk you home,' said David. He didn't think he'd been quite so drunk in his life. But Norma's throwaway remark had somehow crystallised the evening for them, and had set it on a tentative course that was previously not even remotely possible, at least for David. They had refilled their glasses twice more afterwards. Now the night air laid about them like a boxer. 'Where are your digs?'

'Furnace Road,' said Howard.

'Jesus, that's miles away. Never mind, we'll get you there somehow.' They staggered arm in arm towards a railway viaduct. A late express thundered across it, a dazzling necklace of light, blinding and out of focus as a vision. 'Look at that,' said David.

'Brilliant,' said Howard, as if David had conjured the effect for his own special benefit. The train disappeared like a firework hissing into the blackness and left them in star-less silence, together, alone.

'Look,' said David, *'It's another mile to Furnace Road, and I live just up here on the left.'* What had he just said? His mind dredged up the fact that there was only one bed at his disposal. There was the floor, of course... They'd sort it all out when they got there.

David was on a level of consciousness that was new to him. He unlocked the front door of the darkened house *and propelled his companion upstairs. In his room he put on the light. Howard immediately dived onto the bed as people in his state do, but he dived rather tidily to one side, leaving a space next to him, and into that space David, with only the briefest pause for thought, slid his own body. 'Come on,' he said, playing the put upon host, 'let's get you ready for bed.' And he began to unbutton Howard's shirt for him.*

'Hey David,' murmured Howard, 'have you come home tonight?'

'Maybe,' said David.

'Maybe for the first time,' said Howard, though mainly to himself.

Howard looked even better naked than he did when clothed. He was a half-size bigger than David in every respect: height, muscle development – and cock. Though David was pleased to notice that the discrepancy of size in this department was not so great as to be threatening. They were both fully hard by now. Both circumcised. And David noticed Howard's cock was wet. But, checking with a finger, he discovered that the same went for his own.

'You can fuck me if you want to, baby.'

David's astonishment at hearing himself addressed as baby by a handsome naked man not two years older than himself only increased his excitement at the novelty of it all. Though he'd never had sex with a man, he wasn't ignorant of the options that this kind of sex could involve. He'd spent three years at drama school after all and was now a member of a profession some half of whose male practitioners were gay. He was too choked up to answer Howard in words. He gulped and nodded his head. And even if he'd still had any doubts about what his next move should be, Howard's own next move would have made all plain. He rolled onto his back,

The Raven and the Jackdaw

drew up and spread his knees, and with an encouraging smile helped David to roll round on top.

David thought it might be difficult to work his way in but it wasn't. Howard was relaxed by drinking – and pretty well practised too, it has to be said. Within moments David was thrusting deep into his insides and not long after that he came exuberantly. It felt as though a series of waves were breaking over him as he lay face down on the shore of a friendly sea.

He had tried to massage Howard's cock. It was staring him in the face after all. But Howard took his hand away. 'Better idea,' he said. 'Later.'

It wasn't much later. After a short interlude of stroking and kissing, Howard rolled a newly compliant David onto his back and made love to him in a perfect role-reversed action replay of what had gone before. With what remained of his reasoning capability David had thought that this would hurt. And yet, despite the hefty size of Howard's hard-on, both in its length and thickness, David's discomfort was minor and short-lived. He guessed that he was as physically relaxed as Howard had been – thanks in part to the quantity he had drunk. Another thought flashed through his mind: it was as though he'd been born for this moment, as though he'd been looking forward to it all his life. And when, some minutes later, David felt Howard swell and climax deep inside him, he found the hair-trigger of his own cock's workings released again and, with only minimal prompting from Howard's friendly hand, his belly milkily a-flood.

*

But morning changes everything. Especially when you were drunk the night before. Howard left at first light. David stayed, nursing a headache and more. He had woken to find himself a different person from the one who had woken yesterday. Romeo, he thought bitterly.

He was appalled by what he had done. He even smelt different. He got up and had a hot bath. It made no difference. He'd let himself be conned, he thought. The way forward made him feel sick. There was no way back.

All day he planned, scripted and mentally stage-managed his next conversation with Howard. It ought to be in broad daylight, in a public place, the street, a pub. There should be lots of people about, there should be noise. They would see each other, shout 'Hi' and laugh, then go their separate ways, their laughter an unambiguous symbol that last night had been a random, not to be repeated event: a drunken aberration. They would be able to show that they were still friends, that their friendship was all the better for their one shared moment of eccentric behaviour. One day far in the future they might be able to bring it up in conversation over a drink and say philosophically, 'Remember that night? What was all that about, then?' All this David and Howard would convey in their laughing greeting when they met next in the sunshine, in the busy world.

That their next meeting could not be like that should have been obvious. They had to meet that evening at work instead. They did not share a dressing-room and, though David hoped right up to the last minute they might run into each other in the corridor before curtain-up, they eventually met for the first time on stage, in full Elizabethan costume and make up, with rapiers and daggers complete. They wore handsome matching smiles but there was lead in David's eyes and heart.

After the show David got changed. He stopped being an actor, hung his Romeo and his triumph on a hook and wiped his role from his face with removing cream. In jeans and trainers he joined the queue in the fish and chip shop like any other young man, indistinguishable from the rest. You might have driven past him on your way home from the theatre, still talking about his

The Raven and the Jackdaw

splendid performance, seen him queuing there and, never noticing, driven on.

David walked home, eating as he went, and bumped into Howard, quite literally, as he was rounding a corner. 'Sorry,' he said first, then seeing who it was, 'Hallo,' flatly. He thought, fate.

'I thought it might be you,' said Howard with as little enthusiasm.

They stood together in a shop doorway, sharing David's chips. 'I don't know what to say,' said David.

'Doesn't matter,' Howard said.

'I meant about last night. I behaved a bit out of character. I don't usually do ... you know ... the things we did.'

'You don't usually give in to spontaneous natural desires, you mean?'

'I don't mean that. Fuck you, Howard. What I meant to say was, I shouldn't have behaved the way I did. If I gave you misleading signals, then I'm really, really sorry. Please accept that.'

'Misleading signals? A hearty fuck, jubilantly given, and another one just as enthusiastically received... If those were just signals I'd like to know what constitutes a declaration of ... of whatever.'

'You twist my words,' David objected. 'I'm not gay.'

'OK. No problem. You're not gay. You slept with a man last night. Live with that. You'll be in good company. All over the world a million men are doing just that – living with that apparent contradiction, and that's just since last night.' David smiled in spite of himself. 'Well, I can live with that too,' Howard went on. 'And I still think you're gorgeous.'

David hadn't known Howard thought that. He hadn't mentioned it before. It made David feel slightly better. 'Those chips weren't enough,' he said. 'Guess we'd better go back and get some more.'

Outside the chip shop, a fresh bundle of supper in their hands, David said, 'May as well go back to my place to eat them, I suppose. Since it's just round the corner. What were you doing round here anyway?'

'Coming to call on you.'

'Why?'

'Not sure. To try to put things right between us, I suppose. That is, if I could. Maybe just to talk, to say hallo. Oh, here's a wine shop. I'll call in and get a bottle to keep us company.'

'In case we run out of things to say?' David meant to sound sardonic but it didn't quite work.

They didn't run out of things to say. They talked until the small hours and until the bottle of wine was a distant memory. David said, with what he wanted to be a weary sigh, 'I suppose you may as well stay over if you want to. We don't have any surprises for each other any more.' Standing face to face beside the bed they began to undress each other, and neither was in the least surprised to find the other displaying a full and frank erection when at last their most intimate reaches were revealed..

This night they made love to each other more gently, more tenderly, yet somehow more intensely as they each fucked each other – just as on the previous night – and then got fucked, turn by turn.

They stayed in bed till nearly noon, then spent most of the next day together. In the evening when they met on stage again their eyes shone bright and clear once more, and it was those of Juliet that Romeo's gaze could not meet.

*

In the days and weeks that followed, the theatre company came first to realise and then to accept that they had become a couple. Even Sian knew a fait accompli when she saw one. And little by little David

The Raven and the Jackdaw

began to understand that he was falling in love. He knew Howard deeply now: physically, through their bedtime sexual explorations, and personally, emotionally, through their conversations, through just being together. And everything that David knew about Howard was now wonderful. He would have died for him. And yet he would have to part from Howard – he had no illusions about this – when the run of Romeo was ended. Howard had a boyfriend in London, and Howard would go back to him. He always did.

*

David walked into the theatre bar. The last performance of Romeo and Juliet was finished. The room was full of hold-alls, flight bags and backpacks. Howard's was among them, David's not. He alone had had his contract renewed. He had been rehearsing with the new company – rehearsing for a musical – all his daytimes for the last month. David didn't care particularly for musicals. But musicals were going to be the thing, people told him. How lucky he was, they said. Being in a premiere. There was the chance of a London transfer...

Howard had bagged a couple of well-paid commercials, with a little help from his agent, and would soon be smiling encouragement at the consumer from a corner of the consumer's own living room. Right now he was sitting across the bar room from David, his luggage between his knees. David called across. 'Pint of best?' He'd reached the front of the bar queue.

'Small whisky only. Lots of M6 to cope with.'

David went and sat with him. 'I don't want you to go. I shall miss you.'

There were people all around them. David didn't care whether they heard or not. It was a common enough Saturday night scene.

'Miss you,' said Howard. He touched the back of David's hand for a moment.

'I think I've been in love with you,' said David, understating his case somewhat.

'I think I can say the same.' Howard's voice was soft, almost breaking. *'But what is love without loss? Nobody wins with love. If you are born to love you are born to lose.'*

David looked at Howard's glass of whisky. *'Sure you're OK to drive?'*

'To love is to lose. Love is loss. That's all.'

David finished his drink and got up. *'Have a safe journey,'* he said, then smiled wryly. *'I must love you and lose you now. See you again some day. Actors' paths always cross and re-cross. Hope so anyway.'*

Howard stood up and they embraced and kissed for quite some time. None of the people around them batted an eyelid. Then David rumpled Howard's hair, turned and left the room.

The Raven and the Jackdaw

SIXTEEN

Jason phoned me during the evening. Checking that I'd had a safe drive back from Stockwell to Bristol. Checking that I was all right. It meant a lot. It meant a lot to me because that simple gesture showed me that I meant a lot to him. That despite the distance that the years and the miles and his engagement to Anna had placed between us I was still important to him and always had been. This knowledge abated my misery more than a bit.

But Jason's concern for me – his love if I may put it like that – could have no impact on Alastair's suffering and I felt wretched about that. Alastair had mentioned some of his schoolfellows to me by name, and I hoped that one or more of them might be close enough for him to confide in. But I couldn't know that. I wished that I could be the one he could confide in, but there was no realistic hope of that. I could of course defy McNeil senior and boldly pick Alastair up in my car at the school gates one evening after class. I'd have the chance to have a chat with him, at least, and ask him if he was all right, but if that was any kind of victory at all it would be very short-lived. I couldn't kidnap the boy – at least, I wouldn't – and so his father's threats would very quickly be carried out. I would lose my job at the BBC. With it would go all hope of working there in the future. And, although I was too young to be able to have sex legally with other males, of any age, I was not too young to have to answer for myself in an adult court and to be named in newspapers. I might well go to prison. Even if the authorities were more lenient than that, the damage would be done. And none of the above would be of the remotest help to Alastair. Reluctantly I had to accept that Alastair now had to deal with the fallout all by himself.

That our relationship, our love, had become, in one brute moment, a thing of the past.

In bed that night I had to make an effort not to whimper. I wished Jason could be lying next to me, enfolding me in his strong arms. Tonight he couldn't be, and for the foreseeable future could not. He slept with Anna tonight, and probably would do for the remainder of his life. I knew, though, that I had his love. I would have to be content with that.

The Square Metre grew into bit of a success. After each of the next few episodes were aired Jason phoned me on the pretext of saying how much he'd enjoyed the programme. We both knew, though, that he was checking up on my well-being and state of mind. He'd be listening very carefully to the way I spoke, the things I said, my tone of voice, interpreting those faint signals, forming a picture of my mental state for himself. A couple of times I saved him some of the trouble. I said, 'I'm doing OK, by the way. I really am all right.' If any of my housemates were listening they wouldn't know what I was referring to, but Jason would, and did.

Doing The Square Metre helped to keep me sane during that dark time. As the weeks passed it grew easier and easier to find things in the little plot that I could talk about. A golden king-cup flower, then ladybirds, cockchafers, zooming bumblebees and roosting moths. Mice of various species, birds often, a weasel once. As spring moved towards summer I took to presenting the programmes once again in shorts. My twentieth birthday came and went...

I couldn't help wondering if Alastair was allowed to watch my programmes. If I was a weekly presence in his living-room, to his parents' annoyance – or did he have his own TV in his bedroom? During the first few days after the shipwreck of our relationship I'd driven around

The Raven and the Jackdaw

the roads of Clifton, and near his school – feverishly and unwisely – in the hope of catching a glimpse of him, perhaps sitting alone on a low wall as I had once found him near the bridge. But I never did see him and after a few days of this deranged behaviour I stopped doing it.

I saw my brother at Easter, during the short vac. When we were together we were very friendly and harmonious. But there was no question of our sleeping together or having any kind of sex. We mentioned Alastair only briefly, and only once or twice. A little more often than that Jason would ask me again, 'Are you sure you're all right?' I assured him that I was. Though I did add once as an afterthought that I wasn't getting any sex. He shrugged and smiled sympathetically but said, 'These days there's not much I can do about that.' This exchange took place in our parents' garden. Anna and my mother were inside the kitchen and could see us if they looked. I could see what he meant.

I began to notice after the summer term had started and I was back at Bristol full time that an odd thing had happened. I had "come out" to friends and fellow students during the time I was with Byron, but somehow, since I'd become a TV presenter and was no longer just a student, it was as though that fact had been put back in its box. It was the same (perhaps) as if I'd had a limb amputated. There was a suddenly erected little barrier between my sexuality and other people's. Only the bravest among them, I thought, would try to overcome it.

There was no question of my having anonymous sex in places like public toilets either, even if I had wanted to do that. Byron, to whom I owed most of my knowledge about gay lifestyles, had told me that many of the people who went in for that particular pastime were married men who would travel some distance to visit a "cottage" in an area where they would be unlikely to be recognised. A different part of the city, or another town altogether. Well, that wasn't possible for me. In order to be really sure I wouldn't be recognised I would have had to go somewhere like the Republic of Ireland or France. Those were the two nearest places... Obviously I wasn't going to do that.

I had lunch a few times with Will Lumsden and his partner Jeffrey. They were always pleasant, convivial occasions and I looked forward to them – a little more each time, perhaps. They must have noticed that I was *very single*. I know that phrase is both logically and grammatically incorrect, but it serves to make the point. I was without girlfriend or boyfriend, or any particularly close friend of either sex. A good-looking boy with a career as a TV presenter ahead of him rattling around Bristol like a single pea in a drum. Presumably it was because of this that Will and Jeffrey invited me to go on holiday to France with them at the end of the summer, after the final programme in The Square Metre series had been shot.

We went to the town of Vannes on the south coast of Brittany. Actually the town lay at the upper end of an inlet from the Golfe de Morbihan, which was itself a huge inlet. Several miles across, but with a narrow exit to the sea, it was a vast lagoon of the kind in which Venice sits, with a dozen or more small islands in it. It was difficult to compute the number of islands. Some were so low in the water that they were islands only at the bottom of the tide, others were so small that they answered better to the description of rocks. Their presence, sometimes just below the water's surface, made navigation an exciting challenge. We depended heavily on our accurate reading of the charts.

It was a sailing holiday, you will by now have realised. We didn't sail all the way from the Bristol Channel, round Land's End and Cape Finisterre. That would have

The Raven and the Jackdaw

taken a fortnight. We took the car ferry from Plymouth to St-Malo and drove (Will drove – it was his car) across Brittany from north to south. When we got to Vannes we put up at a hotel that Jeffrey and Will had booked, and for the daytimes hired a boat.

I'd never sailed before. I soon learnt. I wasn't sure I would enjoy it. People had told me cautionary tales about their own experiences: sitting miserably on a plank in the freezing cold with a wet arse. But I didn't have to worry. That didn't happen to me. I took to the business of sailing like a duck to … well, you know what. I learnt to steer; I learnt to navigate with compass and marine charts; I learnt to set and trim the sails; I learnt to tie a few new knots they hadn't taught me in the Scouts.

The weather on the north coast of Brittany had been a little autumnal and damp. The south coast of Brittany was a different pair of sleeves, as they say in France. The skies were still summer blue, and the sun was summer hot. Out in the Gulf, among the islands, learning to sail, I felt myself in heaven. As you threaded your way among the islets they changed in perspective and shape from minute to minute as magically as the view inside a child's kaleidoscope. Bright green, bright blue, bright white… Some of the islands had houses on them, others ancient megaliths. Others were uninhabited except by colonies of seabirds – which Will and I peered at through binoculars and competed to name correctly if we could.

Past remote Locmariaquer, famous for its oysters, we headed west to the town of Auray, snug in its estuary and tucked away within the Gulf. On three days we braved the open Atlantic, nosing our way out of the sheltered Gulf into the Bay of Biscay, visiting La Trinité and, at the end of its long isthmus, remote Quibéron. One day we headed due south across the open sea to the Isle of Houat. The name made English speakers smile, including French people who spoke our language. 'You went to What?!' I might have been alarmed at undertaking such a major voyage (we had to get up early in order to be back before dark) in such a small boat. But the breeze was light and the swell was gentle, the air pearly with September light. It might not have been an exciting sail for an experienced sailor but I was new to it all and I found it quite exhilarating enough. I loved the vivid closeness of the sea and the birds that flew across it, low enough to brush their wingtips against the tops of the waves and to be eye to eye with us. I loved the way the distant land horizon would disappear for a moment, every half minute, behind the nearer, lumpier horizon of the sea, then float back up. None of this could be experienced from the deck of a big ferry, which had been my only experience of crossing the open sea to date. Almost best of all was the vast smell of it. Close up it smelt like an enormous tray of opened oysters. And when we ate oysters at some mid-day port of call, or at dinner in the evening, those brought back the sense of being at sea, close to the water in a small boat, so strongly that I began to see the one as the microcosm of the other, the ocean as one apparently limitless oyster, the oyster the concentration of the substance of the whole sea itself.

The town of Vannes was gorgeous, its centre a warren of half-timbered houses that dated back hundreds of years. A major hub of trade and politics in the Middle Ages it was now a sleepy backwater, dozing in the sun like an elderly princess, and frequented by discerning tourists (like ourselves) and sailing types (ditto) and fisher-folk.

Our hotel had a pleasant surprise in store for me. His name was Jean-Christophe. He waited at our table on our first night and I could see him studying me with interest (we were the same age and, I guessed shrewdly, shared the same sexual orientation) and trying to work out what my relationship with Will and Jeffrey was.

He was a very attractive boy, I thought. He had very straight hair, thick-growing and shiny black, which he parted on the left. He was very slender. (I'd noticed on earlier, family, holidays that all French waiters were pencil-thin. I imagined it must be an essential qualification for the job.) He would probably be quite tall eventually, but he hadn't – I was pretty sure – finished growing yet. Beautiful lips. His eyes were very bright and lively. Grey in colour… All right: nobody has grey eyes. They were at the bluish end of the spectrum we call hazel. But grey was the impression I got. If I'm honest with myself I have to say that, although built on a slighter scale and having eyes that were grey rather than chestnut-brown, he looked much like my brother had done just a couple of years before.

On our second night Jean-Christophe not only waited at our table but, as luck would have it, was on late bar duty. Hardly anyone used the late evening bar and nobody lingered long in it. Except that I did, after Will and Jeffrey had gone to bed, that second night. 'What time do you finish?' I asked Jean-Christophe brazenly and then, even more brazenly, pawed lightly at my crotch. I'd never done such a thing in my life. It was the sense of release, I guess, that I had from being recognised everywhere and having to behave myself on account of my BBC job.

To my delight he pawed lightly at his own trousers and said he'd meet me in the car park in ten minutes, when he put the bins out. He was as good as his word. We pleasured each other, rather briefly, in the shadows behind a big shed, standing up.

Over the days, or rather nights, that followed we grew more ambitious. When the coast was clear he'd come to my room in the middle of the night, and once I went to his. I'd never before thought about the fact that hotels have backstage areas just as theatres do. Yet of course that must be the case. I discovered a looking-glass world in which the meagre replaced the grand, the small replaced the large, the dull and dingy replaced the opulent. His room was tiny and his bed narrow. That's why we only slept there the once.

Something I found refreshing about Jean-Christophe was that, when I told him I was a TV presenter and perhaps a rising star in the BBC's little firmament, he didn't care a jot. He liked my face, my physicality, my personality, and he liked my cock. Unlike people I met in England he wasn't afraid of me because he'd seen me on the screen. I found great relief in that.

The trouble with holiday sex, I discovered now for the first time, was that it tends to lead to holiday romance, something which is of its nature finite. I tried not to let that happen between Jean-Christopher and myself. I didn't want the heartbreak. I was still suffering from the pain of my rough separation from Alastair back in March, and didn't want to add to it. I tried ... but was only partly successful. I couldn't help but grow fond of Jean-Christophe. I know he grew fond of me. We swapped addresses when we parted at the end of that holiday and, yes, that parting hurt. It hurt me, that is. I don't know if it also hurt Jean-Christophe but I imagine it did. Probably quite a lot.

Will and Jeffrey must have guessed what had gone on between Jean-Christophe and me though they never commented or asked. But they were particularly solicitous towards me after that parting and on the journey back. I was grateful for that. I was also grateful that neither of them had made any kind of pass at me during the whole fortnight. They had kept to the self-imposed rule that I had broken in the case of Alastair.

The Raven and the Jackdaw

When I compared their unimpeachable behaviour to mine in that regard I didn't exactly feel proud of myself.

I returned from that holiday feeling relaxed and almost happy, despite the fact that I pined a bit for Jean-Christophe. But I also returned with the impression reinforced that if I was ever to have a love-life or a sex-life, I would have to leave the shores of my home country, where I was an on-screen visitor to everybody's living-room, in order to have it.

In my third and final year at university I made the second series of The Square Metre. I studied. I had no sightings of Alastair. I didn't stay in touch with Jean-Christophe. And though I saw Byron from time to time we met now as friends, not lovers. He had one of those by now; their relationship looked fairly permanent from where I stood. They shared a London flat.

I graduated and was adrift in the big wide world at last...

Actually I was not adrift. I was luckier than most. The Natural History Unit gave me a new job. I would be making a number of programmes in a major new venture in which Will would also be taking part. I would be sent to a variety of locations, some abroad and for weeks at a time, in pursuit of unusual wildlife. My spirit of adventure might be tested, I was warned. There would be rough terrain to deal with, rough places, sometimes, to sleep in at night. I found that I was up for that. The money that went with the year's contract made my eyes light up. I was a young bachelor. I had nobody to spend it on except myself.

I spent some of it on the rent for a small flat, quite high up in a block that overlooked Bristol harbour. I was no longer a student; my housemates had moved out of the Redland address soon after graduating; it seemed the right moment to take this new step into adult life.

Having a place of my own had some downsides: when the flat needed cleaning there was nobody but me to clean it; the evenings could be a bit lonely if I wasn't going out with friends or colleagues. On the other hand, if I wanted to bring someone back with me they would no longer have to run the gauntlet of appraisal by my housemates.

Actually, I very rarely brought anyone back for sex or to spend the night. Something had been going on during the last couple of years, of which I'd had more warning, perhaps than most. This was because I had a brother who was almost a doctor, working exhausting hours on the wards at Guy's. He had told me, almost casually, two years earlier, about a cluster of odd cases in San Francisco. A number of young men had gone down with pneumonia around the same time; some of these had developed rare forms of cancer. One thing they all had in common was a homosexual orientation. They hadn't responded very well to treatment.

'There's the US for you,' I said. 'Everything that can happen eventually does happen – over there.'

'Yes,' Jason had agreed. 'But remember what we always say about the weather. What they get over there comes here after a little wait.'

'That's an old wives' tale,' I said. Although I took his point. 'Anyway, you can't catch a disease just because you're homosexual, surely. Over the centuries there's been no evidence of that.'

'You could if it was sexually transmitted,' Jason said.

'Pneumonia sexually transmitted?' I said. 'You're kidding.' But the mention of the cancers had alarmed me a bit. However, there wasn't very much about it in the British media, and I didn't give the matter much thought. But at Christmas that year Jason mentioned that a first case of the odd syndrome had been diagnosed in the UK. They called it GRID. It stood for gay-related immune deficiency. Eventually it was found that you didn't have to be gay to get it. Women could catch it from bisexual partners. You could get it from infected blood. Babies caught it. The acronym was changed in September 1982, just two months after the first GRID-related UK death. The new acronym was AIDS of course.

Perhaps it was just as well that I had been pretty well celibate during my last eighteen months at university. By the time I met Jean-Christophe I was fairly certain, along with most of the medical profession and the media, that the carrier of the virus that wrecked people's immune systems was seminal fluid. For that reason Jean-Christophe and I never went as far as anal intercourse, and for some time afterwards I didn't do that with anybody else. Until some bright spark hit on the idea that gay men should wear condoms for the purpose, and the spread of the disease slowed rapidly as a result.

I thought of Alastair a lot. With a great deal of pain as well as fondness. I never caught sight of him anywhere about the place, even though I automatically peered into the centre of any group of teenagers I saw if I was driving around Bristol or travelling on foot. I had no way of guessing if he was a sexually adventurous teenager or not. Nor whether his tastes still ran to those of his own sex or whether, like my brother, his compass needle had swung round in his mid-teens towards the opposite. I hoped that, whatever the case was, he knew enough to be careful. But I could do no more than hope. His conspicuous absence from the streets of Bristol for a year and a half began to make me wonder whether his parents had upped sticks and, with him in tow, made a new home somewhere else. That they might have left Bristol – because of me? I found that a dismaying, desolate thought.

SEVENTEEN

Birds are not stupid. Most of them. When the migrant species leave western Europe for Africa in the autumn they funnel down the Iberian Peninsula and Italy, crossing the Mediterranean sea where it is at its narrowest: from Spain across the Gibraltar Strait, from the Italian mainland across the Strait of Messina to Sicily and thence, perhaps stopping off at a smaller island en route, to Tunisia. The brightest of all of them hitch lifts for some of the way by settling among the rigging of southbound ships and if they are lucky get fed crumbs by passengers and kitchen staff. That autumn I was sent to the Strait of Gibraltar, with a cameraman, a sound technician, my director and a Land Rover, to film some of this.

To say that I enjoyed the experience would be an understatement. We stayed at a small hotel among the hills and cork oak forests between Tarifa and Algeciras. By day we drove around in search of migrant birds, large and small, and filmed them. In the evenings we drank slightly too much. Who cared? We were young and fit and able to handle it.

I saw storks for the first time in my life, flapping majestically out to sea in skeins of thirty or forty. We could see their immediate destination very clearly, just a dozen miles away across the water: the mountains of Morocco and, in front of them, the Bay of Tangier. In the early morning or late evening sun we could even make out the white houses of Tangier's Kasbah and the buildings around the port. If we could see all this no doubt the migrant storks could see it too. I hoped that gave them comfort as they flew above the unforgiving element beneath.

Among the cork oaks we found almost every species in the book. From three-inch-long wrens and goldcrests to large raptors – harriers, hawks and falcons – that would eat the wrens and goldcrests if they could. The late autumn weather was warm and sunny. While I was out there I heard that a third series of The Square Metre had been given the go-ahead, and that I would again be fronting it. I was in clover, and so was my bank balance.

The migrant birds programme was given an hour of prime TV time. My brother phoned me after he and Anna had watched it. He was very complimentary, and we had a long chat. He had decided not to specialise, and work towards becoming a consultant, he told me, but to become a GP instead. A few more years would pass before he could expect to achieve this.

I had time on my hands that winter, knocking about Bristol, waiting for the next series of The Square Metre to kick off. I was sent abroad a couple more times – to the south of France to film a wild boar hunt, and to Lapland to film reindeer in the all-day Christmas dusk. But still there were gaps between engagements. I filled the time by starting to write my book.

I hoped that, in trying to commit to paper a sanitised account of my relationship with my brother I would be able to sort it out in my head. And elsewhere. I had the dismaying knowledge that, except in the blessed cases of Byron and Alastair, whenever I had sex with anybody or shared any physical intimacies with them I always found myself wishing for the touch, the contours, the scent, of Jason instead.

Yes, I had moments of thinking that the things I had done with him were wrong – perverted, deviant – just as he had thought at one time. Well, he'd told me one time. He might have had the thought more often than that.

But beyond those things I think I was afraid that my feelings towards my brother had so skewed my life and being that I could not love anybody else.

Perhaps for this reason I was very hard on the character of the older brother in my novella: James as I called him. My real life brother was going to get married. In this extract James, the Raven, is already married – unhappily, the reader is expected to infer – and, having sired two children, is in the throes of an extra-marital fling with someone else.

****

James had seen his brother at work several times. He invariably felt proud of him as he watched the show but afterwards, standing awkwardly amid the bustle of cramped dressing rooms he never knew quite how to say so. He discovered that people really did scream, 'You were wonderful tonight, darling,' at one another and, anxious not to say more than he honestly meant, usually ended up saying far less.

This evening he had been to see David in All My Sons at Birmingham. It was a long drive back in the dark. Jenny was asleep when he got home. It didn't make much difference these days. He made himself a sandwich and ate it and was just going to bed when the phone rang.

It was David. He sounded drunk. 'We never talk to each other,' he was saying. 'Never properly. We didn't tonight.'

'Do you want to talk now?' James hoped he didn't. It was one o'clock.

'Not on the phone. But soon. Sometime.'

'OK. Sometime soon. All right? I think you'd better get to bed now, though.' James put the phone down. He hoped he'd sounded friendly. David was very odd.

*

James had to work late. At least that was what he told Jenny. Actually he was having a meeting with Karen

The Raven and the Jackdaw

from Graphics at her flat and it had very little to do with work. It was a very civilised little affair, this. There was candlelight, gin and tonic and Vivaldi beforehand and cigarettes and conversation afterwards.

'Why don't you leave her?' Karen asked, just as she always did.

'Because of Richard and Simon,' James replied, as he always did. 'And I suppose there's a kind of loyalty that increases with time even though the original reason for that is diminishing at the same time.' He changed the subject. 'I saw my brother yesterday. He's doing great things at Birmingham. This time in a play by Arthur Miller. He was very good. He always is, thank God.'

'Why thank God?'

James shrugged. 'It's a difficult way to make a living. That's all I meant.'

'A friend of mine,' said Karen on a little breath of cigarette smoke, 'had a boyfriend who was an actor. She found he became impossible to talk to as time went on. Is David like that?' Seeing a hint of puzzlement on James's face she went on, 'I ask because there's always something in your voice when you mention David. Doubt? Hesitation? Something like that.'

'David has always been difficult to talk to. I find, anyway. He rang me up after I got back last night. At one in the morning. Said he wanted to talk to me. He sounded pissed.'

'Actors usually are,' said Karen. 'Perhaps he finds it equally difficult to talk to you.'

This had not occurred to James. 'Maybe.'

'And did you talk?'

'I told him to go to bed.'

'I rest my case,' said Karen. She took a delicate pull on her cigarette. 'I find your brother fascinating.'

'But I've hardly told you anything about him.'

'That's the fascination,' said Karen. 'I shall have to meet him one day and get to know him myself.' She got up and crossed the room. Her silk dressing gown was not quite tied at the front and the candle-light cast its shadows there. It was the shadows, James decided, that he liked the most.

James sighed. 'I wish... I wish I could give it all up and start painting properly. Doing the stuff I want.'

He said this often, especially after a few drinks, and Karen was used to it. She always said, 'That's simply what everybody wants.' This time she didn't. Perhaps she was tired of hearing it. 'Why don't you?' she asked instead.

****

'Do you know what a lammergeyer is?' Will asked me. We were at the Whiteladies Road studios, having coffee in the canteen.

'Yes,' I said, which surprised him slightly. 'It's another name for the bearded vulture. It's quite rare and a few live in Spain. I know because Peter Scott showed a film about the bird in the Look series a few years before I was born. Happily it was shown again some years later. I watched it when I was still quite small, I think.'

'It must have made quite an impression,' said Will.

'It did,' I said. 'It was called The Ibex and the Lammergeyer, if I remember rightly.'

'You do,' said Will. 'We're going to have another go at it. The lammergeyer nearly died out but was reintroduced. We're leaving the ibex out of it, though. Unless you happen to see one.' The ibex was a kind of mountain goat. 'How are your rock-climbing skills?'

'I've never done any rock climbing,' I said. 'I suppose it's never too late to start.'

The Raven and the Jackdaw

'Excellent,' said Will. He meant, I supposed, that my positive attitude was good. He finished, 'Because you're fronting it.'

We got a couple of episodes of The Square Metre in the can ahead of time before setting off that next spring. We put the Land Rover on the Plymouth to Santander ferry, sailed round the tip of Brittany and down through the Bay of Biscay, which was still in fairly brisk motion in the aftermath of the winter's storms. I was afraid I might turn out to be a poor sailor as I looked ahead to twenty-three hours on the heaving sea. I was relieved to discover that this was not the case. Out of the four of us it was only the sound technician who suffered from seasickness. But the poor guy suffered enough for the four of us, and spent nearly the entire voyage in his bunk. He recovered as soon as we landed, though, and took his turn at the wheel as we headed south. Past Valladolid and Salamanca, two names for historians and romantics alike to conjure with. We were heading for the Sierra de Gredos.

There was another name that set the hairs bristling on the back of my neck. For that inhospitable range of mountains, lying east-west between Madrid and the remote town of Caceres, was the setting for most of the action in Hemingway's monumental novel about the Spanish Civil War, For Whom the Bell Tolls. I had read the book while at university and been so deeply shaken by Hemingway's vivid descriptions of the horrors that human beings had perpetrated on other human beings that I was almost physically sick. The words *Sierra de Gredos* rang through my head like the clanging of a cold cracked bell. It tolled for me.

We saw it long before we got there. Sierra is the Spanish word for a saw, and that is exactly what the profile of the mountain chain looked like when it first appeared in front of us, tearing its way up out of the plain, fifty miles ahead of us, jagged teeth uppermost. At last we began to climb into the range's foothills. Until we reached the beautiful little town of Béjar, and there we stopped.

Béjar became our base. It was where our guide lived. And we certainly needed a guide. Over the following days he navigated our way up unpromising-looking mountain tracks above the tree line and, when we headed away from our vehicle on foot, up rocky and almost invisible pathways that were known only to him, it seemed, plus a few goats. Our guide, who was called Toni, knew not only the mountain tracks and pathways; he also knew where the vultures lived.

Of all the species of vulture in the world the lammergeyer is probably the only one you might imagine wanting to keep as a pet. It is one of the few that doesn't have a bald head or a naked neck. Instead it has a mane of golden plumes like a cockerel's. It doesn't have a comb or wattle, though. Instead it wears a mask of black feathers around its eyes that runs down on either side of the beak to join up in a little black goatee beard beneath. You could imagine it is wearing a rather heavily framed pair of pince-nez, or lorgnette. It has a rather dashing look that becomes also slightly comical when it turns to look full face at you, like a child's face in a bandit mask.

Each pair of lammergeyers controls a vast area of territory, from which the pair will see any interlopers off. In the section of the Sierra that rose south of Béjar we could only expect to find one pair of birds. Fortunately, with their nine-foot wingspans and their habit of soaring high above the mountain passes they were not difficult to spot.

They don't eat rotting carrion. Nor do they take lambs, as their German-derived name would suggest. They pick

The Raven and the Jackdaw

up the bones of dead animals and drop them from a great height to break them. Then they pick the marrow out and eat that. In places where there are tortoises, like Greece, they pick those up and drop them with the same end in view. The playwright Aeschylus was famously killed when an eagle dropped a tortoise on his bald head, mistaking it for a rock. His eagle was probably a lammergeyer, most people now think.

Our first sighting came on our first afternoon. It thrilled all of us. The cameraman, Nick, pointed his equipment up and filmed it as it sailed above our heads, turning repeatedly and coming back. He filmed in a state of feverish excitement, it seemed to me, and it was with equally feverish excitement that I took the microphone and spoke. You couldn't mistake its silhouette, I told an unknown number of future viewers: no other bird of such a size had a diamond-shaped tail like that. It was truly beautiful. Everyone who might watch the programme when eventually it was aired would have to agree with that.

The days that followed were full of luck for us. The weather stayed clear and bright. (It was piercingly cold too above the tree line but we had expected that.) We saw both birds. When they flew close together Nick was able to frame them both in the same shot. We filmed them on the ground, wrenching leg-bones from the carcase of a dead goat. We filmed them rising on their mythic wings to drop their booty into rocky gorges. Thanks to the miracle of the zoom lens we filmed them descending, apparently as endlessly as Lucifer, then landing beside their loosed burdens and picking the marrow out.

We filmed their nest.

Lammergeyers lay their eggs in the dark days of winter, in profoundly inaccessible cliff-side nests. By now the eggs should be hatched, with any luck.

Wonderfully, our guide Toni knew the spot. We set off towards it with two expert rock-climbers from the town. They followed our Land Rover in a pick-up truck, with winches, blocks and tackle in the back. Up, up, upward was our journey. We were going to descend on the nest from above. *We* meant Nick the cameraman – and me, with a small hand-held microphone and mini-tape-recorder in a pocket.

I watched the tripod winch apparatus being assembled on the edge of the cliff. I couldn't help but think of a gallows. I had never been more terrified of anything in my life.

They let us down over the side in a double harness and with a double set of ropes. Don't look down was what everyone said, and I didn't. I was quite scared enough without doing that. To give myself courage I tried to think of my brother on the day he climbed across the top of the school roof. It may have helped a bit, but it didn't entirely cure my fright. Halfway down I started to tremble uncontrollably. Nick must have seen it. 'Do you want to hold me?' I heard him say matter-of-factly. He was ten years older than I was. I didn't answer, but I did hold him, only relaxing my grip when we landed on the ledge. Holding Nick through the last minutes of our descent together was the most wonderful sensation that at that moment I could have possibly felt.

Then fear left me. I was transported by the sight just a metre or two from my feet. Baby birds of prey are called eyasses. There were two such on the flat platform of twigs and branches in front of us; they were white-downed, with prominent claws and beaks, and skeleton wings that they waved towards us. They weren't afraid. Nothing had ever landed on their little planet without bringing food for them to eat. We would be their first disappointment in life. After a time we heard the sound of one of their parents yelping overhead. Nick, still

The Raven and the Jackdaw

crouching by the nest where he'd been filming the eyasses, pointed his camera up. To steady him I held him tight.

When we'd filmed as much as we thought we could without overstaying our welcome and upsetting the parent birds too much we yanked on our ropes, giving the signal we'd arranged with the others, and were hauled back up. As our feet left the narrow floor of the ledge Nick said to me, 'Do you want to hold me again?' Again very matter-of-factly. 'Yes please,' I answered equally casually, and as we slowly ascended I did.

That day's filming was the high spot of our trip. In the snug safety of our hotel that night, around a fine log fire we all got just a little bit drunk.

It would have been remarkable if we had all got through the weeks of filming in such a hostile environment without any of us sustaining a cut or a scratch. And we did not. Although it happened on our very last day of filming, and it wasn't very serious when it did. But it happened to me and so I have a very clear memory of it. I'd grown used to scrambling about on scree, and going on all fours up steep slopes. Practice had made me – not perfect – but competent, and perhaps a little blasé and over-confident. Yet what happened could as easily have happened on the driveway outside my Bristol flat. I turned an ankle when a stone tipped over as I put my foot on it and I fell flat on my face. Had I been on the driveway outside my flat I would no doubt have hobbled inside and taken the lift up. But out here, among the crags of the Sierra de Gredos, I couldn't do that.

It was good not to be alone. The Land Rover stood parked no more than a quarter of a mile from where I'd gone sprawling, and I had the other three alongside me. It was Nick who picked me up and asked if I thought anything was broken. I said I thought not. And it was

Nick who was the first to wrap one of my arms around his shoulder to take the weight off my injured ankle as we walked back. My other arm went around the director's shoulder. It was left to the sound guy to carry the camera as well as his own equipment.

Back at the hotel they found a cold spray for my ankle, and gave me aspirin to ease the pain and reduce the inflammation. It was late afternoon by now. I told the others I would lie down in my room for a bit, as I felt rather shaken up. I'd be down in time for dinner, though. If I didn't appear, would one of them kindly come and wake me up?

I must have gone to sleep. A knock at the door brought me back. I said, 'Come in,' then looked at my watch. It wasn't time for dinner yet. My visitor was Nick. He closed the door behind him. 'I brought you this,' he said. He held out a packet of frozen peas. 'Donated by the kitchens,' he added. 'You don't have to eat them afterwards. Budge up.' He sat down then on the edge of my bed, his bottom pressed against my hip. He arranged the packet of peas across my bad ankle and instep. Then he turned his face towards mine and smiled very sweetly. 'Is there anything else you want?' he asked.

'No,' I said. 'I'll be fine. I'll be down in half an hour or so, to join you for a pre-dinner drink. But, like I said before, wake me again if I don't make it. I wouldn't want to miss our last night.'

'I'll make sure you don't do that,' Nick said. Then he put his hand on my thigh, rather to my surprise, and rubbed it for a moment. Quite high up. For a second he looked searchingly into my face.

'Thank you for the peas,' I said. 'That was a nice thought.'

'Quite all right,' said Nick. Then he gave my thigh a final squeeze and got up off the bed. 'See you at the bar in thirty,' he said. 'And if you're not there I'll come back up.' He walked across to the door, turned and smiled at me again as he walked out through it and was gone. And that was all there was to it.

Sierra de Gredos, Sierra de Gredos. The mountains retreated behind us as we drove away from them the next morning, diminishing in scale until they were no bigger on the horizon than a bow-saw's blade of teeth. But the syllables continued to clang in my head. An old cracked bell that tolled for my past, and for my future – or for a part of my future, though I couldn't know that yet.

I hadn't taken the half completed manuscript of my novella to Spain with me. I planned to settle back into it when I got back. In between filming episodes of The Square Metre, and before my next trip abroad – it would be to the Caucasus, to make a film about another rare bird, the great bustard – I did just that. But during that brief quiet time in Bristol something happened that would make me change the course of the story's narrative. I got a phone-call from Byron in London. He'd had some terrible news, he said. A close friend of a close friend of his – it was not someone he himself had been to bed with, he was careful to point out – had been diagnosed with AIDS (it was always still spelt with a full set of capitals in those days) and was not expected to live.

EIGHTEEN

There hadn't been a family Christmas like this for – David couldn't remember how long. He was usually away somewhere in pantomime and Mary was in Canada. James, Jenny and the boys used to visit Hundredhouse for a few days each Christmas and catch colds with Hector. But this year David had no panto, He was out of work for once, but not unduly worried by that. He had done a few episodes of a television series during the year. His had been only a small part but the money was a treat after the theatre. And now he was a celebrity in the village pub as a result; he rather enjoyed that. Mary was here too because she wasn't in Canada. Lawrence and she had split up. Then Lawrence had died shortly afterwards. Everybody was being extremely nice to Mary. Nobody was asking what she was going to do next.

How different David had become, Mary was thinking. Though he was getting on for thirty he still looked remarkably youthful. Mary guessed that in his line of business this must be an asset. But that look of melancholy that she remembered so well, that he had worn like a badge through the later years of his adolescence... It had gone. To be replaced by something else. A look of... Mary tried to think how to describe it to herself but it wasn't easy... In the end resignation was the best word she could come up with.

'I had a chat with Toby the other day,' Hector announced to the room, a propos of nothing, in the middle of Christmas dinner. Nobody could think who Toby was.

'Toby took over from me at the school. It seems they're expanding the art department.' He looked at James. 'I've asked him to look in and meet you.'

The Raven and the Jackdaw

'Dad,' James said in an aggrieved voice. 'Why? I'm not a school teacher. I don't want to become one. I certainly don't want to bury myself down here in the middle of nowhere.'

'Well, your mother and I did,' said Hector. 'And here is where you were brought up. But I'll leave that. It's just a thought I had. And I don't think they're looking for a full-time teacher. Rather, it's a plan to use local artists on a very part-time basis and, at the same time, encourage them in their own work.'

'I'm not a local artist, Dad. I've got a perfectly good job of my own. I don't know why you're suddenly leaping into my career plans like this.' James had though been thinking gingerly of finishing with his job and going freelance and Karen, whose existence the rest of the assembled company were unaware of, had been urging him to do this. It was not, however, the moment for mentioning any of that.

'I'm not leaping into your career plans,' said Hector. 'I've invited my successor as headmaster round for a drink and I'd like you to meet him. That is not the same thing. Correct me if I'm wrong.' Nobody did.

Later, David could hear his brother and sister-in-law discussing the matter in their bedroom while he lay next door in his own bed. Wattle and daub never were very soundproof.

'You're not to think of it,' Jenny was saying. 'It's just a ploy to get us down here so that I can spend the rest of my life waiting on your father hand and foot.'

'I wouldn't let that happen,' came James's voice.

'Then you are thinking about it.'

'I didn't say that.'

'He treats me like a servant. As though I was something the cat brought in.'

'He does not.'

'You choose not to notice.'

'I've been thinking of going freelance for a long time, actually,' James said next.

'But not down here, eking out pennies in a village school.'

'It isn't a village school. It's the second biggest comprehensive in the county as a matter of fact.'

David tried not to go on listening. He pulled the blankets up over his head.

*

'There's something I ought to tell you,' said Mary, pouring milk onto her muesli primly. This portentous start to the day made David want to giggle. Boxing Days had a bad history. 'When I go back to Canada I'm going to be received into the Roman Catholic Church. I've been accepted provisionally for the novitiate with a nursing order in New York.'

There was total incomprehension on every face. 'What's received?' asked Simon.

'She's going to become a rock-cake,' said Richard.

'A nursing order?' asked Hector slowly.

'I'm going to become a nun,' said Mary with a very straight face.

David and James each caught the other's eye. They both began to laugh.

'Shut up,' Hector shouted. He had turned black in the face. The laughter stopped.

'I'm going to be a nun,' Mary repeated, very quietly but with steel in her voice.

'Have you gone out of your tiny mind?' Hector asked her. 'Have you forgotten the Reformation? Have you gone stark staring mad?'

'The Reformation?' This was David, laughing again now at the absurdity of the question but at the same time indignant. 'The Reformation's got nothing to do with anything. We're not in a classroom, we're in the real world in the nineteen-eighties. Or is the whole family

crazy? Mary's going to be a nun. God alone knows why. I can't begin to imagine why myself, but at least let's say good luck to her!'

'Yes, of course,' said James. 'Good luck.'

'Thank you,' said Mary.

'This bloody family!' said Hector and got up from his chair. He stalked out into the garden.

'Will he be all right?' James asked.

'You're all round the bend,' said Jenny. 'Stark raving mad, the whole lot of you.'

'I just admire the work they do so much,' said Mary simply.

'What's the Reformation, Mum?' Simon asked.

****

I had moved things on in time a bit, for reasons that had to do with the circumstances in which the various characters would find themselves towards the end of the story. The fictional James and David were now about nine years older, respectively, than Jason and me. The real me was not yet twenty-two when the friend of Byron's friend was diagnosed. I phoned my brother, partly to tell him that news, although he'd never met Byron, but more importantly to ask him what the latest theory about the incubation time for aids was. 'A year ago we thought it was about a year at most. This year the thinking is, well, it can be two years. We actually know that. But next year… Well, I think you can see where this is heading…'

I certainly could. In that last extract from the "novella" the subject of religion made its first appearance. It hadn't done so before. I wasn't a religious person. But around the time I was writing it … a lot of gay men were thinking about religion, at least a little bit.

The family were together again only four months later. The ring of chestnut trees around the village church was just breaking into leaf. Mary arrived by taxi. Her brothers were relieved to find that she didn't look like a nun in the least. There was no wimple, no trailing rosary, just a sensible tweed suit with a tiny gold cross on the lapel of the jacket. With genuine surprise James said, 'They don't shave your head?'

The three of them stood together in the church again. How small it seemed, when it had once seemed so big. Jenny and her children were not there, though Hector was. At least the part of him that had eaten and drunk, begotten children and cultivated his garden was. In front of them, surrounded by flowers, in a highly polished wooden box. The irascible teacher, loving father and lifelong romantic had gone somewhere else. In a gingerly hopeful gesture his coffin would lie next to his wife's.

'At least,' said the vicar afterwards at the farmhouse, 'he was spared the suffering of Isabel.' He took another smoked salmon sandwich. 'A heart attack. So very sudden. Not a bad way to go. Not really. I try to tell people ... people whose loved ones have died in other circumstances ... after long illnesses perhaps ... who knows what they may have been spared in a possible future. The mercy of God is a strange thing.'

It certainly was, thought David. People spent a lot of time having to apologise for God. It was as if they had a friend who was intellectually brilliant but who always behaved like a complete cad. 'He means well,' they would say of such a friend, or, 'It's his artistic temperament,' when you wished they had long ago left him to his own devices.

The Raven and the Jackdaw

A neighbour spoke in David's ear. 'At least your father had the pleasure of seeing you on the telly before he went. We did enjoy that. You were so good as that insurance salesman.'

'I wasn't the insurance salesman.' David had said it before he could stop himself. 'I was the ticket clerk.'

'Oh,' said the neighbour, wrong-footed for a moment. But only for a moment. 'We thought you were both good,' he came back.

'You know something, David?' This was Mary's voice. She was Sister Concordia now, but they couldn't possibly call her that. She had explained that they weren't expected to. 'You're not getting any older. You never put any weight on. Is my little brother the reincarnation of Peter Pan? Have you discovered the secret of perpetual youth?'

'It's the healthy life I lead,' said David. 'Mind you, I had a touch of flu in January, which took a long time to get over. I might have lost a bit of weight as a result of that.'

There was a supercharged, rather intense quality about David today, Mary thought, that hadn't been there at Christmas. 'You're in a show in London, James said.'

'Right. Doing a new play at the Canonbury. I have to be back for the half tonight.'

'Will James ever take the plunge, do you think?'

'Go freelance, you mean?' said David. 'Be a painter? Not while Jenny's around.'

'He just needs a little push perhaps. I know father tried and made a balls-up of it.' David blinked, hearing a nun use the word balls-up. Then he remembered she was still his sister first and foremost. She went on. 'Somebody or something ought to give him that push. James needs to do something for its own sake. It's not so bad to have a go at something and fail at it as it is to cop out before you start.'

'Are you suggesting I should be the one to push him?' David asked.

'No. Only that something needs to happen. I end up talking about myself of course. It just needed one thing to push me, you see.' She didn't elaborate.

David didn't try to press her. 'I can't begin to understand what you're doing or why you're doing it,' he said. 'But I wish you all the best.'

'I'll remember that,' said Mary, half smiling. *'Now do be an angel and get me another drink. Whisky if there's any left.'*

David tried to imagine his sister in two days time, in a convent, an ocean away, in New York. It was so impossible it made him laugh.

****

By the time I came to write that last scene Byron's close friend's close friend was dead.

****

David was feeling exhausted by the time he reached the theatre. Funerals were always a draining experience. But he felt tired more often these days. Perhaps he hadn't properly shaken off that bout of flu. Perhaps it was simply the winter. Winters seemed to last for ever these days. Where were the lovely springs he remembered from his childhood? But that was being very subjective. He had to face it: he wasn't that young any more. You couldn't maintain a ten-year-old's pleasure in March sunshine all your life, nor could you expect to have the energy level of a teenager when you were ten years beyond that stage of your life. Once the show was over he would try to get an early night.

The Raven and the Jackdaw

There was a note in his pigeon-hole inside the stage door. I used to know your brother. I was coming to see the play tonight anyway, then I saw your name written up outside. If you're likely to be in the bar after the performance I'd love to meet you. If you'd rather not, or have something else to do, I shan't be offended. *David couldn't read the signature but managed to elicit from the stage-doorman that the visitor had been a young woman.*

She came over to him at once and bought him a drink. That was the positive side, David thought, of Women's Lib. Her name, she said, was Karen. David hadn't heard of her. They talked about the play for a few minutes and then about James. It wasn't necessary for Karen to explain that she'd once been the other woman in James's life and that she no longer was. David understood all this instinctively somehow and was oddly excited by it. She was an attractive woman and nicely dressed. 'You're not a bit as I imagined,' *she said after a bit.* 'I expected someone more extrovert: bigger, louder – more actorish I guess.'

'A dreadful old ham in other words...'

'I'm ever so pleased you're not.'

David thought, I'm being flirted with. It was a pleasant thought. He said, 'Did you come on your own?'

'With friends. They're over there.' *She pointed.*

'Oughtn't we to join them?'

'In a minute. I wanted you to myself for a few minutes first. I hope you didn't mind that.'

'Not at all,' *said David.* 'Though I'm sorry if I don't appear too lively. I spent today at a funeral. My father's. James's father's too, of course.'

Karen was visibly startled and upset. 'I'm sorry. So, so sorry.' *She touched David's arm lightly.* 'You should have said.'

'It happens,' *said David.* 'Heart attack.'

'What'll happen to the lovely old house?'

'Have you been there? Do you know it?'

'No, of course not. I heard about it. Once saw some photographs.'

'It belongs to the three of us jointly. You knew we have a sister, I suppose. It hasn't been decided what happens next. We'll probably sell it but it's just possible James might want it for his family. Dad was trying to persuade him to go down and teach at the school he used to be headmaster of. If James did do that... Well, in that case I imagine he'd have to buy my sister and me out.'

'I haven't seen James for so long. I miss him.' Karen sounded as though she meant it. Again she touched David on the sleeve.

A pity James was saddled with Jenny, David thought. He already liked Karen better than his sister-in-law. She would have suited James very well, he decided. On the strength of their ten minutes' acquaintanceship.

'May I join you?' A small be-suited figure stood beside them.

'Of course,' said David. He turned back to Karen. 'This is Alec. We knew each other years ago in Glasgow. In rep. When I'm in London I stay at his flat. He also just happens to be the manager of this theatre – as you can see from his tidy appearance.'

Alec stayed for no more than a minute. There was a problem he had to see to – to do with one of the fire exits.

'I remember that you were in rep,' said Karen. 'That's when I first heard of you. James had been up to see you once – three or four years ago now, perhaps – and he was in a flap because you'd rung him, insisting you needed to talk to him, in the middle of the night.'

'Good heavens! You remember that?'

The Raven and the Jackdaw

'I was curious about you and it stuck in my mind. I got the impression that the two of you had a communications problem. Did you ever have that talk?'

'No, we never did.' David laughed. 'I wouldn't have rung up at all if I hadn't been drunk.'

Karen smiled thoughtfully. 'You're gay, aren't you, David?'

'Why do you suppose that?'

'A sixth sense, perhaps. You're not camp or anything, but you are... Well, am I right?'

'That or bisexual. Something like that.'

'You shouldn't talk too loudly about being bisexual these days,' said Karen. 'It's not as fashionable as it once was. Tell me about Alec.'

'Alec? Your sixth sense can't be very well developed if you thought...'

'I didn't really. Just making sure. You're not spoken for, then, at the moment.'

'Actually ... no. At least, not by Alec.' David paused an instant. Then, 'Am I in the process of being picked up?'

'Hmm,' said Karen. 'Picked up might be too strong a way of putting it. But flirted with, yes.'

'How delightful, then,' said David. 'Though I feel I ought to warn you that the process might not meet with total success.'

'Even a partial success might be something,' Karen said. 'But perhaps we should join my friends now. I'll introduce you. That is, if you don't mind.'

Karen led the way across the floor of the theatre bar. In her wake she seemed to trail something intangible, something exciting, in which David imagined himself gambolling, as he followed her, like a porpoise.

NINETEEN

Through the BBC I was asked if I would give an interview to one of the Sunday newspaper supplements. The administrator who contacted me about this added helpfully that it was probably time I got myself an agent to handle this sort of stuff. I hadn't given any thought to this. It was the first time I'd been approached for anything more major than an autograph. It was only a few months, after all, since I'd stopped being a student. I was lucky enough to be fronting one series and some episodes of another one. I had no reason to suppose this run of luck would last: that a lifetime's career would come of it.

We did the interview in a room at the Whiteladies Road studios. I didn't really want a sharp-eyed journalist peering round my small bachelor's flat while we talked, and making comments about it in his piece.

In the event it wasn't a he but a she. I found her very easy to talk to and I got the impression that she was straightforward. That she wouldn't just be charming to my face and then slag me off, or twist my words, when she came to write up her notes and transcribe her tape. I was right. When eventually I read her piece, heart in mouth, I found that she had presented me in a very nice light. Better than I deserved, I thought. Before she started her tape-recorder she had asked me, 'Do we talk girlfriends at all...?' And I'd said, 'Off-limits, I'm afraid.' Although I said it with my nicest smile in order to sugar the pill a little I remained afraid that she would take her revenge for that refusal in her article, but she did not.

The most interesting thing about that interview was actually a conversation I had with her as I was seeing her to the door afterwards. 'What do you do with your time in between your foreign trips these days?' she asked.

The Raven and the Jackdaw

'Making The Square Metre can't take up every hour of your working week.'

'Well,' I said, 'I don't really think about it. It's not long since I was a full-time student.'

'You might find time hanging heavily after a few more months,' she said. 'You're very articulate. You could write accounts of your safari adventures and sell them to magazines, I would have thought.'

This possibility hadn't crossed my mind till then. 'Yes,' I said doubtfully. 'But I might find I'd already said everything I had to say to camera, and I'd end up repeating myself.'

She turned and looked at me with a twinkle. 'Look,' she said. 'It's journalism we're talking about. People don't mind if you say the same things twice. It's not a Charles Dickens novel.'

'Oh, I am writing one of those,' I said. The words just popped out.

Mischievously she chose to misunderstand. 'You're writing a Charles Dickens novel?'

'No, obviously,' I said, and we both laughed. 'But I am toying with a sort of novel. Probably just a novella, actually. Semi-autobiographical...' I stopped. I was talking to a professional writer. I heard myself sounding naive and pathetic.

'Hmm,' she said with a slightly downturned mouth. 'I wish you the joy of that. But the other thing...' Her tone brightened. 'Articles about your overseas trips. I could have a word with my editor. See if he has any useful thoughts. Or contacts. It might bring you in a bit of money.' She left it there. She could have gone on, *'...which a novella based on your early life will certainly not.'* Kindly, she didn't. She did suggest I should get an agent, though, which made her the second person to have said that in a week.

Jason was wonderfully complimentary about the programme I'd done on the lammergeyer, and also about the one I did a couple of months later featuring the great bustard, for the making of which we had flown all the way to Rostov on Don and camped out on the plains in tents. He was most impressed with my performance on the rock ledge at the side of the lammergeyer's nest. 'You're very brave,' he said.

'I wasn't brave at all,' I said. 'I was actually quite frightened. I only managed to do it because I remembered how you'd climbed over the school roof that time. You'd set the standard and I didn't want to let you down. And actually, on the descent in the harness I was shaking so much that the cameraman asked me if I wanted to hold him, and I did.'

Jason gave a little light laugh of surprise. Had we been face to face rather than on the telephone I think he would have rumpled my hair at that point. 'You didn't look frightened in the least,' he said. 'Courage means knowing that you're frightened and dealing with it. Which you did.' He didn't comment on my mention of the school roof episode but I knew that he was deeply touched by what I'd said. 'I'm very proud of you,' he finished.

After that resounding 'Hmm' from the journalist, a sound which rang in my ears every time I thought about my little effort at an autobiographical novella, I found it very difficult to go on with the book. Weeks passed and I couldn't bear to touch the incomplete typescript or even look at it. But eventually I did.

I'd been contacted by a magazine called Popular Nature, of which I'd never heard. This was thanks to the editor of the magazine that had run the feature on me. They wanted me to write an article about my expericnce of filming the lammergeyers. Their acceptance of my

The Raven and the Jackdaw

piece would, however, be conditional on the BBC's allowing them to use stills from the film we had made, including a shot of me. I spoke nicely to the right person in the administration at Whiteladies Road. I asked the people at Popular Nature to get in touch with her direct, and let them sort the details out between them. They came to an arrangement, happily for me, and I got to write my piece. I was more than happy that they didn't want anything too sternly scientific. I saw myself much more as a field naturalist than as a boffin in a laboratory, with a library of species distribution charts and a head full of the taxonomy of Linnaeus. Having written my article eventually, and while I had the typewriter out, I felt emboldened enough to go back to The Raven and the Jackdaw. And this is the section I then wrote. It was set a few weeks after David's first encounter with Karen.

****

A Hawaiian goose, neck outstretched along the ground, saw off the two starlings that had dared to approach the largest piece of bread. The child threw them two more, smaller, pieces as a consolation. Ducklings filtered in and out of the shady places among the daffodils. Couples sprawled in the sun. It was the first day of that year that you could comfortably sit without your shirt on.

'You're wonderfully slim,' said Karen, running her forefinger down David's bare back – a little diffidently: the picking-up process had not met with total success so far. 'Even your brother was showing signs of a little surplus around the waistline when I last saw him.'

'Which was when?'

'Over a year ago now. I'm still sad about it. We'd lasted over three years, if you can use the word lasted

about something so very ... extra-marital. But there was no future in it.'

David was nodding gravely. 'Because of Jenny.'

'And the kids of course. Ultimately I suppose I was being unfair to them, by being around, by harbouring any kind of thoughts – plans I suppose I mean – that involved your brother. So I stopped seeing him and it nearly broke my heart. I thought him very beautiful. Not just physically. There's a kind of stillness about him that's rather unusual. Something almost Oriental.'

'I understand,' said David. 'It's something I can't describe either, and it's grown in him over the years. We used to think it was laziness when he was younger but it developed into quite a different quality. And yes, he is beautiful.'

'I suppose you would be aware of that,' said Karen after a short pause for thought.

'More than aware.' David began to pull up little handfuls of grass. 'I was once in love with him.'

'I see. That must have been awkward.'

'It was. For a long time. Perhaps on some level I still feel that way about him. But it's not a problem any more. The world is a bigger place now than it seemed then. So all that has become a story from a very distant past that might almost seem to belong to someone else.' He turned and looked at her closely. 'It's something I've never talked about to anyone, actually. Except to you.'

Karen smiled carefully. 'I'm honoured in that case.'

David stood up suddenly. 'Fancy an ice-cream? You can't spend an afternoon in St. James's Park without one ice-cream at least.'

A cloud crossed the sun and a shower blew through the trees towards them. The ducklings burrowed beneath their mothers' wings but the human couples sat it out and permitted the rain to splash their bare shoulders. Then in time the sun returned.

The Raven and the Jackdaw

****

I might not have been Charles Dickens, but then I don't think I was trying to be. There was no real contest.

The Raven and the Jackdaw story was a bit vague as to the actual years in which things happened. There have been two references so far to David's unusual slimness and his managing to move from one end of his twenties to the other without gaining any weight. Plus one reference to the fact that the action had moved into the nineteen-eighties. David was an actor, and gay. He moved in circles where aids was known about. Though, as I remember from my own experience of theatre and TV circles around that time, it was not much talked about unless you found yourself close up to an individual case. And even then it was not much talked about.

But my novella hasn't mentioned the aids epidemic yet. Perhaps David was secretly worried that he might have picked up the virus somewhere and that it was lying in wait inside him, biding its time like a mousing cat. He may have been in denial about it. We shall never know, because he was a fictional character and I didn't write about any thoughts along those lines he might have had. David might or might not have been secretly worried by all of that. But I know that I was.

We read in those days that people who'd caught aids in the San Francisco bath-houses and other places of the sort had often had hundreds of sexual partners, if not thousands. My own score was meagre in comparison. I could have counted my sexual contacts up to that time on the fingers of my two hands and the toes of one foot. And yet I knew that you only had to be unlucky once. What kept me calm in those days was the knowledge, tested and re-tested on the bathroom scales, that I wasn't losing any weight.

No-one close to me had been diagnosed with the condition. Nor had any of Will Lumsden's friends, I supposed, but then it was not a subject we ever talked about. If a friend of his or Jeffrey's had had aids – well, they could have kept the information from me if they'd wanted to, I guessed. And nobody who was close to Byron either. Apparently. Although a second person whom Byron knew had told him that someone he knew had caught it.

Caught it when, though? We all knew how by now. But it was the unknown quantity of the incubation period that was the terrifying bit. My own sexual activities around that time were curtailed to mutual masturbation. Nothing more adventurous. I think that went for many other people also. I wasn't even prepared to allow myself to be penetrated anally, or penetrate someone else, while wearing a condom, in case the condom split. Even so, I had a sense that perhaps we were all of us taking extra care to shut the stable door after the horse had left.

My article in Popular Nature was well received. Another magazine contacted me, via the BBC, to ask me if I would do an article for them too. As a change from lammergeyers and bustards I found myself writing this time about the herring gull. There were plenty of those in Bristol for me to look at. It was better, I found, than writing about snails' teeth.

There was other news from the BBC. There would be a new series next year and they wanted me to take part in it. I said yes. We signed the contract.

The next bit of news was less welcome. There would be a fourth series of The Square Metre but I would not be fronting it. They wanted to angle the show more clearly towards a younger audience and it would be shown during an earlier evening slot. I would be twenty-three, going on twenty-four by the time that next series went out. A little long in the tooth. They would be looking for someone a little younger than me to present it.

The consequences of that string of decisions by the Natural History Unit were enormous. Enormous in so far as they touched my life, that is. One of those consequences – something the decision makers could not have foreseen in their most delirious imaginings – was that, just a few months later, I went to the special clinic and took an aids test.

TWENTY

James stepped indoors from a beautiful May evening. He had been working late again. Someone called Linda this time. Jenny called from in front of the television, 'There was a call for you. Someone called Karen.' Luckily she couldn't see the startled-rabbit expression appear on his face. 'She's a friend of your brother's.'

James composed his features quickly. A different Karen, obviously. 'Oh? Any message?'

'It's to do with David. He's in some state or other. You're to ring her back.' She gave him the number and the startled look returned. It was not a different Karen.

'What sort of state? Did she say? Is he all right?'

'She didn't say. You'll have to ring and find out.'

James swallowed hard. This was going to be awkward.

Karen was splendid as the total stranger. James blessed her silently. 'I'm sorry to worry you but I think he may be having a nervous breakdown.'

'A what?' James wondered if he'd heard right. David had sounded fine on the phone a couple of weeks before.

'He's lost his job.'

'But he's an actor...'

'They've had to replace him. I think you ought to go over and see him. Make him go away for a bit if you can. He needs a break or something. But do go.'

*

James did some thinking in the car, driving round to the flat his brother shared with Alec. He sincerely hoped that his brother wasn't ill or cracking up, but Karen's saying, 'Make him go away for a bit,' had struck a chord with some ideas of his own. If David needed a breath of country air, for instance, it might not be a bad thing if it were up to James to see that he got it.

David answered the door. Alec was out.

The Raven and the Jackdaw

'Karen says you've got a problem,' James came to the point as soon as David had invited him in.

'I don't know what to say,' David said.

'Tell me about the job.'

'I couldn't do it. Couldn't rehearse. Do you want tea or coffee?'

'Why couldn't you rehearse?'

'I couldn't breathe.'

James smiled. 'I suppose that is rather essential.'

'We're doing a play about Scott of the Antarctic. I told you about it. There's this effing-great sledge we have to pull around. Heavily metaphorical. And literally heavy. I could pull the bloody thing in the first week of rehearsals but not in the second. I just couldn't get breath enough.'

'Couldn't they have let you out of actually pulling it?'

'That's not the point. Acting's a very physical thing. If you can't do it you can't do it.'

'You seemed all right the other week.'

'I wasn't pulling a sledge then. It's all very well to be able to do the shopping and climb the stairs without getting puffed but if I can't do my bloody job...' He found he was close to tears so he stopped talking and laughed instead.

'When did all this happen? Your being sacked, I mean.'

'Today. They were as nice about it as anything. They said they'd carry on paying me provided I saw a doctor.'

'And have you?'

'No. I'm not registered in London. They wanted me to see the theatre doctor but he wasn't available today.'

'I see. Listen. Here's a suggestion. I have to go down to Hundredhouse tomorrow. Remember the man at Christmas who Dad said wanted to make me a schoolmaster? Well, I've decided to talk to him after all. Come with me if you want to. Get a bit of country air.

We'll get you well again. You can see old Doctor St-John. And keep me company.'

'What about Jenny?'

'She won't be coming. Anyway, I want to talk to you about Hundredhouse. Decide what we're going to do with it.'

*

'I have to go to Hundredhouse tomorrow,' James told his wife, not quite truthfully. 'David's been ordered to rest. Country air and all that. I'm taking him there for a few days.'

Jenny found this hard to swallow. 'You're what? It's been empty for two months. You'll both get pneumonia. And why you? Why can't he go by himself?'

'He's not very well.'

'Why can't this Karen woman take him? If she's his girlfriend.'

'I'm not sure that she is. Anyway, friend she may be but I'm his brother.' It was the first time he had made anything in the way of a protective gesture towards David. Even now he'd done it in support of a lie or at best a half truth. He was aware of the irony. It might have made him feel lousy. But it made him feel good.

*

James's battered escort ground down the motorway. David felt himself enjoying the drive. The scenery stood out in sharper relief than usual; the farms and cottages that speckled the landscape seemed more than usually welcoming; the startling green of May and the whites, pinks and yellows of its blossom seemed almost to recapture in their degree of brilliance the painted memories of childhood. There was a vividness and a poignancy about all this that David appreciated but could not account for.

They reached the turn-off and threaded their way towards the village. As they drew near they crossed a

The Raven and the Jackdaw

stream. A flash of dazzling blue arced across the road. They both saw it. It was a kingfisher. 'We're home, James,' said David drily.

Home was an empty shell now. Home, that mysterious alchemy of house and family, had once worn an air of permanence: rocklike, complacent, perhaps, but enviable nonetheless. Yet the concept of home floated away on the wind when its time came, like dandelion down. Isabel and Hector were dead and Mary was incarcerated in an unfathomable alternative existence in New York. There remained the Raven, with a talent he couldn't begin properly to fulfil because of the demands of his own family: the Jackdaw, whose own career had reached an impasse because for some reason he couldn't breathe; and the empty house.

The grass was high on the lawn and the pink brick path full of weeds. Dead daffodil heads still stood where no hand had tidied them and the hawthorn hedge was a mad green shock. The house stood expectant, holding its peace. Frozen in time yet full of ghosts. In the garden were the voices of their parents, young and excited. 'We'll make our own wine, cure our own hams, bottle fruit...' The house was cold and damp and for a minute James thought he had been stupid to come. But David was visibly cheered and that gladdened James. In the kitchen stood Hector's coke-fired Aga, successor to the ancient range but now seeming an outmoded thing itself. James found sticks and coal and soon had it lit. David, who seemed to be having no trouble now with breathing or anything else got a roaring fire going in one of the front rooms and started fetching logs from the old wash-house. There was nothing the matter with him at all, James thought. It was all psychosomatic. With confidence he made two phone-calls. One was to Doctor St-John's receptionist; the other was to the school, to arrange to meet his father's successor at about the same time. Then, after a moment's thought, he made two more phone-calls. To Jenny and Karen respectively, to say they had arrived safely.

David felt well, happy and comfortable. The Red Lion did an excellent steak these days and the brothers dined there happily and enjoyed a few pints with old neighbours among whom David's slender television celebrity was still current. Returning home they resurrected the living-room fire and sat over it before settling down in front of it in sleeping-bags for the night. James had reasoned that a day's warmth would be needed to air the bed linen upstairs. They could move up tomorrow. Now James talked a bit ramblingly about his future. If he moved down here to Hundredhouse... It would depend on how well his chat with the headmaster went the next morning. The school job would give him a basic income, and leave him with time to paint. He would focus on landscapes and wildlife. David found himself frowning as he heard this. His brother had never been very interested in, and was not knowledgeable about, wildlife. However, he let James talk. Hundredhouse would be a wonderful place for the boys to grow up in. (But what about Jenny? David thought.) David could keep his share of Hundredhouse if he wanted to, or else let James buy him out. Either way it would still be a home for David, a place in the country, his retreat from the world. The future grew rosier and rosier in James's slightly beer-foxed imagination as he drifted towards sleep. There was something he wanted to ask David, something to do with Karen, but he could no longer remember what the question was.

*

They stayed three days at Hundredhouse. To the surprise of both of them it was a good time. James was engaged to start work at the school in September. David was examined by the doctor, who diagnosed nothing

The Raven and the Jackdaw

more alarming than nervous exhaustion. He gave David a sick note for a month and sent him off for routine X-rays and blood tests. A phone-call came, telling him he'd got a part in a radio play for which he had recently auditioned. 'At least I won't have to pull sledges on the radio,' he said. But he felt he could pull a sledge anywhere now. The weather made such a difference. May nudged over into June on the second day at the farmhouse, and quite by chance, with a sudden change of wind direction the too-long winter clicked into summer on the same morning. By the time the two brothers returned to London the house looked lived in once again, the lawns were cut and the hedges trimmed.

But a few days later David got a phone-call from Doctor St-John. He wanted to see him again and would appreciate it if James could be there too. James was slightly surprised by this but agreed to drive David down to Hundredhouse for the second time in a fortnight. It actually suited him quite well. His unilateral decision to move the family down to Hundredhouse in the expectation of a part-timer's salary had not gone down well with Jenny. It was looking as though it might take her a few days to get used to the idea and James was not too sorry that he could be out of the way while she was doing this. On the plus side Richard and Simon had been delighted at the prospect of a move into the country. It would all sort itself out in the end, James thought. Things always did.

*

'We've known each other a long time,' said Doctor St-John, leaning back in his chair and pressing the tips of his fingers together. 'Your father was one of my dearest friends in the neighbourhood.' The doctor was being unusually expansive, David thought. It was true that he had known Doctor St-John all his life, but he had never had more than the briefest conversations with him and

certainly didn't think of him as a family friend. 'Anything and everything I can do for you, be assured I will,' the doctor went on.

'What are you talking about?' David heard his brother ask.

The doctor did not answer James but kept his eyes fixed on David. 'I've had the results of your blood tests,' he said. 'Blood tests are more informative than they were even a year ago. Do you understand me?' The doctor stopped and looked at him even more intently. 'Are you at all prepared for what I have to tell you? Do you have any suspicion – perhaps based on your personal lifestyle – about what your condition is?'

'Perhaps I have,' said David in a voice as small as a bird's heartbeat. He felt cold. A sweat broke out on his brow and under his arms.

'We'll talk about this sensibly,' said the doctor. 'You're not a dead man. You're alive and quite well. But I'll not pretend the result of your test is encouraging. At some point in the past it appears that you've come into contact with a virus. You probably know of your condition by its acronym.' He said this in a very matter-of-fact way and then smiled at David, judging that he did not need to spell the acronym out.

There is a moment of hiatus – David thought about this analogy later – between cutting your finger and feeling the pain, seeing the blood spurt. There is a moment when nothing happens and all looks to be normal and unchanged, the accident never to have happened. The deeper the cut the longer seems the hiatus. So David would remember this moment, the moment when the doctor stopped speaking and smiled at David and David had time to think, I'm still here, I'm still all right. He heard the noise of a sparrow chattering urgently about some other matter altogether on the guttering outside the window. After that the pain started.

The Raven and the Jackdaw

The doctor began to speak again in a kindly, measured way but the words meant no more to David than the twittering of the sparrow; there was a roaring in his ears that blocked the words out or turned them into nonsense. There was another noise too that he couldn't understand. It was his own voice trying to speak, trying to ask questions to which his own heart already knew the answers. Finally there was the sound of somebody sobbing. Tears were flowing hotly on his cheeks. David thought they were blood. He could see nothing but a sheet of red.

'It was a very spectacular faint,' said James in the car, driving back. 'One minute sitting up and being very sensible, the next you'd nose-dived to the floor.'

David was matter of fact now. Panic was in the background now. 'I'm going to die, James.'

'So am I, David,' James said gently.

'I know that. But you've no idea how or when. I have. It's not a lot of fun knowing that.'

'I don't suppose it is. The doctor says you're to lead a normal life for now.'

'That may not be too easy soon.'

'Then we'll just have to look after you, that's all.' He said this lightly and David challenged him.

'Who's we?'

'Jenny and I. In the last resort, me of course. In the end, me.'

'You talk as though you've known all along,' said David. 'You act so unsurprised by everything. As though you'd been planning for today. Did you know?'

'No, I didn't. And yet... I have some idea of what life in your world is like. I read the newspapers. Then I see you getting ill...'

'It isn't true that we all have thousands of partners...'

'I didn't imagine it was. Don't worry about what I might think. Or about anything else. You're going to be

all right.' They both knew that last remark was nonsense; they were both glad it had been said.

*

They called it the phony war. David was said to be dying but there was no sign of him actually doing so. The days were hot and David worked in the garden. Not too hard, but usefully. Had there been a sledge he could probably have pulled it, he optimistically thought.

James worked out his notice in London, driving back to Hundredhouse each night. Jenny would move down when the school holidays began, she said. David would do his radio play in a month's time. If he were well enough. He thought he would be well enough for that.

How wonderful those days were. Each one a jewel on a necklace that you handled in the dark. One day you would reach the end of the necklace and your thumb and forefinger would close on nothing. In the meantime you touched and sensed each one as though you had never lived before, with a kind of frantic joy. All day the cuckoo called feverishly.

The nights were different. They were full of ghosts. A soft American voice in David's ear said, 'They've got this thing back home. It'll be here in a couple of years. Thank God I got out in time.' Though he obviously hadn't. David had tried to trace him but without success. He saw a naked man, emaciated beyond belief, stretched out on a wooden cross.

David would come to, shivering and drenched with sweat. He hadn't worn pyjamas since his school days but had had to go back to them now. Sometimes he would lie, half conscious, in a drenching, disorienting fog; sometimes he imagined himself imprisoned in his own rib-cage, which then became a tunnel without an end, a funnel without an outlet. The walls ached and groaned. He was in a submarine that had dived too deep. All would burst, splintering...

The Raven and the Jackdaw

There were times when sleep catapulted him into clear spaces – clear places with a view, a view down from peace and blue sky, though without sun and without sound. Below him lay the human race and – here was where this dream made its promise of peace – the people below him, rather than he, were impoverished, emaciated, ridden with the ills and the guilt of the world: the world that he had escaped. This was the dream from which he would choose one day not to awaken. But – during that run of hot June mornings at least – he always did.

TWENTY-ONE

I was curious as to who my successor as presenter of The Square Metre would be. Inevitably there was a certain amount of vanity involved in this. Would the new kid be as good-looking as I had been judged to be at nineteen? Would he too make a point of doing the warm weather stuff in shorts? I learnt in the autumn, while chatting in the admin office, that the studios had found someone. That he was a first-year student in the zoology department of the university. I reflected that it was easier to fill a post when you knew exactly what you were looking for and where to look. I had been a second year student when Will had scouted my talent out. He didn't teach the first-year students, I remembered. Nor had we discussed the subject of my successor. Will might have had nothing to do with the new choice. I would ask him anyway, for curiosity's sake. With this in mind I asked the woman in the office what the new chap's name was. 'Alastair McNeil,' she said.

I nearly fell to the floor. I had to try and hide my gob-smacked look. Alastair had disappeared from the planet more than two years ago. Now here he was, right under my nose at the university and, in a few months' time, about to take over my old job. I spent the rest of that day turning those astonishing facts over in my mind almost feverishly, wondering what I could do with the new information, what I should do, and what I would.

Alastair's father had forbidden me to contact his son again on pain of reporting our relationship to the police and my employers, and exposing me in the press. I did a quick calculation: Alastair had recently turned eighteen. His father no longer had any legal right to determine who might contact him and who might not. However, were I again to have sex with him before he was twenty-one I would still be breaking the law as it then stood. It

The Raven and the Jackdaw

was all a bit of a muddle. But in practical terms, I knew that if I were to get in touch with Alastair and his father discovered that, my life could still get very difficult.

I wrote Alastair a letter. A fan letter of sorts. I wrote that I'd heard about his arrival at the university and about his good fortune in being selected to take over from me in my old job. I addressed the letter c/o the university zoology department and wrote *To await collection – do NOT forward* on the envelope. I typed the envelope (though not the letter inside it) as a precaution: I didn't want my handwriting to be recognised, by remote chance, by Will or by the office staff.

I could have written c/o the Natural History Unit, but couldn't be certain how often Alastair would be going to Whiteladies Road before filming of The Square Metre got going in the spring. When it did our paths would inevitably cross in the canteen or in the corridors, but spring was months away – it wasn't even Christmas yet – and I didn't want to wait months.

Cautious I may have been about addressing the envelope but I threw caution to the winds in the letter itself. I gave the address and telephone number of my harbour-side flat. I ended the letter *With Love*. Then I sat back and waited, like an angler who has cast his line. I was prepared for the possibility that Alastair might not reply to my letter: that was his choice and his right. But I thought it extremely unlikely that he'd show the letter to his parents.

He did not. He rang the bell of my flat, and was standing outside the door when I opened it.

For a second we didn't know if we would touch each other. Shake hands. Hug and kiss. We just stood there. Then suddenly we hugged. Then we kissed. Out on the landing. 'The downstairs door was open,' was the first thing Alastair said. 'I just came up.'

I said, 'I'm glad you did.' Then, 'Come in.' He did. I shut the door. Then we were alone together, sharing the intimate space of my flat. We stood staring at each other. Neither of us knew what to say. We took refuge in a further kiss.

Alastair had grown, but not a lot. He'd been an inch or two shorter than me; now he was, as far as I could tell, exactly my height. Still slim and feather-light. Still blue-eyed and blond, of course. He was looking carefully at me, between kisses, looking for and registering the changes in my appearance just as I was clocking the changes in his. We wanted to know more. Soon we had our hands inside each other's shirts, checking the increased size of each other's nipples. Then those hands undid the fastenings of waistbands, undid zips and strayed into underpants…

'You've grown,' I said. I knew that I had too, but wasn't expecting him to register that. I'd only travelled the years from nineteen to twenty-two; he'd gone from fifteen to eighteen, a journey of a much more epic sort.

Somehow we were both clever enough to know that talking had to wait. We undressed each other wordlessly and took each other to bed. We did nothing more adventurous than we had done during those happy months nearly three years back. But I knew that if we were to go on seeing each other we might well want to at some future date. It was after we had both come hotly on each other's tummies that I took the private decision to have an aids test.

I got up and made us instant coffee, dealing with the boiling kettle naked – at some risk to myself. Then I hopped back to join Alastair beneath the duvet, from where we sipped our coffee like any couple enjoying a morning's lie-in, and then at last we did begin to talk.

I learned that one of my wilder surmises had been correct. Alastair's family had indeed moved away from

The Raven and the Jackdaw

Bristol in the aftermath of their discovery of what had happened between us. The father had taken up a new teaching job in Exmouth, and Alastair had been transferred to another school, with all the emotional upheaval that entailed, on top of everything else. I was horrified to think I had wreaked such havoc – and yet somewhere inside me a small rat-like version of myself was disgracefully pleased at the discovery that I possessed the power to wreak it.

More importantly, though, I was concerned about what had happened to Alastair after we'd been cut off. Had his parents made life tough for him? On the contrary, he said, they had tried to kill his memories of me with kindness. Spoilt him rotten: sent him to Switzerland on a ski-ing trip; that summer let him holiday with a wealthy French family who showed him St-Tropez and Paris.

'Did you enjoy all that?' I asked him doubtfully.

'Yes,' he said brightly. 'Very much. But it didn't make me forget about you. How could it?' He gave a thoughtful little laugh. 'But you?' he asked. 'You must have been very hurt. Or were you too grown-up for that?'

'Oh Alastair, sweetheart,' I said. Something huge inside me was beginning to ache. 'Nobody ever grows too old to be hurt.' I told him how, hours after reading his father's letter I had driven to London and thrown myself and my hurt at my brother. 'He comforted me wonderfully,' I said. I didn't go so far as to spell out the exact nature of that wonderful comfort. So there was no need to mention that Jason and I hadn't had sex together since.

'But now here you are in Bristol,' I said. 'Where I live and work. Your parents can't be unaware of that. I've been on the telly from here every week.'

'They weren't too happy about it,' Alastair said. 'But I'm eighteen. They couldn't stop me coming to Bristol on the grounds that I might run into you. But I did tell a bit of a lie. I said that it wouldn't mean anything to me if I did run into you. And that I didn't want to see you.' He gave my cock a firm, deliberate squeeze under the duvet as he added, 'Though of course I did.'

I wondered if there had ever been anyone on the planet so brave and principled that they'd never told such a lie to their parents. George Washington excepted, of course.

The discovery that Alastair had wanted to resume our relationship was deeply stirring. It was more than enough. I didn't imagine that he'd kept himself for me, in the sexual sense, for two and a half years and of course he hadn't. He told me about one or two of his romantic and / or sexual adventures. I imagine he was a bit selective. I know that, in telling him about my own, I was.

What was a bit difficult to deal with, though, was the information that he was currently sexually involved with one of his male housemates. He shared a house, as I had done, and it was only a few streets away from where I'd lived in Redland; I smiled when he told me that bit. I thought, though, that in terms of what was accepted or tolerated things must have changed even in the short time since I'd left university. And in spite of the aids epidemic. 'I hope you're being careful,' I said.

'Don't worry,' he said. 'We only do what we've been doing this afternoon,' he said. 'We don't do anything dangerous.'

'I'm glad,' I said. 'But for heaven's sake go on being careful.' Did that sound as though I was giving my blessing to his other relationship? I mustn't get ahead of things, I warned myself. Be thankful just for this afternoon. Regardless of my wishes the future would take its own course.

In the early evening we went out for a drink in one of the harbour-side pubs. Would people who recognised me wonder what I was doing, out with a first-year student? I found that I didn't care in the least.

Alastair came to live with me. He kept his room on at Redlands, returning there every day or two to pick up his post. He didn't tell his parents he'd moved in with me and I didn't blame him for that. Nor did I probe him as to whether he still had sex occasionally with the other boy who lived there. He spent all his nights and quite a lot of his free time with me, and that seemed to me quite good enough. Not every twenty-two-year-old gay man gets an eighteen-year-old boyfriend.

As luck would have it no foreign trips were planned for me between the time he moved in with me in November and the New Year. We had time to settle in together before the Christmas vacation inevitably parted us. And it was during that time that I took my aids test. Not in a rural surgery, with the bad news being given to me by a superannuated general practitioner, but in a purpose-designed new clinic. One calm and reassuring nurse (female) and one shining needle. I watched the small phial filling with crimson liquid and wondered anxiously what horror lurked in its opaque depths.

And then, throughout the longest fortnight of my life, I waited.

****

'I'm amazingly well today,' David announced. 'Take me to see the machines.'

'What?' James was cautious when David asked odd questions. One day, he feared, verbal communication would no longer work. David would have retreated into a different world. 'Machines?'

'Mother used to call tractors machines when we were little.' David laughed with a sound that scratched. It was

early September. 'I want to see some scenery. Can we go and watch?'

It meant a journey in the car, bundling David in with his sticks and blankets, but it wasn't really difficult.

'It doesn't feel the same, does it?' said David. 'These huge cutters. Remember the little grey Fergies and the Fordson Majors?'

James helped David sit down on the prickly yellow stems. The chilling early dew had gone and the ground was warm with the sun.

'It smells the same.' Green shoots pushed up at the base of the stubble. You didn't see them till the corn was cut. Soldier beetles crawled up them in pairs, engaged in the only pursuit that soldier beetles seem fond of. 'And it tickles just as much. You look happy, Raven.'

'Sorry.'

'I'm glad you do. That makes me cheerful too. It's an awful strain, knowing everyone around you is going to go all mopey.'

'It must be. I try not to be.'

'Well, I'm in a good mood today too. Sitting here watching the harvest. I remember watching the haymaking when I was five. Then I felt I was experiencing my last summer, with school – whatever that might turn out to be – lying in wait for me at the end of it. Whenever I dwelt on that thought it made me miserable. This time I almost certainly am seeing my last harvest and it doesn't make me sad at all.'

'You funny bugger. You're amazing. You really are.'

'Not at all. I've been through most of the black bit. Oh, I know there's more to come. And the end bit's going to be awful. But so it is for everyone, whether they die from brain tumours or bullets. OK, I'm happy today. Tomorrow I'll be frightened again and hurting perhaps. But the good times are better than they were a few months ago. Perhaps better than they've ever been. You

The Raven and the Jackdaw

must remember I've told you that. You'll need to remind me I said it, some day when I need a bit of encouragement.'

'Stop,' said James, and looked away for a moment.

'Sorry,' said David.

'Don't keep saying sorry like that.'

'Sorry,' said David.

'Living in the country always meant more to you than it did for me,' James began suddenly. 'I mean, when we were children. I liked it, of course. But I liked it for what I could get out of it. I enjoyed the fresh air and the freedom and on fine days I might notice it was beautiful. But I also resented the inconveniences – you know, no cinema, no buses. I missed my friends in the school holidays. I used to get bored. You never got bored. I don't think you were capable of boredom. That made me a bit jealous of you. You loved the country for its own sake, loved it on wet days as well as on fine ones. You made a friend of it as I never did. You knew the names of all the birds and the trees and the grasses. You knew where they lived and why. You knew what they were doing with their lives. It was all a closed book to me. Now of course I'm regretting all that ignorance. I look back on my country childhood... I look back on it and it seems as though I learnt nothing. I didn't know a linnet from a yellowhammer. But now I'm beginning to learn all that. My paintings are beginning to work – at last – and in part it's due to you.'

'Come on!'

'Well it seems like it. Now you can't do your work any longer mine has suddenly got better. Can you explain that?

David took a breath. Then he tried to. 'I suppose I managed to enter a different world for a few years. The Jackdaw became an actaw and Dad, if he were still alive, might grudgingly admit I made my point. I broke away from everything that had gone before… I mean I broke away from you, if you think I'm being oblique. I lived for my work with a kind of passion that would be ridiculous if it wasn't for the saving grace that I turned out to be quite good at it. I suppose I was ambitious. But that wasn't the main thing. It was the now I loved. I just loved acting, loved being on stage. I used to hate it when everyone clapped at the end of the evening because it meant I had to come down from where I'd been and just be me again. It was a strange world, that now. It really was now then. But now it's then. And I no longer miss it. I'm home now. For the last time. Perhaps for the first. The first time I slept with another man he said, "You've come home tonight, David." But I hadn't. Not really. You don't discover where home is till you've left it and come back. You did the same of course – by getting married.' David stopped for a moment. 'I'm being insensitive.'

'You're not,' said James.

'You must have regrets…'

'About Jenny leaving?'

'I feel very much to blame.'

'I know that. But it would have happened anyway. Your illness – my taking on the care of you – just provided the necessary push.' It was James's turn to stop. After a moment he went on, 'I suppose it's not my business but did you and Karen…?'

'No, Raven, we didn't. I won't have that on my conscience. So, if you were thinking you might ever…'

'I wasn't. Honestly,' said James.

The honestly seemed excessive, David thought.

****

That scene, the next to last chapter of my novella, got written – though heaven knows how I did it – during the fortnight during which I waited for the result of my aids test. During that time I continued to have sex with Alastair (though doing, in his words, nothing dangerous) and Alastair was lovely and gentle with me, knowing what I was going through but not upsetting me by talking about it. He had no need to take the test himself, he said. He knew what he had done and with whom he'd done it. He'd told me the details and I believed him. It wouldn't have cost anything – I mean it wouldn't have cost any money – for him to have got tested if we'd thought he needed it.

My results came, banally, like exam results, in an envelope. Which I opened in Alastair's presence. My test had proved negative. I wasn't going to die in the immediate future. If I wanted to fuck Alastair I could do so with a clear conscience. We celebrated the moment – it was in the afternoon of a day in early December – by doing exactly that.

Shortly afterwards I wrote the final chapter of my "novella". It was too late to let the Jackdaw share the clean bill of health that I'd been given. There was only one way in which the story could end, and I did the best I could with it. It would come over as unreal and sentimental, I guessed, but I was beyond caring. I was euphoric in the new knowledge that, unlike the Jackdaw, I wasn't going to die just yet. I wrote it in the spirit of someone who is giving thanks for his life. Giving thanks for Alastair's presence in that life. Giving thanks for the existence of my beloved brother.

TWENTY-TWO

You could call my brother Doctor Jason Whitcomb now and it wouldn't be a joke. That was his title now, and he had a salary to prove it. On the other hand he was still in training. It struck me, following Jason's career with a brother's concern and interest, that the training process of doctors was pretty well endless. It seemed like hill walking. You arrived panting but triumphant at the summit of your climb only to see a higher peak rising inexorably ahead. Jason knew by now that he wanted to work as a general practitioner. Yet the best part of five years' training still lay in front of him before he could accomplish this. Two years of very varied work in hospitals would be followed by three more during which he would work under close supervision in general practice. When I found myself thinking this process was very hard on my beloved brother I answered my concern with another one. Did I want my future GPs to be thoroughly trained or not? And besides, although Jason's earnings didn't quite match mine at the moment his salary would rise automatically during the next five years, which my earnings would not. When he actually became a GP – assuming he did – he could be assured of a good income for the rest of his working life. It was something that I, for the moment a freelance TV presenter and writer of magazine articles, could not necessarily expect.

Jason had been engaged to Anna for more than two years. In the coming spring they would be married. That gave our parents – especially our mother – plenty to talk and think about. And plan for. Had she not considered the activity indecently premature she would already have started knitting baby socks.

But Jason's impending marriage also focused Mum's attention on me, the son who wasn't about to wed. I wasn't very happy to be the target of this particular searchlight. 'You haven't brought a girl home yet,' she said to me that Christmas. 'You're very welcome to. You must have a whole entourage of female followers. Doing the job you do.'

'I do have fans,' I said evasively. 'And a few women friends. But I don't think of any of them as Miss Right – if that's the expression. If I brought just anyone here for you to meet... Well, you'd read too much into it, I know.' And so would the girl in question, I suddenly thought. Wildly I then imagined myself bringing Alastair home to meet my parents. Announcing that I was gay and that this was my eighteen-year-old lover... It was out of the question. The year was 1984. Homosexual acts had only been legalised seventeen years earlier. Even now they were still illegal if either of the consenting partners was under twenty-one and – believe this or not – if nobody else was present under the roof of the building in which the acts took place. My father had been born in 1919. I could not announce to him that I was homosexual and had an underage boyfriend to boot. He had fought in the war. He would have said that he hadn't risked his life, and seen his fellow soldiers die, for this.

My brother was a different matter. I chose a moment when we were alone together, walking down to the village pub, to say to him, 'Remember that boy I got into trouble over, a couple of years back?'

'I could hardly forget that,' he said. He turned to me with a very meaningful look. Its meaning was that neither could he forget the night we'd spent in bed together as a consequence.

'Well,' I said. 'Brace yourself. We're back together. He's a student at Bristol University now. He shares my flat.'

'Bloody hell,' said Jason. 'You don't believe in doing things by halves.' But he threw an arm across my shoulder in a manly sort of way, just for a moment, as we walked. It meant, I knew, that if things went pear-shaped I could be sure of his support.

'Not only that…' I went on. I told him how I'd managed to get back in touch with Alastair because of the extraordinary circumstance of his taking over from me as presenter of The Square Metre.

Jason found plenty of questions to ask. 'Are you being careful?' was one of them. I told him about the aids test: that the results had come back negative. 'I'm very happy to hear that,' he said, turning to give me a smile that was quite gorgeous. He asked me how old Alastair was now, and frowned when I told him, although he had probably already done the calculation in his head. 'You're still going to have to be careful,' he said. 'You're a high-profile TV presenter. At least you must be easily recognised in Bristol. Swanning around the place with a kid… People will always talk. Even the ones who say they won't. You could still come a hell of a cropper with the parents.'

'I know all that,' I said sombrely. 'I just have to look out for myself.'

We'd reached the door of the pub. Jason stopped. 'Are the two of you in love?'

'Yes,' I said.

'Then nothing else needs saying.' Jason pushed at the door and in we both went.

Jason was now working as a house officer at King's College Hospital in Denmark Hill. It was about the same distance from Stockwell as Guy's, only in the opposite direction. But he was released from time to time – sometimes for weeks at a stretch – to spend time at other hospitals which led the field in some particular area of medicine. He went to the Hospital for Tropical Diseases in central London – a secondment for which he needed a number of injections in advance – and he went to Papworth near Cambridge, a hospital where the most advanced heart surgery was being pioneered and carried out. ('It's really cutting edge,' he said. That wasn't my awful joke; it was his.)

At the beginning of February he phoned me up. He was being sent to the Bristol Royal Infirmary to observe new cancer treatments. We both managed to avoid repeating the cutting-edge joke. He hoped we could see something of each other while he was down there…

'Where are you staying?' I broke in to ask.

'Nowhere yet,' he said.

'Then stay with me and Alastair,' I said immediately. 'We've a spare room, remember'. Jason had been down once; he'd seen the flat. 'Won't cost you a penny. Don't say no, for heaven's sake.'

He didn't say no. We spent the rest of the phone-call discussing dates and arrangements. When we'd finished Jason said, 'Anna wants a word. I'll pass you over.' Which he did.

'Only to say,' I heard Anna's bright voice – a voice I liked, 'that I've heard about Alastair and I think that's lovely. I'm looking forward to seeing him on TV when his series starts next month. And in case you're wondering, no, I don't think eighteen's too young for you. He seems absolutely right. I'm so glad you can put Jase up when he's down your way. That sounds perfect. Anyway, I'll hand you back.'

Jase, I thought. Jase! I'd never called my brother that.

I told Alastair about the arrangement when he came in later. 'I hope that's all right with you,' I said.

'Of course it's all right,' he said. 'Quite apart from the fact that it's your flat. I've always wanted to meet your brother. If he's anything like you he must be very nice.'

'He doesn't look like me,' I said. 'Though we may be alike in other ways. I'll let you be the judge of that yourself. But he is very nice. I can vouch for that.'

The next day, quite by chance, I ran into Will Lumsden in the street. 'Oh good,' he said. 'You've saved me a phone-call. Have you time for a coffee?' He looked around among the nearby shops for a suitable place. 'There's something I'd like to discuss.'

Over milky coffees Will told me about it. There was going to be a book based on the Square Metre series. 'Ideally it will be written jointly by you and the new chap who's going to be presenting it from next month. It'd have both your pictures on the front. Alastair McNeil's the new chap's name. Have you met him yet?'

I couldn't help savouring the reply I made him. 'Yes, I know him. He's my boyfriend, actually. He lives at my flat.'

'Good lord,' said Will. 'Why am I always the last to know anything? You certainly kept that under your hat.'

'Only doing what you told me to, Will,' I answered with a poker face. 'Years ago, right at the beginning, you hammered home the warning that I needed to be discreet.'

Alastair was delighted when I told him. He would be getting an official letter in the post. In the meantime I was able to tell him about the money we were being offered and he was even more delighted when I spelt the numbers out. The time-frame wasn't too daunting. We had until October to finish our part of the job. The book would go to press quickly and be in the shops in the run-up to Christmas. We would have access to transcripts of all the episodes of the first three series, and the use of the BBC's secretarial services. There would be a supervising editor who would decide on the overall structure – chapter headings, what to include, what to leave out – and our job would consist mainly, it seemed, of licking sentences into shape. I was resigned to the fact that I would probably have to shoulder the brunt of the task. I was the more experienced presenter, the more experienced writer... I was the older one. Simple as that. I would willingly do more than half my share of the work if need be. I loved Alastair and that was all there was to it.

I was concerned, though, about the idea of our two faces appearing together on the front of the book. Were they thinking of having two separate photographs of us, small ones, perhaps, against a background of insects and plants? Or a great big double headshot? I was concerned for Alastair. What were his parents going to think when they saw that in the front windows of the shops? I was concerned for myself too. What would his parents do to me when they saw it?

I shared my anxieties on this front with Alastair. He was quite sanguine about it. He was four years younger than me; for him Christmas – viewed from early February – was still a long way off. 'Anything could happen before then,' he said blithely. 'Let's worry about it when it does.' I didn't like to say so but I was pretty sure we'd be doing that.

I was quite nervous when the moment came for Alastair and Jason to meet. Introducing the two people who meant the most to me in life... I was afraid they wouldn't take to each other. And when I wasn't worrying about that I worried that they might take to each other so much that I got left out of it.

Neither of those scenarios came to pass. Jason pressed the buzzer at the street door. I spoke, then let him in with an answering buzz. By that time Alastair had gone haring down the stairs. Seconds later I heard their chatter coming up from below, then they came into view, still chatting happily, Alastair gamely struggling with Jason's big suitcase. Jason, encumbered only with a briefcase and a supermarket bag, smiled at me and shrugged. 'He would insist,' he said.

While Jason unpacked I fine-tuned the cooking of the dinner that was already in the oven. I'd started it hours before. It was Lancashire hotpot with pickled red cabbage: something which Jason loved. Our mother used to do it for us. I was pretty sure that it wasn't part of Anna's repertoire. I incorporated all those extra bits that some people don't like: mushrooms, black pudding and kidneys. Alastair was happy with all of those and I already knew that Jason was. Happily – as I've mentioned before – he didn't allow his vocation to interfere with his taste for the cholesterol-rich.

After our meal we went out to one of the quayside pubs and passed a jovial end-of-evening. It was wonderful to see Alastair and Jason bonding so well and so easily. When we went to bed, all a little fuzzy, Jason in the spare bedroom and myself wrapped around Alastair, I drifted off to sleep with a feeling of great contentment, thinking that life didn't get much better than this.

Over the next week or so our evenings continued to be much like this. Alastair was out at lectures a lot of the time. When he was at home with me we worked together on the Square Metre book. Jason spent long days at the Royal Infirmary, but was always back at night. Me, I found myself in the role of house mother. When alone at the flat I pressed on with the Square Metre book on my own – I'd known that would happen and I didn't care a jot – and combed recipe books for interesting things to cook.

The Raven and the Jackdaw

In the middle of Jason's stay came the big day for Alastair – once again it was February the fourteenth – when he would face the camera for the first time in earnest. The first episode of The Square Metre, series four; the first one on his watch. He was anxious, of course, as well as excited and keyed up. 'What happens if there's nothing there?' he kept asking. 'What happens if that's the case?'

'There's always something there,' I said. I was the reassuring older hand at this.

'But how can you be sure?' he insisted.

'Well if there really isn't,' I said, 'just talk about the grass. Talk about the surface of the water in the pond. Anything you like.'

'I can't talk about grass for twenty-five minutes,' he said.

'Course you can. It's what actors call Doctor Footlights.'

'Adrenalin might be another word for it,' put in Jason with a knowledgeable twinkle in his voice.

'You can still count yourself lucky,' I said to Alastair. 'I once had to give a paper on snails' teeth.'

Jason and I were behaving like parents whose child is about to go to school for the first time, I noticed. I didn't say that to either of them but I was rather charmed by the thought.

On the morning itself I drove Alastair to Whiteladies Road. Jason – who actually had that day off – came with us in the Mini, hunched up rather, in the back. When Alastair got out Jason moved into the front seat. We tried not to watch Alastair's departing rear view as he made his way towards the studios' main entrance. We were getting even more like those first-day-of-school parents. Jason shut the door of the car, with the two of us inside it. 'What do we do now?' he said.

I laughed. Neither of us had given any thought to the day that lay ahead, so preoccupied had we been with getting Alastair ready for his first day's filming work. After a few minutes discussing the possibilities we decided to drive out of the city. We went to Weston-Super-Mare and had a bracing walk along the promenade beside the mud. As soon as we could do so without feeling silly we went into a pub and had a ploughman's lunch. But the charms of Weston are not at their brightest in February and by three o'clock, having admitted defeat, we were back in Bristol and back at the flat.

We stood in the living-room and looked at each other. Jason rubbed at the muscles at the sides of his waist. 'Stiff with all that walking in the cold,' he said.

'Perhaps I'd better warm you up,' I heard myself say. The words had popped, apparently unbidden, out of my mouth.

We used Jason's spare-room bed, although it was a single. Apart from my feeling that if we were to use the double bed I shared with Alastair I would somehow be being even more disloyal to my partner than I already was, there was the practical issue: we didn't want to leave telltale traces, stains or personal odours, about the place. In a nutshell, we didn't want to be found out.

I didn't even think of asking Jason, then or later, how he would square this with his conscience given that he was getting married to Anna in a couple of months. His conscience was his own to deal with. Mine already had enough on its plate.

Conscience or no conscience, we enjoyed this reprise of our carnal relationship. Three years had passed since we'd shared our bodies in this way in a bed. That last time too, Alastair had been the catalyst. Interestingly, though, Jason's physicality felt different from the way it had done when I'd last encountered it. Of course we'd

The Raven and the Jackdaw

both grown older and I, at any rate, was still growing bigger, but really, I well knew, it was my intimacy with Alastair, developed over the last few months, that was responsible for that. It was like the way your own car feels different when you return to it after driving somebody else's for a bit.

Alastair made his way home by bus. We weren't going to mollycoddle him that much. But we were all over him as soon as he got in. Back in the role of those first-day-at-school parents. How had it gone? Had he felt nervous? Had the square metre yielded up anything beyond water and grass?

Yes it had, he told us. There had been some big beasts. A squirrel had trotted across the square metre on its way to drink. A kingfisher had perched on one of the corner posts for quite a long time, preening itself. It had whistled as it had flown off. All this had been captured on film. Then there had been a good old rat. There had also been a beetle of a type that neither Alastair nor any other member of the crew could identify, despite poring over illustrations in the big reference books they'd brought. They had decided to be honest about this. They filmed the beetle. They filmed themselves perusing the reference books. Then Alastair, looking directly into the camera, had asked if anyone watching knew what it was. If they did, would they please get in touch? From memory he had given the Whiteladies Road address.

'Well done,' I said. 'I take my hat off.'

'Will there be thousands of letters?' Alastair asked a bit anxiously.

'Not thousands,' I said, drawing this knowledge from my own experience. 'A couple of dozen, probably, from kids – and nutters who've no idea what they're talking about. Then there may be one from a real expert. Two or three at the most. Somebody at the Natural History Museum… Or Will Lumsden himself, of course.'

Jason and I took Alastair out to a restaurant, like proud parents, to celebrate his first success. We spoilt him rotten that evening. We were also trying to make up to him for our betrayal of him – though it was mostly my betrayal of him – in doing something in his absence that he didn't know about. Yet.

When I went to bed with Alastair that night it felt different somehow. I'd taken the precaution of having a shower – I'd actually shared that shower with Jason – before Alastair came home from work. But the shower hadn't put everything right. I still felt like a louse. I hugged Alastair very tightly as we drifted towards sleep. Held him so tightly that it hurt – for both of us.

The next time that Jason had a day off there was no opportunity for us to repeat our misdemeanour of the previous week. I had an appointment to keep at Whiteladies Road. They wanted a progress report on the Square Metre book. Alastair was excused this meeting: he had lectures all day. I would be there on behalf of both of us.

'Help yourself to anything you want from the fridge,' I told Jason as Alastair and I left. 'Tea and coffee … well, you know where all that is. And if you find yourself sitting around with nothing on the telly, help yourself to anything you like from the bookshelves.'

In that last sentence lay my big mistake.

TWENTY-THREE

'You haven't got aids, have you?' was the first thing that Jason said to me when I returned to the flat. Alastair wasn't back from the university yet. Jason was alone in the living-room. I'd read the expression "ashen-faced" in descriptive works of fiction. Now for the first time in my life I found myself looking into an ashen face.

I felt my stomach clench in a knot. 'No. We talked about that at Christmas. What made you ask?'

He answered in a tone so neutral that it hurt. 'I read your book.'

'Which book?' I asked. I was stalling, playing for time, hoping against hope. I knew which book.

For answer he picked the hundred-page typescript up from the floor beside him and held it up.

'You weren't supposed to read that,' I said quite sharply. 'It's private. It wasn't in the bookshelves. It was in a drawer in my desk.'

'I was looking for stamps.' His voice continued to be toneless. 'I'd promised Anna a postcard. I remembered I hadn't sent her one yet.'

'It was private,' I repeated. 'It was in my desk.'

'It wasn't a letter,' Jason contested. 'The front page says "The Raven and the Jackdaw – a Novel – by Barnaby Whitcomb". A novel is hardly a private document. Though for a novel it's a bit short.'

I was angry with myself for writing the word novel instead of novella. I'd meant to write novella but when the moment came I hadn't been able to bring myself to type the last two letters. I was now beginning to get upset. I felt cruelly exposed and horribly embarrassed. I wished I'd never even written the book.

'Has anybody else read it?' Jason asked.

'No,' I said.

'Not even Alastair?'

'Not even Alastair.'

'Good,' said Jason. But I knew he wasn't going to leave it at that.

'Why did you ask about aids?' I asked.

'Because I was pretty sure you'd never had the experience of being told you'd got it. The way the doctor gave the news… The way you've written that is rubbish. We're trained in how to break bad news to people. We don't do it like that.'

'I had to…' I was going to say something like *I had to make that bit up* or *I had to guess* but Jason interrupted me.

'You weren't thinking of publishing it, I hope,'

Nothing was further from my mind at that particular moment. 'I might have thought about it…'

'Well, you can't. It's quite obviously about us.'

'I fictionalised a lot of it.'

'But not enough of it. You're a public person. You're on people's TV screens every week. I'm hoping to become a GP. I'd never get there if people knew I'd been portrayed like that in a book.'

'It is fiction,' I protested. 'People assume that novelists have made things up. Nobody thinks that Patricia Highsmith is a murderess or that Ian Fleming actually did all that stuff.'

'It isn't fiction,' said Jason. 'You've written about our relationship. Something that was just between us and very private.' His use of the word *was* cut me like a knife. 'But you've distorted it. You've distorted me, and everyone else you've put in the book. Our parents dead, for God's sake! Mother dying of cancer. It's too horrible to think about, let alone write about it in cold blood.'

'It wasn't our mother,' I said. 'It's a woman called Isabel who doesn't exist. Our Auntie Sonia died of breast cancer. I used that experience.'

The Raven and the Jackdaw

'Which is almost worse. You take reality and your warped imagination and mix them up.'

I thought that was what all fiction writers did – but this was not the moment to mention that.

'But it's the way you've written about me that's got to me the most.'

'It's not you,' I tried. 'It's a character called James.'

'Yes,' said James. 'A character with a name just two letters different from my own. A character who's exactly two years older than the main protagonist. With black hair and brown eyes. You've taken me as your model and twisted me – turned me into an uncaring idiot.'

'Uncaring?' Jason's use of that word had shocked me. There was nothing uncaring about James in the last chapters of the book.

'I didn't abandon you on your first night at boarding school for a start. You walked out of the dormitory in a huff.'

'That was because you'd said we couldn't sleep together. You may not have abandoned me but at the time it felt like it.'

'And the people who're going to read the book – the countless thousands you may have in mind – they're going to work that out? You've made me totally un-academic – which I was not. And an ignoramus about the countryside…'

'I've made James into a brilliant artist if that's any consolation,' I said in a take-it-or-leave-it voice.

'And why St. Andrews? Glasgow? Of all places.'

'I had a boyfriend called Byron who went to work in Glasgow as an actor. You knew I used to go up there to see a friend a few years back. St. Andrews because I liked the red academic gowns they wear on University Challenge.' I thought that might raise a smile from my brother and ease the tension a bit, but it did not.

'As for the ending – James spiriting David away to the farmhouse and surrounding him with all the choicest furniture – that's simply pinched from Howards End. You know, when the elder sister takes the younger one there after she's got pregnant and crazy Miss Avery has unpacked all their things and furnished the place…

'And talking of getting pregnant, to add insult to injury you have James's prick getting him into trouble and having to get married. When in real life it was *your* prick that nearly got you into trouble with Alastair's parents and the police. You're the one who's been careless in that way. Not me.'

'Sorry,' I said. 'But that part is fictional…'

'Well obviously it is. I know that. But imagine me as a GP in a few years' time. My patients wouldn't know what bits of the book were fictional and which were not. I'd be the doctor who knocked up a barmaid at twenty-one and whose brother wrote it up in a book.'

I said, 'I may yet be in trouble with Alastair's parents.' I hadn't brought this up with Jason yet, though I'd meant to. Now didn't seem a worse time than any other. I told him about the projected cover of the Square Metre book. I actually had some news on that front. The subject had come up at that day's meeting – which by now seemed to have taken place days ago. They were planning to use two separate mug-shots of us against a background of the square metre itself in close-up: grass and other plants with creepy-crawlies dotted about. (I'd guessed that right.) That was better than what I had feared more – a single photo of the two of us, arms around each other's shoulders perhaps – but it would still be enough, I thought, to upset Alastair's parents.

To my surprise Jason was reassuring on this point. 'If they use separate photographs then there's no proof that the two of you have even met. Technically, all that's happened is that Alastair has taken over your old job.

The Raven and the Jackdaw

Margaret Thatcher took over Jim Callaghan's old job. Pictures of the two of them appeared on the same page of all the newspapers. Nobody's ever suggested that meant that something was going on between them.'

I was surprised into a bit of a chuckle at that, and that did ease the tension a little. But a moment later Jason returned to the subject of my manuscript. He had laid it back on the floor again by now, which I was pleased about. By this time I wanted to do nothing more than pick it up from the carpet and tear it into shreds. I didn't do that. It would have looked absurd as well as melodramatic. (I didn't mind people close to me knowing I was gay but I would have hated to be thought camp.) But the bigger reason why I didn't do it was that it was already too late. The damage to my relationship with Jason had been done. He had yet to tell me the worst part of what he had to say, though I knew he was going to. It was coming towards me now, like a blast of icy wind with hail in it, or a massive cold wave of the sea that would swamp a boat.

'The thing is, Barney, the big thing is... You write about Jackdaw being in love with Raven. At the end of the book you hint ... and I recognise that it's no more than a hint ... that the Raven returns the compliment.' His tone softened. 'I don't want to hurt you, Barney, but you must learn to see the difference between love and hero-worship. And between love and sex.'

I felt my lip begin to tremble and my chest start to shake. At that moment I heard Alastair's key turn in the lock. Alastair came in and saw us. There was Jason, sitting gaunt-faced in the armchair. I was standing across from him, with tears rolling silently down my nose and cheeks.

Jason moved out two days later. He found a cheap hotel near the Infirmary. He only had four more days left in Bristol anyway by then. He said he was afraid of outstaying his welcome with us and 'cramping our style' as he put it. I told him he was doing nothing of the sort and practically begged him to stay. So did Alastair.

Alastair could see that something had very suddenly gone dreadfully wrong between Jason and me. He'd been astonished to see me in tears on his return to the flat that day and had immediately said, as anyone would, 'Is everything all right?' Jason and I had rather ridiculously tried to cover up. Jason picked up the manuscript, rolling it into a tube before Alastair could see what it was, got out of his chair and went over to the desk to replace it in the drawer from which he'd taken it. While I said that we'd been discussing an incident from our family history and got unexpectedly caught out by our emotions. Alastair had the grace to pretend that he believed that and we all busied ourselves very promptly – too busily and too promptly – in preparing for supper.

Jason and I tried to be bright and normal with each other over supper and afterwards but for all our acting skills – and I had once thought that mine were considerable – we failed to convince Alastair. In bed that night, wrapped in my arms, he said, 'If you want to tell me what's gone wrong between you and Jason…' Then quickly added, 'But no problem if you don't.'

'I will one day,' I said. 'Maybe not just at the moment. It's just that he read something I'd written and it upset him. It'll blow over. Storm in a teacup.'

But it didn't blow over. The atmosphere remained tense and the day after the next one Jason left the flat. On his last day in Bristol I phoned the Infirmary and left a message, asking if he'd like to meet us that evening for a parting drink. Perhaps he didn't get the message. He didn't reply to it at any rate, and so left Bristol without saying goodbye to us. The next time I saw him was two months later. At his wedding. We didn't have much in the way of a private chat.

A week after Jason's departure from Bristol I decided I was being unfair to Alastair, keeping him in the dark about what had happened. I told him in bed – the place where we tended to share our most intimate confidences – that I had written a short piece of fiction that involved two brothers. I'd written it for my own amusement, and had no thought of trying to get it published. It had no literary merit. By chance my brother had come across it and read it. He had thought it must be about himself and me and – although I'd assured him it wasn't – had taken great exception to it.

'He must have taken very great exception to it,' said Alastair. 'To hardly speak to you for two days, then flounce out, and not even say goodbye when he left Bristol. Whatever did you write in it?'

'A bit difficult to explain,' I said. Actually it would have been easy to explain. Just dreadfully embarrassing.

What Alastair said next was exactly what anyone would say if they were in his position. 'Can I read it?' Stupidly I hadn't realised that he was going to say it.

'I suppose so,' I said, taken aback. 'But read it some time when I'm not around the place. It's in my desk. Third drawer on the right.'

'I know where it is,' said Alastair. 'I saw Jason put it back there after I interrupted your discussion about it.'

That was that. A week passed during which I didn't know if Alastair had read The Raven and the Jackdaw or if he hadn't. Either way, he said nothing at all about it. But then came the day – this time it was my turn to come back to the flat from somewhere I'd been to – on which I knew he'd read it. He was sitting in the living-room watching television. But when he saw me he jumped up at once and switched the screen off. He turned to me, and the look on his face was almost identical to the one

I'd seen two weeks earlier on my brother's. I knew then that he'd read my story and that we were in for a re-run of the scene I'd had with Jason.

'I've read your story,' Alastair said.

'Yes,' I said despondently. 'I can see you have.'

'It's very sentimental,' he said. 'It's like *The Country Diary of an Edwardian Lady* with aids added.' That bit really hurt. 'And it's not very well written. The ending's mawkish. But the thing is … Jason was right. It's so obviously about you and him. It's no wonder it upset him. But it's told me something else about you. I mean about you and Jason. The two of you have sex together.'

I felt my skin prickle hotly. 'Umm… When we were kids…' I tried to begin to say something that would soften it. To lie in other words. But he cut me off.

'That day I spent filming. When I came back I thought the two of you were behaving quite weirdly. The way people behave when they've had sex together and are trying to pretend they haven't. I thought, no, it's impossible. I'm imagining it. And I tried to make myself go on thinking that in the days that followed. Even though it was difficult. Because you seemed so close. Closer than normal brothers. Closer than you'd been when Jason first arrived in Bristol. Now I know I was right. It's in your book. You've simply sublimated it, cleaned the act up. No sex, just emotion and – your word – love.'

Which cut me like a knife.

I sighed. 'I don't know what to say. It's true. We used to have sex together. It was a long time ago, though. But yes, we did do it that day when you went filming. We were feeling happy because it was your big day. Like two proud parents. We got a bit carried away… We shouldn't have.'

'In our bed?' Alastair asked, ignoring my apology.

'In Jason's.'

The Raven and the Jackdaw

'Out of concern for my feelings?! That was jolly decent of you, I must say.'

'I've said I'm sorry. Anyway, it won't be happening again, if that's any consolation. You saw what happened between Jason and me after he read the story. In any case, he's getting married.'

'Hmm,' said Alastair, ignoring that. 'Don't think I'm blaming you. You or Jason. I'm no saint either. I've occasionally had sex with Alan since I moved in with you.'

I sort of knew this. Alan was the housemate that Alastair had slept with before he'd come to live with me. Alastair went back to Redland to collect his post quite often. I'd chosen to turn a blind eye to what else he might do while he was there. I said, 'I think I knew that. Don't worry about it.'

'Thank you,' said Alastair. 'Look, as I've said, I'm not blaming you for anything. It's just that I've got this nasty feeling inside myself now – and it won't go away – about you and Jason. It's like a pain somewhere in my middle.'

'Sorry,' I said. Sorry isn't the hardest word, it's the easiest. The hard bit is to make it work miracles for you. It wasn't going to do that on this occasion. We looked at each other in silence. We were still both standing. 'Look,' I said, 'if you'd like to move out for a bit – I mean back to Redland – to have a think about things, I won't mind. Come back when and if you feel like it.'

'I don't know,' Alastair said uncertainly.

I said very softly, 'Will you kiss me?'

I didn't know if he would, but he did. Rather thoughtfully and slowly, and we stayed standing as we did this – for quite a long time actually – swaying a bit and once or twice nearly losing our balance.

Then we tried to return to normal. Made tea. Watched TV. Had supper. Went to bed together. Made love rather desperately.

Over the next few days things became easier. We seemed to have patched things up. The day was approaching on which Alastair's first episode of The Square Metre would be broadcast. I was looking forward to watching it with him and was planning to shell out for a bottle of champagne to drink together while we watched it. (It had been homemade beer for my first episode, three years earlier.) Then Alastair dropped a bit of a bombshell. 'My parents are insisting they want to watch the first episode with me.'

'What?' I said. 'They want you to go all the way to Exmouth for the evening?'

'Not exactly. They're planning to book a hotel for the night in Bristol. To come and watch the programme with me at Redland.'

'Oh bloody hell,' I said. But I could hardly argue. If someone's parents wanted to show their pride in their only son on such a major occasion it would have been churlish of anyone to find fault with the way they chose to do it. But I couldn't possibly go over to Redland and join them. I'd have to watch the programme on my own. I wouldn't be drinking champagne, though. I'd save that for when Alastair came back later. 'You will come back afterwards, I hope?'

Alastair made a maybe sort of face. 'I don't know. They want to take me out to dinner afterwards. Then I imagine they'll drive me back to Redland. It'd be a bit late to…'

'Yeah,' I said. 'I can see that.' But I said it with a heavy heart. By this time I knew exactly what the score was, and that Alastair was trying to let me down gently. When the day came I did watch the programme on my own. I did drink champagne with it. I drank the whole

The Raven and the Jackdaw

bottle. Alastair didn't come back that night. He never came back again. At least, not as a lover, not as a partner. He came to the flat sometimes when we needed to put our heads together over the book we were working on. It was all very civilised, and very friendly. He'd stay for tea or coffee and a chat, but not for intimate conversation or for sex.

And so I came to realise, albeit slowly, letting myself down gently as the weeks passed, that through doing nothing more than write a book in which I'd incautiously worn my heart on my sleeve a bit too bravely, I had managed to lose the two great loves of my life in the space of a fortnight.

TWENTY-FOUR

The final chapter of that fateful novella. Heart on sleeve. Though I guess that one man's heart on his sleeve is another man's mawkish. At least that was what Alastair thought of it. Anyway, here it is.

****

It was dark. Isolated lights appeared among the fields below. Did one of them belong to Hundredhouse? The plane was sliding imperceptibly lower and the lights drew closer together as roads, villages and towns coalesced to become London. Mary saw Windsor Castle float beneath. Moments later wheels had lightly kissed tarmac.

James was waiting at the arrivals gate. He looked thin and careworn; a different, older, figure from the one Mary had seen in the spring and she wondered if he would see a similar alteration in her. He drove in the same careless way, though, one hand lightly on the wheel, and she was pleased to find him unchanged in that.

The light was on above the front door; the crumbling brick path caught your heels in the same old pot-holes, and you still had to duck under the familiar overhanging apple bough before you went in at the low, wide door of the farmhouse. The same pictures hung on the walls. They had never hung straight. They never could, for the upright wall-posts were neither straight nor at right angles to the ceiling, and the floor was not level either. But among the familiar old pictures were some new ones. Mary looked at them closely.

'I'll get along now,' said the old woman who had been sitting by the fire, knitting, when they came in. 'He's been asleep most of the time. No trouble at all.'

The Raven and the Jackdaw

'The runner beans are frozen,' said James when they sat down to eat. 'From the shop. Remember how Dad used to salt ours down for the winter in those earthenware crocks? He never believed in deep-freezes. For him progress stopped exactly where he wanted it to on any given occasion. Cars were triumphs of engineering but electric toothbrushes decadent. Anyway, the rabbit is local. Remember that child at Kingsbank? He's grown up enough now to shoot. You may find a few pellets.' They started to eat.

'I don't want you to think I'm doing a lonesome hero act down here or anything like that. I get out. Up to London to see friends and things like that. The neighbours are all great.'

'The stew's excellent,' said Mary. 'I never knew you were such a cook.'

'I'm not,' said James. 'There's a whole bottle of plonk in it.'

They finished their meal and James began carefully to dissect a small joint of rabbit and to cut up potatoes and beans. They went upstairs, James leading and carrying the tray, and turned into the smallest of the three front bedrooms, the room the brothers had shared as boys. It was clean and smelt fresh. Most of the finest ornaments and furnishings in the house, Mary saw, had been brought together in this room. James must have painstakingly sorted and chosen the things with which David was to be surrounded. She was touched but also a little disturbed by the thinking that seemed to underlie it. She thought of the pharaohs entombed with wealth and beauty uselessly around them. It was a thought that grew to a chilling intensity when she saw David.

He lay on his back in a wide bed, between immaculate, unruffled sheets. He wore a neat, closely trimmed beard and his hair looked cared for, the neat brown curls forming a fine frame for the face. But the face was mask-

like even now and death played hide-and-seek among his features.

'Hallo, Mary,' David said, waking quite suddenly. 'Have you come to talk about salvation?'

'Sense of humour unaffected, you notice,' said James.

Next morning brother and sister took a walk. The ground was hard and splintery with the deep frost that had been working on it for several days without let-up. Needles of crystal sprouted from every grass stem and every twig was defined with steely precision by a crest of ice.

'Those paintings were a surprise, James,' said Mary. 'No-one would think you hadn't been studying birds all your life. It's not just that all the detail is right; there's real life in them too. Each bird is acting in the way of its own species, wearing the right expression, almost thinking the right thoughts. You haven't just borrowed all-purpose birdlike poses to hang the shapes and details on. I've come to expect your work to be good – to be interesting as well as professional – but last night I was really surprised. I do think they're the best things you've done yet.'

'Thank you. They're actually beginning to sell now. I can't pretend I'm not interested in that aspect of it. There's lots of interest in them in the places that matter. And it's entirely due to him, of course.'

'To him?'

'To David. I started doing landscapes and stuff. Birds used to turn up in them but I didn't know the first thing about them. David taught me. I did a rather Christmas-cardy one of a blackbird eating holly berries, I remember. I showed it to him, thinking he'd be impressed. But he wasn't. It wasn't truthful, he said, and he asked me what the blackbird was doing in the holly bush. Eating berries, I said. But why was it there? Colour, I said, and composition, and I added a few more

The Raven and the Jackdaw

technical terms to impress him. He told me that holly berries are very bitter; that birds only eat them when they are nearly starving and that what I had produced didn't reflect that in the least. For him the picture didn't work. Then he used some jargon from his field of work to impress me. Motivation and so on. Yet I suppose he was right. He's made me think – no, feel – more what I'm doing. Perhaps he's helped in some other way too.'

'Like what?'

'I don't know. I can't explain.' James looked pensive for a moment.

'Well it seems to have worked, whatever it was. You never painted like that before.'

They trudged on across the frost for a minute in silence. Then James said, 'I'm glad you came. You came at the right time too. It's getting more difficult. He had a few days in hospital in October, but apart from that I've managed – with lots of help, of course.'

'You've done incredibly well. It doesn't get any easier for the professionals either, you know.'

James said, 'It was stupid of me to wait so long before telling you what was wrong with David. I thought you'd be shocked, ashamed, wouldn't understand it. My ideas about nuns were a bit out of date, I realise. It was only when I saw the article in the paper about your convent and the work you were doing...'

'You should have told me straight away. I could have helped you both quite a lot,' said Mary gently.

'Perhaps you should have told us straightaway what kind of nursing you specialised in. Then we could have...'

'Perhaps I should have. And I would have done if I'd known about David. But I wasn't sure about myself until I started doing it. I wasn't sure I'd be up to it. I needed to prove that to myself before going public about it. It *was a big challenge to face. Though I hardly need to tell you that.'*

'I had the challenge thrust on me. You rushed forward and picked it up voluntarily. Without any prompting.'

'Wasn't there? I don't seem to have been very honest with you. My credibility as a nun may wear thin with you soon, I'm afraid. I couldn't face explaining things to Dad. I was a coward. Mind you, I wasn't a nun at that time ... if you think that makes any difference ... I don't... But you think I was unprompted... I wasn't unprompted. AIDS was what Lawrence died of. I did have a motive.'

'Lawrence...?'

'Soon after we split up he drove his car off a bridge. He lived. But among the many pints of blood they gave him...'

'You needn't go on. I had no idea. Oh Mary, I'm sorry.'

'We became friends again. A different sort of friendship. He never really got well again. It all happened exceptionally quickly...'

*

A week later James brought a dead bird in from the garden. It was fresh and clean and frozen quite stiff. It weighed almost nothing. It was a redwing. James showed it to Mary. 'Strange birds, redwings,' he said. 'They're almost indistinguishable from thrushes until you see them this close. The same white breast, the same spots, the same brown back, but look at this one. You never saw so dazzling a white on a thrush, nor a brown so rich and chocolaty. Look at its head. It has a clear pale stripe above the eye where the thrush just has a jumble of freckles. And then, when you spread the wing – see – look at that glorious colour. All the under-wing is the colour of blood. I found another one dead last week. I read up about them. They live in Scandinavia and only

The Raven and the Jackdaw

come to Britain in the coldest winter months. And yet they're not even as tough as ordinary thrushes. Why this upside-down-ness? You'd think they'd live further south and come here only in the summer. Yet I find it fascinating. Strange, bright-coloured thing, arriving with such panache, such fecklessness in the autumn, then dying in the winter. It's so pointless it's breathtaking.'

'Maybe,' said Mary slowly, 'they come to teach the art of dying to a world that's nearly forgotten it.'

James did a great many sketches of the dead redwing. He worked with a concentration that bordered on the ferocious. The results, Mary decided, were both beautiful and workmanlike.

*

David was having one of his good days. James had just carried him downstairs. There had been snow in the night but sunshine filled the room now. Alec had telephoned for a chat from a world of bustle and urgency that David now had trouble remembering or making sense of. He found the chatter tiring but Alec not; it was the fact of the phone-call that cheered him, not its content. Now he was talking to Mary in the urgent way that, on those occasions when he was fully awake, was becoming more and more a part of his manner. 'Has James talked to Karen about you?'

'I've heard the name. I don't know who she is.'

'She was one of his girlfriends. While he was married. She was nearly mine but I had a headache. He doesn't bring her down here. He thinks I'll be upset. You must make him marry her.'

Mary laughed. 'You can't make people marry each other. And he is still married to Jenny, in case you've forgotten.'

'There'll be a divorce.'

'How do you know? She might want to come back.'

'She won't,' said David with conviction. 'He doesn't want her anyway. Don't let him rattle around here on his own. He'll go barmy.'

'I'll remember what you've said, but I'm not a dating agency.'

'Ring her up. Tell her...' David closed his eyes for a second, then reopened them. 'I'm tired now. I talk too much.'

'Then go to sleep.'

'Don't forget.'

'I promise.'

In the evening David had a temperature and complained of stomach pains. They got worse as the hours went by. Mary telephoned the doctor; James stayed with David. David couldn't keep still now and writhed in the bed. His face glistened with sweat and his eyes were wild and frightened. It seemed to James that he had been here before. This moment was not happening for the first time: David with him, those frightened eyes...

David was speaking now. 'What have I done? What did I do? Short life...'

'What have you done? Earned a living. Made hundreds – thousands – of people happy.'

'So? I was ambitious. More than you knew.'

'I knew.'

'I wanted to leave something. Children. Not be part of the family tree of a virus. Perhaps books. Not just the fading echo of a round of applause.'

'You'll have left me,' said James.

'Left you behind. I meant created.'

'I repeat: you'll have left me.'

'What do you mean?' David asked.

'Everything. And you may have more to teach me yet.'

'Don't understand you. Dying people allowed to talk riddles. You not.'

The Raven and the Jackdaw

James took David's hand in his. 'Back in the summer, when we sat in the stubble field, talking, you said something like, "I'm happy today. Tomorrow I'll be frightened again and hurting. But the good times are better than they've ever been." You said I might need to remind you that you'd said that – one day when you needed encouragement. Do you remember saying that?'

'Yes,' David murmured, then grunted as a spasm of pain ran through him.

James went on, 'Well, now it's me that's saying it. Tomorrow, or one day soon, I'll be frightened and hurting. It'll be your job to remind me that the good times are good.' In his mind James saw the frightened eyes of a badger in the winter hedgerow, its coat blood-matted, snarling, arguing with death. But the badger had calmed down when the gun was pointed at its head. It seemed to bow. Some of the terror left its eyes…

The doctor arrived. Mary beckoned James away from David's bed and took him downstairs. 'Are you sure you'll be all right after I've gone?' she asked. 'You may have a lot more of this to go through yet. Can you cope? Really?'

'Of course,' said James.

'You told me the other day that I was uncommonly ready to pick up a certain burden. Remember? Well, it occurs to me that so were you.'

'Perhaps. We always have reasons for doing things. Sometimes we know at the time what those reasons are, sometimes not till much later.'

Mary frowned. 'Can you elaborate?'

'This will sound callous, but in a way David's illness came at the right time for me. In the sense that I needed a break. From my job. From Jenny. I wanted to start again. It actually suited me – I'm being very selfish here – to bring David here and look after him myself. Everything else then fell into place. But there was

something else… There was another reason why I did it. I've only just started to realise it in the last few minutes… Do you remember a dreadful Christmas, a miserable Boxing Day when we were growing up, when David was sick at breakfast and he and I didn't speak for days?'

'Yes. I wouldn't have forgotten that.'

'David had told me he was in love with me. I couldn't handle it. We never referred to it again. We'd seen a badger horribly mangled in a wire. We had to have it shot. I'd forgotten about the badger. It came back to me just now, though. I kind of saw it…'

'I'm not quite following about the badger bit, but I'd sort of guessed how David felt about you. I didn't know he'd actually voiced it.'

'What I'm finding out now,' James went on, 'and it's a new thing for me, is that when he gets hurt → David, I mean – then I get hurt…' He stopped.

'Perhaps what you're trying to say is that you've grown up suddenly. Perhaps that's his legacy to you. In return, of course, you've given him back, briefly, a childhood that he never wanted to leave behind in the first place. The building-blocks that go towards what we call a grown-up. There were yours and there were his. Maybe not quite enough for both of you. So now you're inheriting the lot…' She changed the subject. 'I suppose you know that he'd like you to get it together with Karen?'

'He always did like things to be tidy.' James tried to laugh, but found himself crying instead.

*

'Just an ordinary little bug in the tummy,' said Doctor St-John. 'Like we all get from time to time. Plus a pretty hefty bout of panic. Nothing more than that. I'll have him admitted to Reading General in the morning as a precautionary measure but he should be home in a few

The Raven and the Jackdaw

days. Well… As you know, there's always a maybe. He'll be fine tonight, anyway. I've given him something to relieve the symptoms and something else to make him sleep.'

The Raven climbed the stairs slowly, alone. He stood for a long time in the Jackdaw's bedroom, looking dully at the dark window. The curtains had not yet been drawn shut. There was nothing to see except his own reflection, a thin, pale ghost, faintly superimposed on the blank night. The room was silent except for his own breathing and David's; the two were not quite in synch. At last he crossed the room and closed the curtains, shutting out ghost and night. Then he went back to the bed, touched his brother's brown hair, then very slowly bent and kissed his forehead. He looked for a while at the familiar face, now relaxed with sleep, and turned towards the door. There he turned back and called, 'Goodnight,' very softly before putting out the main light. A small light was left. A night light, that would burn dully through till morning light. In his mind a painting of a redwing was taking shape. Again he heard his breathing and his brother's. Two sets of footsteps travelling together, not quite in step. Then, as he still listened, one set of footsteps stopped.

TWENTY-FIVE

Jason's wedding that April could have been an agony for me. I went to it without a partner. I just had my parents. They were the bridegroom's parents too, though, and it was their big day because of him, not because of me, so I was very much an also-ran in family terms. I couldn't even comfort myself with my slender TV celebrity. Nobody is a celebrity at someone else's wedding. The bride and groom are sun, moon stars and planets, filling the sky. It's right that it should be that way. I tried not to be jealous.

Jason and I found that we were on speaking terms, and that was something. Not that we talked about anything deep or serious. Certainly not about the state of our relationship. We exchanged bits of brotherly banter during the few minutes we spent together. (I wasn't his best man: one of his medical student friends from Cambridge was.) I did manage to tell him, though, that Alastair and I had split up. He was kind enough to say, 'Oh God, I'm so sorry,' touching my forearm as he spoke, and I knew that he meant it. Whether it would cross his mind at any point afterwards that he might himself have something to do with the breakup I couldn't guess. It was good to know that we were friends still, but that only went a small way to counterbalancing my sadness at the knowledge that we could no longer be close.

What saved the occasion from being even more painful was a job offer I had had a few days earlier. It would involve several weeks filming in southern Spain, starting in a month's time. At the end of May. I jumped at it.

The theme of the series was wildlife that lived in towns and cities. From a purely scientific standpoint we could have chosen a selection of sites that included, for example, Corby, Loughborough and Crawley. But we

The Raven and the Jackdaw

didn't. We were going to Seville, Granada and Córdoba instead. The beauty of the places we visited would have no impact on the wildlife: the series would not be compromised in terms of science. But the viewers would be cheered no end by the scenery – it was sure to help deliver good viewing figures – and it would cheer us, the team who would fly down there, too. The weather would be better in Córdoba than Crawley. It would cheer me especially. I needed it. The knowledge of this impending adventure bore me up through Jason's big day. Thanks to it I survived the church service in Tunbridge Wells – that was where Anna's parents came from – and then the reception in a splendid hotel on nearby Mount Ephraim, whose grounds boasted views across half the weald of Sussex.

You couldn't fly from Bristol to Seville in those days. Even from London you couldn't fly there direct. We took off from Heathrow around four o'clock in the afternoon. To Santiago de Compostela on Spain's north-easternmost tip. There we went through Spanish immigration and customs and then re-boarded the plane we had disembarked from an hour and a half earlier. We flew down across a corner of Portugal and the un-peopled expanse of Extremadura in the dusk and then the dark. I managed to identify the Sierra de Gredos, which we passed just before night fell. I pointed it out to the sound man, who was sitting next to me, as the location of the film I'd made about lammergeyers. I didn't tell him how those syllables, Sierra de Gredos, had seemed to toll in my head like a bell. But I had only good memories of my time there. If a bell were tolling for me still ... perhaps it was a nice bell. Then the Sierra was behind us and night came down on Spain.

Seville at last appeared from nowhere like a Catherine-wheel of light. By the time we got to our hotel it was after ten o'clock.

The day had been exhausting. We'd eaten on the plane. My body clock was telling me it was time to go to bed. I'm sure the same went for everyone else's body clock but none of us was going to admit that. We were young (ish) and we were in southern Spain, a place where the evening did not finish, but was only beginning, at ten o'clock. Our director, Thomas, knew the city well, he said. He knew the oldest tapas bar in it. El Rinconcillo, at the end of Calle Gerona. He wasn't sure he could find the way there on foot in the dark, though. We took a taxi instead.

El Rinconcillo was everything we could have wanted at that moment. An oasis of light in a dark street. Inside were walls of azulejo tiles coloured blue and cream and chestnut. Above the tiles the walls were a comforting yellow ochre. Wooden lattices closed off the view into the kitchens as in a Moorish harem. Massive bar counters had the prices of our rounds chalked on them in front of us. There was no question of sitting. We stood at the bar in a lively din of chatter that rose in volume as time went on, and in a fug of blue cigarette smoke that also thickened during the evening. We ordered tapas of all kinds and drank Rioja.

There were five of us. Thomas, the director, was a new boy on the block. He'd been head-hunted from Anglia Television in Norwich. The sound engineer was someone I'd worked with before occasionally: an Irish chap called Fergus. The fourth member of the group, the cameraman, was someone I knew slightly better. He was Nick, with whom I'd descended a cliff-face once – in the Sierra de Gredos – and had held him for comfort on the way down and on the way back up. I hadn't forgotten that he'd also rubbed my thigh once when I was lying in bed after being shaken up by a fall a few days afterwards. I had worked with him a few times since, although not very often. He hadn't been the cameraman on The Square Metre, though he had been the first cameraman I'd ever worked with – on my first two nature garden slots, in Bristol and at Slimbridge. The fifth member of the group was a young man called Tim. His job title was production assistant. One of the reasons he'd been chosen for this assignment was his fluency in Spanish.

When we were filming away from Bristol we were put up in nice hotels – except for the rare occasions when we were in the middle of nowhere, as we'd been when filming bustards in the shadow of the Caucasus mountains, and had to sleep in tents. And usually, in those nice hotels, we were given a single room each. This time however, there had been a bit of a hitch. The hotel we'd been booked into turned out to have only three rooms available by the time we pitched up. Rather than make a fuss or try to find somewhere else late in the evening we agreed that two of us would double up. Nick and I had known each other longer than the other three, so we volunteered to share a twin-bedded room for the night.

We were hardly aware of each other's company in the end. We had both drunk copiously. We tumbled into our separate beds, turned the lights off and went to sleep at once. When I awoke in the morning Nick had already gone down to breakfast, having turned the bed down very neatly, I noticed, in order to air it before the chambermaid took it all apart.

We had come to Seville in order to make a programme about the lesser kestrel. It's a rather rare species. It looks much like an ordinary kestrel except that it's smaller – as you might expect. It's also much more vocal, mewing and yapping to draw attention to itself, and unlike its larger relative it is social. A large and long-standing colony lived among the pinnacles and belfries of the cathedral in Seville – itself one of the most impressive buildings, and the largest Gothic church – upon the planet.

The BBC, thanks to its high international standing, reaches the parts that ordinary mortals can not. So doors were opened to us – in the most literal sense. We found ourselves squirming through tiny portals that were normally kept locked, through gates as narrow as arrow-slits. They led off spiral turret staircases, or were accessed along dark corridors between inner and outer walls of stone – secret corridors that were themselves normally shut off. We stood on sloping sheets of lead and zinc, amidst carved spikes and finials that were normally viewed only by steeplejacks, by the kestrels themselves and, so the medieval master masons believed, by God.

The kestrels were surprised to see us emerging onto the floor of their world from subterranean regions they could have no concept of. Surprised but not unduly alarmed. They kept a wary distance from us, but were not as distant as all that. Getting close enough to film them was not too difficult, at least in that sense. On the other hand the spaces we were moving in, around and through were hostile. We all had to be contortionists. We also had to be extremely careful as we moved. None of us wanted to be the one who fell from a hundred-and-fifty-foot-high roof. As I had done years ago when filming lammergeyers on their cliff-side nest I thought of my brother, remembering how he had found the courage to scramble over the school roof, and used that memory as the driver to screw my own courage to the sticking point.

It is easier to be brave when not alone. I was lucky in having not only the memory of my brother's long-ago

The Raven and the Jackdaw

exploit but the very real presence alongside me of Nick. If he could reach out along a ledge to film a promising scene, then I could slide along the same ledge to turn and face the camera and comment on it. If he could wriggle his way through a tortured crevice in the stonework then I could also do it. I could do no less. I was slightly smaller and thinner than he was in any case.

We could have walked back to our hotel easily after our day's filming, but because of the expensive equipment we had with us – and because of its bulk – we took a taxi the short distance through the narrow streets. I had assumed that by the time we arrived back at the hotel the previous night's accommodation mix-up would have been sorted out. I guessed that Thomas would have done something about it. But he hadn't. He apologised profusely. He said he'd assumed that Nick and I would have sorted the thing out. He shouldn't have made such an assumption, he said. He was in charge and should have shouldered that little responsibility himself, or at the very least asked his assistant Tim to do it. Nick and I both laughed at him and said it really didn't matter. We had spent the whole day virtually rubbing shoulder against shoulder. It wasn't going to worry us if we found ourselves adopting a similar position for a second night.

In fact our shoulders were going to be even closer together than they had been the previous night. We discovered when we went upstairs to clean up before going out to eat that someone on the hotel's staff had taken it on themselves to push the twin beds right up together. We burst out laughing when we saw this. 'They must think we're a couple,' said Nick.

'Do you want to help me pull them apart?' I asked.

Nick sighed. 'It's hardly worth the bother,' he said. 'Unless you really want to. I'm OK with the way it is.'

'So am I, in that case,' I said, thinking no more of it.

Nick was married. I'd seen his pretty wife a couple of times when she'd come to the studios, and I'd met their kids. They had a pair of twins, one boy, one girl. Lots of people, when told this, would ask facetiously if they were identical. The joke must have worn a bit thin for Nick by now but he had a very tolerant, sunny disposition and always laughed gamely, warmly, when the silly question was asked.

I had seen the twins once. They were two years old. Other people's children stay the same age in your mind if you don't see them often and so it was with a shock that I learnt, when I routinely asked after them in the course of that evening, that they were in their first year at school. We were standing together at the thronged bar of La Rinconcillo, We had got separated slightly from the other two by the jostle of the noisy crowd and the blue mist of cigarette smoke. 'You started young,' I said with a little laugh.

Nick pulled a face. 'Not that young. I was twenty-four when I got married. The twins came along a couple of years after that.'

'So now you are…?'

'Thirty-two,' Nick said.

I made the only possible answer. 'You look very good on it.' Though it was true. He did.

'And you?'

'Twenty-two,' I said.

He smiled mischievously. 'And you look good on that.'

Actually I was going to turn twenty-three in a fortnight; I was looking even better on it than he thought. I didn't tell Nick that. I raised my glass of Rioja. 'Cheers,' I said.

We were pretty tipsy by the time we went to bed. Once there we were indeed very close. Simultaneously we clicked off our bedside lights. I said, 'Goodnight. Sleep tight.'

Nick didn't respond to that. Instead he said, 'I was very impressed by you today. Scampering about on that roof. Cool, calm and collected...'

'I only did that because you did,' I said. 'You're the cool, calm, collected one. I just saw your example and tried to live up to it. I wouldn't have done that by myself.'

'Thank you,' Nick said. His voice had changed. It sounded very soft, yet suddenly emotionally charged up. That was the first moment at which I guessed – dared tentatively to guess – what might be going to happen next.

It happened at once. I felt Nick's bare arm come round my bare shoulder: his warm skin on mine. I placed the palm of my hand over the back of his as he palmed my chest. 'You're very sweet,' Nick said. His voice was very quiet.

Duvets had made this situation marginally more comfortable than used to be the case with sheets and blankets. There was only the crevice between the two single mattresses to be careful of. We were careful of it. We each ran a hand exploringly down the other's chest and belly till we encountered the other's tingling erect cock. At that point I climbed boldly across onto Nick, a pirate boarding a captured merchantman, and we started to kiss.

Later, after we had brought each other to a climax and Nick had mopped us both up with a corner of the sheet I stayed in his bed, waking just often enough, for a second or two each time, to understand that Nick was cuddling me through the whole of that night.

In the morning we found it difficult to leave the bedroom. We couldn't stop kissing each other while we were shaving and dressing and, even when those preparations were complete, every time we made the self-denying decision to head for the door and the stairs we found ourselves going back for more physical contact. My head was telling me this had been a one-night stand and, given that Nick was a happily married man and a father, could never amount to anything more than that. But the intense experience of these morning-after minutes in the bedroom seemed to be giving the lie to that piece of knowledge. I was experienced enough to know that mornings-after were not usually like this.

Despite the delays we were the first of our party to arrive at breakfast. Though Thomas arrived a minute later. He saw us and came over to the table but didn't sit down with us at first. 'I'm going to talk to them at reception before I join you,' he said, leaning over. 'I'll get you separate rooms for tonight. Sorry about…'

Nick stopped him. 'It's all right. We're happy with the way things are. No change of arrangements required. Do you get our drift?'

Had he said – Do you get *my* drift? – Thomas might not have done immediately. But the *our* drift did the trick. Thomas tried not to look flabbergasted. 'Oh, right, guys. I see. Well, OK, then. Nothing more to be said.'

'Especially back in Bristol,' Nick said smoothly, and Thomas nodded his acquiescence as he sat down with us. I admired Nick's sang-froid. Cool, I thought, was probably the English word for it.

It is seldom possible for a new relationship to move seamlessly from a first experimental sexual encounter into honeymoon mode. Yet that was exactly what happened in our case. Usually one of you at least has to go out to work, if not to return to another home that's miles away for a matter of weeks. The practicalities of adult life nearly always see to this. But for Nick and me…

The Raven and the Jackdaw

Quite by chance, or by stroke of fate, we were gong to spend the next few weeks in each other's company for almost every minute we were at work. We would be eating together – with the rest of the crew of course – and drinking in the same bars after work was finished. We would also be sleeping together, I knew, because Nick had boldly staked that claim when he spoke to Thomas at breakfast. We had already discovered that we were comfortable with shaving together, side by side at the wash basin and smiling at each other in the same mirror; happy to stand side by side admiring each other when we pissed. The only minutes during which we'd preferred to keep a shut door between us were those when we'd needed to defecate.

Whether our new and surprising relationship would survive this twenty-three hours and fifty minutes per day proximity, though, would be another matter. Many a relationship foundered on it; that was common knowledge. I could only shrug my shoulders inwardly. Wait and see, I told myself. And because I was in Spain – although the phrase isn't really Spanish – *Que sera sera*.

Because I was in Spain. Because I was in a beautiful place. Because Nick and I both were. This must have helped. We spent the next few days in Seville. Again crawling around the leads of the cathedral roof in pursuit of ever better shots of the kestrels that flew around us and mewed and yapped. We grabbed hold of each other often while we were doing this. Our fear that the other might fall was mostly imaginary: a pretext for frequent physical contact. But that itself was a cloak for a deeper fear: the fear that we might lose each other in a less physical sense. It was too wonderful to be true, we thought, and we clutched at the experience, as we clutched at each other, afraid – terribly afraid – that it was a dream as insubstantial as a cloud that would evaporate.

We climbed towards the clouds inside the Giralda – the Moorish minaret that was now the bell tower of the cathedral – and peered down from among the bells at the birds that flew beneath, skimming the glossy tree-tops inside the courtyard of the oranges. We roamed the back streets and the crumbling Roman walls of the old city filming the lives of the resident black redstarts – they are birds resembling and related to robins, mainly black in colour but with strikingly bright red tails. And all the time, all through that charmed week, the sky was a heavenly blue above us. And where the jacaranda trees were blooming, in the Gardens of Murillo and around the Gate of Jerez, their airborne florets made the sky look even bluer than any sky ever was.

Having arrived in Seville by plane and, when not on foot, we used taxis to get around the city. We hired a Range Rover for the rest of our Andalucían odyssey and crammed ourselves and our equipment into it. We headed out from Seville eventually along the road to Granada. Along the same route that Washington Irving had taken a century and a half before, though we travelled it more quickly and in greater comfort. And in better weather. Irving made his journey in April and it rained a lot. We made ours as the cuckoos that called everywhere were changing their tune from two notes to three, while May changed up a gear into June. It made all the difference.

Granada meant the Alhambra. That wonder-of-the-Moorish-world palace, or series of palaces, on a cypress-grown hilltop. The place that Washington Irving had made famous after he lived there and wrote his collection of magical tales about it. Alhambra, I knew, meant *the red one* in old Arabic. But though the oldest surviving block of the rambling fortifications is indeed

The Raven and the Jackdaw

red my impression – formed then, during my first exploration of the place, and reinforced by memory and by many subsequent visits – is of whiteness: of a magical filigree artefact carved out of whalebone or ivory. I was still only twenty-two. I had never seen anything more beautiful in the whole of my life.

The series we were filming was all about nature. But it had a sub-text, which was about beautiful buildings and beautiful landscapes – the man-made backdrops against which nature did its stuff – and we cheated those into it. We filmed the Alhambra. We strolled in its scented courts after the tourists had departed. We recorded the frogs that sat smiling and barking on water-lily pads in its basins and fountains. We filmed the swifts and the humming-bird hawk moths, the kites and the falcons, the painted lady butterflies, and the scarlet flowers on the pomegranate trees that were the symbol of Granada. I was doing all this with the man whom I slept with, the man I was falling in love with and who was falling in love with me. And I was getting paid for it. I could have imagined nothing more perfect.

During those heavenly days in Granada we stayed in a hotel that was tucked away among the very buildings of the Alhambra. Tim, the production assistant, had phoned ahead to change the single rooms that had been booked for Nick and me for a double. That room was beautiful, old and beamed. The door into the bathroom, an old one made of chestnut, had a sliding hatch in it, through which the person inside the bathroom could communicate with anyone on the outside of it. Nick and I played with this like children. When I remember that room now I see and hear Nick and me laughing.

If I've created an impression of Nick and me at work together, scrambling on rooftops and roaming courts and alleyways filming, just the two of us, that may be misleading. Fergus the sound man was always with us and so was Thomas. Tim the production assistant also was quite often, though sometimes he was elsewhere, fetching or buying or arranging something, ironing out little local difficulties in his fluent Spanish. Yet the impression of just Nick and me together is not a false one. That is how I remember it all these years later. Nick and I together, just the two of us. Sometimes the truth lies deeper than the facts of the situation that surround it.

Long before we left Seville Nick and I had got to know each other's histories. Even on the morning after we'd first slept together Nick had said to me when we were back in the bedroom after breakfast, 'You're hurting, aren't you? Something's happened to you recently. I noticed the change in you last month. One day when I bumped into you at the studios.'

'You were watching me even then?' I answered. I was taken aback but also flattered.

'I've always been watching you,' Nick had said, smiling. I told him about losing Alastair. That startled Nick. He hadn't known that Alastair had been mine in the first place.

'That's good,' I said. 'It means there are still a few people around the place who can keep a secret.'

'We may live to be glad of that,' said Nick thoughtfully.

It was difficult to explain how I'd come to lose Alastair without explaining about my brother. I prevaricated. 'We split up because I'd written something – a sort of private diary – which he read, and it upset him. I think that's all I can tell you for the moment. Maybe when I know you better…'

'You don't have to tell me anything you're uncomfortable with,' Nick had said gently. 'I'm not the Spanish Inquisition.'

The Raven and the Jackdaw

From Granada we drove down from the mountains and along the valley of the Guadajoz to Córdoba, where we filmed – much of the time by night – the colonies of bats that inhabited the Moorish wonder of that city – the Mezquita. The vast building's forest of horseshoe arches, with its cathedral plonked incongruously in its centre (like the gingerbread house, I've always thought, in the story of Hansel and Gretel) hardly needs describing these days. Anyone who hasn't been there and seen it can simply conjure up a picture of it on Google.

On one of those nights in Córdoba, after filming the noctules in the cathedral's belfry, we'd gone to bed at four in the morning but still weren't ready for sleeping. Nick and I exchanged a few more of the confidences that lovers do in the early stages of sharing their life histories, talking about previous sexual experiences. These days we'd progressed from ambiguously twin-bedded rooms to frank doubles. It made the sharing of those confidences – like the sex we enjoyed together – that much easier. Nick told me on this occasion that he had once had sex, while a teenager, with one of his male cousins. He hoped I wasn't too shocked by the information. I said I wasn't. Then I took my courage in both hands and asked him if he was ready to hear the reason why Alastair had left me. To hear what I had written. 'But be careful about saying yes,' I warned him. 'It's a bit of a Pandora's box. It caused Alastair to give up on me. I don't want the same thing to happen…'

Nick, who lay already with his hand around my shoulder, now squeezed it. 'It won't happen. I won't give up on you. Whether you tell me you've committed a murder or shagged your brother.'

'I haven't committed a murder,' I said. I could already feel the relief pumping into me like morphine. I told him the whole story. By the time I'd finished the sun was rising.

'I'd like to read it one day,' Nick said. 'That's if you'll let me.'

'I'll let you,' I said. Suddenly I burrowed my head into his chest and armpit and started crying. 'Oh Nick,' I said, 'I love you.'

We are all radioactive parcels of outgoing love. Remove one object and we beam out to another one. It's surprising then, given that love is such an abundant commodity, that we manage to be so bad at handling it.

Nick sighed with his whole body. 'Thank God for that,' he said. 'I love you too. I thought you'd never say it.'

June again. You've already had twenty-two Junes without knowing what they were. But this one you're going to appreciate and in the years to come will long to escape back into. In your fond memory the palm trees will grow taller and greener, the sun warmer, the sky bluer, and the Raven's – Nick's – grin wider as he peers down from the hay cart at you – peers across the cathedral roof at you – from a distance measured in galloping years. And the image will grow ever more vivid as time leaches the accidents of mundane reality out of it and leaves you with... With what? With the essence of a smiling face, sunlight on his black hair, and a sky of the deepest, hottest blue.

The Raven and the Jackdaw

TWENTY-SIX

I wrote in The Raven and the Jackdaw about the melancholy that tinged the rapture of those days in June just after Jackdaw turned five: a melancholy induced by the knowledge that he would soon be at school. I returned to the thought when I described the fictional Jackdaw's last summer of life, conversing with his brother James in a reaped cornfield. It wasn't a new or original thought. After all, it is a part of everybody's life experience. It was mine that June of 1985. And it was Nick's. The glass of our days was emptying. Our tour of Andalucía was running out. We clocked up Baeza and Jaén. We filmed eagles and snakes. We did the palm groves of Elche, full of lizards and mice. We went to the hottest place in Europe, – the frying-pan of Europe – the town of Écija, where terrapins cooled off in the water beneath the river bridge. Then it was back to Seville, to return the hired Range Rover and spend one last night before catching the plane back. Back to Heathrow. Back to Bristol. Nick to return to his wife and children. Me to my empty flat.

'It's not the end, it's the beginning,' Nick kept reassuring me. But he was having to repeat the mantra about thirty times a day by the time we got to the end of our tour. It was easy for me to want to keep things going, difficult for him. I had grave doubts about the truth of what he was saying; that was why he had to keep upping the dose by repeating it.

I won't dwell on the misery of that parting at the studios in Whiteladies Road. It was as painful a parting as I'd experienced in my life. Especially as Nick's wife, Lois, was there with the children, full of joy at seeing Nick again, to witness it.

There was still no email in 1985 for most people, and no mobile phones either. Communication between pairs of people whose relationship was secret remained difficult. The saving mercy for Nick and me was that we were both employed at Whiteladies Road. We might not meet there every day, but we each had a pigeon-hole there, and could write each other notes, which we sealed, of course, in envelopes. It was back to the days, nearly four years earlier, when Alastair and I had left notes for each other between bricks near the school gates.

You don't know someone truly, perhaps, until they've put their thoughts about the two of you into a love letter addressed to you and you have read it. I won't quote from Nick's. Suffice it to say that they were long and beautiful. We didn't exchange them every day – we didn't go to Whiteladies Road every day. I know that Nick thought my letters to him were lovely: he told me so. I thought his were gorgeous.

We had already agreed that we would work individually at the task of getting work on another new series that would take us abroad, or at least a long way from Bristol: of working together again, and sharing hotel rooms, and continuing our relationship from the point at which we'd had to break it off. It meant, on my side at least, taking someone very senior into my confidence, and asking for their help. With great apprehension as to his response I told Will Lumsden about Nick and me over lunch with him and Jeffrey one Sunday. I told him of our plan: that working together away from prying eyes was our only hope of continuing with our relationship.

'But he's married,' Will said.

'I know,' I said. 'But we're in love.'

Will sighed. 'And that sanctifies everything?'

'I know what you're thinking,' I said. I felt my heart sink.

'What about Alastair?' Jeffrey asked gently.

The Raven and the Jackdaw

I said, 'I'm afraid we split up. He's gone back to the house-share he used to have. He's in a relationship with one of his house-mates.'

'Young people,' said Will. His tone was more sorrowful than collusive. 'And what about the book?'

'Don't worry about that,' I answered, glad to be able to say something that would please him. 'We're still good friends. There's no animosity. We're still working together on it.'

'Well, that's something, I suppose,' he said. He frowned for a moment at the bottle of Beaujolais that stood on the lunch table, then he reached for it and topped my glass up. 'Back to your request for help. Getting you and Nick contracts to work together on future projects. I can't promise anything. But I'll see what I can do. Have discreet words in discreet ears and see if anything comes of it.' He looked at me across the table warningly. 'No promises.'

The university wound down for the summer vacation. Alastair divided his time between his parents' home and Bristol. When he was in Bristol it was to make episodes of The Square Metre and while he was doing that he also came to my flat – that had not long ago also been his flat – and we worked in a friendly fashion on the Square Metre book. And when he wasn't there I was at a bit of a loose end. I had no new TV projects to keep me occupied. I wrote ever longer love letters to Nick, and tried a few magazine articles, which I sent around to various publications on the off-chance. I travelled to London a few times, catching up with Byron (he still had his lovely partner) and with my brother and his wife. They all knew by now that I'd split up with Alastair. But I hadn't told any of them, yet, about Nick. I even spent a couple of weekends with my parents. Though I told them even less. All of them had seen the new presenter of The Square Metre doing his stuff on TV. All of them thought he was doing a splendid job, was a worthy successor to me, and looked deliciously nice. All of them. Even my father, who had no idea who Alastair was. Although he didn't actually use the words deliciously nice.

I saw Nick only once in all that time – I mean during the long, university vacation, summer months. We found we were going to be at Whiteladies Road on the same day – thanks to our note-in-pigeonhole correspondence – and arranged to coincide there. Then we went down the road together to a pub where we had a very quick pint. It was an exquisite torture. We didn't dare risk touching each other. We managed a quick kiss – though nothing else – in the gents'. We talked. That was something. And we could smell each other, which was unexpectedly good. But Nick couldn't stay out long. Lois would be wondering where he'd got to and question him about it. I asked him, had he never before had dalliances with men, during his seven years of marriage? He'd answered this question before, when I'd asked him it during one of our first evenings in Seville. No, he'd said then, and he repeated his answer now. Not since he'd been married, though he had done before that. But since he'd married Lois, no. I was his first.

I had to make do with that small nugget of comfort after we parted at the pub doorway and I walked back alone to my flat.

But in mid-September I got a phone-call from the studios. They wanted to make a series about the wildlife of southern France. Would I like to front it? I said I would. I hoped against hope that they'd engaged Nick to be the cameraman, but on the phone at that moment I could hardly ask. I wrote Nick an excited note.

And got one back. Yes, it looked as though we would be going to France together in the autumn. He thought the focus would be on the Camargue marshes – in other words, the Rhone Delta. *That means wild horses and*

The Raven and the Jackdaw

mosquitoes, I wrote in my note back. We would see each other at the first planning meeting. With any luck have a drink afterwards. I added, *It's my turn to buy the next pint.*

But before the planning meeting could happen, something else did. My mother died suddenly of a massive stroke.

Over the years I've met a number of professional fiction writers. More than a couple of them have told me that an uncanny thing can happen after you have written a novel, say, or a short story. It tends to come true.

Not the whole thing, obviously; not every brick and stone of the construct. Just bits of it. The trouble was, those writers told me, that you could never know which bits would come true and which would not.

'So if you wrote that your main character won millions on the football pools you couldn't guarantee that the same would happen to you?' I queried facetiously. This particular conversation took place before the National Lottery was started up.

'I can't say that it wouldn't happen,' replied my interlocutor with a poker face. 'But, no, you're right. You couldn't guarantee it.'

It isn't a very remarkable thing, actually, to foretell in fiction the death of your own parents. You don't need a lot of precognition to foresee that. But, all the same, my mother's death did send a chill down my spine; I really had written of it in The Raven and the Jackdaw, and dwelt at some length on it. The chill on the spine was mingled, however – and I'm glad to say this – with a very real grief. I'd always known that I loved my mother deeply. It took her death to make me realise just how much.

Of course I left Bristol, and Jason took leave of absence from work, to help Dad organise things at home.

The funeral came and went, and then Jason went and, a few days later – because the planning meeting for the new series was imminent – I went. Dad was left to fend for himself, just as Hector had been in my novella. Of course I would return soon, I said. Once the planning meeting was over. To see how he was getting on. Though after that I would be away for several weeks, I knew: filming with Nick in the south of France.

In the Raven and the Jackdaw I had written, about Hector's reaction to his wife's death: *It made a nonsense of his life and he found no purpose in it afterwards.* I was only human: I couldn't help remembering that and wondering how much time my real-life father had left.

I had to ask Nick a question. We found a brief moment alone together between the planning meeting and the all too brief visit to the pub afterwards. I just heaved the question out. 'Do you still sleep with Lois?'

'Sometimes,' he answered. He must have seen a look on my face that I failed to hide quickly enough because he added appeasingly, 'Not very often, though.'

It was like being told by a friend that although he sometimes murdered people he didn't do it very often. Well, all right, it wasn't really like that, but for a moment it felt like it. I had no right to feel aggrieved. Nick was married to Lois and intended to remain so. He'd made it clear to me quite early on that he wouldn't be leaving her or divorcing her for my sake. Those were the terms of our relationship and I'd accepted them. Strictly speaking I was the bad boy anyway. I'd proved a temptation to a man I knew was married and when he gave way to that temptation I'd not only gone along with him (instead of telling him, as a morally upright person was meant to, to leave me alone and stay faithful to his wife) but had managed to fall head-over-heels in love with him as well.

The Raven and the Jackdaw

I hadn't had sex with anyone in the three months since we'd come back from Spain. But that wasn't because of any great moral rectitude on my part. Alastair hadn't wanted to rekindle the sexual element of our relationship. Had he done so – and turned our book-writing sessions at my flat into sex sessions – I would most happily have gone along with that. It just so happened that apart from with Nick and Alastair, I didn't want sex with anybody else.

Well, I did, of course, but that person was recently married and had as good as told me that he didn't love me, so I couldn't entertain that thought.

Alastair and I finished the Square Metre book just before I set off for France. As I had anticipated, I had done most of the work, but I didn't begrudge Alastair that. We handed it in the day before I left. 'Like a university essay,' Alastair said.

The team I travelled with was almost the same as the one I'd gone to Andalucía with. Nick of course, then Thomas the director and Fergus the sound man. The only difference was that the production assistant was not the Spanish-speaking Tim but a Francophone chap called Josh. Happily he was just as easy to get along with, and there was a convivial, almost family, atmosphere in the Land Rover as we set off. Except for the sea crossing we drove all the way to the Camargue. Bristol to Portsmouth. Ferry to Le Havre. Then, after skirting Paris, straight down the road the French know as the motorway of the sun to Provence, to the town of Arles, which was to be our base. We all did a share of the driving. I was deliriously happy – despite the recent death of my mother – because I was back together with Nick. It was the beginning of October and my happiness was only increased by the experience of the weather's growing perceptibly warmer and sunnier hour by hour as we headed south after Paris. I couldn't wait for bedtime – for the moment when I would have Nick all to myself. But *I couldn't wait* is a formulaic expression that, if you trouble to examine it, actually means almost the opposite of what it says. Because, of course, I could wait and I did wait, and the waiting itself, like all kinds of sexual longing, all kinds of emotional longing, was almost the best part. Almost, though not quite. Because when it did come to bedtime that was itself wonderful, and went on being wonderful throughout the night. Right through till morning, when it was time to get up, have breakfast, and go to work.

Say the word Arles and the next two words that will come into your head are probably Van Gogh. Many of the buildings in the town that he painted have been demolished, in separate acts, in what seems a wantonly vandal series of strokes of fate. But still the town seems pleasantly haunted by the painter's presence. The countryside around the town is the same countryside that he painted. The October sun that blazed for us in the sky like a yellow torch was the same sun that shone forth from his canvasses – those southern paintings that have you reaching for your dark glasses because the colour and the power of them is so intense. It didn't cross my mind at the time that what would happen that evening had anything to do with the influence of Van Gogh. But now, looking back, I find myself thinking, though perhaps too lazily, too tidily, that it did.

We drove that day to the area of the Camargue that is a site of such special scientific interest that most mortals can not enter it. But once again, those magic letters BBC had unlocked the bureaucratic gates. We filmed the water. We filmed a swarm of dragonflies that was so big and dense that the insects turned the air to gauze, got entangled in our hair, dropped into our pockets, and dimmed the sun like an eclipse. We filmed flamingos, we filmed egrets... And on this very first day Nick got the shot of the trip – the one we'd all dreamed about but didn't dare to think we'd actually get. A herd of wild horses entering deep water at a gallop and plunging through it, sending up multiple plumes of spray as big and violent as you might see in a hydrofoil race.

The white-maned horses, wild Camargue horses, ploughing through water, tails flying, manes waving among the jetting water founts, are one of the great clichés of the artist's or the photographer's things-to-do list. The image has been reproduced to infinity and sold in Boot's. Yet clichés become clichés for good reason. Clichés become clichés because they are born beautiful and good.

That image of the horses galloping, swimming, through water that came up to their necks, stayed on my retina throughout that day. So strongly was it lodged there that I found it difficult to concentrate on anything else. Nick filmed flamingos, I talked about flamingos, but all the time I carried the vision, and the energy, of the horses in my head. By evening I knew I must do something to discharge that energy, to release myself from the vision's spell. No sooner had we arrived back at our the hotel than I dragged Nick out to an artists' materials shop and bought a block of cartridge paper, a set of pencils of different degrees of hardness, and an India-rubber eraser (just in case...). Thus I found myself fulfilling another cliché, conforming to a stereotype of which the town of Arles had taken full advantage. Presumably because of the impact that the Van Gogh connection had had on the mindsets of generations of visitors it was full of artists' materials shops.

Nick watched me as I drew, sitting behind me in our hotel bedroom, fondling my shoulder occasionally – my left shoulder, obviously: I was drawing with my right –

and occasionally nuzzling my neck with his nose and forehead.

I spent an hour and thirty minutes on my sketch. It wasn't very good. It didn't live up to the original image on my retina. (Though better artists than I could ever be have told me that no work of art ever does.) But Nick, who had no idea that I could wield a pencil at all, was enormously impressed. Though much of that, I know, had to do with the fact that we were in love. 'Can you do a sketch of me?' he asked.

To tell the truth, I wasn't even sure myself that I could wield a pencil. Much earlier I mentioned that my brother and I were both good at drawing when we were kids. That was why I had chosen to turn the fictional James into an artist in my novella. But neither of us had kept this activity up. Our skills, such as they were, had not been developed through effort and practice and had probably, I guessed, grown rusty through lack of use. In the circumstances then, I had probably done well to produce a sketch of such an ambitious subject as a herd of horses at all. I should perhaps have been satisfied simply with that, without bothering about whether the sketch was any good or not.

I think I shared most of these thoughts with Nick before I answered his question. 'I haven't tried to get the likeness of a human face for years,' I said. 'It might come out really awful, and then you'd be upset.'

'I could make a point of not looking at it till it was finished,' Nick said. 'I'd let you decide whether it was good enough to show me. If you didn't like it you could simply tear it up without showing me.'

I though Nick's terms were reasonable. I said I'd sketch his face. 'But not today,' I said. I felt a bit drained after my intense effort. It was time we joined the others and went out for something to eat and drink.

The Raven and the Jackdaw

Later that evening Nick dragged the others along to our room and showed off my wild horses sketch. Of course they all said it was excellent. They could hardly have said anything else.

We did get bitten by mosquitoes. Though we took all the precautions we could. The hotel had provided gauze screens – they were stacked in the wardrobe – which we put up at our windows while we slept. We sprayed ourselves – sprayed each other in Nick's and my case – so thoroughly with insect repellent that the fumes of it got up our noses and made us sneeze and cough, but still the creatures got through our defences, and when they pierced us with their infernal mouthparts it really hurt. They were double the size of the mosquitoes we had already learned to dislike in England, and their bites were nearly as painful as the stings of wasps. The pain would return to surprise us at intervals, for a minute or so each time, even after several days had passed. That we then filmed the giant mosquitoes in close up, as they reproduced, and as they hatched from their pupal shells at the surface of water pools that lay still and stagnant out on the marshes, did not seem revenge enough. That I knew their names in Latin still did not help.

We did not confine our explorations of the marshes of the Camargue to the area of outstanding scientific interest at the centre of it. We visited farmsteads that were scattered about the vast flatness of the delta. We went to small remote towns: one was Les Saintes Maries de la Mer, at the end of a lost-looking road to the sea, and another, a little way inland, Aigues Mortes. The town of "The Holy Marys" was so-named because of an ancient legend that had Mary the mother of Jesus and Mary Magdalen, among others, arriving there by boat, in exile following the death of Jesus on the cross. While the name of medieval-walled Aigues Mortes meant dead waters in old French. A name that sounded sinister enough even without the overtones that our Anglophone ears were bound to find in it of mosquito-borne ague and death.

One day, walking through waist-high grass between two watercourses we came across a semi-derelict small house, approached by a narrow track. We couldn't resist looking inside it, the five of us. Sleeping Beauty's castle in miniature, we thought. It wasn't beautiful in its current state, though it could have become so if someone mad enough to want to live in this remote and desolate spot among the mists and winds and mosquitoes, had wanted to do it up. I felt Nick take my hand unexpectedly as we moved from one abandoned room to another. 'They'd probably let us have this for a song,' he said, equally unexpectedly, his look into my eyes at that moment clearly excluding the others from the thought. 'We'd be all right here.'

It wasn't I that said that; it was Nick. It was the first time he'd ever mentioned the idea of the pair of us living together, even as an escapist fantasy – which this was: I had no illusions about that. But all the same a thrill ran through me when he said it. I didn't spoil the moment by saying anything silly and complicated. (What about the winter? What if we needed a doctor in the night? What about Lois? Are you thinking about divorce?) I simply showed that I accepted the fantasy and liked it. I said, 'Yes,' simply, and was rewarded by another squeeze of the hand from Nick.

That evening I did my sketch of Nick. I'd spent some time observing him even more closely than I usually did, and wondering how I would accomplish this or that little challenge to my technique: eyelashes, say, or the corner-folds of the eyelids. This preparation paid off. The sketch was better than the one I had done of the horses.

The Raven and the Jackdaw

It was good enough to show to Nick. To my relief he liked it too, and showed it off to the others later with pride. It's quite a feather in your cap, after all, if someone takes the time and trouble to do a portrait of you, however simple, without being paid for it.

In the middle of another night in the hotel in Arles I awoke with a start. Nick had leaped on me, wrapped his arms around me tightly, and was gibbering something in what sounded like fright.

'What? What?' I asked.

'There's a thing in the bathroom,' he said. 'It's on the ceiling. With inch-long whiskers at both ends and about a million legs. I think it's a scolopendra. They can kill you with their bite.'

A little learning is a dangerous thing, though to be fair to Nick, although he didn't have a degree in zoology, he had learnt more than a little about the animal and plant kingdoms in the course of his job: he actually knew a lot. The scolopendras are a branch of the centipede family. Some are frighteningly big and – Nick was right about this – can deliver a very nasty bite. In southern climes they have an unpleasant habit of concealing themselves beneath the rims of lavatory bowls.

'It's OK,' I said. 'Stay here. I'll go and have a look.'

As I walked naked across the cold marble floor of the bedroom towards the bathroom I became particularly conscious of the nakedness of my feet. I peered through the doorway into the bathroom – the light was still on, as Nick had left it. I saw the creature on the ceiling, immediately above the cistern. It was exactly as Nick had described it: it was about the size of a small cigarette, though it had a pastry-brush arrangement of whiskers at both extremities that nearly doubled its length. I switched off the bathroom light and reported back to the bed. 'It's all right,' I said. 'It's not a scolopendra, though it's in the same family. It's called the house centipede in English. Their mouths are too weak to pierce human skin. They live on woodlice and things. I've left it where it is. It's nothing to worry about.'

We cuddled each other, seizing the excuse of Nick's fright. I didn't think he was as frightened as all that, though. I remembered the night of the thunderstorm when, at the the age of six, I'd first climbed into bed with my brother, and I smiled quietly to myself.

After I had gone back to sleep I dreamed, extremely vividly, that Nick and I were riding at a gallop across the Camargue on big white stallions, bareback. There were other people riding with us, but Nick and I rode the fastest, and we had the biggest, fieriest mounts. We soon left the others behind and were dashing excitingly through mountain passes, making our way towards a high peak, beyond which a vast expanse of country lay spread out below us…

I wouldn't need to read Freud on the meaning of dreams to interpret that.

In the morning the house centipede had gone. Nick was mildly worried by its disappearance. He looked behind bits of furniture, and pulled pictures away from the walls, squinting behind them to see if he could find out where it now lurked.

'It's gone,' I said. 'Forget about it.'

'Yes, but where's it gone?' Nick said, on his knees now, pulling up a mat. I laughed at him, and he laughed back at me after a moment. This was what living with somebody meant, I thought. Living with Nick. I couldn't get enough of it.

The Raven and the Jackdaw

TWENTY-SEVEN

Parting from Nick on our return from France was not quite as difficult as it had been when we'd come back from Spain earlier in the year. We were surer of each other now and had had the foresight to make a few plans for the future. We had been assured that many further foreign trips were already in the pipeline. While Nick, who did a good deal of other camera work on projects that did not involve me, decided that he would invent a few additional jobs that would take him away from Bristol overnight. The invention would be for the benefit of Lois only. He would spend those fictional nights away with me at my Bristol flat. He thought that he could probably get away with doing that nearly once a week during the gaps between our genuine foreign trips. And in addition to that he would get into the habit of staying behind after work at the studios for a drink with his colleagues before setting off for home. Other men did that routinely and their wives accepted it without much fuss. Why shouldn't he do the same? he said. The mates he stayed behind to drink with would be me, of course. We could meet up two or three times a week in this way. Either in a pub or – if time allowed – at my flat. In a difficult situation these arrangements seemed about as good as things could ever get. I would be seeing Nick almost every day and, with luck, having sex with him, and sleeping with him, at least once a week. We put all those plans into operation immediately on our return to England that autumn and, despite our fears that theory might not easily mutate into practice, it did.

'Can you paint?' Nick asked me on one of our first evenings together at my flat.

'No,' I said. 'Or perhaps I should say, I don't know, because I've never tried.' Nick smiled at that. 'I mean, I used poster paints at school during art class, as I'm sure you did. But that's about it.'

'I was thinking,' said Nick, 'that paint is simply a medium, a technique. You've already got the talent. That was clear from those sketches you did in Arles.' In addition to the drawings I'd done of the horses and of Nick's face I'd done another one of him, this time a full-length nude portrait. 'I'm simply thinking of your future income,' he went on. 'And what you might do between filming jobs now that the book's finished. To keep you out of mischief.' He reached across my thigh and playfully squeezed the place in my jeans-clad crotch where he thought my cock might be. He got it wrong, accidentally squeezing one of my bollocks by mistake and making me yelp, but it was the thought that counted.

'Thank you for the thought,' I said when I'd recovered. It was a good thought. I was making what I considered very good money, and had been since before I'd left university two years before. But I was earning on a freelance basis. And every freelance worker lives like Damocles on the throne of Dionysus, waiting for the sword to drop.

'It'd be another string to your bow,' Nick said. 'I was thinking about Sir Peter.' He was referring to Peter Scott, who was very successful as a wildlife painter as well as being a broadcaster and naturalist.

'I'd have to learn to paint,' I said. 'Go to classes or something like that.'

'Exactly,' said Nick. 'But you've time on your hands now. You've got the money... You've also got the background and the contacts. Thanks to your TV fame you're having a book published. I'd have thought you could easily sell paintings of ducks.'

'Ha-ha,' I said. But I took Nick's suggestion to heart. I made enquiries at the public library. I asked colleagues

The Raven and the Jackdaw

at the BBC and at the university. A week later I was enrolled for an evening painting class.

I would have expected my father to die before my mother did. For various biological and lifestyle reasons that is usually the case. I had also assumed that my mother, when drawing up her will, would have left my father everything she had. Jason had made the same assumption, I discovered when the matter came to be discussed after her death. It was not something he and I had previously talked about. We did know vaguely that our mother had more money in her own right – family money, that is – than Dad had. But that was another thing we never talked about. So we were in for a surprise when, after Mummy died, the terms of her will came under the spotlight. Jason and I made the discovery that she had set aside a substantial sum of money for each of us.

A decade and more of runaway inflation was just coming to an end, though at that time no-one could be entirely sure of that. People who had trusted to savings-account interest to keep their nest-eggs intact had seen those savings wiped out. The only kind of asset that had seriously increased in value in recent years had been real estate. Jason and I found that we needed quickly to make a decision about what to do with our mother's gift to us. There was no question of leaving the money in the bank and making leisurely and informed decisions about what to do with it at a later date. Safe as houses is a cliché that must date back a good few centuries. In 1985, to Jason and me, it seemed to make complete sense.

As luck would have it we heard about a pair of cottages for sale one village away from where Dad lived, where we'd been brought up. They were old farm cottages, about two hundred years old, of weathered red brick, with tile-hung upper storeys. They had been labourers' "tied" cottages in the days before mechanisation did away with the need for all but a tiny number of farm staff. They were halfway down the track that led to the farm where, years ago, Jason and I had witnessed a trapped badger being shot: one of the real-life incidents that had made its way into the Raven and Jackdaw book. You could see the farmhouse's gables through the trees a couple of hundred yards away

The cottages were an attached pair and quite pretty, almost chocolate-boxy, to look at. One was called Holly Cottage, the other – for God knew what reason – Burnt Oak. Not many years had passed since estate agents stopped describing rural properties of their sort as modernised or un-modernised, code for whether they had indoor bath and toilet facilities or not. This pair of cottages had been modernised – in that sense. Both cottages had indoor bathrooms and lavatories, as well as Rayburns in their kitchens. This "modernisation" had taken place in the late forties, we guessed. Nothing much had been done to the cottages since.

Jason and I went together to look at them, along with Anna and Dad. Our mother's legacy consisted of two separate though identical sums. We were under no obligation both to use this money in the same way, let alone to buy a pair of attached cottages, becoming the owner of one each. But we did. The opportunity was there, arising at exactly the right time, and it seemed to make perfect sense. Jason bought Holly Cottage and I bought Burnt Oak. Having bought them we rented them out. Because neither of us lived nearby we did not want the hassle that went with being hands-on landlords. We put the matter in the hands of a local estate agency, accepting the fact that they would take a substantial cut of the rent. We could shrug our shoulders about that. Neither of us was desperate for the income. The important thing was to have something made of bricks

The Raven and the Jackdaw

and mortar that either of us could if necessary realize as cash – or even live in – if at some point in the future things went wrong for one of us.

This, my first adventure in house buying, brought me back into contact with Jason quite often over a period of a few weeks and the contact was friendly enough. While I no longer felt I could fully open myself up to him I did feel able to tell him that there was a new man in my life, and who he was. To my surprise Jason told me that he knew what Nick looked like. 'About ten years older than us, with straight dark hair; your sort of height but stockier. Same nose as I've got, but broader in the face.'

'How do you know that?' I asked, astonished.

Jason reminded me that, just occasionally, the cameraman in my series had appeared on camera himself. It was one of those things we liked to do on nature programmes. The director or production assistant might aim a video camera at Nick while he was filming me, or even catch him with the big camera when he wasn't. He was part of the team, the thinking went, so why shouldn't he have a few moments of on-screen presence? 'I noticed him because he was rather handsome, to tell the truth,' said Jason. He added hastily, 'From your point of view, I meant. I might even have thought he'd be nice for you to have around you... Seems I was more right than I thought.'

'He's lovely,' I said. 'And absolutely right for me. Only trouble is, he's married and has two five-year-old kids.'

'Oh Barney,' said Jason, shaking his head in a parody of despair. 'You do pick them. Whatever shall we do with you?'

'What's wrong with married men?' I parried. 'You're married for a start.' That was a cheap and nasty little dig, and we both knew it. But I couldn't resist taking that tiny revenge on Jason for flouncing out of my life simply because of what he'd read in a book.

Jason was gracious enough, and lovely enough, not to respond to that last remark. He shrugged. 'All I can do is wish you luck with it, I suppose, and hope that it works out for the best.' Then quite suddenly he said the most wonderful thing ever. 'I know I was a bit harsh on you about the ending of that book you wrote. Some of it was quite well written. And you've got Dad down to a T. But for God's sake don't try to get it published. It's not that well written, and we'd both end up as laughing stocks.' So far, so nice, but that wasn't the wonderful bit. The most wonderful thing ever came next. 'But if you ever did get aids, or anything like that, I would take you in and care for you. I promise. I couldn't do anything less.'

I didn't try to touch him and I managed, by not even allowing my lower lip to quiver, not to show him that inside I had fallen completely apart. 'I'd do the same for you,' I said. In a rather low voice.

Later that evening, back in Bristol, I flicked quickly through The Raven and the Jackdaw, trying to guess which parts of it my brother might have thought were the well written bits.

I had delayed handing the "novella" to Nick. He had assured me as long ago as May – the night I'd come clean about my feelings for my real-life brother – that he would have no trouble with it. But my experiences with both Jason and Alastair had made me cautious. Still, that November, after a month of seeing him on an almost daily basis, I was confident enough to hand over the manuscript. My confidence was not misplaced. He enjoyed reading it very much, he said. 'Yes, it's sentimental,' he said. 'Alastair was right about that. But what's wrong with a bit of sentiment? In today's world, especially. I didn't have any problem with it.'

The Raven and the Jackdaw

Some people have written at length about the difference between the noble purity of sentiment and the base metal of sentimentality, but I decided not to draw attention to the distinction at that particular moment. Nick liked The Raven and the Jackdaw because he was in love with me, and he liked my drawings for the same reason. It was as simple as that. Equally simple was the fact that, because I was just as much in love with him, if he hadn't liked them I would have been deeply upset.

I continued with my painting classes throughout that winter. Interruptions came only at Christmas – which I spent at Dad's – and in January, when I went abroad again with Nick, filming the winter wildlife of the Atlas Mountains of Morocco. Christmas alone with Dad was a penance. Jason and Anna were spending this first Christmas of their married life in Tunbridge Wells with Anna's parents. That I ended up doing all the cooking for my father and myself was not one of the penitential elements of that Christmas: because it gave me something to do it was a blessed relief. As for the Atlas Mountains... If anybody imagines that January in that part of Africa might be a cosy billet they should try it some time. On the other hand I had Nick with me. Because of that I was cosy enough, and warm enough. And happy beyond belief.

I had seen Alastair shortly before Christmas. I'd asked him how the cover of the Square Metre book had gone down with his parents. 'They pursed their lips but said nothing,' Alastair said. 'They praised the book's contents, though. They seemed determined to kid themselves that I'd written the whole of it.'

'Nobody kids themselves like parents do,' I said. 'They're past masters of the art.'

Alastair told me he'd been engaged for the next series of The Square Metre, though it would begin not in February this time but in March. The February slots had always been the most difficult ones to fill with interesting stuff. 'Why don't you join me at painting classes?' I asked him teasingly. He declined with a laugh.

In The Raven and the Jackdaw I allowed ten years to pass before Hector's death came along to complement his wife's. Fate was less kind to my real father. Only two years were left to him before he joined my mother in the stillness that ends all life. As in the case of the fictional Hector it was a heart attack that did the job.

It was my brother who said it. Jason, newly qualified as a GP, Jason who knew about heart attacks and their causes, found words for a feeling that lay deeper than any understanding of science. A feeling that was shared by both of us. He said, 'He died of a broken heart.'

'I know,' I said.

The truth was that we both felt we'd been judged by our father's death at the age of a mere sixty-eight and convicted of neglect. You can never do too much for your parents. But we hadn't done nearly enough. Remorse has a healthy appetite. There were just the two of us for remorse to feed on and remorse very easily ate both of us up.

We hadn't visited often enough. We hadn't stayed long enough when we did visit. We'd counted down the hours till we could decently depart and, though phoning dutifully once a week each, we'd kept those calls indecently short. We both cried more than once in the days after Dad passed. Never in each other's presence. But the evidence of our ever so private tears was present in our faces, though un-commented on when we met. I wanted to think I was weeping for my father, and I'm sure Jason had the same wish. But I know, now that I'm much older, that – I won't presume to speak for Jason

The Raven and the Jackdaw

here – I at any rate was weeping for shame, and for myself.

I longed to be able to ask Nick to Dad's funeral. I wanted him to stand next to me, black-suited and straight-backed, supporting me in that all-eyes-upon-it front pew seat in the church. Jason had Anna to stand, kneel and sit next to. I was happy for him that he had that. But I had just myself. I hadn't actually asked Nick if he would come with me. I didn't want to hear the words, brought out in an agony of divided loyalties: 'You know I can't. I'm sorry. What would Lois think?'

Our father's funeral took place on October 15th 1987. A strange strong wind, quite warm, was blowing as we stood at the graveside. It increased with intensity as the hours passed. During the small hours of the night that followed, southern England was struck by a full-blown hurricane for the first time in centuries. We awoke to a landscape of felled trees, closed roads and blown-down chimneys, and instructions on the radio not to go out. It seemed somehow appropriate.

It's an ill wind that blows nobody any good. The hurricane brought me a few days' work, which meant a few days sharing a hotel room with Nick. Reports started to come in of wild boar roaming the devastated woods of East Sussex. They were getting into people's gardens, trampling and rooting up: doing what any gardener would consider serious damage. Apparently, several enclosures in which wild boar were kept around the region – being farmed for their meat – had been damaged during the night of the hurricane and numbers of the animals had escaped. Our team, as I liked to think of us, were sent down to make a programme about it. We put up at a wonderful ancient hotel in the picturesque town of Rye, near the sea, on the border between East Sussex and Kent.

We had filmed a wild boar hunt in France a few years earlier; we knew that the animal we were looking for was dangerous. Now, in Sussex, we met up with local farmers and they helped to put us on the track of the fugitives. Much of our work had to be done, with thermal imaging cameras, at night. Traipsing hopefully around dark woods yielded no results. We struck lucky when we shifted our focus to the gardens of houses on the edges of woods that the wild pigs were known to frequent. One of the properties where we eventually got good sightings and good footage was an empty cottage, almost a shack, whose owner had recently died. The farmer who had found the place for us explained that the authorities were having difficulty tracing the old man's descendants. Meanwhile the empty house was deteriorating month by month.

This made me think of my father's death, naturally, and occasioned a new bout of filial guilt. But also I found myself taken back to an abandoned house in the Camargue, isolated among reeds and tall, wild grass. The two ideas coalesced in my mind and gave rise to a completely new thought. I didn't share this thought with Nick; it was too soon; for the time being I kept it to myself.

Driving back from Rye, our mission reasonably successfully accomplished, we passed near Tunbridge Wells. 'This is where Jason's just about to start work,' I said to Nick. 'I think I told you. His wife works as an anaesthetist in the local hospital. It's near where her parents live. Now Jason's bagged a job as a GP at a local medical centre. Simply on salary at the moment. One day, I think, he'd like to buy into the practice as a full partner.'

'That would cost something, wouldn't it?' Nick said.

'It would,' I said. 'But don't forget, we're waiting for probate on Dad's estate.' Even saying this out loud brought a tiny new pang of guilt. 'Not that Jason's said anything to me about joining up those particular dots.'

Nick saw the point and left it at that,

Dad had lived frugally, especially in his last years. He had taken no holidays since Mum's death, and continued to live in the same small cottage that Jason and I had known all our lives. But as we began to talk to the solicitors who were working on his will, it gradually became clear that he was a man of more financial substance than we'd thought. The terms of his will left his entire estate to be divided equally between Jason and myself. We had already agreed that we would sell the cottage and split the proceeds: there was no good reason for either of us to want to live in it – it was roughly equidistant from Tunbridge Wells and Bristol – about eighty miles from each. And we still had a foothold in the area in the form of the pair of ex-farm cottages – Holly Cottage and Burnt Oak – that we'd bought. What came as a surprise to us was the extent of Dad's portfolio of shares and bonds – augmented by the residue of Mum's estate: she hadn't left the whole lot to Jason and myself.

Half a year passed before probate was granted. Then we put the cottage we'd been born in up for sale, and separately put two large cheques into our bank accounts. Jason's plan, which he told me about, was much as I had expected it would be. He would negotiate to buy a partnership in the practice where he worked and, moving out from the flat he and Anna now rented in Tunbridge Wells, put down a deposit on a fair-sized house. Anna, by this time, was carrying their first child. The house the two of them eventually settled on had four bedrooms. I wondered how many children they were planning to have.

'Why do you want to buy a house in France?' Nick asked, with a degree of astonishment in his voice, when I told him what my plan was. 'If you went over there to live ... we'd see even less of each other than we do at the moment.'

I was glad that that was the first thought that had popped into his head.

'All sorts of reasons,' I said. 'Don't worry, though. I'm not going to be giving up this flat.' I gestured around me. We were sitting on the sofa together, drinking coffee. I returned, mentally, to France. 'It'd be good for holidays. I mean, you could go there with Lois and the kids. I could paint there. Find inspiration in the landscape and the wildlife. It'd be an investment. Bricks and mortar being the best sort. It'd be fun looking for a place. I'm sure you could find an excuse to come out there and help me do that. And there'd be the fun of doing the place up. Again, I'm sure you could wangle your way into coming and helping me.' You could lie to your wife was what I meant.

England's supply of "un-modernised" cottages had run out. The people in search of rural idylls and houses to convert in their own images, those who a generation earlier might have plundered the rural housing stock of the Home Counties, were having to go further afield. The newly retired were homing in on purpose-built small villas on the Spanish Costas, the more independent-spirited were tackling renovation projects in rural Portugal and France. One part of France was beginning to be especially popular: a trickle of Britons, year by year, were making second homes, retirement homes, even first homes, out of rough and ready cottages in the Dordogne département. Houses whose owners had died, and which had been left to sons and daughters who lived far away in Bordeaux, Lyon or Paris. Quite like my

The Raven and the Jackdaw

situation, and Jason's, vis-à-vis our parents' cottage, come to think of it.

'I'm thinking about the Dordogne,' I said to Nick. 'I mean, that was my first thought. I'd take your views into account, of course. We can think about it together, plan it together, do it together…' I tailed off. 'The money's come to me,' I said. I heard myself sounding rather serious. 'From my parents. I wouldn't be expecting you to put money into it.'

Nick rolled halfway onto me on the sofa, wrapping his arms around my neck loosely and giving me a casual kiss. 'I do love you,' he said.

'I love you too,' I said. What I didn't say was that somewhere among my deepest and least worthy thoughts lurked the idea that the prospect, for Nick, of sharing a property with me in deepest France might be the catalyst that was needed to make him leave his wife and his – now eight-year-old – twin kids.

TWENTY-EIGHT

I went to painting classes, on and off, for three years. Only then did I approach the BBC to ask if they would consider publishing a coffee-table type book of my work. By then I had collaborated with Alastair on a second Square Metre book. There was really no need for me to be involved in that: the programme was very much Alastair's by now. But I think the editors were worried that, if it were left entirely to Alastair, the deadline might not be met, or the grammar might be slipshod... Perhaps I'm doing Alastair a disservice. But I can think of no other reason why the powers that were at that time were so amenable to publishing a book of paintings by someone who, though well enough known as a TV presenter, was an unknown quantity as an artist.

The book sold well, to my surprise, and on the back of that I mounted an exhibition of the original paintings at a gallery in Bristol and sold nearly all of them within a fortnight. I was still buoyed up with that success when I went house hunting in the Dordogne with Nick.

Yes, we went out there together. Nick told Lois that he was going out with the rest of our team to look for locations in which to film wildlife. That had never been part of Nick's job, or mine, but Lois seemed to be satisfied with this explanation for his week's absence. I'd heard it said that wives always knew, at some very deep, perhaps subconscious, level when they were being lied to. But what did I know? I'd never had, had never been, a wife.

By this time, the end of the nineteen-eighties, there were a number of estate agents based in Britain who specialised in handling property deals in France. Nick and I crossed the Channel armed with a dossier full of details of properties to look at, and we didn't hesitate to call additionally on French estate agents when we arrived. We inspected everything from eight-bedroom *manoirs* to ruined cowsheds that were in need of extremely imaginative treatment. We drove up the river, from the elegant wine town of Libourne among the vineyards near the sea, to the magically preserved centre of Sarlat, nestling among folding hills where truffles abounded in the dark oak and walnut woods. Unsure at the end of that glorious week of exactly what it was that we wanted we allowed ourselves the luxury of not making an immediate decision but returning two months later for a second look. I had grave doubts as to whether Lois would wear this second trip, but somehow she did.

In the end we plumped for a three-bedroom stone house, a hundred or more years old, just outside a pretty hamlet called Le Breuilh. The tiny village lay on the edge of the Dordogne's flood plain, a few miles west of the market town of Sainte-Foy-la-Grande. Our house – it was technically entirely mine but we thought of it as ours and called it ours – was situated a prudent ten metres up the hillside behind the hamlet. It had a secluded garden, and was distanced just enough from neighbours by a small pony paddock on one side and a finger of vineyard on the other. There was work to do on the interior, but not too much. It was perfectly liveable in; kitchen and plumbing all worked perfectly, and the roof didn't leak. Over the next couple of years Nick and I updated the kitchen and bathroom – with a bit of expert help – and changed the main element of the colour scheme from dingy brown to light-reflecting white, with the help of a few cans of paint. We were both in love with the place. Probably because, despite the passing of the years, we were still both in love with each other. I've always wondered whether the difficulty of our situation, and the fact that we couldn't be together all the time had something to do with that.

Gay men notice the passing of time less than other people, I suspect. They can quite easily go into denial about it, until an accidental glance in a mirror they aren't prepared for catches them out. That and the growth of other people's kids.

Nick's twins were in their teens when he brought them out with Lois for a holiday. I wasn't there at the time, although Nick said it would be fine with Lois. I explained that it wouldn't be fine with me. Lois and he would share a bedroom, naturally, whether they had sex or not. I wasn't up for sleeping in the room next to that.

Jason first brought his two children over while they were still quite small. Like Nick he had a boy and a girl. They weren't twins, though, but had been born two years apart. When he and Anna stayed at Le Breuilh I was sometimes there and sometimes not. I didn't have a problem with their sharing a room together. That may have been inconsistent of me, but life's like that. Alastair came over with his long-term partner; they'd met when they were both twenty-three, clicked, and stayed together ever since. One night, to my surprise, I found myself having sex with the pair of them. When Byron came to stay with his boyfriend, I did not. Again, call me inconsistent, but life's like that.

The threat of aids had receded, it seemed. The rise in European cases was no longer exponential. Those of us lucky enough, by the merest chance, to have escaped the disease's first onslaught knew what to do to protect ourselves from future mishap. And Nick and I were particularly careful. Because of Lois.

Nick didn't leave his wife. But we somehow managed. Nick's continuing marriage was, in a way, the grit inside the oyster of my life. Forgive this over-elaborate metaphor. Time smoothed it over with pearl and it became simply an odd, no longer a painful, feature of my life.

The Raven and the Jackdaw

I spent plenty of time with Nick, anyway. When we were both in Bristol we still met up, as we'd done for years, at my flat, and when we were in France ... well, we were together in France. We still worked together. We travelled the world, or at least some of it. The series we were involved in grew bigger and more ambitious. With bigger budgets, additional cameramen and more back-up. Our trips abroad were longer, and took us further afield. To the forests of the Congo, to the Gobi Desert, to Patagonia and the Andes... I added rock-climbing to my skills. Up to a point. I would never make an assault on Everest, but I learned to be good enough – as Nick was – to meet the increasing demands of my job. I no longer got frightened when abseiling: no longer could I use that excuse to hold tight to Nick when descending together, sharing a harness.

My relationship with Nick was an open secret among the people we worked with. The production assistants might come and go as the years passed but they all knew to book a double room for Nick and me wherever we went, or to billet us in the same two's-company tent. We were seen very much as a couple and out of loyalty to us none of the team ever told Lois. It could easily have been the other way around. Morally speaking it probably should have been. But thankfully it wasn't.

And when I found myself alone in France, as happened sometimes, I would paint. Exhibit and sell my work back in England, and turn photographs of my paintings into books.

Nick and I had never been the kind of gay men who went to clubs. I had become a minor celebrity at nineteen, and for that reason hadn't wanted to risk finding myself in the papers and out of a job. Similarly, Nick was already married by the time he was really sure of his gay orientation. It would have been hard for him to explain to Lois that he wanted to go out to a gay night-spot. Then, after we got together, we never felt the need to go to such places. We had each other and, most of the time, found that to be enough. Being seen together in gay bars or clubs would still have been a bit risky in Britain, even now, although abroad we could have got away with it. A prophet is never honoured in his own country, but a minor TV celebrity is seldom recognised outside it – which can be to his advantage.

I'm not sure exactly when the following incident occurred. I can try and date it by thinking of the age of Nick's children. They would have been in their early twenties, I think. That would have meant Jason's kids were of college age, and Jason himself about forty, with me not far behind. Nick – gosh! – would have been approaching fifty.

We – Nick and I – were in France and had gone into Bordeaux to enjoy an opera. (Should one say *hear* or *see* an opera? I once heard a blind man who was a British government minister say that he liked to *go and see* an opera. Perhaps it was quite a profound remark.) It was more than fifty miles from Le Breuilh to the centre of Bordeaux, so we had decided to make a night of it, booking a hotel, leaving the car at the station in Sainte-Foy, and taking the little train that followed the Dordogne to the great river port.

We dined early, before the opera started, and then sat back and listened – or watched. It was Mozart's Magic Flute, sung in French, of course, but who cared about that? Afterwards we were too high on the experience of Mozart's wonderful music and the sheer craziness of the story that it set to want to go immediately to bed. We walked around the streets a bit, looking for somewhere to have a nightcap. We found ourselves by chance outside a gay venue called Le Pollux. We looked at each other, shrugged, and went in, paying our dues at the door.

We were older by some ten and twenty years respectively than anyone else in the place. We didn't want to make an exhibition of ourselves by taking to the dance floor, so we ended up standing at the bar, drinking an absurdly expensive cheap Cognac. At least there were two of us.

A minor TV celebrity is seldom recognised outside his own country. But seldom is not the same as never, and this night somebody recognised me. He was English, aged about thirty, very presentable, and he approached us with a smiling face. 'Hope you don't mind,' he said. 'I knew I'd seen your face. Had to think for a moment, seeing you out of place, so to speak. You're Barnaby Whitcomb...' He stopped for a second while a doubt hovered on his forehead. 'Or if you're not I hope the floor will swallow me up...'

'It's OK,' I said to reassure him. 'Fairy, thou speakst aright. I am that merry wand'rer of the night.' What made me go quoting Puck from "The Dream" heaven knows. It was twenty years since I'd played the role as a student. Although I'd remained slim I no longer looked remotely like Puck. 'Sorry,' I said. 'Bit of Shakespeare. I can never resist.'

'I really love your programmes,' the young man said. He turned towards Nick, waiting for some explanation of who he was.

'This is Nick,' I said. 'Senior cameraman on our roadshow. You'll have seen him too. They occasionally let him blunder into shot.'

'Of course,' said our new friend. 'I thought he looked familiar too.' Though he might just have been saying that.

Sometimes I thought the world was divided into two types of people: those who watched and enjoyed my nature programmes and those who did not. There were times when I loved the one type and loathed the other. At other times it was the opposite way round. Tonight I liked the first lot. I liked this chap. Now he said, 'My name's Nicholas too, by the way.' He giggled. 'I often am, too.'

'Often are what?' I asked.

'Knickerless,' he said. Then, 'Sorry. Was that in very bad taste?'

'In a place like this it's about par for the course,' I said. 'But it's a terribly old joke.'

'Tell me about it,' said Nick.

'I'd better tell you,' I said to Nicholas, 'that I'm not "out" to the general public. Even at the BBC it's a well-kept if well-known secret. I'd appreciate it… We'd both appreciate it if…'

'My lips are sealed,' young Nicholas said.

We chatted for a few more minutes. Nick bought Nicholas a drink. And another one for the two of us. At enormous expense. Then Nicholas said to me suddenly, 'Do you have a brother?'

'Yes,' I said.

'Called Jason?'

'Yes,' I said. I could feel a frown developing on my forehead.

'You don't look a lot alike. Mind you, there is a bit of a resemblance if you look closely.' He added very quickly, 'You're both very good-looking in your different ways, of course.'

'You know my brother?' It was half question, half statement.

'We had sex together once.'

I am lost for clichés when it comes to describing the astonishment I felt on hearing that. At the time I was lost for words too. 'You what?' I said.

'Sorry,' said Nicholas. 'Have I put my foot in it?'

'Not exactly,' I said, recovering myself. 'It's just that my brother's straight – at least I thought he was – and he's married…'

'It's not as unusual as all that,' I heard Nick say. I wasn't looking at him but I could imagine his poker face.

The space we were in, which I had thought of as being quite brightly lit, now seemed full of long shadows and dark recesses. I asked Nicholas, 'When did this happen… And where?' If Jason had given both his names to Nicholas, as he must have done in order for Nicholas to guess at our blood relationship, the encounter couldn't have been as casual as all that.

'In Birmingham, a few years ago, at a medical conference.'

'Good heavens,' I said. 'I had no idea…' I tailed off, but then came back with a new thought. 'Are you a doctor, Nicholas?'

'Ear, nose and throat,' Nicholas said.

'Oh right,' I said, then added, 'E.N.T.,' so that he'd know I had a little medical jargon at my fingertips. 'Jason's a GP.'

'Yes,' said Nicholas, 'I know that.'

I longed to know the details. How had they picked each other up? Had they spent a whole night in the same bed? Nicholas looked about ten years younger than I was. Ridiculously I found myself beginning to feel jealous. Had Jason fucked Nicholas? Had Nicholas fucked Jason? Or had they not gone as far as that? Unless I was going to get to know Nicholas better I wasn't going to be able to ask.

'What are you doing in Bordeaux anyway?' my Nick then asked young Nicholas.

Nicholas grinned a bit sheepishly. 'Another medical conference.'

I wondered if there would be a way to see more of Nicholas over the next day or two – or even perhaps tonight – but Nick suddenly took charge of the moment, as he sometimes did. He was the older member of our partnership after all. Just occasionally he liked to flex the muscles of his seniority. 'Well, good hunting at Le Pollux, Nicholas. It's time we drank up and got to bed.' And, though he gave us all time to shake hands first, he very quickly led me out of the place.

I hadn't really entertained thoughts of Nick and me taking Nicholas back to our hotel for a threesome, but I would have liked to talk a little longer, to exchange business cards, perhaps, and somehow to have found a way to explore this new area of my brother's life of which I'd been given a startling if intriguing glimpse .

Out in the street it seemed very cold suddenly. Though that was hardly to be wondered at. It was October, and my watch said one o'clock.

'Sorry to drag you out by the scruff of your neck,' said Nick. 'I just thought that if we went on talking about Jason... Well, I think there are some things in life, and some people, that it's better to forget.'

I was tempted to say I disagreed in this case. But I bowed to his longer experience of life. He was nearly fifty, I was not. I kept my mouth shut on the subject and we walked back to our hotel through the chilly streets, admiring the city's floodlit spires and towers and white-faced houses.

Over the years Nick and Jason met each other occasionally. Once over lunch in London when we all three happened, for different reasons, to be there on the same day. Then twice at the house at Le Breuilh when a visit from Jason and Anna and the children overlapped by a few days with Nick's. They got on splendidly – though, as Alastair said when told this, they didn't have a lot of choice. Nick knew that in the distant past I'd loved, and slept with, my brother and Jason must surely have assumed that I would have told Nick this. For me the little friendship they struck up, even though it was born out of only a few meetings years apart, was a special sort of bonus.

I remember the three of us sitting in the garden at Le Breuilh one afternoon, enjoying one more glass of wine than probably we should have had. We were sort of celebrating the completion, by me, of a painting of goldfinches fluttering above teasel heads. 'You should take a leaf out of Barney's book,' Nick told Jason. 'Take up painting. Barney says you were very good at drawing as a kid. At least as good as himself.' He jerked a thumb in my direction with a little laugh. 'Very therapeutic.'

'I know,' said Jason. 'It's a good way of helping busy, stressed people to relax. The only trouble is … busy, stressed people don't have time to relax. That's why they're stressed. When would I find time to paint?'

'When you retire,' suggested Nick, then added facetiously, 'or get struck off.'

'Ha-ha,' said Jason. Then he turned to me. 'Shall I hit him or would you prefer to do that?'

Never during those few times that the three of us were together did Nick or I bring up the matter of the young doctor we had met in Le Pollux. Nor did I mention that surprising meeting when Jason and I were alone together. If the story that Nicholas and Jason had had sex together were untrue then Jason would be outraged that I'd taken it even sufficiently seriously as to mention it. If it were true, then Jason might be more than embarrassed to discover that I knew he'd had sex with a man who wasn't me; with a person who wasn't his wife. He never showed any sign of getting onto that subject. In the end it wasn't my business, or Nick's, but only his.

We had good relations with our French neighbours, Nick and I. One was a farmer – with whom, years earlier, we'd got off to a very good start. Access to a pair of his fields was by means of a narrow track that ran between our garden and the little protruding tongue of vineyard next to it. One day we happened to see him approaching the closed gate to the track at the wheel of a tractor, while we were actually standing next to the gate. It was the easiest and most natural thing in the world to open the gate for him, sparing him the need to brake and stop the tractor, dismount, open the gate and then climb back up, before repeating the whole procedure when he got inside the gate. We simply shut it for him after he passed. But that tiny gesture unlocked everything for us. The very next day we were invited to his ramshackle farmhouse to partake of walnut liqueur and his wife's almond cakes. As the years passed he couldn't do enough for us. Little presents of vegetables would appear on our doorstep. If he had business in Sainte-Foy or Saint-Émilion he would ask us if there was anything we wanted. And he must have spread the word around that we were good news. For immediately after that gate-opening episode all our other neighbours thawed towards us. They had us in their houses, we had them in ours. And when we could we returned favour with favour. Not everyone in rural France had a computer in those days. But we did, and we earned our position in the small society we lived among by helping our new acquaintances get hold of useful information from the internet.

What our neighbours made of our relationship I wasn't sure. They had probably not come across gay couples setting up house together in remote villages, and might not have realised that that was what they were looking at. Especially as Nick was sometimes at the house with his wife and children, whom some of them met. Then

The Raven and the Jackdaw

there were the visits of Jason and his two kids... Our neighbours probably thought our arrangements a bit bizarre, but then put that down to the fact of our Englishness – an elastic cloak that could be made to cover every kind of oddness. They found us agreeable, ready to pitch in and help, ready to enjoy a joke and laugh at it even if it wasn't very good, ready to get stuck into conversations on any subject in our very indifferent French. And that was probably enough.

There were a few years during those two and a half decades when our visits coincided with the haymaking in the fields behind our house. Then we would give some token help to our farmer friend, throwing bales up onto the tractor-drawn trailer that went round to collect them. We were even allowed to drive one of the tractors once, taking a turn each.

The last time that we did this was in May 2006. It was May because haymaking takes place a good month earlier in southern France than it does in southern England. It was May the sixteenth to be precise. While I didn't remember the year, let alone the date, of that encounter with the young doctor called Nicholas in Le Pollux – because there was no reason to – I would never forget this date.

It was a beautiful evening. The trees were a luminous, translucent green, wearing that almost golden freshness that belongs to only a few days each spring. The coils of the Dordogne could be seen below in the distance, cut into sections by stands of poplar trees, by a sprawl of agri-glasshouses and the smaller sprawl of an out-of-town supermarket.

Nick and I had been shopping earlier and then, because life is made to be enjoyed as well as to be worked through, we'd spent the afternoon lying in the garden with our clothes off – but with plenty of sun-cream applied to the vulnerable bits. A field away the cuckoo called incessantly, while orioles and hoopoes could be heard occasionally, the one kind fluting, the other pooping, among the poplars. When afternoon began to turn to evening we put our clothes back on. From the bedroom window we spotted our farmer friend – his name was Thierry – out in the field, loading hay bales onto the cart. 'Is he up there on his own?' Nick said, tucking in his shirt.

'Looks like it,' I said. It was unusual enough to comment on. Normally one or other of his now hefty sons would be with him. 'We can't leave him to do all the driving and all the picking up,'

'No, obviously,' said Nick. 'He'd be there all night.'

Fully dressed we tramped down the stairs together, round the corner of the house and up the track. We walked up to where Thierry was and announced, without asking why he was working unaided this evening, that we had come to help.

Thierry accepted our offer with a grin. It was agreed, in a single sentence taking less than ten seconds to pronounce, that Thierry would drive, I would pick the bales up from the ground and pass them up to Nick, using a pitchfork. Nick would be on the trailer, stacking the load.

The situation took me back, of course. The memory was all the clearer for the fact that I had once written about it. Nick had read The Raven and the Jackdaw, and now he remembered the scene very clearly when I reminded him of it. 'A bit purple-prosy, if I remember rightly,' he said. 'But there was a lot of feeling in it too, I think. You were trying to write what you felt about your brother at the time. Right?' This did not all come out as a single speech. It came between puffs and grunts as Nick unloaded the bales from the points of my pitchfork and arranged them in the neatest stack he was capable of…

The Raven and the Jackdaw

Raven was allowed to scramble up on top of the load and ride back across the field. He climbed like a monkey up the bars that leaned outward from the back of the trailer to keep the load in place and soon he was securely in position on top. Mary had said emphatically that she would prefer to walk. Jackdaw stood on the ground looking from his sister to his brother and back again. There was his brother miles above him, grinning like a gargoyle, framed in hay and sunshine and a vast blue sky. There was the picture that he would keep for ever. There the grin, the snub nose and the laughing brown eyes. There was his brother suddenly calling out, 'Come on, Jackdaw.'

It didn't happen quite like that this evening. Nick was already on the trailer, building the load from the bottom. He climbed slowly only as the load grew beneath him, while I had to reach ever higher with the pitchfork. Fortunately the field was small and the number of bales was not enormous. Otherwise I would have run out of strength and breath, and run out of pitchfork. At last we were finished. Thierry sat at the wheel of the tractor, I stood on the ground, looking up at Nick who was looking down at me – yes, grinning like a gargoyle – crouched on top of the bales about five feet above my head. Then he turned away and called to Thierry, 'You going to give us a ride back?'

'Of course,' said Thierry jovially. 'I'll even get off and open the gate. *(Je démonte même; ouvre le portail.)*

Then Nick looked down at me. He said ... I'm hesitating as I type this, almost shaking with the feeling it gives me to write it ... he said, 'Come on, Jackdaw.' Yes, he really did say that. There was no-one else to hear it. Thierry was on the tractor at the other end of the trailer, the sound of the engine stopping his ears. I've sometimes wondered if perhaps I imagined I heard Nick say that. But no, I didn't imagine it. Yes, Nick did say it.

There he lay with Raven and the men, his heart thumping and his clenched fists holding on with the grip of panic, but happy beyond belief. High on this perilously rocking, sweet smelling mountain of hay, under the cloudless blue dome of the sky, close to the Raven in the afternoon sun, this was where he had to be. Here he had found what he most desired and now he wanted the ride never to end. Raven and he could ride on top of the wain till the end of time. For at the end of the ride lay the end of everything.

I scrambled up the bars at the back of the trailer easily. As I approached the top I must have appeared to lose my balance. Though Nick was fully aware of my prowess, modest though it was, as a rock climber. He would have known I wasn't going to have trouble getting on top of a hay cart. He reached a hand out towards me. I took it, almost for form's sake, though probably more out of affection and that other, more complicated, thing that we call love.

I didn't give my whole weight to Nick. Not even half of it. If I pulled on his hand at all I did so gently. So what happened then is still a bit of a mystery. Nick must have lost his purchase on the surface of the hay-load, lost his balance and toppled forward. From where I was it looked as though he – like a springing tiger or wolf – was taking a plunging leap above my head from the ledge or edge of a cliff.

He still held my hand. He wrenched me off the rear bars – like wall bars – of the trailer, and I fell painfully backwards to earth. My shoulder was dislocated at the very least. I cried out with the pain, as well as the surprise of it. But Nick made no sound at all. He only fell ten feet, and his legs fell across me with a painful thwack. But he came headfirst off the top of the trailer and headfirst he hit the ground. I was glad for him that he had no time to cry out. With luck he had no time to

The Raven and the Jackdaw

feel pain or even fright. An experienced rock climber doesn't expect to die in a fall of ten feet. But die he did. In the blink of an eye. He had broken his neck.

The Raven's grin grows wider as he peers down from the hay cart, from a distance measured in galloping years. The essence of a smiling face, sunlight on black hair and a sky of the deepest, hottest blue.

TWENTY-NINE

Poor Thierry! Among the whirlwind of feelings that must have buffeted him when he leaped off the tractor and saw the catastrophe that lay sprawled at his feet would have been the thought that this was a workplace accident involving two people, one fatally, who were not covered by his insurance. Poor, blind Thierry. The big thing that he didn't know was that he was a witness – or as near as damn it to a witness – to not just one death but to two. I might have done little more than break an arm but the finality of that moment was as absolute for me as it was for Nick.

Lois… I'll have to come back to Lois in a moment.

It was Jason who saved me.

I phoned him, broken arm or no broken arm, and God knows how I got a signal, from the floor of that field, before the ambulances arrived and while Nick's body lay, still warm, on top of me.

The next morning, waking in the Bordeaux hospital, waking late after a morphine-induced slumber, I saw him … Jason, I mean … at my bedside. He held me while I cried. And then we talked. That is to say, my brother told me what we would do.

Lois arrived just two hours later. Jason dealt with her. He had never met her before, and he didn't muddy the waters now by letting her know that he had three times met her husband, even staying with him for days at a time in the same house. He told her that Nick and I had been asked by the BBC to examine my house in France, its garden and environs, as a possible location for a programme about French wildlife. He told her the truth about the actual accident. He gave her as much comfort as a total stranger could. In the evening Ian, one of Nick and Lois's twins, arrived to take care of his mother. He was now twenty-six. He came to my bedside and said kind words to me. Though he kept giving me a rather cagey look. But if he'd harboured suspicions over the years about my relationship with his father he was decent enough now to keep them to himself.

It was Jason who phoned Will Lumsden – now in his late sixties but still working – to ask if authorisation could be given retrospectively to turn the last few days of my stay with Nick in France into a bug-hunting trip. Otherwise the insurance situation would be problematic. There would be the cost of flying Nick's body back to England for cremation or burial – whichever he might have willed, or Lois wished. Will had seen the point and said he would do what he could.

It was Jason who sorted things out with Thierry. In the presence of a representative from the French Farmers' Union Lois and I signed papers that stated that Nick's family and I would not be pursuing Thierry in the courts; that Nick and I had not been employed or even asked to help him with his hay baling, but had wilfully insisted on helping him, despite his repeated requests for us not to. We all crossed our fingers and hoped that this document would never come to the attention of the British insurance companies. It was a blessing for Lois that she would not have to rely entirely on a possible insurance payout in connection with Nick's job. Nick had taken out a hefty private insurance on his own life, and that looked pretty safe.

It was Jason who actually arranged, with the hospital authorities, the transport of Nick's body back to Bristol once the post-mortem had been carried out. It was Jason who helped to shut up the house in Le Breuilh, put my car away in the garage, and flew back with me after a few days in hospital had made me well enough to travel. He took me to his and Anna's house in Tunbridge Wells, made me comfortable there and, at meal times, cut up my food for me on my plate.

It must happen to thousands of people. Death catches them out while they sleep in the wrong person's bed, or are on holiday at the wrong person's address. It happened to Charles Dickens. His body had to be taken by coach in the middle of the night from the house of a woman friend on whom he had inconveniently died, and returned to his home in another part of Kent, where his death was then decorously announced. But being among such numerous company – and such exalted company too when it came to Dickens – did nothing to make my situation easier to deal with. Still less did it do anything to assuage my grief.

Sierra de Gredos, Sierra de Gredos. The unyielding, ten thousand foot high, chain of rock that was Hemingway's metaphor for the inescapable cruelty of life / death came often into my mind. High in that inhospitable range I had first clasped Nick to me in fear, descending to a cliff ledge on a rope. Sierra de Gredos: those dark hard syllables echoed in my head like the tolling of a cold cracked bell. It tolled for me. It tolled for my intrepid rock-climber boyfriend who had died falling off a hay cart: it tolled for Nick. It tolled for *us*.

I went to the funeral in Bristol. I remembered how, ten years earlier, the French President Mitterand's funeral had been attended by both his wife and his long-standing mistress. I didn't mention this to Lois. This was a day for the public display, and comfort by others, of her grief. It wasn't something she would have wanted to share with me as an equal. I had to button and steady my lips, keep my eyes dry, and grieve in secret. Lois spent quite a bit of time with me at the gathering in a Bristol hotel afterwards. She said it was wonderful of me to attend, given my own plaster-cast state. Either she really had no idea still, or she was doing a magnificent job of pretending that she hadn't. Jason didn't come with me. As far as Lois was concerned he had never met Nick, so

The Raven and the Jackdaw

his presence might have struck her as slightly odd. The less that Lois was presented with in the way of oddness the better, Jason and I both thought. Still, I missed my brother's support at the funeral. I didn't sit with Lois and her family and Nick's but about four rows back, with other BBC freelancers and staff. I could have done with Jason beside me, black-suited and ramrod-straight, just as I could have done with Nick's presence at the funeral of my father all those years ago. Actually, I could have done with Nick beside me now. At his own funeral! I knew I would go on missing Nick for ever. I would never, ever, get over Nick.

I stayed at Jason and Anna's until the plaster came off my arm. Then I returned to my Bristol flat. When we parted at the station Jason, for the first time in twenty-one years, gave me a kiss.

Some things became true retrospectively. Those days in Le Breuilh during which Nick met his death became an official reconnoitring trip. The insurance company paid out. And we really did make a series based around my house. It ran for six episodes and was called The Hectare, in a nod to the long finished series, The Square Metre. In another nod to that series, Alastair and I presented alternate episodes. There were new cameramen, and a new director. But every one of them knew who Nick was and what he had been to me and they were careful with me on that account – especially in view of the location's sensitivity – or rather, my own sensitivity to it.

During the years that followed I spent most of the time that I wasn't away on foreign filming trips at my place in France. I painted lots, and sold lots. I didn't find another Nick. But I wasn't looking for another Nick. There could never be another Nick. I managed all right for sex, though. Because I didn't live full time in Le Breuilh I needed occasional help with the garden there. That had been the case all through the years when Nick and I had shared the place. Following his death I was careful about the young men I employed in this capacity, choosing shrewdly. In several cases my careful selection process paid off and my young gardeners were able to oblige me in more than the care of my roses. One of Thierry's hefty sons was included in that little coterie. A minor TV celebrity is seldom recognised outside his own country. Which can be to his advantage. I might have been heading towards fifty but I still looked young for my age and was slim and fit.

I saw little of Jason in the years after Nick's death. The renewed closeness that was born in the immediate wake of it did not last, though God knows I'd been infinitely grateful for it and still was. Of course we didn't have sex together while I stayed with him and Anna at their Tunbridge Wells house. The cuddle he gave me when I was in my hospital bed, lost without Nick and crying for him, and the kiss he gave me on the platform of Tunbridge Wells station were both one-offs. Jason was a doctor as well as a brother. It seemed that once I'd had the plaster taken off my arm he felt I needed to start standing once again on my own two feet. He didn't want me to go on needing him. And he didn't really need me. He had Anna for that.

My filming jaunts continued to take me far afield. South Africa, New Zealand, the Far East... I learned that there is no end to learning things in life, and that that is one of the most wonderful things about it. I continued to learn new things about animals and plants. In my role as a painter I went on learning about light and colour, and about technique. I even learnt things about language, something that I'd never considered a particular interest of mine. About the way that animals' names are pronounced, for instance, in the places where they live.

The Raven and the Jackdaw

The puma, for example. In South America, where it comes from, they say poomah, which sounds lovely, not to say cuddlesome, while a jaguar, pronounced by a South American Spanish speaker, becomes a hachrwarr – with the ch as in Scottish loch. It is clearly an onomatopoeic name, mimicking the animal's snarl that is almost a purr – something that is not remotely evident from the English way of pronouncing it. I loved discovering little things like that.

In France – at any rate in Sainte-Foy-la-Grande – the English newspapers still arrived one day late. I could watch the news on television, and I did, and I could have read the English press on my phone or on my lap-top and been up to date. But I liked the experience of reading a solid, made-of-paper, newspaper. I liked the comforting rustle of it, familiar since childhood, as I turned the pages. I liked to sit in the garden at Le Breuilh on a Monday, reading through the news and features in the English Sunday press.

I was doing this one day in early spring – there is such a season in southern France, unlike in England, and it is rather nice – when my eye was captured by this on an inside page. A small article began: *A Tunbridge Wells GP has been suspended from his job by his partners while complaints about inappropriate behaviour with three young patients are investigated. The doctor, who can not be named...*

Oh dear, I thought. A GP in Tunbridge Wells... It would be someone my brother knew. I skimmed the article to see if the name of the practice was given. Again, oh dear, I thought. It had happened at my brother's practice.

The memory came back to me of a young doctor called Nicholas who had told Nick and me in a Bordeaux club, some ten years ago now, that he'd had sex with Jason while at a medical conference. Even if what he'd said was true – and I'd spent much time in the intervening years doubting that it was – the event in question had involved two consenting adults who happened to be doctors. It had not been a question of doctor and patient. Of doctor and patients. Of doctor and young patients. It was the word young that sent a shiver down my back.

I did something I had never done before. I typed my brother's name into Google. His name popped up in three or four contexts. All of them, I was relieved to see, were quite innocuous, not to say commendable. Not only did his name appear, along with a photograph, on his practice's website, but he was mentioned in connection with a number of charity and fundraising events. I didn't remember, if I'd even known, the names of all the doctors who worked with Jason in his practice, so I couldn't tell whether any name had disappeared from the list. At least his had not. I let out a breath of relief.

Later that day I re-read the article. It gave me a cold, unpleasant feeling. Turning the pages to find the right one I experienced the physical sensation I would get on the rare occasions when I had to handle a slug. I hadn't remembered whether the sex of the three young patients had been mentioned. I found that it had not. Neither had their ages. In fact the article gave away very little. I found myself almost memorising what little there was of it, trying to tease significance from each and every word, as well as from what was left unsaid.

I thought about phoning my brother and directly asking him what was going on. Was this suspension of a colleague doing damage to the practice … meaning, doing damage to him. But I dared not pick up the phone to him. Supposing, just supposing, the suspended partner were not some other fellow but Jason himself… What would I say to him? What would he say to me? My

The Raven and the Jackdaw

imagination balked at even trying to picture the embarrassment, to both of us, of that.

I decided to keep my thoughts and worries to myself. But I followed the news very attentively in the days that followed. A week passed, and although I combed the British press more thoroughly than I'd ever done before, via the internet, no further mention of the matter was made anywhere. I looked everywhere, so I was pretty certain of that. When nothing appeared in the following Saturday's newspaper I felt a further access of relief. It seemed that the matter had fizzled out, had been a misunderstanding perhaps. A storm in a teacup. Idly I googled my brother's name again. The references to him that I had seen the previous week were all still there, unchanged. No new ones had been added. I clicked on the website of his practice. His name was no longer there. Neither was his photograph.

I felt my hands trembling as I stared at the computer screen, willing the photograph and the name to come back. They did not, of course. I sat there and I didn't know what to do. I had no more idea what to do next than if I had been a four-year-old. I needed someone to talk to – in English. But there was no-one. There was no-one, anywhere, whom I could trust with this stick of dynamite. I wanted Nick with me. Strong, handsome, older, Nick. He might have known what to do – whether I should now contact Jason perhaps? – or he might not. But even if he didn't know he would have put his strong arms round me. He would have held me and taken care of me and I – though Jason might not be – I at any rate would have been all right.

As things were I was very definitely not all right. And if I was in a state about this, how much worse must it be for Jason? How would Anna be taking this? Would she be standing by him? Would her arms be round him, protecting him? In the way that I so much wanted now to be protected by Nick? Putting jealous thoughts aside for once I hoped very much that she was supporting, holding him. Then I wondered whether, if perhaps she wasn't doing that, my brother might for once need my support and help.

I decided I must phone him, however difficult a task that was. I spent a long two hours working out what I would say to him. Going through possible conversations in detail. If he said that, then I would say this. If he said the other, then I would say that. And so on. It was a Sunday evening. At seven o'clock French time, six o'clock British, I picked the phone up.

Anna answered. I gave my name in a friendly way, though without embellishment, and asked if I could speak to Jason. 'He isn't here,' Anna answered. 'He's in London, staying with friends.' Then she hung up on me.

I waited a further hour, hardly managing to bear myself with patience. Had I rung back immediately she would have known who it was and would probably not have answered. As it was there was a possibility that these days they had a house phone that would display either my name or my number. I placed my hope in the possibility that they did not.

At the end of the hour I dialled the number again. Anna picked up. I didn't give my name this time. I didn't want her to put the phone down before I had a chance to ask my question. I came to it with brutal directness. 'Do you have his friends' number?' I asked.

'No,' she said. Then, 'Try his mobile.' And again she hung up.

I should have thought of that at once. But I rarely phoned Jason on his mobile. I hadn't done so in years, I thought. I looked for a number for him in my phone but couldn't find one. He might well have changed his number since I'd last rung him on it. But then, wouldn't he have notified a brother of the change if he had? I finally tracked down a mobile number in my old address book and rang it.

He answered. In the sudden emotion of that moment I forgot all the speeches I'd prepared in readiness. 'Jase,' I said, 'It's Barney. Are you all right?'

'No,' he said.

'I thought not,' I said. 'I saw what was in the paper last week. I knew it was you when your name disappeared from the practice website. But you're with friends. Is that right?'

'Yes,' Jason said.

'Can I do anything…?' I asked, tailing off.

'No,' Jason said. 'You can't.'

'Do you want me to come over?'

'It wouldn't do any good,' Jason said.

'I could just be there,' I said.

'It wouldn't do any good.'

'Are your friends looking after you?' I asked. 'What part of London is it? Do I know them?'

'Yes,' Jason said, just about managing to answer my questions in the right order. 'And it's Chiswick. You may have met them in Cambridge.'

I felt I'd gone as far as Jason would allow me to. Reluctantly I wound up. 'You will tell me if you need anything from me, won't you?'

'Of course,' he said.

'And we'll keep in touch. See you soon, I hope.'

'Bye for now,' said Jason.

'Bye, Jase,' I said, and we both hung up. This was the first time ever that I had called him Jase.

I was reduced to watching from the wings. Reading the papers in other words. I felt as though I was watching a plane crash in slow motion. Knowing exactly how it would all end, but not being able to do a thing to prevent it or to help.

A young man had been involved in each case. I use the word man advisedly and with some relief. All three had been eighteen or over at the time of their involvement with my brother, although in two cases only just. Nevertheless, no law had been broken; my brother would not have to go to prison, or even to court. It was a question only of professional conduct – or misconduct. That involved the General Medical Council. They might have kept their deliberations secret. Unfortunately, though, there were enough people in Tunbridge Wells who knew enough and were happy to talk to the press. His name came out. You take someone to your house and have sex with them while your wife is out. Or you go to theirs and have sex with them while their partner or parents are out. I accept that not everyone has done this – but I know that a very large percentage of us have. It doesn't seem sordid but merely high-spirited, a sign of health... Until we come to read about it in the press.

I felt for Jason. My heart went out to him. How easily it could have gone like this for me after Alastair's parents read the riot act when I was nineteen and Alastair was a fifteen-year-old blond morsel of jailbait. I reminded Jason of this in an email but he didn't answer. I emailed him quite often, in fact, but he seldom replied. I phoned occasionally to check how he was. He seemed to appreciate my phoning and to appreciate my concern for him, but he spoke only briefly when we talked. I asked him at intervals during those terrible few months if he would like us to meet up but he said each time, probably not.

In April I had to go away to work. To film animals in the forests of Borneo. It was truly the back of beyond as far as communications were concerned. Now I could only wonder, in a nearly complete news vacuum, how my brother was faring. I returned to the news that my brother had been struck off the medical register and had

had to sell his share in the practice. At least that would give him some cash, I thought. He was going to need that. Anna was now in the process of divorcing him and was expected to be able to hang on to the house. At least the two kids weren't kids these days; they were both in their mid-twenties. You had to be thankful for small mercies, I thought.

THIRTY

I sometimes dreamed about Nick. I knew very well that I hadn't pulled him off the top of the hay cart. Neither on purpose – God forbid!! – nor by accident. But my dreams at the beginning seemed less convinced of that. During those first few days in the Bordeaux hospital I would wake distraught and in tears, having dreamed that I'd yanked my partner to his death and that – as I had found myself thinking once before, after the death of my father from loneliness – Everything Was All My Fault. During those days in the hospital and afterwards I had had the comfort of Jason's frequent presence. I had been able to pour my heart out to him. I'd heard his reassuring voice. 'Take no notice of dreams. They're part of the adjustment process. Part of the grieving process. In time they'll fizzle out and stop.' And in time they did stop. Just as my brother had said they would.

But now that he was in dire circumstances himself, isolated and cut off from Anna, I wanted to be able to return my debt. It hurt like hell to know that I couldn't do that. To know that he didn't want that. I hoped that those friends of his in London had been good to him while he stayed with them during those first few weeks. I tried to recall whether I knew them from Cambridge days or not. But I failed to. It had been a very long time ago, and my memories of Cambridge were full of people. Too many to remember or even remember the names of.

Jason couldn't stay with friends indefinitely. He told me on the phone – for he wasn't so withdrawn from me as to give me no information at all about himself – that he was moving into Holly Cottage as soon as the current tenants' agreement ran out. I asked him, naturally, how he intended to earn his living. He said he wasn't sure but – and he managed to laugh as he said this – among other things that he was doing to keep himself occupied was learning to paint.

Not long after we had bought them Jason and I had both spent money on our two cottages. Prompted by the estate agency that managed them for us we had their bathrooms and kitchens brought up to the standards that, by the last decades of the twentieth century, tenants had come to expect. The improvements, the agency had told us encouragingly, would mean that we could expect to receive higher rents. And indeed we did.

Having made those improvements to my property it was only too easy to sit back and consider the work was done for ever and that nothing more would have to be done to the cottage for as long as I lived. But houses don't stay standing up unaided for ever. They constantly need patching and propping up. Perhaps a month after Jason moved into Holly Cottage I got a letter from the estate agency – it had been sent to Bristol and forwarded from there to France – to let me know that there would be a short gap between tenants at Burnt Oak. There was also a list of minor repairs and renewals that ought to be tackled if the cottage was to remain in good shape. The list was attached to the letter. Would I like the estate agency to put the work in hand at this juncture, before the new tenants arrived?

I looked at the list. None of the items was major. Some exterior window frames needed painting, a couple of tiles had slipped. There were a few other things to be done but nothing that would be difficult to fix. If I let the agency sort things out the contractor they engaged would charge them heftily. They wouldn't haggle. It would be in their interest, after all. When they passed the cost on to me with their administration charge added they would be able to take a larger cut. I decided I would do the work myself, staying at the cottage for the few days it would take me to do it. I emailed the estate agency – it saved the cost of a stamp – to tell them that.

It suited me well, to tell the truth. Jason could not prevent me from staying at my own cottage. I would, I hoped, have a chance to talk to him properly at last. I didn't want to startle him by simply turning up unannounced. I phoned him and told him what my plan was. It was funny, he said. He'd had a similar letter from the estate agent about a year earlier and had done nothing about it. But now that he was living there himself he was catching up on those little things that needed doing at Holly Cottage. It gave him something to do, he said. 'Maybe we can join forces,' I suggested brightly. 'Many hands make light work.' He only said, 'Hmm,' in reply to that.

I didn't know exactly when I'd be back in France. Whether I'd be going back to Bristol when I left Burnt Oak, or if I might be summoned suddenly for another overseas filming trip. I called the caretaker at my Bristol flat and asked him to forward any post that arrived for me to Burnt Oak until further notice.

I drove to St-Malo, made the leisurely Brittany Ferries crossing to Portsmouth, then drove up past Winchester and Newbury to the village and Burnt Oak. I was spared the need to knock at Holly Cottage to let Jason know I'd arrived. He was doing something in the front garden as I drew up. He came up to the car as I got out of it. 'Good to see you,' he said. That was friendly enough, but there was an awkwardness in the air. We hadn't met face to face since Jason's disaster. Uncertain whether we would embrace or simply shake hands we ended up doing neither. We bowed minutely to each other instead. It would have looked almost comical to anyone watching us. 'Would you like to go to the pub and get something to eat in a bit?' Jason asked. I was glad he said that. It was evening and would soon be dusk. A meal on neutral

The Raven and the Jackdaw

territory seemed the best way to deal with this first evening as next-door neighbours. He wouldn't have to come into my house; I wouldn't have to go into his.

'I'd like that,' I said. 'Give me half an hour to unpack a few things and I'll be with you.'

We took Jason's car to the pub. 'I haven't been in there since I've been here,' Jason said. '…If that makes sense. Will I be recognised?'

I said, 'I doubt it, though I might be. Don't worry about it anyway. When did I last go in there with you? Around the time Dad died, I think. Getting on for thirty years ago. Anybody who knew us then will be dead.' That made Jason laugh a little. I was glad of that.

The pub hadn't changed much, but we were perfect strangers there. Jason might have been recognised in Tunbridge Wells but here he was mercifully anonymous. Even I got only a couple of semi-recognition looks. Our conversation grew easier as we drank and ate. I wanted to ask things like, So do you think of yourself as gay now, or bisexual, or what? But I didn't. Those labels didn't seem to mean much anyway, applied to someone whose complexities I knew so intimately. Jason was simply Jason and I was just myself.

I did say at one point, 'If you want to talk about things that have happened…' Jason didn't take the prompt. I had to go on. 'I'd be very happy to listen…'

'Thanks,' said Jason. 'But probably not. Anyway, not tonight. I had some relationships with young men that got me into trouble. But I don't think you've anything new to learn about things like that.'

That was quite close to being a snub but I accepted it. 'Fair enough,' I said. 'I just want you to know I'm here for you. Rooting for you. Whatever the current expression is.'

'Thanks, Barney,' Jason said. 'I do know that.'

We left it there. I didn't expect or need him to tell me that he would be eternally grateful to me for being who I was.

We parted outside our adjacent front doors after arranging to meet in the morning to do some work together on both our houses. Then I went into my cottage and went upstairs to get ready for bed. As I undressed I congratulated myself on my forethought in having turned the heating on before going out.

Drifting towards sleep I found myself pondering the nature of the thing that, for want of a better word, we call love. Our personal love stories, I thought, are small and intimate things. They don't all involve death and bloodshed, though it may feel like it at the time. Our individual experiences of human love more usually resemble small and intricate jewels sewn up inside the lining of a coat. Rarely visible to anyone but the coat's wearer they are burningly precious nevertheless. Even the story of Romeo and Juliet, though exploded open by Shakespeare for the whole world to see, was in essence intensely private. I thought about Byron, I though about Alastair, I thought about Jason – and of course I thought about Nick. The four people I had loved – or still did love. I fell asleep.

Intrepid scrambler among Andean rocks that I was, I would still not have been happy to climb a tall ladder while alone at a remote cottage that was hundreds of yards from the nearest other house. The manner of Nick's death had made me even more circumspect in this. Jason felt the same, I knew. It made sense for us to work together on all those small jobs that required ladders during the few days during which there would be two of us at our semi-detached addresses. One to climb the ladder, one to foot it. One to administer first aid, in the last resort, or call an ambulance.

The Raven and the Jackdaw

So we worked together, that first day – much of the time in companionable semi-silence. I made a point of not plying Jason with too many questions. How did he feel about the ending of his marriage? Had he been in love with the boys he'd got into trouble over? When did he know that he wasn't exclusively attracted to women…? Umm, that was a difficult one. Yours truly was a part of that particular equation, and had been, off and on, since Jason was eight. But even the easier questions were better fought shy of for the present. Did he cook for himself? Had he got beyond the level of all-day breakfasts such as we'd cooked together in Cambridge? Or did he eat out every night? Would that burn holes in his pockets? How was he managing for money in any event? Had both his son and daughter sided with their mother, or were they still on good terms with him? And who were the Cambridge friends who had taken him into their home for a while? I bided my time. Who needed the answers to such questions anyway? If Jason wanted to tell me things, or needed me for anything, well, here I was. If he needed money … well, I had some of that. If he needed it I would soon spot that, being close to him, and I would help him. But I wouldn't wound his self-esteem by prematurely offering that. Those things could wait. As for me, I found that being with Jason again, just having his quiet company while we re-positioned roof tiles or daubed bare-to-the-wood bits of window frame with primer, was extremely nice.

Jason was still a few inches taller than me (now that we were fifty-one and forty-nine respectively that wasn't going to change a lot) and so there were times, reaching up the slope of the roof for instance, when it made more sense for Jason to climb the ladder and for me to foot it. That afternoon he climbed in the sunshine, to tuck back a couple of roof tiles that had slipped. Fortunately they were situated just a few rows above the gutter; had they been higher up the operation would have been trickier and we might have needed to call in an expensive specialist. As it was I leaned forward on the ladder to weight it and keep it steady while Jason worked at the top. My head was more or less level with his trainers, which I could smell faintly. That pleasing faint smell of him hadn't changed in all the years, I thought. Like the smell and taste of Proust's madeleine it brought the whole of my past history with him rushing back. Lazily I reached up and cupped his calf muscles in my hands through the fabric of his jeans. They were like small melons or large peaches. They were as they had always been in the past: achingly familiar and wondrous. Jason didn't react in any way to this. He didn't say anything, nor did his body jerk or flinch. He went on calmly adjusting the tile he was working on until he was satisfied with the way he'd positioned it. And I continued to hold him, continued to cup his calf muscles, until he'd finished.

We went into town for a Chinese that night.

The next day Jason showed me, a little shyly, some of the pictures he had painted. They were mostly peaceful rural landscapes and tranquil farmyard scenes. Working on them must have helped to ease the pain of his heart in the wake of his loss of job and wife. A case of physician, heal thyself. Although they occasionally betrayed their creator's lack of experience I liked them. They were easily as good as mine had been when I started exhibiting. Although I no longer thought those early pictures of mine very good I'd thought them good enough to exhibit back then. Good enough to sell. Good enough to get published as a BBC coffee-table book. And they had sold; so had the book. Of course Jason would not have the benefit of the BBC's patronage to give him a leg-up. But I could still give him encouragement without lying to him. 'They're good enough to sell,' I said.

The post arrived around midday. For me, forwarded from Bristol, came a letter from the Avon and Somerset Police. With a puzzled frown I slit it open. My eye travelled quickly through the letter's preliminaries. My heart nearly stopped when I came to this.

It has been alleged that between November 1981 and February 1982 you engaged regularly in unlawful sexual activities with a minor in the Bristol area.

In view of the sensitivity of any claim of this nature it would be helpful if you could make an appointment to have an informal talk with us at the above address at your early convenience...

I walked out of my front door, leaving it swung open and, without knocking, went into Jason's. I couldn't speak. I held the letter out to Jason as soon as he came out into his living-room from the kitchen. I let him read it. I would let him speak.

'Oh Jesus, Barney. Why the hell...? Over thirty years have passed...'

'Yes,' I said. 'But you know how it is these days. All those cases involving celebrities going way back... People with axes to grind coming forward...' My imagination leaped horribly ahead. I was going to follow the Via Dolorosa along which Jason had already led. But in my case a child – as the media would describe him – has been involved and it would all be very much worse. I saw myself in a police interview room. In court. The ghoulish interest of the media in a downed media figure. The photographs. I foresaw what would happen to me in prison. I wouldn't come out alive. And if by the remotest chance I did survive those years... No more work at the BBC obviously. And the second string I had to my bow – my painting... Who would ever buy a painting by me after this? People who had my canvasses on their walls would take them down and burn them, or heave them into the nearest skip.

Jason recovered his composure more quickly than I did. He said in a measured, confident tone of voice, 'Alastair won't have done this. As for his father, in that dreadful letter he said he never would. You kept your side of the bargain and for all these years he's kept his.'

'His father died last year,' I said. 'You might not have known that. But what the fuck do I do, Jase?'

'We need to think,' Jason said. 'And while we're thinking, have a Scotch.' He went to find the bottle. I sank onto his sofa, too distraught to think.

Jason came back with the bottle, two glasses with ice in them and a plan already half hatched. 'We need to phone Alastair immediately,' he said. 'Find out what he knows, or doesn't know about this. Then take it from there. Step by step.'

I don't know what I'd have done without you is a cliché of the first rank. Never can it have told a bigger truth than it did that day about Jason and myself.

I hadn't been in touch with Alastair for several months. We'd met for drinks at Christmas but since then our paths hadn't crossed. I got him on his mobile at the first attempt. 'Oh God,' he said. 'I should have warned you. I didn't think...'

'Warned me?' I queried. 'What of?'

'It's Mum,' Alastair said. 'She's got dementia. It came on rapidly, after Christmas. She's in care now...'

'She can only be in her seventies,' I said, astonished.

'It happens,' Alastair said. There and then I checked this with Jason, standing beside me. Alastair was right. Apparently it did.

'She's been dredging up all sorts of remembered wrongs and accusations. Most of them are totally trivial. It didn't cross my mind she'd come up with this. Until somebody told me the other day she'd said it. I laughed it off and told them she was imagining it. I should have got in touch with you at once, just in case… I can only think she's been going on and on about it in the care home and someone's picked it up and taken it to the police.'

'She's got dementia but she remembers the dates?!' I felt as though I'd wandered into the pages of Kafka's *The Trial* by mistake. I heard Jason, following my end of the conversation intently, say quietly, 'That happens too, I'm afraid.' Alastair and I talked some more, and arranged to meet the next day, before I had to reply to my letter from the police.

Then Jason took the phone from me and spoke to Alastair himself. 'Is it OK with you if we get a solicitor in on this meeting tomorrow?' I heard him ask. Then, 'Good. I'll get on to that right away and phone you back. We'll have to meet wherever the solicitor – whichever one we can get hold of – hangs out. Bristol, London, Newbury, wherever.'

Thirty minutes later Jason had sorted it. He found a solicitor in Newbury, whose father had acted for our parents. He didn't let the solicitor speak to me, explaining that I was, 'in a state'. When he put the phone down he turned to me and said, 'It means a bit of a way for Alastair to travel, but it won't be so far for us. And you'll be pleased to know the solicitor thinks you've probably nothing to worry about. If Alastair's mother hasn't actually spoken to the police herself, then it's only hearsay based on hearsay.'

'But if the police go round and question her…'

'The solicitor will find a way to prevent them doing that. And don't reply to the letter yet. The solicitor will help you with that too. It's all being taken care of…'

And I was being taken care of.

Jason went to the kitchen and opened a can of soup, switched the oven on and from the freezer produced a semi-baked frozen baguette. We ate at a table in the garden. I never had a lovelier lunch.

By the afternoon it was really hot. We were in late June. No cuckoo called. Sadly the cuckoo was now a rarity and seldom heard. But everything else was as I remembered it.

In your fond memory the grass will grow longer and greener, the sun warmer, the sky bluer, and the Raven's grin wider as he peers down from the hay cart at you from a distance measured in galloping years. And the image will grow ever more vivid as time leaches the accidents of mundane reality out of it and leaves you with… With what? With the essence of a smiling face, sunlight on his black hair, and a sky of the deepest, hottest blue.

That sunny afternoon we did a bit of paintwork touching-up together. For this I stripped off and put on a pair of very short denim cut-offs. I wore nothing else, except for a pair of ancient trainers. Fresh paint comes off the skin very easily in the bath or shower but it sticks to clothes like nobody's business. I didn't even wear underpants beneath the roughly made, ripped-seamed shorts. Though I might have had a second motive for this.

One particular spot was hard to reach. It was a triangular piece of weatherboard in an awkward corner above a piece of guttering. Using the long ladder would have put weight on the fragile guttering and broken it. We solved the problem by using a pair of steps instead. It was my turn to climb up, brush in one hand and paint tin in the other, trying not to drop either or both on my brother beneath. I had to stand on tiptoe on the small platform at the top of the steps. Jason held the steps

The Raven and the Jackdaw

steady with a vice-like grip. Even so, I had difficulty reaching the highest, furthest angle of the weatherboard.

'Step over the bar,' I heard Jason say. 'Stand on the bit of the platform in front of it. I'll hold you. You'll be all right.'

I had no doubt of that. Because I was a rock climber. Because Jason would be holding me. Because it was me. Because it was him.

I stepped across the bar and stood on the front part of the platform. I felt Jason's hands clasp my bare legs. Then, when he had assured himself that I was standing steady I felt his right hand work its way softly up my thigh. His fingers made their way in through the ripped seam of the crotch of my shorts. I felt him caress my tight ball-sac with his fingers' ends, then very lightly touch the tip of my cock. Then, quite unhurriedly, he slid his hand away again, out of my shorts and down my thigh. His hand stopped sliding downwards when it reached my calf. Which he clasped, as I had clasped his yesterday, until I'd finished painting that awkward corner spot. 'So,' he said, as I climbed backwards over the bar, ready to descend the steps, 'where shall we eat tonight?'

THIRTY-ONE

We ate at the local pub again. The evening was sticky and hot. There would be a storm in an hour or two, everybody said. People in country pubs, country-folk, were good at predicting the weather. They would take their phones out of their pockets and look it up.

When we drove back home we could see the lightning flickering at a distance. We pulled up in front of our pair of cottages, got out of the car (mine this evening) and got our front-door keys out. I knew that one of us would say it. It was Jason, it turned out. 'Want to come in for a nightcap?'

We opened a bottle of red and sat on the sofa drinking it. The television news was on, with the sound so low that we could hardly hear it. Not that we were even watching it.

'Come and stay with me in France again soon,' I said. That was some time after we got involved with a second glass.

'I will,' Jason said, slowly nodding his head.

'Actually you could come and live with me there.' I said this lightly, with a laugh in my voice, to show that I wasn't being too serious.

'We could both paint,' said Jason, also with a laugh. 'Live in Le Breuilh and make a living from our painting.' He chuckled again. Protecting us from the possibility that we might both be being serious.

'Nick and I were completely accepted there,' I said. 'Nobody ever questioned our relationship or seemed to want to know the details of it.' I let that hang there. So did Jason.

There was a sudden crack of thunder above us and immediately the sound of rain starting abruptly, like the swoosh of a descending theatre curtain.

The Raven and the Jackdaw

'You were wonderful today,' I said. 'Knowing what to do. Talking to the solicitor. Jason above and beyond the call of duty.' I paused for a moment. Jason said nothing so I expanded a bit. 'As so often. You're always helping me out. Catching me as I fall...' Images of Nick came crowding in at that moment. Of me holding him as we abseiled in the Sierra de Gredos. Of him holding me as he fell to his death. It took me a second to get a grip. But I did get a grip. I said, 'You never let me help you out like that. Sometimes I wish you did.'

'Do you?' Jason asked. Then after a moment's thought he said, 'I guess the human need to give is as big as the need to have. Perhaps I should have remembered that in your case. I've been too proud sometimes to let you ... to let you help me when I could have done with it.'

I had no answer to that. 'I'm just grateful to you anyway,' I said. 'For everything. Ever.'

'Well, we'll see how tomorrow goes,' Jason said, putting a gentle brake on my runaway confidence in his ability to make everything come right. 'We're not out of the woods yet.'

'No,' I said, 'but...'

'See what Alastair and the solicitor have to say for themselves...'

'Of course,' I said. I wondered if Alastair and I would tell the solicitor the truth about things or if we'd be expected to lie through our teeth. Alastair and I would need to meet in advance to discuss this so we could present a united front...

Jason said suddenly, going off at a tangent, 'Don't let the philosophers kid you there's any difference between love and friendship. Amor and amicitia. There isn't. They tried to kid themselves and kid posterity. Have none of it.'

I wasn't sure that I agreed, though I wasn't going to say so at such a precious moment. I'd never before heard

Jason taking issue with a major tenet of western thought before. Though perhaps he did it sometimes when I wasn't around to hear him.

Was he getting drunk more quickly than I was? I looked at the wine in his glass. He hadn't got any further down it than I had mine. I put my arm tentatively around his shoulder. Another, even louder, crack of thunder sounded overhead. Jason didn't react to it in any way. Neither did he make any move in recognition of my gesture. I felt no relaxation of his muscles in acceptance, but neither was there that stiffening of his back that would have told me the overture was unwelcome. He didn't remove my arm, anyway. That was something.

We sat in silence for a few more seconds. Then he said, 'It isn't easy living up to what you want from me.'

That took me aback. 'I don't expect you to live up to anything,' I answered, puzzled. 'I promise.' I tried to make sense of what Jason had said. 'It just so happens that time and time again you've saved my life.'

He took no notice. 'Your expectations were all there in what you wrote,' he said.

'In what I wrote?' I couldn't think what I had written.

'The Raven and the Jackdaw,' he said. 'You had the Raven behaving wonderfully to the Jackdaw towards the end. That's what I have to try and live up to.'

I could hardly believe he'd said that. 'You don't!' I said, appalled. 'Oh, fucking shit! It was a stupid book. Forget it.'

But he clearly wasn't going to forget it just yet. He said, 'Actually the ending was quite moving. But I had a problem dealing with it at the time. I was at Bristol, coping with real, dying cancer patients. I'm afraid the reality was rather harsher than your book was.'

'I'm sorry,' I said. 'I should have thought of that.'

'No worries,' said my brother blithely. 'I've come to think that the whole of our lives – our futures at any rate

– are mapped out by the things we should have thought of earlier.' He reached down to the coffee table and got the bottle. It was a Fleurie, if anyone's interested. 'Top you up?' he said. I let him. Then he topped himself up. I let him. The next day's meeting in Newbury wasn't till two-thirty in the afternoon.

The storm was moving away now. The thunder still rumbled and rattled at us, but from a distance. For a few minutes we sat in silence, sipping occasionally from our glasses. Then Jason said, 'It wasn't only that.'

'Wasn't only what?' I'd lost track of his thoughts.

'Why I wouldn't let you get close up.' Jason was looking intently into his wine glass. As if watching things swimming in it. After a moment he said, 'I was frightened – off and on – by *us*.' He pronounced that last word in italics.

'I was frightened of that too, sometimes,' I said.

'But so much else has happened to us now…'

'I know,' I said.

'To both of us.' He stopped. Then, 'I'm not frightened any more.' Quite suddenly Jason turned and looked at me. So suddenly that the movement quite hurt the arm of mine that was draped round his shoulder. He gave me a look that was urgent, almost beseeching. Looking hard at me, trying to read my face. And when he spoke, which he did immediately, his voice was also anxious, almost beseeching. He sounded vulnerable, scared of a rebuff. He said, 'You can stay the night if you want.'

'I want,' I said.

THE END

****

Anthony McDonald

Anthony McDonald is the author of more than twenty novels. He studied modern history at Durham University, then worked briefly as a musical instrument maker and as a farmhand before moving into the theatre, where he has worked in every capacity except director and electrician. He has also spent several years teaching English in Paris and London. He now lives in rural East Sussex.

Novels by Anthony McDonald

**THE DOG IN THE CHAPEL
TOM AND CHRISTOPER AND THEIR KIND
DOG ROSES
SILVER CITY
RALPH: DIARY OF A GAY TEEN
IVOR'S GHOSTS
ADAM
BLUE SKY ADAM
GETTING ORLANDO
ORANGE BITTER, ORANGE SWEET
ALONG THE STARS
WOODCOCK FLIGHT**

**MATCHES IN THE DARK:
13 Tales of Gay Men**
(Short story collection)

The Raven and the Jackdaw

Gay Romance Series:
twelve short novels among which…
The Paris Novel
The Van Gogh Window
Tibidabo
Spring Sonata
Touching Fifty
Romance on the Orient Express

All titles are available as Kindle ebooks and as paperbacks from Amazon.
www.anthonymcdonald.co.uk

Printed in Great Britain
by Amazon